WHITE WOLF AND THE ASH PRINCESS

TAMMY LASH

WHITE WOLF AND THE ASH PRINCESS

©Third Edition 2020

Book Cover Design by © Jennifer Zemanek/Seedlings LLC
Interior Design by Tammy Lash/White Wolf Publishing

This book is a work of fiction. All incidents and dialogue, and all characters with the exception of certain well known historical and public places and figures, are the products of the author's imagination and are not to be construed as real. In all other respects and situations in the book, any resemblance to any persons alive or dead is purely coincidental.

ISBN Number: 978-1-940155-66-1

Printed and Published in the United States of America

ACKNOWLEDGMENTS

Praise and endless thanks to my Heavenly Father, the Author of All, who wrote for me the most amazing story. Thank you, Abba Father, for adopting me and becoming my 'daddy'. Thank you for writing my story so I could create this one.

A smothering hug to my Jonathan; my husband, Kris. You bravely nurtured each of my raw and bubbled wounds, and you did so with a silent strength. Thank you for patiently waiting for me to come to you. I love you! More hugs to our three gifts: Kelsey, Austin, and Ryan. Thank you for putting up with my back as I spent hours a day tippitytyping. Thank you for your random *White Wolf* quotes. They gave my ego a boost when I felt my work stunk!

Thank you, Mama (Linda Bolhuis), for your stories—the stories I heard from the back seat of our car on long trips, and the stories I heard from my metal chair in our Junior Church classroom. I studied you every chance I got.

White Wolf sparkles and shines because of my amazing editors, Pastor Brandon Crawford (editor first edition) and Savannah Jezowski (second edition). Thank you for your beautiful work. A bazillion thanks to my sister-in-law, Jill Bolhuis, for proofreading edition two of *White Wolf*, and Savanna Roberts and Cherise Taylor for proofreading this third edition. Hugs, all! Thank you, Beta Readers—Linda Bolhuis and Kelsey Lash, for your love and endless support; Savannah Jezowski, for your gentle push to dig deeper and for your patience with my endless list of 'authoring' questions; Casey Quarles, for your contagious enthusiasm—it gave me the energy and drive to finish. *All* your feedback, my dear betas, turned *White Wolf* into the work that it is today.

All basket of chocolates to my talented cover designer, Jenny at Seedlings, LLC for creating my gorgeous cover. Girl, you did amazing!

Matt Harmon, you mended my love/hate relationship with my laptop. Thank you for getting it into tip-top shape to finish this book!

I never would have had the capability to sit still and organize my thoughts if it weren't for my own Dr. Batchford/Mikonan, (Pastor/Psychologist) Harry Borsheim. Thank you for guiding me through my past and showing me how to let the Lord heal it. Panic attacks, anxiety, and PTSD no longer things to be feared. They are nothing but aches from scars. Thank you for helping me to see that willows are important trees, too.

Thank *you*, dear reader, for picking up this book! I hope Izzy's journey is an inspiration to you. May the Lord bless you and keep you on your journey.

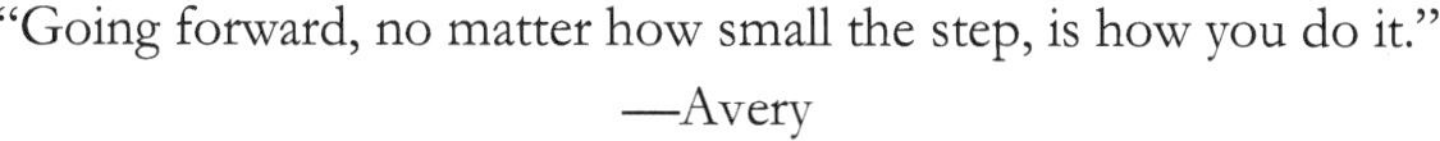

"Going forward, no matter how small the step, is how you do it."
—Avery

To Kris, Kelsey, Austin, Ryan….and Mama.
For your love, support, and company on this book journey

PART ONE

ONE

Jonathan brushes past the open library door and one of the paper leaves on its front coasts to the floor.

We had glued them to the carved barren oak when we were younger. Every time one loses its grip on the door, I fasten it back up. It's one of my favorite memories of our time together. It looks like later I'll be making a fresh batch of egg white glue.

"I got him! It took me a while, but I finally cornered him behind your door." He has his hands cupped. The bat, I assume, is folded in them.

It must be close to morning. I can see a faint line of light between the curtains. The fire's out. I didn't get up to stoke it. Jonathan knew I wouldn't. He didn't know how long it would take to wrangle the bat in my room, so he made sure I was bundled in an extra covering. He lit all the candles on the library table just in case so the room wouldn't go dark.

"Do you want to see him?" Jonathan beams.

"Not particularly," I tell him in a yawn. I sit up on the couch to make room for him because I know he wants to show me. I run my fingers through my hair and toss its weight over my shoulder. It must be an unruly mess, but his look doesn't reveal that. This look is a mystery to me. I've spent plenty of time with him and have gotten to know most of his faces. This one, I notice, came home with him from his trip last summer.

"Help me with this glove." He keeps hold of the bat with one hand while flinging the other about wildly.

"Hold still so I can grab it!" I giggle. "You are *not* going to touch him, are you?" The thought makes me shiver and I scrunch my nose at him to show my disgust.

"Sure, why not? I've never caught one before. He's cute. Look at him." Jonathan moves his thumb back and the bat turns his head towards me. I scream when its beady-eyes find mine.

"Mercy sakes, girl, I've got him. He's not going anywhere," he laughs.

He sounds like Miss Margaret, our head housekeeper and "mother." She uses that phrase all the time. It's catchy—I find myself using it, too. Our clean and orderly Miss Margaret, I'm sure, wouldn't approve of him touching it. When I tell him this, he gives me a crooked smile and airy exhale.

"Of course she wouldn't approve. To her, he'd be a vermin with wings. To me, he's a creature I haven't had the chance to examine before. Come on. If I touch him, will you touch him? Scratch that. This is a dare. I dare you."

Now he did it. He knows what it will take to get me to touch it.

"I'm scrubbing my hands after, Jonathan, and if I get sick, it's your fault. He looks like a mouse."

"I'll wipe your nose for you…deal?" he grins.

When I nod, he tucks the bat's face back under his thumb, and he pulls a wing out between pinched fingers. It looks leathery and bird-like. There are several books here on ships, and this wing almost looks like a sail to me. I tell Jonathan this and he agrees.

"That it does. Good observation. Look, a thumb—just like the drawings I've seen." He nudges into what looks to be a finger on the top of the bat's wing. "All right, your turn. Touch." He raises a brow at my hesitation to deepen the dare.

"Jonathan," I sigh. I'm tempted to back down, but I haven't done that yet with any of our dares. "He's completely and utterly horrific," I moan.

"No, he's not. He's amazing. He's a flying bug trap. They love mosquitos. You hate—*dislike*—mosquitos," he corrects. "So, that makes you and the bat friends!"

He has over-pronounced the replaced word with stretched brows and widened eyes, and it makes me giggle. He looks over his shoulder and flashes me a sideways grin. Miss Margaret is much like a ghost in this house. She can come and go without anyone noticing. Jonathan had changed his word for her. She dislikes us to use the word "hate." She says it's too strong of a word, and strong words can lead to bad things.

"Friends?! I should say not!" I chuckle. This creature will never be a friend of mine. He had me so terrified last night diving about my room, I belly-crawled to Jonathan's room with a blanket over me. No, most certainly we are not friends, nor ever will we be. I reach for the bat's featherless wing but pull back when it trembles.

"I can't!" I shudder in a giggle.

"Give me your hand, I'll help you."

"That's cheating. I'm not doing it on my own."

"I always help you and you always win. Why would this be any different?" He shrugs.

It's true. In all our games, if he wins, he plays on until I win too.

He hasn't taken up my hands since he's been back from his latest journey, and I can tell he's hesitant, but he takes one up and helps guide one of my fingers over the bat's wing.

"Oh!" I shrug my shoulders up into my ears. "That's enough!"

"See. He's not so bad."

"I suppose he's a tiny bit cute—*tiny*." I squint and show him how minuscule it is by leaving the smallest gap that I can between the two fingers that I hold up.

"He's gone from utterly horrific to a tiny bit cute. Mission accomplished. I'm proud of you, Izzy—well done." Jonathan is up and he's heading towards a window. "Open the window for me?" he asks over his shoulder.

"Absolutely!" I hop up to race past him.

"Unless you want to cage him and keep him," Jonathan offers.

"No. Let him be free to have his fill of our mosquitos." I tug open the tall curtains from the window. They're heavy and it takes two hands to handle each side.

"It's morning. Bats are nocturnal. He may zip back up to whatever hole he found in the house and find his way back in," Jonathan warns.

"Or he may just learn to endure the sunshine and flap his little way to some glorious cave somewhere—with an endless supply of bugs and friends of his kind. That's much better than a perch behind a door, wouldn't you think?"

Jonathan's brows pinch. "I don't know. If I were a bat, this place wouldn't seem so bad to me. What would you do, if you were a bat?" He's looking at me in that strange way again.

"*If* I were a bat—and I have no plans on ever becoming one if that will bring peace to your mind, Jonathan—I think I would fly for the cave." I nod with the finality of my decision and against the lie I just told. I wouldn't do that, and he knows this. I get anxious when I venture too far past the stables. My chest tightens until I can't breathe, and my stomach will hurt. If I were a bat, I'd be curled up behind the door just as this one was.

His smile is a lie to what I see in his eyes. They look sad. The brown flecks in his eyes swell when he's sad, and they always threaten to swallow all the green that I love in them.

"Well, then. Maybe he wouldn't like our home here. It would be no different than a cage to him. Let's let him go and let him choose."

He attempts to hide his sorrow by pressing his smile more tightly, but he fails. I know him too well. When I push open the window, he releases the bat, but we can't see its chosen course. The morning is too thick with fog.

TWO

"I'm heading out. I need to get to my spot before the fog burns off. Want to come?" Jonathan asks at the door.

"No. I'm staying in the library today," I say. He expected this answer, but it didn't stop him from asking it. He asks it every time before he goes out hunting. Since I haven't outgrown my fear of straying too far from the house, I think he's hoping for a sudden, miraculous intervention.

"Will you try to come out later? We need to practice. It's been a while."

"I'll try, but no promises. You know what happens when I read," I say.

For as long as I can remember, Jonathan has insisted that I learn to shoot all the weapons here. He asks that I at least try each of them once and know the basics of each. I don't understand the purpose of my needing to know this. Our home is secluded. People rarely visit. The visitors we do get are far from threatening. Regarding his argument that someday I may decide to leave this place for some far-off fantasy land thick with ogres and trolls, I always respond that he's gravely mistaken. I have no plans on ever leaving. I can't make it past the rock wall.

He raises his brows at me and huffs with an amused smirk. "You won't be out."

He knows the power the library has over me. Once I get a book open, it's hard for me to put it down. He also knows about the dare and how close I am to finishing.

"Tomorrow?" he asks. "I wouldn't ask you if I didn't feel it was important. Please don't say you'll try. We both know you won't do it then. Just say yes, please? Tomorrow?"

The smile he wore just moments ago has been exchanged for lines of concern that press in between his brows. The boy that had introduced me to the bat has gone and the guarded adult version is back. I can always see the exchange. It's like watching a storm swallow up a sunny day.

"Tomorrow," I agree with a soft smile.

I can feel the change in myself when the boy is swapped out. It's my fault he's this walled version. This is the Jonathan that feels he must continually protect me, so naturally, I blame myself each time he comes out. When this Jonathan comes, I have the strong urge to run, to release him and to release me from the polite and hollow people we become. I never do because I don't know how to run.

After getting dressed, I have my daily breakfast with Miss Margaret. Today it is her biscuits and poached eggs. I love her biscuits but tolerate the eggs. The insides spill out of the eggs when I cut into them and I find it disturbing. The texture is remedied when I dip my biscuit in them, but Miss Margaret dislikes it intensely when I do this. It's another thing I do that's not ladylike.

Once in the library, I pick up the book I started yesterday and read until my head hurts. I only have a chapter left, so I push through the ache in my skull and the blurring words until I finish. When it's ready to go back where it came from, I ignore the ladder and struggle to place the book back on the shelf where it belongs on my own.

The books on either end are taking turns falling over. To separate the troublemakers, I use the book's edge.

"How did this ever fit?" I groan. I direct the question to the mute wall of books in front of me. I think they're enjoying watching me balance the stubborn one with my fingertips.

Just a few steps away, the ladder, meant to be used for this very purpose, waits for me to give in. I'll take dares in whatever form they come in, mocking inanimate objects included, so I wrestle with the task for a few minutes more. I'm sore-toed and sweaty by the time I get it back in, but I get it. I twist my hair to the top of my head to let the air get to the swamp on the back of my neck and step back to admire how I tucked the fat book in its spot without the ladder's help.

"I win," I announce to the empty room. The loser could care less. It stands there completely unaffected.

I'm still half-teetering in a world ruled by dragons from the book I had just returned. I pull back the curtains that I had shut up and blink back the explosion of light. At what point the sun had decided to make its presence known, I wouldn't know. I always keep the curtains drawn in here and only open them when I'm finished reading or if there's rain. I don't want my book journeys disturbed by the anxious thoughts of the outside world that always come when the sun steps in.

Through squinted eyes, I half expect to see the crimson dragon from my book coasting in flight and reducing the billowy clouds to white streaks with a few powerful pumps of its wings. I'm disappointed when all I see after my eyes adjust is a tiny sparrow fluttering down from a tree branch to peck at a blade of grass.

I did it. I finished the last one. Now what?

The books don't answer when I ask them out loud—but I don't expect them to. I stretch my arms over my head and arch my back like a drowsy cat just waking from its nap and smile. Books only talk when they're open.

I can count on one hand how long it has taken me. It's been three years. I should be as puffed as the sleeves on my dress at having just completed the largest and longest self-appointed dare in history. Correction, the largest and the longest that I'm aware of. I wouldn't know of any other unless it was written down in this library somewhere.

I have just finished reading my two hundred and fiftieth book. No one would argue that reading two hundred and fifty books is a colossal accomplishment. I should celebrate somehow, and the first thing that comes to mind is the quick-footed Irish dance that I have seen Miss Margaret do in the kitchen when she thinks no one is looking. It's a short attempt, and I feel foolish with my bare feet knocking against my shins, so I stop and fall back on my couch.

It was somewhere near book one hundred when a thought sparked. It started as small as an ember's glow. Singular and insignificant like the sound a letter makes alone. By book one hundred and twenty, those sounds piled upon one another and formed words until a nagging sentence was born. Nurtured in my mind, the three tiny words puffed and swelled together like the grains in a pot of boiling oatmeal.

"Who am I?"

It was a question that hung in awkward silence whenever I asked it as a little girl. I never got an answer. Just an uncomfortable smile and the same rehearsed response from Jonathan each time.

"You are Isabelle Gudwyne. That is who you are."

So, as an obedient and dutiful member of the Gudwyne household, I tried to shelve those nagging three words. As days stretched into years and the book count of my dare became smaller, I began to take notice among all the different letter combinations, word pairings, sentences, and paragraphs that there was a common thread. As I replaced each volume in their place, their stories lingered in my mind hours after they were put away. They teased me with their knowledge. Their leather shells no longer held secrets. Something I fear I may never know for myself. I am only aware of my present, while they, however, are complete works with a beginning, a middle, and an end. With each cover that I close, I know someone or something better than myself. Even after reading Jonathan's science books, I know more about the earth's rock layers than who I am and where I come from.

The reason why I can't dance isn't solely from the lack of coordination. It's mostly due to the absence of joy from an only moderately completed task. Somewhere along with the dare, I unshelved my three-worded question and the secret hope was fanned that somewhere in one of these books, I would find my answer. But I didn't find it. Maybe it will be in book two hundred and fifty-one. I can't help but sigh instead of celebrating. Dare or no dare, I'm not finished here.

Outside the library window, I catch a glimpse of movement. The anxious figure in front of the garden's stone bench is Jonathan. He's pacing on the path in the roses that his father planted in memory of Evolyn. He sits briefly to rest his head in his hands but pops back up moments later. I would have thought this back and forth, up and down again scenario funny if I didn't see his face first. He's still bothered, and this troubles me.

This library is Jonathan's and if it weren't for him, I wouldn't have accomplished what I did. He's my best friend and the one who sets most of my dares. He put the idea in my head to try to read all the books in his library. Even he hasn't accomplished that one.

I must not have shut the window correctly after the bat. It's stuck, and I can't get it open to call to him. If he could hear what I did today, it may make him feel better. He always lights up at my accomplishments.

"Tea in twenty minutes, Izzy," Miss Margaret sings. My gasp is the harmony to her knuckled tune rapped on the open door.

"Oh! I didn't know it was that late already. I wanted to help you!" I tell her. I keep my eyes from her on my rushed trip to the couch. I always feel uncomfortable around her when I get caught looking like anything other than she expects. I must look wild and disorderly to her.

The late hour has me frazzled. I race to get my shoes and it's a fight for balance when I skip my stockings and try to cram my bare feet into them instead. The first step I attempt to take is on the unfastened ribbon, and I fall with a thud on the hard floor.

"For mercy's sake, child! Where are your stockings! If you would only keep your shoes on like a civilized person..." A giggle chokes the rest of her words.

I don't find the humor in my taking a spill. I had landed on my right side; the side where I have the most scarring and where it is always tender. Miss Margaret stops laughing when she sees my grimace. I try to hide the pulsing pain in my arm by busying myself with my skirt and ribbon entanglement.

"Oh, my sweet dear! Are you all right?" She rushes to my side to help me to the nearest chair.

"I just had the wind knocked out of me a bit," I say, and I manage a chuckle to reassure her I'm fine.

My hands fly to my loose hair and I gather it to tame it. Miss Margaret ignores my unrestrained locks and sees through my feeble attempts to brush off the discomfort.

"Let me help you, dear." She gathers her skirt to kneel, and she leans in to lace one of my ankle-high shoes when I stop her.

"No, please. I'm fine. I can do it."

She sits back on her heels to study me; her face is lined more with concern than the sixty years that age it.

"If you're sure. I can get Jonathan or the doctor," she says.

I bend down to her to tie my shoes and tug hard at the laces. My face is beginning to feel hot. I don't like the way they baby me so!

"No, honestly, I'm fine. Tea?" I remind her. "I'll be down in a minute to help you."

My smile is weak but it's enough to reassure Miss Margaret. Though the pained expression is still etched on her face, she leaves me to finish dressing. I tie a neat bow and stand to brush the wrinkles from my skirt. I take a deep breath and massage the ache in my arm. I try to punish the flickering flames that taunt me in the fireplace with a glare and hope that this is the trick to keep the tears away for today. It's been eleven years—and these scars still bother me.

It feels good to punch the crushed couch pillows back into shape, and I take extra care in doing so today. When I feel they've endured enough, I position them in the angles Miss Margaret tilts them in when she comes to dust. I scan the room for disorder before going to the mirror to pin my hair back up in the bun Miss Margaret asks that I keep it in.

When I read, I take my bun out. Laying on it makes the back of my head numb if I don't. I like wearing it down, and I like the way the waves tickle my elbows. Mostly, I like that I can hide behind it. My hair covers what clothes cannot. Its thickness and length cover the scars on my neck, and I don't get as many sympathetic looks from the household when it's down. But unfortunately, that isn't very often.

I make sure all the pieces are neatly tucked where they should be and stare hard at my reflection to try to will the tears away. My earlier glare did a pitiful job in damming them up. My reflection blurs as my eyes fill. I roughly wipe the moisture and the thoughts of the fireplace away with my sleeve and try to drown out the sounds that echo from the two children who used to come here to cry. This library was meant to be our safe place, but the flames that live here in the fireplace sometimes make that difficult for me. I know Miss Margaret doesn't like me to use this word, but to say I dislike something just isn't strong enough. I *hate* fire.

THREE

I know I just told Miss Margaret I'd be on my way, but I think it'd be wise for me to linger in the library for as long as I can. Tears make Miss Margaret nervous and she worries enough for me already. My face gets blotchy when I cry and right now, I look like one giant rash. She'll call Doctor Batchford for sure, thinking it's an incurable disease when it's just me doing what I always do.

Jonathan works hard to try to get me to forget. Smiles are commonplace here. Tears are quickly ushered away with dares or games, sugary sweets, or gifts. Rosemary, my darling white speckled horse with a brown nose, is his newest ploy to keep my eyes dry.

He thinks these things will help me to move on and leave the past behind. It hasn't worked yet, and my stuffed wardrobe of unworn dresses is evidence of that. The past he speaks of is the day where we— Jonathan, Miss Margaret, and I—began, here in the cottage, when I came here as a raw, open wound. I think I could move forward if I knew what happened. The past I'm concerned about is my life before here. When I try to look back, it's like trying to read a book missing most of its print. I do know three things. One: I had a papa. Sometimes, I can smell his pipe. Two: I had a mama. Sometimes, I can feel her when my chest is empty of fear. Three: there was a fire

Jonathan knows about my past, but he won't say anything more no matter how much I beg. I used to cry to try to get him to tell me. It upset him every time, but it didn't work. Only adults hate tears. I guess I could try it again. Jonathan is twenty-six, but an eighteen-year-old carrying on in such a way would cause Miss Margaret to summon Doctor Batchford without a doubt. I see enough of him already.

I was taught that adults have zero tolerance for tears. They taught me this lesson themselves when I was rushed up the cottage stairs and placed for the first time in the bed I still use. They didn't have to say a word. Their shushing spoke for them. They were wasting their air with their tea-kettle hushes. I couldn't help it—it hurt. I wasn't going to stop crying for them—they terrified me. The screams I added made them upset, but it wasn't me who they got angry at. They took it out on Jonathan, the boy with the pretty green eyes that I had met months earlier but had already forgotten. He wouldn't stop his crying either, even when they threatened to pull him from me.

"Get the boy out of here. He's making things worse! Alexander, take him." Doctor Batchford shouted the order while pointing the way to the door. He never loses his composure, ever, but that day he did. In his defense, it must have been the sight of my ruptured blisters that forced it upon him. The vision had everyone rattled, including myself.

"No!" The worded scream from me burned out of my throat, so much so that no other sounds should have ever followed again—but more did—when our fingers were pried apart. They were violent sounds, mixed with sobs that I found from deep within. They frightened me as much as they did the men that scattered from the room. I didn't care what I sounded like. I wanted Jonathan back.

Alexander had been a hulking man to me then—large and intimidating. I didn't know he was the sweet man that he is now. I just knew that a monster of a man with a golden mustache had my boy up in the air and he was taking him from me. My animalistic sounds worked, and they forced Alexander to drop Jonathan to protect his ears. Jonathan fell to the floor with a thud but scrambled back to his feet to get to me. The doctor, who was in the process of fixing his glasses, knocked them sideways on his face. As they were adjusted back, two more men scampered out of the room.

Jonathan's arm was caught by Alexander before he could reach me. He begged both men in sobs to let him come back to me.

"I'm sorry. Please. She needs me—let me stay."

I remember his face was drenched. Mine probably looked the same, if not worse. He dried his off with the bottom of his shirt and he took in a few unsteady gasps before reassuring them. "I'm fine! I'm fine! See?"

"It's true, Doc. They have formed quite a bond. I wouldn't separate them." Alexander waited for the doctor to nod his permission before releasing him and he shrugged an apology to Jonathan for manhandling him.

When I got his hand back, my wails were soothed, and this relieved the few adults that remained in the room. Jonathan was the only thing that felt familiar to me and I didn't want to lose him. I knew they wouldn't pull him from me again. I knew what worked.

"Who's responsible for this child?" Doctor Batchford asked. He leaned back in his chair to reach the table beside him to grab a set of fresh bandages before attempting again to pull off the piece that he announced was stuck.

Miss Margaret was near the foot of the bed. I remember her dabbing at her smudged cheeks with her apron before following the lantern over to where it needed to be. With a sigh, she swept her arm across her forehead to catch the beads of sweat she had missed. "Mercy sakes, it's warm in here. Is it warm in here, Doctor?"

"No—it's not. It's freezing. You need to sit, Miss Margaret. I'm afraid a faint is in your future if you don't." The doctor used his foot to drag over a chair for Miss Margaret. He had managed to pry off a corner of my bandage and he didn't want to dirty his hands again. "I need someone to fetch me some warm water. I need to drench this bandage to get it to come off and this is going to bring the girl to chill more than she already is. You there—can you handle that for me? While he's off doing that I need one of you to poke that fire awake."

The doctor had chosen Jefferson to get the water. He had spent his time in the back of the room—dead quiet—twisting his hat into various shapes. I think he was relieved to be excused; his nod to accept was an energetic one.

The announcement of a stoked fire brought me to a fresh round of weeping. Jonathan spoke for me and pleaded over my noise. "She's afraid of the fire. Please, sir, let it go out."

"With burns as severe as hers, it's understandable, but that said, the girl is shivering, and that fire *will* be revived. Well? The child? Who's responsible for her?

Anyone?" The doctor waited for an answer but when he didn't get one, he threw his hands in the air and huffed. "Someone find their tongue, please!"

Jonathan gave my hand a final squeeze before letting it slip from his. This caused me to whimper in protest. "Just for a minute. You're cold. I need to make the fire a little bigger to warm you. Don't look— at the fire or your burns. Keep your eyes on me and don't take them off." I did as he told me. I don't even think I blinked.

"It's Captain Gudwyne, sir. He's the girl's appointed guardian," Alexander answered. He was the only one left to answer any questions besides Jonathan. My cries had unnerved the room that was once full of curious men perfumed in pungent odors. All were gone.

"Edward? Well, where is he? Bring him in." The doctor tightened the rolls in his sleeves and pushed them past his elbow.

"He's not here, sir," Alexander informed him. "Captain Jonathan is in charge now, sir."

"Is that so?" The doctor looked at Jonathan over his glasses. "Where's your father, boy?"

When Jonathan returned to me, he didn't answer the question. He squeezed into my hand instead. My fingers were bunched in his grip, and it was uncomfortable, but I didn't care. He looked sad and I felt sorry for him. To show him how important he was to me, I stopped my whimpering and did a healthy sniff instead. This seemed to help him. He rewarded me with a smile, though his eyes still swam in tears. When he blinked, a wet glop splashed onto our clasped hands.

"No point in pressing the boy, Doc. He's not going to answer you. Leave him be. Just know Captain Edward isn't here nor will he ever be."

Alexander had Jonathan's shoulders in his hands, and he was squeezing them to comfort him, but it had the opposite effect. Jonathan groaned in protest and his knees buckled. Alexander caught him before he crumpled. I didn't complain when he had to drop my hand. It ached from his sound grip.

"Doc, when you're done with the girl, you need to check the boy." Alexander slid a chair underneath him and went to the washbasin for a cloth. The water that was squeezed out sounded like rain, and I wanted it to go on forever.

"Check him over for me, Alexander. Keep him comfortable. Jonathan, am I to believe that a fifteen-year-old has been given a child to raise? How is this going to happen?"

"With my help," Miss Margaret choked from her seat. Alexander and the doctor were then outnumbered. No one else looked well. A sob pierced my throat. This boy was to be my new papa? What about my real one? And Mama? This white-haired lady was to replace her?

"Now that's something I can wrap my head around," he said, "but don't you already have your hands full with the baby?"

"Sir, I'm home now and I'll be handling the care of my son from here on out. I'm much obliged, Miss Margaret. My boy and I appreciate your sacrifice for us." Alexander nodded his thanks to the blushing Miss Margaret, who disliked then, as well as now, any forms of flattery.

"That's good to hear because this girl's wounds are going to require extensive maintenance. Expect a round-the-clock battle with her against pain and infection. Thankfully, the girl seems to be clear of any infection as far as I can see, but if there's open skin, there's a threat of it.

"Sleep will be a stranger to all in this house for a while, I'm afraid. Captain Jonathan, please find your words. I need to know. Who's responsible for this?"

"Responsible for what, sir?" Jonathan asked. He looked sick and it scared me.

He was too far away. I moaned in my stretch to him and reached with my fingertips as far as I could without falling off the bed. He shouldered off Alexander's hands from his lifted shirt and he slid his chair over. It was then we were down to one healthy person in the room. It was Alexander's turn to look sick.

"The bandages, Jonathan. Who took care of her on the ship? I'd like to shake his hand. The care she received was exemplary. This girl should be riddled with infection. The open wounds, though they look fierce to the rest of you, are clean and are already beginning to heal."

"The hand you need to shake is right across from you. It was Jonathan. Don't let his tears fool you. This boy is just as brave as this little girl. No other man would touch her. The few that tried either passed out or emptied their stomachs where they stood. Jonathan was by her side the entire trip home," Alexander said. His eyes looked misty when he said it.

"Job well done, son. I feel confident that you can handle her care when I can't be here. Your hands, my boy, prove to be as capable as mine." The doctor shook Jonathan's hand and looked to Miss Margaret. "You, Miss Margaret, on the other hand, are of a concern to me. Watch and learn. This is quite a job for one person to handle and Jonathan has already handled more than his share. I know what fresh burns look like and you, boy, are of a rare breed to have accomplished what you did. And on your own? Remarkable. Are you ready for lesson one Miss Margaret? Attempting to remove fused bandages without moistening it first will damage the healing underneath. They must be thoroughly moistened. Never pry it off."

Miss Margaret nodded in understanding, though she didn't look at all confident with the future task.

Jefferson came back with a steaming bowl. Doctor Batchford directed Miss Margaret to bring over the washbasin where he washed his hands again from Jonathan's touch. He then instructed her to do so as well, even though all of us knew she wasn't anywhere near ready to help remove any bandages. It took three efforts by the doctor to encourage her closer to me. Each time she responded with a tiny side shuffle.

"You can do this. I have confidence in you. If you could handle bringing Jonathan into the world those years ago, you, my dear, can handle this."

Miss Margaret exhaled a nervous giggle. "All I did was catch him. Evolyn did the rest."

Her words caused Jonathan to seek my hand. He gently squeezed into it to keep his composure. Nobody noticed he had begun crying again. His tears stirred my own. Doctor Batchford resumed his tea-kettle noise. He thought I was crying over the fear of the pain to come with the last bandage. I knew it would throb with the heat of a fire, but I had already felt that and knew a good scream would get me through it. I was crying for Jonathan. I wanted to somehow help him.

"You're such a big girl. So brave." Miss Margaret smiled down on me and feathered a finger across my cheek.

"How old is she, Jonathan?"

He pressed his lips together and lifted a shoulder. "I don't know." He bit into his lower lip and swallowed hard before telling them he heard my name was Isabelle. Isabelle Elizabeth.

"No surname?" Doctor Batchford asked.

When Jonathan lifted his shoulder again, the doctor made his guess with my age. "I would say this little sweetheart is about six or seven. Am I right, Isabelle?"

The doctor was talking to me, but he used a name I didn't recognize. He wanted me to answer him with my age, but I didn't know that, either. I couldn't breathe. I wanted Mama and Papa, but I couldn't see their faces when I closed my eyes. I looked at Jonathan for answers, but he could only blink more tears.

"No fear, Isabelle, this is the last big, bad bandage. It will hurt, I won't lie, but I'll work through it as fast as I can. Shall we begin?" I whimpered a yes and clung tighter to Jonathan. "First we'll soak it and then I'll gently pull it away. Miss Margaret, this soaking part is yours. I'll be right here to assist if needed, but I want you to try this step on your own."

Miss Margaret's hands were unsteady as she squeezed the cloth dry onto the bandage on my arm. It was a large area and took several rags full. Once it was drenched, Dr. Batchford began to peel it back. Jonathan told me not to look, but I did. I screamed to scare the pain away and screamed extra for the sticky things I saw clinging to the underside of the bandage.

"Let her rest, Doctor, please," Miss Margaret begged. "It's too much for her."

"This last section needs more soaking, Miss Margaret. That will give the girl the break she needs. We do not want to prolong this pain any longer than necessary," Doctor Batchford reasoned. "Soak away, Miss Margaret."

"You are such a brave girl. You're nearly done!" Jonathan praised. "The bandage is almost off. When this part is over, we'll take care of your hair and then no more for today, I swear."

Miss Margaret shook her head and grimaced at Jonathan's choice of words. He swore his statement true instead of promising it because even in his younger years, he saw that making a promise meant something. He couldn't guarantee there wouldn't be something unexpected to do to my burns later. Today, Jonathan still feels this way towards his promises. When he makes one, it's done only because he has complete certainty he can keep it.

"In a bit, Miss Margaret is going to give you a pretty new haircut— so healthy hair can grow back in." He grinned at me as if it were something to look forward to. I had never had my hair cut. My braids dangled to my waist, and the thought of having them cut scared me just as much as the rest of the bandage.

"Will it hurt?" I asked him.

"Will what hurt? What's left of the bandage or the hair?" He smiled with the question and tugged my hand.

"The hair."

He let go of my hand to take hold of my braid. "It won't hurt a bit." He let it slip through his hand. Pieces of my braid broke off and fell to the floor. "See?"

I saw the chunks fall, and though I didn't feel it, it didn't change the fact that usually cutting and pain went together. I didn't understand how it wasn't going to hurt. I was afraid.

"I'll go first, Miss Margaret, to show her there's nothing to it," Jonathan said.

"Jonathan, your curls," Miss Margaret pleaded.

"It's just hair and hair can grow back, right, Isabelle?" He comforted me with a wink. I didn't know that hair grew back. I thought once it was gone, it was gone.

"His isn't back," I said with a sniff.

I had noticed Dr. Batchford's hair was thin on top.

This statement made the adults laugh—and Jonathan.

"That's because I'm old." Doctor Batchford widened his eyes and made a funny face. I could feel my lips pulling, and Jonathan noticed.

"Look at that smile!" he beamed. "I didn't know you had one," he teased, and it made me snicker. This pleased him and smoothed his crinkled brow. "When we finish here, if Doctor Batchford says it's ok, we'll go on a little trip down the hall to my favorite room. Doctor, is she well enough to go? I can carry her."

"It's up to our patient. I don't have a problem with that, but please, keep it short. She needs rest and lots of it."

"Yes, sir," Jonathan nodded.

He leaned in and whispered in my ear, to make it look like he wanted to share something with just me. I couldn't remember how old I was, but I knew I was no baby. I knew the others could still hear, but the shared secret filled me with excitement. It was delicious to feel something other than the usual hot pain that beat in time with my heart.

"This room is a glorious place, Isabelle. In it, you can become anything you desire to be and—the places you'll go! Adventure is waiting, but you'll have to learn some things first. Will you let me teach you?"

I nodded and grinned through the pressure on my arm. If he could teach me to be anything, then I'd choose to be a bird so I could fly and find Mama and Papa.

FOUR

"Good girl!" Jonathan and Dr. Batchford both praised in united voices over the sight of the dangling bandage.

"One thing down, one more to go, sweet girl. This part won't hurt, I promise." Miss Margaret leaned down and kissed my forehead, and warmth spread through my body clear to my toes.

Miss Margaret clipped away at Jonathan's hair first. He made silly faces while his chestnut curls piled on the tops of his shoulders. He made me laugh and I think the others enjoyed the new sound from me as much as I did. When Miss Margaret finished, Jonathan guided my hand over the top of his head. It felt spikey and it tickled the bottom of my hand. It made me giggle. When it was my turn, my hair didn't fall in soft mounds like his did. Mine was crispy and it crunched under the scissors. I was afraid to touch my head after, so he helped me. It felt just like his.

"Ready, Isabelle? I think she earned a trip to the special room. Don't you think, Miss Margaret?"

"She most certainly did," she sniffed. She covered her cries with her apron. The ordeal had traumatized Miss Margaret. It changed her that day. Jonathan says this is when her excessive nit-pickiness with the house began.

I, on the other hand, fared better than Miss Margaret. I was more than ready to see Jonathan's special room. To show him so, I held out the only arm I could to him; the other I couldn't. It was heavy in throb under the new bandages.

Jonathan leaned in to pick me up but whispered into my ear to tell me to keep my arm around his neck only and to please keep my weight light against him. Miss Margaret and Doctor Batchford were busy tidying up the room and didn't hear. Alexander opened his mouth to remind the doctor to look at him but snapped it shut when Jonathan shook his head.

I wondered then and still do, why Jonathan chose to not invite the adults to the second secret. I did whisper a "why" to him, but he hushed the question away with the same snake-like noise the big people used.

Jonathan waited in front of the special room's door so I could trace the tree's branches with my finger. He let me fill all the spaces in the carving that I could reach with my touch.

"The tree looks sad, doesn't it? He needs some leaves. Tomorrow, if you're up to it, we can make paper leaves for him to cheer him up. Sound fun?" he asked.

I nodded with such excitement my chin hit into my chest each time it went down. This made him laugh—and me, too. He looked happy. To check, I patted his cheeks, and I couldn't help but hug him when I saw they were dry. This made him tighten and I got a gentle reminder to be careful with him. Somehow, I had helped shoo his tears away. I remember wishing I knew what I did, so I'd know what to do in case they ever flowed again.

"Close your eyes, Isabelle, and don't ruin the surprise by opening your eyes too soon. I want to show you my favorite part of the room. Tight! I can see that you're cheating!" My attempt to sneak a peek with my scrunched squint made me giggle and made Jonathan snicker.

My little heart began to pound when I heard the handle click. The door's creak sent an excited chill through my body.

"I'm sorry," he said when he took my excitement for a shiver. "Should we try this tomorrow? I don't want you getting sick."

"No, plcasc," I bcggcd. "I want to." I gavc him my best smile as payment in the dark behind my lids. It worked. We went forward. Jonathan, completely unaware that he had done so, had just shown me how to soften his heart and win his good graces.

When we went in, his shoes made a different sound in the room than they had in the hall. It had extra notes. He made the sound of an owl and it made the same repeated tone as his steps. My high-pitched hoots that followed his made him chuckle. It was hard to keep my eyes closed; curiosity's pull was too strong. I stole another peek and tried to hide my gasp by disguising it into a yawn. The large room was full of strange things—things I had never seen before—but my gasp wasn't one of fear. It was an intake of joy. I could feel fear didn't live in this room like I felt it did in the other. It could have been because the others were gone, and it was just Jonathan and me. In the short time I had known him, he had done something the others couldn't do—he made me feel safe.

"You can't fool me, cheater!" he teased.

I didn't peek again. I didn't want to ruin any more of his surprise. Our journey ended at my reading couch, where he laid me down and covered me with a blanket to protect me from the chill he thought I had. He asked if I could count.

I didn't know.

"Maybe you'll remember if you hear me start. Count along with me if you can. If not, just listen for five. That's when you can open them. Keep your face straight and your eyes up. Are you ready?" he asked.

He started to count and by the time he reached three, I remembered that four came next. When we got to five, I opened my eyes and squealed. Golden-haired children with dove-like wings flew in a sky of a color I had never seen before.

"The sky—what color is it?" I asked. I'm surprised I had the breath to speak it. The painting in the ceiling brought me to awe that day the same way it does today.

"Turquoise," he answered. He groaned on his way down to the floor, and he took his time in making himself flat next to the couch. He made a pillow for his head with his hands and he gazed up into the painted sky with me. He let me take it in for a few minutes before speaking. "Try not to blink. The clouds will move for you if you don't," he said.

"The children. They have wings. Is that what you can teach me to have?" I asked. If I couldn't become a bird, I thought, growing wings like theirs would do just fine.

"No," he chuckled. "I'm going to teach you to read. That is if you don't know how. The children are cherubs," he said. "They're a type of angel."

"Are they real? Can I have one?" I asked. I leaned over the couch's edge to give him a duplicate of the smile I had given earlier, but the movement to him hurt. Hot pain bit into my arm, and its heat spread up into my neck. When I settled back down, I didn't move again.

"You just can't go out and get one," Jonathan laughed. "But, yes, they're real—you just can't see them. They're invisible. There could be one in this room right now. One could be sitting right at your feet."

I remember curling my legs up to give my invisible angel more room on the couch.

"That one, though," Jonathan sat up and grinned, "is different than the cherubs on the ceiling. He's a warrior."

"What does he do?" I didn't have a clue as to what Jonathan's warrior word had meant.

"He fights bad angels," he says, "but they do other things, too. In the Bible, they delivered messages or sometimes they were sent to help people."

When I told Jonathan I didn't think the angel on the couch went out of the room, he asked why. I told him I felt safe in his special room—outside of it, I didn't. The angel, if he were able to leave the room, would have kept me from getting burnt. My child's mind couldn't grasp the thought that sometimes God allows bad things to happen. He could have intervened, yet He chose not to. He could have sent a whole host of angels or just the one on the couch. He didn't. This made Jonathan's eyes shiny. He got up and held his arms out for me.

"I'm going to show you something—and I probably shouldn't—but it's too fun not to. If Miss Margaret finds out, she'll blister my backside, for sure. But first, let's punish this dragon and his fire."

The couch covered but a small portion of the rug the sapphire, snake-like dragon slithered across. It took up a large square of the room and his golden eyes made me shudder.

"You—are a bad dragon," he said as he walked over its curving body. "Did your flames hurt Isabelle? Your fire is bad, and we don't want it here." Jonathan stomped on the cherry-red flames that tumbled out onto the rug from behind the dragon's forked tongue. He continued his punishing journey to a mouth that was spiked with emerald teeth and he crushed its head under his feet.

"Don't be afraid of him. He won't hurt you. I took care of him— see? Come feel." He crouched low so I could lean down and sink my fingers in the needlework image. The dragon wasn't hot, prickly, or sharp; he felt soft under my fingers. Jonathan had tamed the beast for me.

"Do *not* let Miss Margaret see you do what I'm about to show you," he said with raised brows on his way to the room's ladders. He slid his hand over a table glossed to a high shine, and I leaned down and did the same. When we reached the shelved books in varying degrees of brown, he instructed me on what to do with the ladder that stood at attention in front of them.

"Put your feet here and your hand here." He lowered me on and guided my feet and my hand where they needed to be. He let my bad arm remain limp at my side. "These are ladders to get to the high books. See the wheels at the top? That's what makes the ladder move. In this game, you push off your foot to make the ladder move to the next. You ride them all until you get to the front of the room again. Don't touch the floor with anything other than your push-off foot or the mud monster on the floor will grab you and swallow you up." This made me giggle. "Don't believe me? Put your foot down." His grin grew when I shook my head no.

Jonathan hopped on the ladder behind me and pushed off. Together we rode until we collided into the next ladder. He helped me on and off each one until we made it back to the front of the room.

"Fun?" He sat me down on one of the tables.

I nodded. The room almost made me forget Mama and Papa. It was the noise of the clock that brought the longing back.

I clicked my tongue in time with the noise. It sounded like a hungry woodpecker nosing its way through a tree.

"You can hear my clock," he grinned. "It's over the fireplace. Let me get it for you."

He spared me the sight of the fire and brought back the glass skinned clock from the mantel. Together we admired the energy of the shiny metal gears that moved inside without coaxing from any fingers. While the insides danced, we clicked out the tune the clock sang.

"When are Mama and Papa coming?" I asked when my tongue became tired. One of the hands on the clock moved with a "ker-tick." Next to the rhythmic heartbeat of the clock, it was the only other sound in the room. The minute hand seemed to be the only one willing to answer.

Jonathan didn't want to answer me. He pointed out the farm scene on the Dutch delftware vase from the table instead. I didn't care about the blue cow or the white sky behind it. I missed Mama and Papa. I began to sob for them.

"They aren't coming," Jonathan croaked in a whisper. I couldn't hear his voice over my cries. I had to read his lips. I stopped my ruckus because I could tell he wanted to repeat it. He cleared his throat when he saw I waited for him. "They aren't coming, Isabelle," he said firmly. It was here that the wrinkles I've become accustomed to seeing were born. They nestled in between his brows and stole away his soft, boyish features.

"But I want them," I said in a sniff before letting more tears come.

"I know," he said.

Jonathan wasn't rattled the way the adults had been. He didn't shush me. He didn't get angry, lose his patience, or make promises that he wouldn't be able to keep. He left me to shut the room's door. When he came back, he sat on the floor in front of me. His face was already tear-streaked.

"This room, Isabelle, is a library and it's a safe place. Here, you can cry as loud as you need to and they won't hear. I know—," He roughly wiped his face with his fingers, "—because I come here to cry for my mama and papa."

"Your Mama won't come?" I asked in staggered breaths.

"She can't."

"Your Papa?" I wept the question and began to shiver.

"He won't." For a moment, a flash of anger overtook his look of sorrow, but the latter returned when he saw my discomfort. He went for the blanket and wrapped me in it. "Do you remember anything before today? Do you remember the trip? Me?" he asked. He knelt at my dangling legs and took up my hands.

I didn't—neither of them and this frightened me.

"Well, Isabelle, my name is Jonathan. Don't be afraid. I have some of your memories for you and I'll keep them safe." Jonathan pointed to his head. His soft smile twisted into a pained grimace, and to hide his weeping from me, he dropped his chin to his chest. He kept his sounds inside and the tremble in his shoulders was the only evidence that he cried at all. When he caught his breath, he smeared away what wet he could reach with a shoulder. He narrowed his brows and shook his head. "Most of them aren't nice ones. Not nice at all. These, especially, I want to keep for you. May I?" he asked. "Until you are ready for them?"

I didn't want any of them if they were bad, so I nodded in agreement. My memories weren't lost, I thought. They were just in my new friend's possession. He'd take care of them for me.

"Very good. Thank you, Isabelle, for sharing." He smiled and smoothed back the stubble on the top of my head and announced he was now going to share with me. "This room, beginning today, is yours but it's just one of the gifts I have for you today. I have one more, from your parents, but know this is all I will ever offer you from the memories you're letting me keep. The only life you ever need to be concerned over is the one that starts here—now. Do you understand?"

I remember he made my little hands gently clap in time to his spoken question with help from his. I found it funny. It even made me giggle. I had forgotten what he asked so he had to repeat it for me. Even after he did, I didn't understand it. I would later ask again for Mama and Papa, and even later, as I grew, I'd continue to press him and ask other questions, but Jonathan remained true to his word. He has never shared another detail. Even the smallest of them that I begged him for remain to this day locked tight inside him.

I gave him his nod and he gave me the remaining gift. It was the name he had heard my parents call me. Izzy.

"My mama and papa are gone, too. I'm all alone here. Izzy, will you stay with me?" The way he asked was stronger in plea than an invitation. It tugged at my little heart that day, and it makes my grown one ache.

My nod didn't change the fact I still wanted my mama and papa. Jonathan knew this and that's why on my first day here, he gifted me the library.

My agreement undid him, and this unraveled me further. He didn't use the tea-kettle hushes on me like "they" did. Together we wept. We let the tears come and our united sorrow was the first stitch that bound us together in our inseparable friendship.

"You won't leave me like Mama and Papa?" I remember asking when my tears were spent.

"I won't," he sobbed. He hugged me to seal his oath and cried into my shoulder. "Ever. I promise."

I shut my eyes and fell asleep against him. I didn't want to tell him that I was tired. He would have brought me back to my room. I could tell he needed to stay in the library longer. He had more tears to get rid of than I did.

FIVE

Sometimes it's a hard transition. The fog I feel from a day's long journey in the library can take hours to burn off when I resume the drab life of cottage living.

I would never come out again if I had my way. The early memories I have with Jonathan mingle with the stories in the room, and it makes life here look empty and pointless. There's nothing in the rest of the house but aimless wandering; between sparse extra rooms and carefully manicured outdoor spaces, there is nothing else here. I'd be happy in the library with just Jonathan to visit me. Miss Margaret isn't an option. She won't visit. When I asked for her company in the library to read with me one day, she said the Good Book is the only reading she needed and the only she would ever find time for. She only comes inside to dust or fluff the pillows and she won't even give the books a second glance.

Miss Margaret, I'm sure by now, has the tea waiting in the sitting room. I touch each stair with both feet to slow the trip down to allow my face extra cooling time. Teatime is every day at five o'clock sharp.

When I left the library, the clock read five minutes after. It's going to take me at least another five to make it down the stairs. Perfect. Either way, late or blotchy, I'm going to get smothered—in scolding or concern.

The tea is waiting. I'm glad I'm not the only one running late. Jonathan isn't here yet, either. I must remember to complain again to him when he comes. It's his fault that teatime doesn't taste as pleasant as it used to. We used to drink coffee.

A few years ago, Jonathan brought home our first batch of tea. Miss Margaret was captivated upon the first sip. She was delighted to discover recently that she needn't ask Jonathan to replenish the stock upon his next visit to the orient, for now, she can get the foul-tasting leaves at the coffee shop in town. Oh, how I miss the smell of fresh, ground coffee beans! The smell of mint mingled with leaves is no comparison to the robust scent of coffee. I would much rather drink a bean than a leaf. It seems more logical to me.

I take the seat farthest from the fireplace to wait for Jonathan. Evolyn doesn't mind that I have chosen to sit this far from her; she's giving me the same smile from her place in the oil painting that she gives me every evening. She knows I'll move up closer when Jonathan comes. He makes the flames in the fireplace easier to bear. They don't taunt and jeer when he's here.

The painter has done a remarkable job with his mother. He has captured much more than just her beauty. For the brush to portray her in this light, the artist must have known her. Her eyes don't have the blank stare that the other paintings here do. They beckon the admirer to come closer, and I can feel kindness in them. I love the blue gown that she wears in the painting. The white wispy fabric at the wrists is just as light and airy in person as it is in the painted version. Her dress still hangs in one of the closets. When I was younger, I used to try it on. I haven't visited it in a while. It's because my frame has grown beyond her delicate one.

I walk along the edge of the room to avoid the fire's glow to get a better look at my favorite piece of jewelry. Gleaming from a finger is a copper ring with an unusual emerald green stone. The copper band is different than what most women prefer to wear. Most choose gold or silver. What's highly unusual about this ring is its stone setting. Most gems are like twinkling, colored pieces of glass. This one looks like the polished back of a turtle's shell. I wish again like I always do when I see it, that I could see it in person. She's smiling at me and willing to show me herself if she could only move. I wish I had known her. I side-step, my toe just missing the illuminated section of the floor. I wish she were my mother.

"Breathtaking, isn't she?" Miss Margaret brings in some biscuits and places them on the table next to the tea service. With her hands on her thick hips, she shakes her head. "Too young. She was taken from us too young. She was a fragile little thing, but an enormous heart bursting with gold that sweet woman had. Why if it weren't for that beast of a man—"

Miss Margaret's thoughts are cut short by the sound of boot heels in the next room. Cut short again. There is always an excuse or a problem that causes these types of conversations to stop.

Jonathan steps in the doorway with a sweet, lopsided grin and greets Miss Margaret with a kiss to the cheek.

"Miss Margaret, I've decided today is the day you get thanked properly for forcing us to tea."

He gives me a wink. I smile at him. Force is right. We complain to each other often how much we dislike tea and equally dislike the formal air it produces.

"Thank you for your teacups and saucers. They both have an upside—I get to spend every evening when I'm home, without fail, with my two favorite girls."

Jonathan's hands are behind his back. Occasionally, he'll bring in flowers. A petal that coasts to the floor is the clue that this is his surprise.

This is the longest Jonathan has been home in between trips. The last trip he took was the shortest. It was last spring, and he was home again by the end of summer. I don't think about it; well, I try not to, but I can't help but notice how much time has passed. I know another trip must be around the corner. Each year it gets harder for me to see him go. I don't want him to go. I curl my toes in my shoes to keep myself from crying and I bite into my lip to punish myself. I'm a complete fool. He's not even gone yet—and I don't even know if he has plans on going. I'm wasting tears on a what-if.

Miss Margaret giggles and swats at him with her towel. She then reminds him of his place and how he shouldn't be kissing the hired help. Miss Margaret is help, but she is the next best thing to the mother he no longer has. She knows this, for she wholeheartedly embraced her role as a mother to both of us long ago.

"This is all I have to show for hunting today. It's not venison, but it's something." He reveals the two bunches of flowers that were hidden behind his back. Miss Margaret gasps just as he thought she would. She adores flowers and would have fresh bouquets in every room, every day if she could.

"Oh, they're beautiful—and less work for me. I'll take them!" She says with her nose buried in blossoms.

Both of us chuckle. Miss Margaret never shies away from work. She's happiest when life is bustling and frenzied. The disassembling of a deer on top of her daily duties would have been her earthly version of heaven.

Now that Jonathan is here, I take the chair by the fireplace where the tea service is set. He hasn't taken his seat yet. He's by his mother's picture. Whenever he's near her picture like this, I like to note all the similarities between the two. They are innumerable. His eyes are gifts passed down from her, and today they are their usual cheerful green. Both have hair in curls of brown that match the hue that's splashed in their eyes. His mother's cascades down shoulders that cap a frame that's "dainty like a porcelain doll," Miss Margaret has said, not needing to look at the picture to provoke her memory. Jonathan's brushes the tops of his shoulders and plays often in front of his eyes. Both mother and son have the same pleasant demeanor about them. You can see it in Jonathan's posture and his gait. Light, carefree, and playful. Evolyn's can be read in her parted smile. It's not tight pressed like the others in their portraits. There can't be much of anything of Edward in Jonathan—besides maybe the stronger stature and richer skin color that stray from his mother's—there isn't anything left.

He already has his summer skin and the season has barely begun. Jonathan is the master of the house, and even though he doesn't need to, he works as hard as any of the hired help, and he can be found working alongside them on most days. On many occasions, visitors have thought him to be one of them with his summer tanned skin and rough hands. In the summer months, his skin darkens to the color of the toasted bread Miss Margaret sometimes serves at tea, sprinkled with cinnamon and sugar. In the winter months, his skin lightens and then, at tea, when we compare arms, mine is the darker. Besides Jonathan's, my skin color is consistently darker than everyone's here and among the women especially. English ladies prefer to have snow-white skin. This should be proof enough for Miss Margaret that I'll never be a lady. I can never obtain that pale of skin no matter how much I avoid the outdoors.

"Both of you are late. Your tea is getting cold. I won't keep either of you another second. Enjoy your time and remember what I always say," Miss Margaret grins.

"Proper manners make the tea taste that much better," Jonathan and I finish for her in unison.

Miss Margaret seems visibly tickled to offer up today's mundane lesson in tea. Perhaps she's thinking this is the evening we'll get it right; with no more dares of who can stuff their cheeks with the most sugar cubes or who can balance their spoons on their nose the longest. I hope she isn't holding her breath. We'll be short a "mother" and a housekeeper. She takes my bouquet from Jonathan and snuggles them to her with her bunch. He leans in for a thank-you kiss.

"Oh, you!" She swats. The color in her cheeks spreads down her neck. "Next time, wipe those boots off before you come in from the garden. Honestly, my floors!" She fights a smile and gives him a quick kiss on the cheek before leaving. "Dinner will be ready in an hour. See you two then," She announces without looking back. A new task has already taken her attention.

"Thank you," I say with wide eyes. "Your flowers couldn't have been timed better."

"You're welcome," he grins back. "The curtains were drawn back longer than usual. I had my suspicions you wouldn't make it."

Jonathan falls hard on the chair across from me. He stretches out his legs and crosses his booted feet. The rough motion causes his hair to fall into his lashes. I brush away invisible pieces from my forehead in hopes he'll take the hint. I do wish he would tie up his hair. Curls often fall over his eyes and more than once I have had to sit on my hands to keep from tucking the unyielding pieces behind his ears. It shouldn't bother me that he would rather his mane go unruly. I can't stand to wear shoes and find them to be confining and uncomfortable.

"It was a beautiful day today, wasn't it?" he says. He smiles, and the corner of the eye that I can see wrinkles.

"I had the curtains pulled all day. I didn't see it. Was it?" I ask. "I noticed the sun came out," I say in a shrug. Sunny days for me are not as sought after as the rainy ones.

"What? You missed your most favorite of days. The sun has only just managed to poke his head out. Let me describe what you missed. It was a glorious day, dark and gloomed with the gentlest of mist for rain. This is why you need to go hunting with me. To see these things." He's smiling his lopsided smile. He slides his hands back in his hair and leaves them behind his head to lean back into them. Dark and cloudy days are my favorites, and he knows it. I know what he's up to. He's trying yet another tactic to get me to go outside with him.

"Why you like these kinds of days is beyond me," he says. "They're sad and depressing. Only…"

"…trolls and the like enjoy them," I tease and finish his favorite line to describe the only beings who could enjoy such weather.

I don't know why I love these days so. Maybe because I don't feel as guilty being shut in my library when I should be outside doing the things Jonathan and Miss Margaret force me to do instead.

This makes Jonathan laugh. "You are not a troll." He gives me a soft smile. My repeated fingertip brush across my forehead works; Jonathan combs back the returned wandering lock of hair out of his eye before crossing his arms.

"How's your book dare coming along?" The disobedient curl slips back down into its original position.

"I just finished up today. I've read two hundred and fifty books. Dare complete," I say. I can't help but smile. Somehow, I've managed two successes today; with my book dare and the short but victorious influence I had over his hair.

I drop four cubes of sugar into my tea, skip the spoon, and swirl the liquid around in my cup. I'm not a fan of tea but I like the thought of it. The pretty cups, the steam that's fun to blow on as it rises, and the warmth it gives my cold hands as I cradle it, in the most unladylike way I have been told. Given enough time, Miss Margaret says even the most unpleasant things can become tolerable, even almost enjoyable. I take a sip of the hot tea and make a face. No, still bitter, like I went out back and took a handful of leaves off the nearest tree and poured hot water over it.

Jonathan laughs. He knows that Miss Margaret's attempts with us are futile. We could be cultured if we wished to be, but neither he nor I wish it.

"That is a huge achievement! Well done!" he praises in a clap. "Tell me, what was this prized two hundred and fiftieth book about? I think we should frame it and place it in the center of the mantle as a trophy to the grandest accomplishment of the great Miss Isabelle Elizabeth Gudwyne."

I snicker and smile back at him from behind my steaming cup and glance at the fire behind him. His comment makes me happy. Not the idea of my achievement in a place of honor near his mother's picture, but the fact that he let me have his last name. On my second day here, I cried when I found out I only had two names. He and Miss Margaret had *three.* My tears were dried when Jonathan said he'd share his last one with me. It gave me an identity, a sense of belonging, something I was unsuccessful in finding in my books. But my smile doesn't last. It's not legal. It's not binding. It was just another gift to soothe away my sorrow.

Jonathan's name isn't mine.

He wouldn't like my book choice. I may get into trouble. May— but most likely, I won't. I never get into trouble—well, with Miss Margaret yes, Jonathan, no—but I don't want to put it to the test. When I was little, he put all the dragon books on the highest shelves so I couldn't reach them. He didn't want me reading them. Why? He's good at keeping quiet. He wouldn't tell me. He forgot about them, and I grew. The fire pops and a log shudders when I ask a question to distract him from the book.

"Do we have Savages here?" I ask.

My question catches him off guard, but a smile replaces the pained expression that had slipped across his face for a breath of a moment. It was so fleeting; I would have missed it if I didn't know it was a look that sometimes lingers there much longer.

"I have come across one or two," he says with a grin, and he nods down at my half-laced shoes.

Miss Margaret with a broom in hand has overheard the question from the hall.

"I would say there's one with filthy boots right here in my sitting room." She playfully squints at Jonathan as she sweeps up the moist dirt clumps that have fallen from his boots.

"No, really. Do we have any here in England?"

I'm serious about the question. I have never been past the stone wall that surrounds the property. There could be natives with masks of paint hiding in the trees waiting to attack while I sit here and pretend to care about tea and polite conversation.

"Savages?" Jonathan watches Miss Margaret sweep. Their eyes catch briefly before she scuttles off in a hurry.

"Natives. Red people. The ones that live in the New World. I read they are a savage people, killing entire colonies."

I bite into one of Miss Margaret's biscuits that are heavily brushed with butter. The morsel collapses in my mouth and turns into sugar. When I make them, they taste like hardtack, and chewing them makes my jaw sore.

Miss Margaret says it's all in the kneading.

Jonathan shifts in his chair and looks into the kitchen for help. "Savage is a harsh description, Izzy."

Help doesn't come, though both he and I know Miss Margaret heard and has an opinion. She always has one. He places his folded hands to his face as if in prayer searching for the right answer.

"From what I know, they're nowhere near savage. They're people, just as you and I are."

He lifts an ankle to the top of his bent knee, and as he does, another chunk of dirt falls to the freshly swept floor.

"Think for a moment how these people must have felt with strange ships showing up on their shores. Oddly dressed men speaking in a foreign tongue. Can you imagine the questions that must have raced through their minds? 'Who are these people? Where do they come from? Do they come in peace? Are they going to stay?'" The vein in Jonathan's neck is pulsing. The fire behind him swells when a log shifts.

"Is that how you felt when I came here?" I say with a sly smile. I smother a section with jam before taking another bite. I know what the throbbing in his neck means. My question has made him upset so this one is meant to detract. He either doesn't hear me or wants the conversation to continue.

"Not every colony had problems with these people, Izzy. In most cases, Natives were crucial to the survival of our people. Teaching them to plant and to hunt, to live off the land." Jonathan takes a deep breath, probably to quench the throb in his neck. The fire leaps higher in its confined boxlike space, and Jonathan changes positions. He leans forward and rubs his hands together, and they sound like rustling pieces of paper. "Izzy…"

I don't hear the rest of Jonathan's answer. A memory is coming. I can tell. When I get one, I tingle from head to toe with needle-like stings. Jonathan recognizes them when they come, too; I freeze, and I can't move. He's shifted forward to the edge of his chair, and he's waiting for the faint that always comes at the end.

This time, a returning memory is playing like a living picture book in the fire. It's forcing the firelight to pulse in rhythm with my heartbeat. The already lustrous oranges, reds, and yellows become even more vivid and are too terrifyingly beautiful to turn away from.

Miss Margaret's biscuit turns to stone inside my mouth when I see the images in the fire. People are melting into one another like sticks of butter on a hot plate. Men, women, and children—they're all reaching out with glopped arms and faces contorted in pain. The fire's roar replaces screams that can't be vocalized.

My uneven gasps of breath and the tinkling of my dropped teacup echoes in the narrowing, cramped room that seems consumed with the fire's story.

Jonathan pushes himself up to get to me. A gentle ping and a hollow roll are the last distinctive sounds I hear before my ears press shut.

"Mercy sakes!" Miss Margaret gasps. "Her lips have no color! She's going to faint again, poor child."

Jonathan is the one who guides me to the couch; Miss Margaret's feet are nailed to the floor. My stomach lurches on the way over, and I fear I won't be able to keep down my biscuit and tea. There may be more to clean up than spilled tea and broken china.

Miss Margaret is fanning me with her apron, which I find funny. It's a worthless gesture. Not a whiff of air is coming from it. It just makes her look like a flapping bird. Jonathan props my feet up under a pillow and asks her to get a cool cloth.

"What did you tell her?!" Miss Margaret shouts to the kitchen for a cloth. When one is brought out, she hands it over to Jonathan. The wet feels good against my forehead, and the cool pressure helps ease the spinning.

"Nothing! Absolutely nothing," Jonathan says. My hands didn't feel cold until he gathered them in his. He brings them to his mouth and huffs his warm breath onto them.

"I know exactly which book it is, Jonathan. I'll get it straight away," Miss Margaret promises, but before she does, she bends over and begins picking up pieces of jagged china from the puddle of tea.

How could she know which book it is? She's never in the library but to clean. The thought tumbles through my brain and mingles with the fire's disturbing scene like a turned-over hourglass.

"Is it damaging her to faint like this?" she asks Jonathan as if he could know the answer. "Your mother was a fragile sort, just like our Isabelle. Jonathan, I will not lose her like I did your mother." Miss Margaret's lip quivers and the cup pieces clink as she places them in her apron.

Jonathan shakes his head and hushes her. "She'll be fine. She's strong. She just doesn't know it yet."

Miss Margaret gives Jonathan a reluctant look. A droplet of water escapes from the cloth and rolls down my neck, and it leaves behind a cool, refreshing trail. I want to cry but I'm too weak. Strong. Strong was Jonathan who could handle anything with a silent strength. Strong was Miss Margaret who could work circles around women half her age. I want to laugh at the insanity of Jonathan's statement. I even try to tell him, but nothing works. I feel as if I'm floating away.

Jonathan keeps hold of my hands. It feels as if he's my only tether to a world that is narrowing down to a speck.

I can feel his calloused thumbs roll over the tops of my fingers before my entire body goes numb.

"Jonathan?" Mrs. Margaret stands to show him a ring damp in tea.

It is a copper ring with a green stone.

SIX

By morning the whole house is a buzz. According to the talk, Jonathan and I had become engaged last night. That's what Mary, one of the girls from the kitchen who brought my breakfast tray said before demanding to see the ring. I, of course, had no clue as to what she was talking about. My finger is still as bare as the day I was born.

Mary, a tiny girl of sixteen, blushed three shades of red and apologized profusely when I corrected her. She told me she got her information from someone in the kitchen who was told by yet another who was asked by Miss Margaret to fetch my cloth. Jonathan was seen kneeling and Miss Margaret holding the ring, so my collapse on the couch was read as a faint from sheer excitement.

Miss Margaret and Jonathan came up after breakfast to check on me. I acted like I was asleep. I could hear them talking. Jonathan told Miss Margaret he was going for the doctor, and that I was to stay in bed until I was cleared to get out. He was upset that I wouldn't get my shooting lesson. I heard him say it was to be my last one. Miss Margaret said that if I didn't know how to shoot by now, I never would, and one less lesson shouldn't matter. I almost sat up to ask what all the fuss was over with me and Jonathan's fancy guns but I was supposed to be asleep—so I couldn't. Jonathan put yesterday's flowers on the dresser by my bed and asked Miss Margaret to say goodbye to me for him. He was leaving for the rest of the week and he didn't want to wake me. I wish he had. When he walked out, I nearly jumped out of bed after him. Nearly.

He'll only be gone for the rest of the week. That's days compared to the usual months that it easily could have been. The house will be gloomy and empty with him gone, but this time, it'll be a good thing. The dropped ring and missed proposal could have possibly changed things between us. Why did he have to go and ruin everything? For me, our relationship has been steady and constant like a beating heart. Natural and easy, it is something I never thought about. Now, I fear the rhythm of our friendship will be forever changed when I have to somehow refuse him—that is if a proposal was what I was going to get last night. Why else would he have his mother's ring? I hope he doesn't try again.

I punch the bed pillow and then put it over my face. Why do I have to be such a weakling, fainting like some fragile flower deprived of water? On the positive side, my abilities did save me from a rather uncomfortable engagement refusal.

The fainting spells are starting to become more frequent. Last night was the most terrifying. I had my first full memory—or at least the first full one that I have been able to keep. Usually, I get just a picture of one. This one was a series of pictures—like the flowers Jonathan drew for me on the pages of an empty journal once. He drew each one subtly different. When he let the pages flip through his fingers, the flower looked like it was opening. Unlike a dream that slowly dissipates just moments after waking, this new memory feels like it's a forever part of me just as my skin is. It's as bright and vivid in the post-morning hours as it was last night.

In my memory, people in the moving pictures were burning; but they weren't burning alone. The flames that melted them also melted me.

The floor is cold on my bare feet, and I tiptoe to the water basin Miss Margaret filled earlier. The water is no longer warm and the cold shocks me further awake. I glance across the room and a sad, droopy willow bids me a good afternoon from outside the bedroom window. The sun looks warm, though the early summer temperatures say different. Regardless of its depressed demeanor, the lacey leaves that drip from branched fingertips look longer today after the day-long soak that I missed yesterday. I sloppily splash on another round of frigid water and allow the cold to punish my face. I feel just like that tree. Droopy and sad. A strong, confident oak like the one carved onto the doors of the library is the type of tree I want to be, but I don't have a clue how to accomplish that.

"Oaks can't grow indoors. They need sunshine, soil, and air," I argue with myself.

The basin was filled too full, and I can't keep the water from sloshing over the edges as I make my way to the window. Only half of the water splashes to the bushes below and the rest is either on the floor or absorbed by me. I sop up most of the wet and put on a fresh gown before rushing on back to bed, promising myself it will just be long enough to get warm again, but Miss Margaret changes those plans with a rap on the door. She pushes through with her backside and enters with a tray.

"How are you feeling this afternoon, child? My, my, may we thank the Lord above! You look so much better today. Your cheeks have color."

Her cheerful Irish accent fills the room with the sound of a song. Though a large woman, Miss Margaret carries herself with elegant grace. She's light on her feet; so much so that it makes me wonder if she's barefoot under her skirt, but I know better. Miss Margaret…barefoot? She pauses at my bedside and waits while I adjust my pillow. I fluff it and punch it two times for good measure. A raised brow voices her impatience.

"I think I might sit here a spell and let myself rest up just a bit," she sighs. She pulls a chair to the bedside and drops down. "Ah, how wonderful to get off these aching feet."

Miss Margaret tries to massage her feet—through her boots. The impossibility of her achieving relief that way makes me giggle, and I dip my finger in the thick icing of the cake on my tray for a quick taste. The frosting is smooth, and as it softens, it covers my tongue in a silken coat of sweet. I have a suspicion she wants to discuss last night—Jonathan and the ring. I would rather avoid these subjects altogether. I care for Jonathan and the thought of crushing his heart in a refused proposal is something I don't want to think about.

"Miss Margaret, you and I both know how much you despise sitting still!" I tease. I skip over the healthy lunch items, the potatoes, and venison, and cut into the cake instead. I don't even know if Miss Margaret can sit still. She has as much energy as Tubs.

She laughs at my ability to see through her ruse. She takes the rare slice of idle time to tuck loose strands of wiry hair back into her cap. She pats at the loose bun twisted at the base of her neck to check for further disorder and in proper posture sits tall and upright as if her energy has miraculously returned. It's obvious I had made her nervous last night, and she's still quite worried about me. She never just sits.

"Well, then, how about I *try* to sit for a moment and keep you company until the doctor gets here," she says.

The "doctor" word immediately releases a volcano of energy from within and I let the heat from it flow. I make no attempts to cork its power or hide it from her.

"Doctor?! I don't need to see the doctor!" I all but slam my fork on the metal tray, and the bouncing fork's stem chips the edge of the cake saucer.

I was hoping Jonathan had forgotten or that Doctor Batchford was just too busy today to see me. I dislike his visits. His questions are always the same and they are always directed towards me. I don't particularly enjoy talking about myself, so most of the time I don't, but somehow, he always finds something to write in his notes. He spends much of our visits scratching out ink with his quill pen.

"Isabelle Elizabeth!" Miss Margaret scolds. She makes it clear my behavior is distasteful to her by using both of my names. "I declare, your temper! Your eyes practically boil red!"

Her comment makes me wince. She had once told me that my eyes looked like gemstones to her like the good Lord himself gave me two brown agates. I looked them up in one of Jonathan's geology books. They look like caramel candies swirled with chocolate. When I get angry, the toasted hues step aside and give the red flecks hidden behind them their chance to rule; that's what Miss Margaret says anyway. I've never seen this. When I asked her what my eyes do, she said to picture my coffee when I add milk to it and the way the white swirls around like liquid silk. Take away the milk and add the crimson color of fire instead. Fire in my eyes? I don't like the thought that fire lives there. I wish she'd take back what she just said.

"Your behavior is unacceptable, young lady! Jonathan may tolerate it, but I will not. He's the one who suggested the doctor, so your quarrel is with him.

Though I must admit, I wholeheartedly stand behind him. He *and I* just want to make sure you're all right. A grateful attitude towards our concern is more of what I expect from you."

I apologize but I don't mean it. The towering cake that had just made my mouth water moments ago has lost its appeal, and I push it away.

"The spells are getting more frequent, Izzy. Just for peace of mind, let the doctor look at you."

To defuse the situation, Miss Margaret tries what usually works. A gentle touch. But she makes a mistake; she has put her hand on my arm, and it shifted my sleeve. Contrasted against last night's memory is exposed skin that resembles an odd, patchwork quilt. I despise my arm. It looks like a mish-mash of other people's skin; hues of muted pinks and creams are knitted together with a few healthy patches of my bronze pigment. It disturbs me that Miss Margaret's aged hand looks healthier than the healed burns on my arm.

"Does it still hurt?" Her hand slides from my arm to her lap.

"Sometimes. But not today." I smooth my sleeve back to my wrist and nurture the strong desire to get back into the library. Too many memories of long days trapped in a body consumed with pain are why I choose to spend as little time as possible in my room and this bed.

"Once Dr. Batchford clears you, we'll get you up and dressed. Maybe you can ride Rosemary today," she says. Miss Margaret gets up to tug at my bedcoverings until all the wrinkles are smoothed out. She's keeping something from me. She's excessively primping. My face must be scrunched. She lets out a sigh and sits back down. The loose thread on her apron now has her attention.

"I feel we are failing you. Most of what interests you lies within the boundaries of that dark and gloomy library. It's not good for you to be sealed up in there like a caged bird. I fear it's causing you more harm than good. The world is much bigger than the one you've made for yourself out of dusty old books." She wraps the loose thread around her finger and pulls it free. It gets tucked in her apron pocket where I would have let it float to the floor.

"I'm perfectly happy and content in the state I am in, Miss Margaret." I hope she notices that I paraphrased a piece of Scripture for her, to prove all the time in the library to be beneficial, though I never read that. I just remember that line from one of the nightly readings with Jonathan.

Though I have little desire to go outside and pursue other interests, the truth is that I know deep within my heart, at some point, I'll have to. Miss Margaret is right. I'm a caged bird with one song. Books. If I truly want to find out who I am and find out what the world is like beyond the ink, I'm going to have to venture outside and not just to the gardens and stables, but past the stone walls to the unknown. My stomach flutters at the thought. I wish an anxious spirit could be extinguished as easily as a candle's flame.

"I have no desire or need to go beyond our gates," I lie, no longer believing the statement to be true.

A moan vibrates past her pressed lips. She crosses her arms and studies me. "You met one challenge this week. May I lay another so soon at your feet?"

"You want me to go out there," I guess. I stretch up to look out the window, and the nature that peeks back fills me with the urge to cry.

I slam back down in my bed to punish my stomach's swelling ache. I was wanting out of this bed but being "out there" for too long fills me with anxiety. I know I just decided that I need to try at some point, but it had *just* been decided. I need more time to mull it over; to take the plunge when I feel truly ready. I can't decide which is worse, lying here remembering or going out there worrying. But stomachache aside, I am not one to turn down a challenge.

"For the rest of the week, just until Jonathan gets back, no library and no books. Well, except for the Good Book of course. As with the out-of-doors, you don't have to go past the stables. I just want you outside, young lady. A large dose of English summer air will do you good." She narrows her eyes. "Did you happen to include the Bible as part of Jonathan's dare?"

I grab my pillow and put it over my face and moan.

"Aye, Izzy! The most important book in Jonathan's library and you haven't even cracked open the cover." She flings her hands in the air in disbelief.

I spring upright to defend myself. "*That* I did, Miss Margaret. I read the first handful of chapters, but then all the 'begats' came." I roll my eyes at the thought of long lists of names that no person should have to pronounce. "I don't know those people and I don't care to know them." Miss Margaret gasps but her reactions to my behavior have long ago ceased to bother me. It just adds extra energy to my tongue. "I just don't understand it. I figure I hear it every night from Jonathan. That should be enough." I don't add that I rarely pay attention when he reads. That would be pushing her too far.

Miss Margaret's face is as red as a summer beet. I have gone too far. She opens her mouth to answer but changes her mind and leaves the room instead. Her returned startles me upright. Pressed against her chest, in a protective embrace, is a book.

"It's time you're given back what belongs to you. This was your mother's." Her round cheeks maintain their smudged color, but the rest of her face drains when she holds the book out.

"Your mother." The two words sound unnatural and strange together. Visibly uncertain, she lets me take the charred book from her.

The little book, smudged with ash, looks pitiful and injured resting on my clean bedcovers, but it's a handsome, well-made book, even with all the damage. The edges of the red leather cover are curled back and blackened by flame, but the cream pages inside the protective cocoon are still clean and crisp. Threads matching the cover were used to bind the pages together. It was done with such precision and care that not one page is loose, even under such apparent trauma. Flipping through the pages, I notice that it isn't like any other book I've ever seen or read. Though the gold stamp on the front reads "The Holy Bible," the inside is written in a language I can't read.

"Jonathan need not know I gave this to you." She whispers it although she doesn't need to. He's not here, and the walls certainly won't tattle. Jonathan will be none the wiser if neither of us says anything. She takes my hand and squeezes it. "To keep the past away from you is most difficult, and every day it becomes more and more unbearable. Jonathan expressed the first night you lay in this bed that you are never to be burdened with your past. He says it is to be his burden to bear and his alone. But these fainting spells—I wonder if the good Lord isn't deciding for us what is best for you. I feel your past is trying to make itself known."

I have always known my past was something to be forgotten. Jonathan's daily habit of distracting me from it has always made that clear.

Inside the cover, a name is written in a flourishing script. My finger becomes an inkless pen that traces over the swirls and swooshes of my mother's signature.

"Her name was Elizabeth?" I say. My mouth didn't feel like it moved any when I asked it.

I have her name. I had a piece of her with me all along and I didn't know it.

SEVEN

"Yes it is, sweet dear. You have your mother's name." Miss Margaret sits and doesn't even take notice that the picture on the wall beside her is slightly askew. "And those golden threads in your dark hair? You share those with her, too. Her hair was the color of sun-ripened wheat, Jonathan has said. A mighty fine woman she was. Brave, Izzy, just like you."

"Do brave people faint?" My question drips with sarcasm and it pierces Miss Margaret. I wish I knew how to bridle my tongue.

I wonder if my mother would be disappointed in me. I know how disappointed I am. I haven't come across anyone like me in the books I have read, and I'm beginning to think there's something wrong with me.

I wrestle with the desire to throw the singed book as far away from me as possible, but part of me wishes to hold it tight to me and never let it out of my sight again. I choose the latter and press it close. The thought of having something that was my mother's sends a soft feeling over my body, like when Miss Margaret brushes my hair. A piece of the Bible's edge falls loose, and its crumbs litter my bedcovering. The dislodged piece and the smell of smoke-soaked leather cause my neck to prickle with fear.

"How did she die?" I didn't need to ask. The Bible's condition is clue enough. If Miss Margaret fails to answer, it will make what I guess to be true less real.

I hope she remains silent. Let a faint bring on the memory of my mama when I'm ready.

Miss Margaret forces a smile. "You are so much like Evolyn. Do you know she loved the library as much as you do?" It is an odd response to the question I asked but welcome.

So that's why Miss Margaret doesn't like to visit the library. I had always known there was a strong bond between the two women and that she had and still has an intense dislike for Jonathan's father. Evolyn died young. I wish I could summon the courage to ask what happened to her, too, but I already feel I've pushed Miss Margaret beyond what she's comfortable with—as well as myself.

"Child," she says, "may this quench some of your hunger for answers; but know, this is all I am going to offer. I promised Jonathan I'd remain mute over your past, but with his—I never made such a promise. I must share it. It's been so hard to carry the sorrow I have for her alone. Mercy sakes, I don't know how the boy does it," she says in exhale. "Jonathan's father wasn't always an evil man. Greed drove Edward to shatter my sweet Evolyn's heart beyond repair. His behavior killed her." Miss Margaret presses her apron against her mouth to stifle her sob.

I apologize to her and inwardly scold myself over my attitude with her. Could it be possible? Can you break someone's heart to the point of death? It sounds like a story out of one of my books. I can see the sweet, dark-haired beauty from the painting curled up on the library couch clutching her aching chest. Poor Queen Evolyn and her pierced heart! What poison dagger did the King use to force her to leave her beloved young prince behind?

"So that's why Jonathan refuses to speak of his father. It explains his struggle with the wealth left behind, too," I say. The silence is awkward, but I wait through it in hopes Miss Margaret will keep her guard down and share just a little bit more.

She nods. "Only a few things from the original estate remain. What there is here is just a fraction of what the Gudwyne estate used to be. Jonathan was right to have moved us here. He was but a boy, Izzy. A child. At fourteen, the good Lord blessed him with the wisdom to move us here—away—away from that place while Edward was gone on one of his trips. The beast's imprint was everywhere there—like a stain. We couldn't get him out," Miss Margaret shudders. "Jonathan has not only taken care of you, my sweet. He's taken care of me as well. I owe him more than I can ever repay. The boy is all Evolyn. He's nothing like his father. Edward has done unspeakable things. Horrible things, child. Things that will never be repeated in this house. Jonathan has taken great pains to keep the past away from you. Let it stay there. Away."

Without thinking, she squeezes my arm. Though a gentle gesture, she pulls away as if my scars have burned her through the material. She's looking at me, but it's not me that she sees. She's lost in memory, and I wish it were possible to peek inside her head. She becomes aware of her lapse, and she pats at her cheeks to speed up the waking process.

"It must weigh so heavily on that poor boy. Please know that Jonathan is doing everything he can to care for you in the way he thinks best. Trust him. We can be thankful to the good Lord that His judgment has already taken care of the Captain. He's gone. Let us keep him and the past burning where he is."

Determined to change the somber mood, she smacks her hands to her legs. A smile seals the finality with the subject.

"But *you,* my dear, bring the boy out in him. I see it. He is full of such life when he's near you. When he's with you, he seems lighter."

I can tell Miss Margaret is struggling with her loyalty to Jonathan and their bond of secrecy with the love she has for us both. She, as our "mother", wants what's best for us—for me—and for the time being, silence to my past is still the best decision in her mind.

"Now, for the rest of the challenge. There's more," she grins. "I would like your two hundred and fifty-first book to be your mother's Bible."

A sparkle pushes past the soupy gloom that had been in her eyes. She has been trying to get me to read the Bible since my book reading challenge began. I honestly have had no desire to read the Bible. Miss Margaret and Jonathan's God is my God as well for the simple fact that I want to be in heaven with them and not left alone to burn in hell. That's enough for me, and that's all that I want from God. To me, He's as invisible as the angel from the library couch when I was six and just as unhelpful.

"Complete my two tasks and this is yours," she says as her face flushes. "Jonathan doesn't know that I still have this." Again, Miss Margaret lowers her voice. I resist the urge to remind her Jonathan isn't home.

She pulls a necklace out from under her blouse. Still fastened around her neck, she holds out the pendant for me to see. "Jonathan made this for me when he was just a boy. An amazing piece, isn't it?"

Pinched between her fingers is a gold chain and dangling from it is a strange yet spectacular metal owl. The metal bird, shaped of dull silver, twists merrily in the air and ogles me with gear eyes. The teeth around them are comical and look like whimsical lashes. Tucked against his sides are copper wings buffed to a high shine.

"Watch this." Miss Margaret's eyes widen when she pushes down on the copper beak. The bird comes to life with flaps to the wings and eyes that whirl in a dizzying circle.

"Jonathan made that?" This piece of Jonathan forces me to sit up straighter. I'm not sure how to feel. It's an exciting discovery, but I don't like secrets.

I watch in amazement as the brilliant toy begins to wind down and drift back to sleep.

"Yes, he did. He doesn't know I still have this," she smirks. "Oh, my dear, the things that boy could create! He would spend hours in the cellar tinkering. With his father gone most of the time, he needed something to busy his mind, and his inventions did that for him."

"The clock in the library?" I ask. The gear work matches the style of the owl. I would bet tomorrow's cake that Jonathan has made that, too.

"Made by Jonathan. Breathtaking, isn't it? That's the only other surviving piece of his work."

She tucks the owl safely back in its place near her heart. Neither of us is willing to give up our thoughts to speak. I try to picture a young version of Jonathan hunched over in creation for hours the same as I curl behind a book. Miss Margaret, I imagine, is seeing the same similarities. The thoughts have a grip over her attention. She doesn't get up to adjust the curtains, stoke the fire, or reposition the flowers in the vase near the washbasin. Miss Margaret, for once, is still.

When she does wake from the spell of memories, she pounds her strong hands into her legs with a clap and pushes off to stand. "Now, do we have a deal?"

To seal it, she does so in the custom that Jonathan and I seal all our dares. She spits into her hand and holds it out for me. I see a new side to Miss Margaret that I never knew existed, and I find it delightful.

"Deal bonded and sealed, only broken when won," I spit and take her hand. Maybe reading my mother's Bible will bring me closer to finding out who I am—and who she was—and accomplish two tasks at once. Somehow, I'll find a way to read the strange language. The owl is as good as mine.

EIGHT

I was cleared by Dr. Batchford that afternoon, though he wants to come back in a few days to check me again just to make sure. He never shows worry or concern, but he does seem perplexed as to why the fainting spells are becoming more persistent. After I told him what I saw in the fire, he looked intrigued. His theory is the same as my own. The fainting is a result of returning memory.

I get dressed and make my way down the twisting, mahogany staircase. I stop after a few steps to check one of the stair rungs. The thin, jagged crack is still there from my heel when I had to save myself from certain death while attempting a dare of Jonathan's. Jonathan's laugh echoes in my memory as my own bounces down the staircase and into the foyer.

"A sound that makes my heart sing, Izzy-girl." Miss Margaret swipes her rag across the foyer table and disturbed pollen clouds up and tornados in the air. "I remember the day perfectly when Jonathan dared you to slide down that railing. You were a wee little thing. Only ten?" She guesses. "He made it look easy, didn't he?" Miss Margaret shakes her head and chuckles at the memory—*now*.

He had demonstrated how to slide down by whooping with arms out like a bird in flight. He had indeed made it look easy, just like with everything else he does. Well, it wasn't easy and apparently, it's even more difficult to do while wearing a dress. I made it only a couple feet when my dress bunched up underneath me and sent me careening over backward. I caught myself with the back of my knees and there I hung, upside down, my ankles and feet clinging to the banister with my skirt clean over my head. Jonathan roared in laughter at the sight of a headless girl in pantaloons. Miss Margaret on the other hand was not pleased.

She adjusts the fresh blooms and places the taller ones toward the back. Mis Margaret's sly smile rounds her pink cheeks into balls. "On your way outside, I presume?"

"Yes, ma'am, I'm going to pay Rosemary a little visit. Why don't you rest while I'm out? You look tired." I wrinkle my brows at her to show my concern.

"Mercy sakes, why? I feel fine." She places her hands on her hips, and her eyes narrow in her attempt to figure out how I have come to that conclusion.

"It's the necklace. Carrying around that heavy owl all day has to be a burden. But fear not dear madam, soon you shall be released from your shackle of fatigue." I offer her a curtsy and a grin.

"Off with you, silly girl!" Miss Margaret attempts a scowl, but a laugh opens it into a smile. She guides me through the foyer, and she pushes me out the door towards the direction of the stables. "Give Rosemary a kiss for me!"

The stables are beyond the gardens. Evolyn's rose garden is off the path first. I notice the empty stone bench and it makes me miss Jonathan, even though earlier his absence had relieved me. When he's away, the house feels eerily quiet. It's not that there's endless chatter here. Neither of us does well in that area, though Jonathan is better at conversing than I am. His presence and good nature are what adds volume to the house. When we both feel chatty, though, we can get in great debates over silly things like the existence of tree fairies or why we have to wear shoes. Jonathan's reasoning as to why shoes are important is to keep grass from growing on the bottoms of our feet. He said grass seeds stick and they can grow from skin. Though he said this with a straight face, I knew he was just trying to be funny. I can tell when he's teasing. His arms cross and his nostrils flare. Even so, I wore shoes that entire summer.

Beyond the roses are squares of flowers in mixed varieties. Foxglove with its tiny pink bells are my favorite, and white primrose with yellow pupils is a close second. For Rosemary, I choose the magenta blooms from the Fireweed garden. I think they will look sweet tucked into her mane.

I follow the stone path and make sure to not step on any of the seams. This can be achieved only with precise foot placement and deep concentration. I make it to the stable and am close to winning when I collide with Tubs. Our heads knock together in a dizzying thud, and both of us end up on our backsides.

"Your head is as hard as a cannonball! My skull feels like it's cracked clean in two!" Tubs is on the ground rubbing into the pained spot with his hat.

"Yours is the hard one, Alexander Hackett!" My head hurts, too, but I can't rub into mine. I'm on the ground struggling through another skirt entanglement.

"Still not it," he says in a grin. His life-threatening injury is suddenly forgotten. "And besides, that name belongs to Papa. I told you, you're never going to guess."

I've been going through the alphabet trying to guess Tubs' real name. I am back in the A's. Tubs is a nickname his father gave him. Alexander Hackett traps in his spare time when he isn't in the stables or tending to the livestock. Tubs had gotten into one of Alexander's traps and it snapped shut. It pinched the tip of the two-year-old's thumb clean off at the top knuckle. Unable to pronounce the 'th' in thumb, his 'tumb' was a wound he was proud of, and he would hold up his nubby appendage to anyone who showed any interest. The toddler's 'tumb' sounded more like 'tub' and thus his nickname was born.

I offer Tubs a hand and help yank him to his feet. As he brushes himself off, I smash his hat back over his orange curls.

"Hey!" He hollers and swipes at me but misses.

Tubs is an adorable thirteen-year-old. His powder blue eyes and creamy white skin remind me of Dutch vases in the library. Tubs' most notable feature, however, is his freckles. Hundreds upon hundreds of them are speckled across his face and spill down the front of his neck. I have always imagined that to achieve this precious work of art, God had pulled back His paintbrush and let the bristles randomly splatter.

"Come to see Rosemary finally? She sure misses you, you know— it's been almost a week."

"Looks like I have some lost time to make up for then, don't I? What do you think, Rosie, braids and flowers today?" The brush is on the same stool I left it on. When I brush into Rosie's mane, her muscles quiver. I wonder if she just caught a chill like I get when Miss Margaret brushes my hair.

"Jonathan gone again?" Tubs asks. He resumes his chores, removing the dirty hay from the barn, but can't resist planting a big kiss on the handle of his pitchfork. "'Oh Jonathan, must you go? I love you so.'" He looks at me and bats his almost invisible carrot-colored lashes.

I roll my eyes for him, deep, to show how annoyed I am at how fast the false news has traveled. "Yes, he's gone but he'll be back in a few days. In the meantime, you're stuck with me. I'll be spending most of my time out here if it's ok with you."

I tell my young friend about Miss Margaret's challenge and pull apart Rosemary's mane. The brush can only detangle so much; I've neglected her mane for too long. She shakes her head in disagreement at having her knotted sections tugged apart but settles down when the braiding starts.

"Sure, as long as I get my chores done. I've gotten scolded by father twice this week for running off before things got done." Tubs jaw drops down to his neck as he lowers his voice to mimic his father. "'Work first, leisure second.'" He forgoes the needed break between sentences and continues without need to add a breath. "Why don't you help? We can get done quicker—then we can go fishing!"

"How far is it?" I ask only to appear interested. I don't want to go. The stalls are far enough for me today.

"Not far. Just past the woods. It'd be good for Rosemary to stretch her legs a bit. It'd be a nice ride for her. You can handle it. I know you can. Let's try."

He knows the reason behind my hesitation. "I don't know, Tubs," I say. Fish are in ponds and ponds are beyond the rock wall.

"Come on. Please? If it gets too bad, we can always turn around."

"It will get 'bad' and we will turn around," I say with a point from Rosemary's brush. "But, for you, Miss Margaret, and Jonathan, and whoever else wishes me discomfort, I'll try again. And if—*if*—we make it to the lake, you have to put the bait on and take the fish off." I spit and hold my hand out for Tubs, and he shakes it with a grin. Rosemary's mane is finished so the flowers are next to get tucked in. "Rosie, what do you think? Clean your house and then go for a ride?"

I scratch the bridge of her nose and kiss her. Rosemary stomps her foot and shakes her head from side to side as if to reply. But really, I know she is just trying to free herself from the braids.

"Looks like it's a yes," I announce Rosemary's answer, and Tubs responds with a twirl and a whoop.

He hands me his pitchfork and scrambles to get another. I tie my skirt in a knot below my knees and begin to toss clean hay in the emptied stalls. Working alongside Tubs and the swishing sound we make as we dip our forks into waiting hay is a pleasant distraction that keeps thoughts away from the discomfort to come.

It doesn't take us long to get the barn done. Tubs gathers his fishing gear while I lead Rosemary to the whitewashed fence outside. I climb a wrung and grab ahold of braided mane before throwing my leg over. Miss Margaret would rather I ride side-saddle, like a lady, but it feels odd to have my legs facing one direction and my torso the other. She's not here and will never know. I lean over and wrap my arms around Rosemary's neck. I inhale the scent of her. Her strength beneath me is soothing to my belly's growing ache. It knows in just a matter of minutes we'll be outside the stone walls.

"You ready?" Tubs' hands are full of his pole and pail. I scoot up closer to Rosemary's neck to make room for him. "It's going to be fun, Izzy." He climbs the fence and hops on the horse's back behind me.

I squeeze into her side with my legs to give her the sign we're ready to go. She shakes her head and adds a snort, accepting the invitation to come along on my first fishing adventure.

The flittering in my stomach creeps into my chest, and my dress suddenly feels two sizes too small. Rosemary lopes her way through her fenced run. Anxiety crescendos and forces me to pull on her mane once we make it out of the property gate. "You can do this. I won't let anything happen to you," Tubs says. He squeezes his arms tighter into my waist.

He means it. Tubs is a brave boy. He spends most of his time outdoors and most of it alone. I feel the tears again. This is ridiculous! I'm eighteen for mercy's sake! I must have said this out loud because Tubs makes fun of me.

"You sound like Miss Margaret! Here, let me help you."

He pinches me on the arm. Hard. Thankfully, it is my left because if it was the other, I might have hit him.

"Ouch! What's wrong with you?" I look back at him and scowl while massaging the pain away.

"Just trying to take your mind off what you're thinking about," he chuckles from behind. "Try this," he offers. "Focus on a spot. Father said yesterday the reason why my chores are so shoddy is because I don't focus. He said if I worried about my work as much as I do about my fish, the stable would be a sparkling fortress. He told me to focus on the task at hand until it's finished. *Then* I can think of my fish—for a few minutes, that is. Then on to the next task, concentrate, think fish. Task, concentrate, fish; task, concentrate, fish..."

"I got it," I interrupt. I tug on Rosemary's mane to turn her around, but Tub stops me by grabbing my arm.

"Pick a spot up there in the meadow. Where do you want to make it to?" he says into my back.

I look over the waving grass and notice a lone tree standing leafless in the middle.

"There," I point. "To that sad, little tree."

That's me. In the center of the field. I'm not as convinced as Tubs that I can make it.

"All right then. To the sad, little tree. Onward, Rosemary!" He then whispers to me. "You got to make her go, Izzy. When you're ready."

I squeeze Rosemary's side before I have the chance to think things through, and together, the three of us cross the meadow. I keep a steady eye on the lonely, barren tree in the distance and work hard to ignore my pounding heart and the pressure that builds around it.

I'm on my first adventure, Tubs reminds me, in between all the fish chatter. He explains that if the fish are still in their beds of lily pads and pond grass, they'll be biting something fierce. His attempts at distracting me aren't working; I'm far too concerned with not dying. For two miles we travel this way: me picking a spot, Rosemary obediently leading, and Tubs chattering enough for the three of us.

We make it to Tubs' lake. The fish aren't in their beds as he had hoped. I'm the only one who gets a bite, but I scream and shake off our only fish when I feel the strange tug on the line. Tubs is as patient as a thirteen-year-old can be. He mumbles under his breath about girls not knowing a thing about fishing and packs up the bait and hooks. He doesn't stay down long. Tubs never does. His freckles light up and his eyes swell at a new idea.

"You want to see something gigantic?" He asks.

I don't want to sound like an echo and ask how far again. Thankfully, he chides on and doesn't require an answer yet. He's merely throwing the line in the water.

"Do you want to see where Jonathan used to live? It's amazing." Tubs raises and lowers his brows in play. He looks silly widening his eyes with them. His toothy grin tugs at the line he just threw at me. "You think you know him? You don't. He's full of secrets, you know."

That comment catches me and now I'm helplessly dangling with curiosity on his hook. I momentarily forget my fear of going even farther from home and begin to mount Rosemary when he stops me.

"We'd better leave her here. We have to walk through the woods to get there, and they're pretty choked with raspberries. Those thorns will be vicious enough for us to deal with, let alone lead a horse through it. It'll be a walk, but I think we can get back home before dark."

Tubs lifts his shirt and unwinds the rope he's wearing around his pants.

"You're not going to lose your breeches, are you?" I laugh. I watch him unwind the rope and loop it to the ground, and its length appears to be endless.

"These pants are a year too tight. They're not going anywhere. This rope is for my adventuring." He keeps unwinding, at least three more times. "You never know when you're going to need some rope."

He ties a loop at the end and drops it over Rosemary's head. He ties the other side to a tree, leaving plenty of slack for her to wander a bit and to allow her access to a late afternoon's feast of grass.

I remember the library clock and Miss Margaret's story about her owl and ask Tubs if Jonathan's old home happens to have a cellar.

He beats back a low branch with a thick stick, ready to lead us on to our next adventure. Rosemary is too busy with her nose buried into her snack to acknowledge the sharp noise with anything other than a tail flick.

Without turning back he shouts, "Does it ever!"

NINE

It was a wise decision to leave Rosemary behind. The woods are inhospitable. Where trees aren't, wild raspberry bushes are, thick with ripe, juicy berries that stain our clothes and jabbing needles that tear into our skin. Tubs whacks away at the reaching vines with his stick while I stomp down the ankle-high ones. Both of us enjoy taking our revenge from the lingering stings that tarry after being scratched. This place isn't one in which you can stroll like in the gardens at home where the stone paths are clear of plants that bite. I discover the importance of picking up my feet a little higher than usual while walking. Dragging them is dangerous. Earlier, a vine wrapped around my ankles had sent me straight to the ground like a downed tree.

Every few feet, Tubs turns around to check on me. In between the questions, I manage to forget about the ache in my stomach. It's when he asks how I'm doing that the discomfort comes back. I thank him for his concern but ask him to stop. Once the back of him is all I see, the ache miraculously goes away.

Eventually, the woods and overgrowth begin to thin, and we come upon a road, or what is left of one. Two tracks are visible where weeds have been worn away from the pounding of wagon wheels. Erosion from yesterday's daylong soak is eating away at the road and making slow but steady work at smearing it away. A slender trail slithers down the road's edge, transporting rushing water that's anxious to join the river below.

The road is fragile and my foot slips down the soft portion of its edge. Rocks are freed from their muddy graves, and they roll down the incline just to become lost again, this time in the belly of a dark and tangled wood. Before scampering away into the forest's undergrowth, a chipmunk hesitates in front of me and puffs his cheeks while making a bird-like chirp of warning. In his haste, he must have caught his tiny foot in the puddle he hopped over. The reflection of the tree line sways in the ripples left behind. Nature's warnings are everywhere. I can't help but feel everything is fleeing from the direction we're going.

Tubs stick has gone from an axe used to fight off thorns to a staff to help him climb the decaying road. It's a straight uphill climb. It could very well be a ladder to the sky. I keep this thought to myself and I don't share it with Tubs—I don't have any air left to. He's up ahead and is climbing the hill with ease. My lungs feel like withered grapes. When he notices my struggling, he searches the woods for a stick of my own. I'm grateful when he tosses one to me. It helps take some of the strain off the steep incline. My legs scream for a break, but I ignore their pleas. I'm nearly there. When the top of the path begins to round, I can see more cobalt sky than dirt. The new color encourages me to push forward. When I reach the top, I don't celebrate with the insane whoop Tubs does. Gasps are all I can manage.

The sun is beginning to go down, but it doesn't seem tired in the least. Its early evening rays illuminate the forest floor with a renewed vigor as if to give the world one last glimpse of its handiwork. Unusual white flowers with three petals bob their heads in the breeze and cast shadows of stretched-out versions of themselves in the clearing ahead. I collapse onto them, and their disturbed pollen is carried away. The air is heavy with a nose tickling fragrance that makes me sneeze. The shout from it echoes and startles a nesting finch. She flees for safety in a tree near the decaying ruins that lay just ahead. Past my heaving chest, I notice the sun is eager to play a game of peek-a-boo behind a crumbling stone tower attached to the remains of a castle.

"Trillium," Tubs says, hushed, as if not wanting to wake the sleeping, stone giant. He lays down next to me on the flowery mattress. "He planted them here for her."

"Who?" I ask. "Jonathan?"

"No, Captain Edward. For Mrs. Gudwyne." He props himself on an elbow and breaks off a flower from its stem to spin it between his fingers. "He got them from the northern territory in the New World. Not too many people venture up there yet, meaning us English folk, that is. Father says it's mostly French trappers and a handful of missionaries for the 'Reds' that bother to go up that far past the colonies. These flowers don't grow anywhere else but this spot right here." He lifts his hand to show me. My tsk of disbelief makes him laugh. "The place where you can find them is shaped like a mitten! We have a map of America at home and father showed me. A Dutch map. He and I are Dutch, did you know that? Well, he is. My mama wasn't. So that makes me only part Dutch."

Tubs rambles on and I let him. He will get to the point eventually. It's enjoyable just to lay here, and I'm in no hurry to begin walking again. My feet ache something fierce in these shoes. I try to flex them in the stiff leather but it's not easy to do.

"You think your feet hurt in those? Father has a pair of wooden ones that he wears in the stables. I tried them on and it's like trying to walk with logs stuck to your feet." He sends the flower into the air by spinning it between his hands, and it twists in the air before falling alongside the rooted ones. "The flowers. They now grow here, for her," he says, finally finding his way back to the Trillium story. He nods his head toward the tired castle as if she were still there, with a backdrop of sky that is now heavily streaked with pink and orange.

I imagine a square-shouldered man on his knees planting the frilly blossoms under the same colored sky but doing so at dawn instead of the coming night, to surprise his bride when she awoke. I count the castle stories that are still standing. I get four, six if I count the tower that is on the right side. I wonder which window she gazed out to discover the surprise that was brought back for her.

Glassless windows ogle past us with empty stares. Like Queen Ravenswood's hair from my favorite fairytale, vines hang out of panes resembling her trailing, green locks; except hers were decorated with various wildflowers of the forest. They cling down the sides of the building, gathering in clumps at the ground below, and grow up the collapsed roof which resembles a jagged crown. Under the consuming vines where it is visible, blackened rock peeks out. I wonder what happened. Aren't castles nearly indestructible? I envision the great flying serpents that Herodotus wrote about. Maybe they had sprayed the mansion with molten flame and brought it down to its ruin.

Tubs is ready to move on and he offers me a hand up. He jogs ahead and stops in front of a huge hole partially concealed by weeds and grass.

"There are several of these scattered around and hidden like this. We have to watch where we walk."

"What are they?" I ask. I squat to get a better look down the dark abyss.

"Holes for pigs." He says this as truth, and I laugh at him. He huffs at my disbelief. "Do I know something you don't? It's genius, Izzy! How do you bring down a place this big without no one seeing you, no one knowing?"

I blink back at him.

"You live in a library, for mercy sakes, Izzy! You dig tunnels under the castle and pile in the pigs! Light them up, and you have a fire that can burn silently for days, weakening it from the inside out!"

"How do you know this?" I ask, disgusted at the thought of blubbery pigs used as tinder to feed a fire.

"Father and I have a trap line around here. He told me this used to be Jonathan's house. He told me to keep that bit to myself and to keep away from here." The look he takes over his shoulder is spawned by guilt. He managed to disobey his father's wishes twice in one sentence.

"Let's go, Tubs. No need getting you into trouble. I've seen enough."

I hadn't, I was just concerned about Tubs. Surprisingly, the thought of learning more about this secret side to Jonathan far outweighs my anxious feelings, but I can't continue at the cost of getting Tubs' backside bruised.

"No, this is important." Tubs straightens. "If he wants to marry you, and you say yes, you need to know who he is."

His fast-lipped energy is harnessed and a softer Tubs is exposed. I want to give him a smothering hug, but I restrain myself. Boys find hugs from girls disgusting, so I hug him mentally instead.

"Father will understand when he catches wind of you and Jonathan. He'd want you to know, I'm sure of it."

Tubs is a good friend to be concerned of my engagement to a man who has secrets. Jonathan may want to marry me, but I don't want to marry him.

What Jonathan feels towards me can't be love and what I feel for him can't be that, either. My books have told me what love is, and what we have isn't at all what they speak of. The women in my stories are helpless, smitten beauties with no thoughts or opinions. They rarely frustrate their men, and they always have nothing but sweet sayings on their tongues for their princes. I fail miserably in all those areas. The men who love these living dolls fight dragons all day and speak of nothing else but their undying love for their princesses. Jonathan hasn't slain any dragons for me, nor has he even uttered a breath of love. No, if a proposal was what I was going to get, he's lucky my faint intervened. He's wrong in wanting to marry me. He's in dire need of a trip to the library to be set straight.

"There's no engagement, Tubs," I tell him.

I won't explain further. I don't have to. Boys don't care about the particulars of how love works, and it is enough for him because he gives me a shrug and asks if I still want to see. I do, so he leads the way through the tall grass.

We high-step through the waist-high grass, and the movement sends hundreds of seeds with hairy tops floating through the air and swirling about our heads. I follow Tubs' crushed path meticulously because there are several more hidden "pig mines." I had walked too close to one and the edge gave way. Now he makes sure to lead a wider path around the ones that remain. These are frightening, hungry-looking holes, and neither one of us wants to be the one to satisfy their appetites.

The front door to the castle stands as a tall as a foreboding guard. It's made of tarnished copper turned turquoise, but the scales of the serpentine dragon that slithers down the front is the metal's healthy, golden bronze. The serpent is enough to make a stranger turn back from the doorstep. Yellow, jeweled eyes place a deadly dare to any hand brave enough to lift the knocker that pierces his flared nostrils. I don't go any further than the bottom step. It's just a sculpture, but something about it makes my body feel charged with something other than nervous energy.

"Creepy, isn't it?" Tubs isn't afraid and he runs his hand over the dragons curving body. "It feels cold like you would think a snake would feel. They're not, you know. They're warm to touch." He puts his face right up to the dragon's extended tongue and he sticks his out.

"It's the same as the dragon on the rug in the library," I say, noticing the similarity. Without a doubt, this castle once belonged to the Gudwynes.

The serpent's attempts to protect the castle from strangers is a futile one, for the walls surrounding it have crumbled away. I agree with Tubs when he says it's too dangerous to go inside. There are floors, but there are more holes than solid structures. Two doves are brave enough to test fate and both peck at the littered white marble in search of dinner. Their conversation of coos and the crunching of rock from our cautious steps fill the void of Tubs' usual chatter.

I feel like a trespassing stranger peeking in between piles of rocks into something that had once belonged to my beloved best friend. Once upon a time, Jonathan and his family lived in pristine splendor just on the other side of the decay where I stand, where marble once gleamed, and glass sparkled. I knew he held secrets of my past, but I thought I knew all there was to know about him. Now I'm wondering if I know him at all.

"If I'm going to show you the cellar, we'd better get going. The sun's going down, and when it goes down, it goes quickly. Bushwhacking our way home in the dark is not going to be pleasant."

Tubs leads the way along the back of the castle, hopping over clumps of tangled weeds and broken stone. I leap over them, too, though not as gracefully with my slippery boots and dress. My dress is tied in a knot at my knees and out of the way, but it is still too cumbersome for exploring. Exploring—just like a hero out of one of my books. My heart leaps within my chest. For the first time, I feel something other than anxiety.

It surprises me when we reach the edge of the back wall of the castle. We keep going.

"Aren't cellars usually underneath the house?" I ask. Tubs can't hear me through his leaps over the debris.

We squeeze through the remains of a garden of abandoned evergreens. At one time, they probably were clipped religiously into smooth walls to form a maze, but today they are wild branches of green choking out the paths. At each elbow of the maze, a crumbling statue points in the direction in which to continue. A girl made of stone with pipe curls and a missing arm gazes with longing into the distance while pointing the way with the other. She looks heartbroken at having to send her newfound company away.

"Tubs! Do you know where you're going?" I shout. "Shouldn't the cellar be under the house?" He's too far ahead of me to hear. He's already free of the maze and near an octagon-shaped building.

He answers with a wild arm gesture to hurry me up. As he waits by the building's door, he rubs a spot clean on the window.

"We don't have time to go in. Maybe next time." He says with a glance at the fading sun. "Take a peek. It's a pool. It still has fish."

If there are fish, they don't have the pool to themselves. Chunks of ceiling jut out from just under the surface. As fast as a blink, something jumps and twists in the air and leaves only a circular ripple for me to point out to Tubs.

"Told you. It's good fishing there." He huffs on the glass to clean a larger spot and rubs it with his sleeve. "Up there. See the waterfall?" When he points, he leaves a print behind in the film of dirt. "That's how the pool gets fresh water for the fish. The water never overflows because it's constantly circulating. I don't know how it works," he shrugs then taps his temple, "but I know it's genius."

The water is frothy where the waterfall pierces the surface, and the sound of rushing water beckons me to go in and dangle my feet. I change my mind when I see another ripple. Do fish nibble toes? Tubs is in a hurry and is already well on his way without me. He doesn't even turn his head when he shouts for me to hurry.

We don't stop again until we reach a cluster of interwoven trees. Their trunks are twisted, making them look as if they had tried to dance together and forgotten their imprisonment to the soil. Tubs ducks underneath a branch and disappears into the trees' thick canopy. I follow close behind and find my nose touching the tip of his bushy head.

There isn't much room between the trees and the odd door in front of us. It's wide and circular at the bottom and narrows to a point at the top. Rusted hinges hammered into the shape of hands hold the door to its frame. There is no door handle, just a rusted keyhole in the shape of a yawning mouth.

Tubs pushes on a stone in the wall, and a key tumbles out and lands at his feet.

"I saw these trees and thought they'd be fun to climb, and when I crawled under, I found this door." He makes a face and wriggles his shoulders. He squints and pulls his mouth to his shoulder to try to get a look at his back.

"Doggone, my shirt!" he exhales.

Just under his right shoulder, a coin-sized amount of blood has dampened his shirt. There are no rips in the material that would suggest injury. The staining doesn't make sense. Tubs shrugs and flashes me a smile, but it's not his. It doesn't have its usual shine.

TEN

"The walls aren't that wide. About as wide as my leg." He attempts to hold his leg out to show me but there isn't any room.

"They don't need to be any wider than that. There's a stairway that leads straight down and then back underneath the house. That's how the trees hide the entrance so well. I bet it was meant to be a secret escape or something. Are you ready?"

He waits for my nod and inserts the key and gives it a turn. The door clicks and yawns awake and exposes a deep throat of dark.

"Now, this is going to be a little tricky." Tubs steps onto the first step that leads down into nothing but inked black. "We only have a few minutes to reach the bottom before the lights go out and then we'll have to crank again."

Against the wall is a box with a handle. In a circular, clockwise motion, he cranks the handle. The gears inside clink together and above our heads, along the angled ceiling leading down, a line of lights appear. The faster Tubs cranks, the brighter the lights begin to glow. More powerful and constant than a candle's flickering light, these could more closely be compared to the sun. The captured fragments of light are encased in round, clear balls and they hang from stiff rope. They dangle just over my head and I can easily grab one if I want. I hesitate before touching one and

decide it safer to flick at it with my fingers. The clink reveals they're made of glass.

"We have to go quickly. The next crank box isn't until the bottom and these lights won't stay lit long."

Tubs leads the way in a gallop down the stone stairs. True to his word, at the last step, the balls begin to wane. Just when we're about to be blanketed by the dark, Tubs makes the next set of gears sing. This time, a long hallway made of stacked, rounded stone awakens in the light. Beads of moisture disturbed by my hand trickle down the wall and stain the dirt below. Tubs' shoe leaves a print over others, but some look larger than his fresh ones that have been placed on top.

"How often do you come here?" I ask. I hope the tracks are all his. I don't want to get into trouble being somewhere I shouldn't.

"Enough," he says. "But I'm not the only one who visits." He turns to flash a grin to show me he isn't afraid. His freckles are as orange as the glowing veins in the glass balls above him.

Before the balls of light nod off to sleep, I catch a glimpse of reflective shine in the room ahead of us. Tubs reaches into the dark room and muscles the first box. Once the gears clink, light appears, but Tubs stops when the lights are just at a pale glow.

"Here are all the boxes." He walks around the room and points them all out for me. "When the lights begin to dim, run to the nearest one and crank. It's easy at first but harder as the lights charge. When the balls are full, the handle won't turn any farther."

He stops at one of them and cranks the handle fast, showing how easy it is when the lights are near death. He grimaces and slows down when the lights reach their full charge.

He skips to the middle of the room and twirls under a ceiling crammed with dangling glass balls. In a variety of shapes and sizes, each hangs from varied lengths of twisted twine. Teardrop, egg, and tubular—the ceiling is in the whimsical glow of a hundred motionless fireflies.

"With lights like these, you don't ever have to be afraid of the dark!"

"No, I wouldn't," I say. I'm too distracted by the ceiling to see where he is, and I bump into him. I'm blind to the surroundings below the glass balls with bellies of light.

They're already getting warm. I can feel the heat before my fingers touch them, so I brush only my tips along the bottoms. The gentle nudge from the sweeping motion sends them into a swaying dance. The melody of pinging glass makes the damp room feel less gloomy. I have always hated the darkness, but with these lights, every shadow is chased from the farthest corner.

Darkness is no more. The entire cellar is lit in glorious light. If Jonathan had these here, at this home, why weren't they dangling from my own room's ceiling? Or in the library and every room at the cottage? He knows how much I dislike the dark.

"Tubs, are we under the house?" I ask. I run my hands over a long table. It's cold to the touch and made of a mirror-like metal. I can see my reflection in it. Tubs doesn't answer. He's juggling, and he's trying to keep three bolts in the air.

Giant versions of the square-toothed gears used for Miss Margaret's owl support the table's weight. There are three of these magnificent tables running the length of the room. Baskets of gears, levers, nuts, and bolts are stashed neatly underneath each table. Large candlesticks stand at the foot of each table, each with a glass eye on top. I tap one of them with my finger.

"It's a light, like the little ones hanging," Tubs says. "There are threads in them just like the others. The hand cranks seem to be just a temporary, emergency thing. They don't generate enough energy to light these larger ones. There has to be something bigger that runs everything. I mean, I wouldn't want to be cranking every handful of minutes."

Tubs kicks one of the bolts he had dropped with his shoe and sends it clanking into the table leg. He tosses the other two in the basket they came from and answers my last question.

"We're somewhere near the middle, between the castle and the door we came in. That metal door over there opens to a hallway that leads to the castle, but you can't use it. The walls are all caved in." He walks to the other side of the room and begins to randomly open drawers and cabinets. "I'm thinking at one time or another weapons and ammunition used to be stored in here. See?" He holds up a musket ball between two dirty fingers. "It's a safe distance from the castle if something should happen to blow up, and it's well hidden from enemies. Pirates, dragons, or..."

"Savages!" I laugh and play along.

"Yes!" Tubs passionately agrees. "It'd be easy for the men of the castle to get in here if there were a threat of battle, and they can flank the enemy from the back by using the secret entrance. Brilliant!"

He's pretending a metal bar is a gun and he points it at an invisible enemy. He throws the musket ball while making a wet, explosive noise, and it lands with a thud against a bulking wardrobe. There are five more. The oak giants look like the guardians of the secret room. Pairs of two are placed against the three available walls. The fourth wall contains the metal door that had once led to the castle.

Each wardrobe has its own unique story chiseled out of the face of their door, much like the pumpkin Jonathan carved for Miss Margaret one fall. He carved a figure of a fox holding a basket and put a candle inside. It was beautiful the way the light escaped out of the picture. For the wardrobes, there are no candles to light them from the inside, and the dark that peeks out from the doors makes the carvings look like sketches outlined in ebony ink. It doesn't take me long to recognize that the wardrobes' tale can only be properly read by combining them all.

"The creation story," I say on the way over to a wardrobe. Tubs has seen all this before many times. To keep himself entertained, he scoots across the floor on a high-backed chair on wooden wheels after me.

He hums. "Never noticed that before. You're right. There's one missing, then," he says. He points out the last wardrobe with a man and woman surrounded by animals. "The seventh one, the day the Lord said it was good and he rested." He pushes off and speeds towards a table. There, he plants his feet on top and leans back in his chair far as he can without toppling over. He points over to a wardrobe with the rod of copper he had picked up. "Did you notice the keys in the locks?"

Each keyhole has a coordinating key that matches the cabinet's design. The first is a simple strip cut out of the top of the key, the next a curling wave of water. A tree is on the third. The remaining are stamped with a sun, a bird with his wings around a fish, and the last, a deer standing over a sleeping wolf. The last key has an additional element, however. A piece of bone is tied through the key and sways in the air when I hold it up to Tubs.

"Do you know what this is?" I ask. I take notice that in the depiction of Adam, his ribcage isn't symmetrical.

"A stick?" Tubs guesses. He makes a swishing noise with his makeshift sword and doesn't seem interested in the least. He stands up a couple of bolts on the table and knocks them over with the rod.

"It's supposed to be a piece of Adam's rib. That's how God created the first woman. From a piece of man," I say. Tub scrunches up his face.

"Girls," he chuckles. "God would have done better to keep them uncreated."

I get him back by knocking his feet off the table, and it nearly knocks him over backward in his chair.

"Serves you right messing with a girl," I tease. The cabinet is just beckoning to be opened. I turn the key to unlock it and put it in my skirt pocket for safekeeping. The inside is disappointing. There's nothing in it but litter and dust.

"Just a few more minutes and we have to be going," he says. Tubs begins to pick up his mess and returns things the way he found them. "Don't want him to know someone was messing with his things," he says as he lays the copper rod back in the middle of the table exactly how he found it.

"This place is still being used? By who?"

I look in one of the drawers that Tubs left open. This room is no longer the armory that Tubs says it once was, stocked full of cannons, guns, or bows. It looks more like a workspace now. I didn't need to ask Tubs the question. I have found the answer myself. A sketch of a man in strange armor has dimensions and measurements scribbled in familiar handwriting. The dot in the middle of every "o" makes it unmistakable as to who these belong to.

"Jonathan," Tubs answers while cranking the nearest box to return the lights to their brightest glow. "Most everything is cleaned out, except for the baskets stashed under the tables and a few rogue pieces here and there. Like the stuff in that drawer. Neat, isn't it?"

He is now looking over my shoulder at the assortment of sketches. They range from the whimsical—metal fireflies with smaller versions of the cellar lights in their tiny bodies and birds with gleaming gem eyes and copper feathers; to the practical—teapots and clothes irons with clocks and spiral metal tubing. There are even sketches of weapons. Stringed bows with gears and pins, swords of varying blade lengths with copper and gemstone embellishments, and guns so small you can hide them in an undercoat pocket. All the sketches have notes scribbled in Jonathan's penmanship, and his looping initials penned in every corner.

"You thought you knew him, Izzy, but you don't. I've seen him meeting in the garden house with some rough-looking men. Some are men who work at the cottage, but the others, I think they're seamen. Sailors. I heard them all talking in the barn one night when they thought I was in the stable house asleep. Well, I wasn't. I was in the loft trying to coax a barn owl down from the rafters with a mouse. Have you seen him yet?"

Tubs is off subject again and carries on about the owl. He says the books are right; they can turn their heads completely around. He tried to do it but when he did, he heard a pop so loud he thought the men below could hear it.

"They didn't know I was up there, and I heard them talking "sea" things. When the best time to sail is, which ship of Jonathan's would be best to take, the cargo, those kinds of things. I told father what I heard, and he said I should mind my own matters, that the company Jonathan chooses to keep is his business. He said my business is Rosemary's 'business' and he'd tan my hide if I spied on the master again." He rubs the back of his leg. "And he wasn't lyin' either."

The lights dim and go out. We had forgotten to crank. My eyes feel like they're as big as my head as I stretch them wide to try to see. Tubs orders me not to move and says he'll find the crank. That won't be a problem. I have no desire to move. In moments, a light grows, but it's in the hall. Tubs must have cranked the wrong box because the wrong room is lit.

Tubs' eyes are as big as the balls on top of the candlestick lamps. He's nowhere near a crank. We gawk at each other like two street urchins who have just stolen a loaf of bread. I force my feet to move, and I grab Tubs by the shirt and drag him with me across the room to the wardrobe that I had unlocked earlier. The sound of boots clopping down the stone steps echoes in the long corridor.

The wardrobe is spacious enough for both of us, and the decorative carving provides a place to peek out without fear of being seen. The wardrobe has a strange smell and the floor is crunchy under our feet. What didn't get kicked out when we rushed in tickles my hand as I adjust my skirt to sit on my knees.

The lights dim just as a figure appears in the room's doorway. The darkness lasts for only a few moments. After a couple of manic whirls of the squeaky crank, the light reveals a sturdy, well-dressed man. He places a lantern on the nearest table and lights it as well as a pipe. From the far end of the corridor, presumably from the top of the stairs, a voice shouts the man's name along with a set of orders.

"Come on, Jared! Make haste, will ya? How does it look down there?"

"Gimme a minute! I just got down here!" He barks.

Smoke billows out of his mouth with the shout and more pumps out when he takes a couple more puffs from his pipe. When it's lit to his satisfaction, he removes it to wipe the spittle from the corners of his mouth with his fingers. He grumbles a complaint against the impatient voice at the top of the stairs before shoving the pipe back in. His fingers disappear into his dark beard as he digs into his chin, and it's with a groan that he pulls a comb from the inside of his jacket. He rips it through his beard, all while managing to keep the pipe out of the way by manipulating it with his lips. The frantic grooming seems to ease the mad look in his eyes, and once the comb is tucked back, he gathers his hair with stubby fingers and gives it a few twirls around his hand. When he lets go, the thick hairs stay together in a pointy clump down his chin. He uses the lantern even though the ceiling balls still have plenty of glow. This gesture shows his knowledge of the short life span of the lights. Unlike Tubs and I, he wouldn't get caught groping in the dark once the artificial suns turned back to empty glass.

"It was probably that scatterbrained brother of mine that forgot to lock the door. That man would leave his teeth if they weren't stuck in his head!" His chuckle is wet and crackly. A sure sign the man is never apart from his tobacco and pipe.

Jared begins a clockwise inspection of the room. Starting at the far end, he checks the remaining wardrobes, which are easily unlocked with a turn of their keys. He peeks under tables, looks in corners, and even inspects places a person couldn't possibly fit, like a skinny drawer and a couple small, round barrels.

Though he made earlier attempts to tame his beard, wiry strands are already beginning to loosen from the twist. His physical features are rough, and he looks like a raven in peacock's clothes.

The dust and webs from the cellar are things he's not happy to deal with. Occasionally, he'll check his boots for blemish. Sticky webs are brushed off the sleeves of his long coat with gloved hands and grumbles of smoke. It's comical to see such a thick man so afraid of dirt, but I can't help but think that he could be someone of good influence to Jonathan. His hair is neatly tamed by a ribbon of the same navy as his jacket.

I nudge into Tubs when I feel a tug on the bottom of my dress, and I tell him to get his filthy shoes off me. If I go home with a tear, Miss Margaret will throw a fit. He barks in a whisper that he's nowhere near my dress and that his feet are tucked under his backside. I stiffen and freeze and force myself to resist the urge to fling the wardrobe doors open and break into a wild dance. Though my eyes fail to see, my mind has a vivid picture of what is making the journey up my dress and sounding the occasional high-pitched squeak.

The gentle pressure continues up my back and stops near my arm, where I feel a wet nose and the tickle of whiskers—or so I think. My skin is on such high alert, the tiniest drop of dust can send me into a thrashing fit. I grab onto Tubs' arm and squeeze. His rasped "owwwww!" pairs with my matching "ewwwww!" and our frightful chorus of airy cries summons the attention of Jared, who is near the collapsed tunnel door at the far side of the room. Just before the bulbs blink out, I catch a glimpse of the handsomely dressed stranger slinking towards our wardrobe like a hungry cat. With the lights out, the lantern appears to float in the dark. The carrier is no longer visible, and the fog from the pipe bounces against it like a flame-hungry moth.

This reason alone is why I like my library. I can go on a thousand adventures and never once be any worse for wear. I feel, see, smell, and taste every adventurous task; yet in the end, I always end up on my comfortable couch in the middle of the library. I squeeze Tubs' s arm even harder. This time it's not out of fear over a curious, tiny monster, but this grip is to punish him for getting me into this predicament.

It takes both of Tubs' hands to loosen my grip. He gropes around in the confined dark for the little explorer. I no longer feel pins clinging to my sleeve, but it doesn't bring the relief I had hoped for, for now, one predator is exchanged for another.

Jared is close. He has the lantern held up to rounded cheeks that look as if they're stuffed with Sunday dinner. They're a sickening watercolor of the bird he resembles in blues, purples, and greens.

"I know you're in there!" He spits. His missing lips release the slurred words. "There's no point in hidin'."

An open smile reveals why he sounds so strange. He doesn't have any teeth. I slide back into the farthest reaches of the wardrobe and wait for the door to burst open. In its place, instead, is a blood-curdling howl.

Tubs is hysterical, laughing as much as one can while trying to stifle all sound. He shakes me in breathless excitement at being able to provoke such ear-piercing shrieks from a grown man.

Tubs had dropped the squirmy mouse out of one of the carved opening at the top of the wardrobe door and it had landed on Jared's shoulder. The light show from the zigzagging lantern is entertaining, and Jared's screams are sounds I never expected to hear from him. I agree with Tubs. It is rather amusing.

The ceiling balls pulse to life and spotlight a twirling Jared. His coattails flap with his frantic bushing all while keeping his pipe pressed between his lips. The growing sound of boots fills the hall and drum into the cellar, and in moments, a group of men appears in the doorway with sticks, rocks, or anything one could find in such a hurried state.

"Mice! This place is infested with those cursed vermin! One attacked me. Rabies! I'll be gettin' rabies!" Jared all but sobs.

From the cluster of men, laughter rings out. One steps forward and hits the disturbed man on the back.

"Jared, you'd think that after all your years at sea, you and the rodents would be friends!"

A rush of heat flushes through my body, and my limbs suddenly feel weak at the sight of Jonathan.

"Come now, it's the poor mouse we should be concerned about. I'm sure one taste of you is going to do the little fellow in. Hackett, clean out his war wound. We wouldn't want him frothing at the mouth while at sea."

The man I thought I knew takes a strapped pack off his shoulder and tosses it to the balding Alexander. From behind a blonde mustache that hasn't changed since I was six, a low voice booms and pierces through the wardrobe.

"Yes, sir, Captain. Come, Feral Jared, but be mindful. The poor mouse's mother may be coming for revenge," Alexander jokes. He leads Jared to the nearest chair and pushes him down into it.

Tubs is right. I don't know Jonathan.

Poor Tubs. He doesn't know his father, either. His face couldn't be pressed any closer to the wardrobe door.

ELEVEN

Tubs' quick thinking saved us from being discovered. He had found the mouse that had been exploring my sleeve. He squeezed him out of Adam's head, right onto the top of Jared's. It was funny and both Tubs and I would have been lost in a fit of giggles over it if it weren't for the room full of men.

I only recognize half of them. They're from home, and either work outside in the gardens or with our livestock. I've never had the opportunity to talk to any of them. They never look up when I pass, and their work suddenly seems to become more interesting to them when I'm around. Jared is one of the new faces. It wasn't until Jefferson breathlessly popped through the door that I noticed the similarities. Jefferson Fenway works in the kitchen with Miss Margaret.

He was the first to come to Jared's aid.

Jefferson's head is topped with the same mop of dark, silver kissed hair, but instead of a wiry beard, he has sideburns that are as bushy as squirrel tails. He has the same narrow eyes as Jared, and they glare at the near-mirror version of himself for his lack of restraint over a rodent. It's unmistakable once they are side-by-side that they're brothers, though Jefferson is considerably thinner and his complexion healthier. The punches to each other's arms and the criticizing banter are the other giveaways.

Sometimes we treat those closest to us in the most unpleasant manner. That's what Miss Margaret says anyway. I have never observed this with Tubs and his father, and Jonathan would never treat me like that. Tubs adjusts his position in the wardrobe and the heel of his shoe crushes my pinky finger. The nauseating pain makes me instantly sweat and my eyes tear. I fight the urge to cry out and stuff my finger in my mouth in hopes the warm saliva will do something beneficial. Even now with an uncomfortable heartbeat in my finger, I couldn't hurt him back on purpose, even if we weren't trapped in a wardrobe surrounded by men in a secret cellar.

"We're going to need more mice," Tubs jokes.

It is a lame attempt to keep me calm. I groan back at him. The rest of the group surely wouldn't be bothered by such a thing. This is my first adventure, and so far it isn't going so well.

Jonathan shoulders through the men to get to the far end of the room and announces over the chatter. "We need to get the weapons counted, checked, and loaded onto the wagon. Jared, I need you and Jefferson to keep watch out here—for more mice."

Jared sneers while Jonathan flashes a grin at the others as he unlocks a wardrobe and disappears within. His comment has roused a chorus of snickers. The back must be a doorway to another room because when the men enter, the sound of their laughter becomes muffled as they file in like ants marching into a hole.

"There's just two of them left. One of them is Jefferson and he's nothing to be afraid of. When their backs are to us, we'll sneak out. We're going to have to get out of here. It's going to be dark soon," Tubs whispers close to my ear. I shudder and rub away the tickle from his breath with my fingers.

I nod in agreement, and my stomach flips at Tubs' announced time frame. I don't want to be wandering the woods at night, even if it's with company.

"Where'd you get the clothes?" I hear Jefferson ask Jared with a mouthful of apple. He has pulled it out from inside his worn jacket. "What?" Jefferson suspends his answer with an open mouth at Jared's glare. He chuckles and covers his mouth to keep in the apple when he remembers his brother's missing teeth.

"London. That's where I've been since. Getting some culturing." Jared opens his coat to show Jefferson his complete ensemble.

"Is that so?" Jefferson sputters, spilling spit and apple after another bite. It seems to me he took the extra bite on purpose.

"And it'll be me cooking on this voyage, Scarecrow. I need to show off my new skills."

The announcement brings both men to a spirited disagreement over cooking duties. Jefferson points out that he has been head cook at Captain Gudwyne's for all these past years and that he has been cooking not only for the house but for the entire staff.

"That, Jared, is good 'nuff practice for 'nybody. I ain't got to go to London. I got no complaints stayin' with the others and the Captain. I learned everything I need to know from Miss Margaret 'cept the secret to her biscuits. Can't nobody make biscuits like Miss Margaret." Jefferson wipes his lips with a handkerchief that he pulled out of his trouser pocket. "Gets my mouth waterin' for 'em just thinkin' about 'em."

Both men go on comparing recipes and cooking techniques; each trying to outdo the other in knowledge and experience. When the shoving starts, Tubs takes the opportunity to make his escape, and he scampers across the floor as fast as a four-legged spider. He motions for me to follow when he reaches the safety of the doorway.

I crawl out and close the door behind me before making the uncomfortable trek across the stone floor. My skirt provides no cushion on the uneven stones, just problems. I'm nowhere near as fast as Tubs; but then again, the boy isn't wearing a skirt.

Jared wallops Jefferson's chin when he mentions the lice in his beard, and it sends his brother sliding across the top of the table in front of me. My knees catch on my dress, and it pulls the material tight beneath me. The forced stop causes me to fall forward right into Jefferson. Nose to nose, I'm more alarmed with the disturbingly large piece of chewed apple in his mustache than being discovered.

Jared lifts the half-dazed Jefferson off of me by grabbing a fistful of his jacket. Like a silly marionette, his feet dance crazily beneath him.

"What have we got here?" he says. His pursed lips made the pipe bob wildly with the question.

"It's a girl," Jefferson says with a head shake and a squint. He rubs across his nose with the side of his hand, and fingers get lost inside a mustache that's as dense as his sideburns.

"I see that Jefferson, I have eyes!" Jared lets go of his brother, and he crumples to the floor like a discarded hanky.

Jefferson recognizes me and begins to tell his brother.

"Wait a minute. Miss Izzy, wha..."

Before he can finish, I stomp down with my heel as hard as I can to the top of Jared's boot. The unnaturally strong rodent-fearer had yanked me up to my feet by my hair, and I expected to look back and see a fistful of it still in his hands when I wrangled free. I make it to the stairs with my dress gathered in my arms, a little too high for Miss Margaret's taste, and thoughts of her crowd out the fear of getting manhandled again.

My beastly dress trips me up the stairs, and Jefferson finds my ankle amidst all the material and pulls me down.

"Shh! Miss Izzy, I jus' want to talk to ya." He presses a hand over my mouth to keep me quiet. It tastes like salty apples. I relax a little when I notice his face isn't surly and sour like his brother's. This eases my struggling, and when he releases me, I'm able to appease Miss Margaret's inner scolding and cover my exposed ankles.

"Are you going to let me go?" I direct my question to Jared who has appeared behind his brother. Both men have the same dove-grey eyes, but Jefferson's are soft. Jared's are as cold as the tabletop he sent his brother across.

"Nope. You're comin' back down with us to see the Captain." He reaches across his brother to grab me, but Jefferson smacks his hand away.

"She's no trouble. She won't say a thing, right, Miss Izzy? You didn't see 'r hear nothing."

"Miss Izzy, is it?" Jared peeps farther over Jefferson's shoulder to get a better look at me but gets pushed back.

"Not so close. You keep those pets of yours to yourself. I don't want 'em!" He moves a safe distance away and swishes his fingers through his hair to shoo off any visitors just in case.

"My, you grew. That's what little ones do, I suppose." Jared stretches his sunken mouth open and scratches the side of it with his comb.

"I'm lettin' her go, Jared. Tattle to the Captain if you want, but I'm lettin' the girl go," Jefferson says. "We don't need no added trouble right before we leave."

"Who put you in charge? I'm the one here who has say," Jared huffs. "I should drag her on over to Captain Jonathan just so I can see the look on his face. I deserve some joy today and that would bring me a wagonload of it. The girl knows nothing. Why else would she be sneaking around? He hasn't told you a thing yet, has he?"

"He hasn't told me what?" I ask. My question is bold. It is uncharacteristic of me to ask it. Jared's a stranger and a scary one at that, but this concerns Jonathan, and my curiosity far outweighs any fears I could conjure towards him.

"So, he hasn't told you yet," Jared grins. "Some Captain he is. He's nothing at all like his father. A coward—that's what the boy is. A soft coward," he spits. "You're crazy if you think I'm going to answer anything for you. Jonathan deserves the full honor of that." He snickers with another pull of the comb.

"Let's let her go," Jefferson pleads. "Give the girl just a few more days of peace, please?"

"You're just as squishy as the Captain!" Jared jeers. "Fine. Let her go. She's gotten an eye-full today. Here's hoping it'll make things even more difficult for the Captain when he finally fills her in. Good call, brother. This makes me quite happy." He adds a smile. He looks like a hairy snake.

Tubs appears in the doorway that looms above. I can tell the sun is going down. He's illuminated in the tints that the sun washes the sky with right before it plunges behind the horizon; colors like fire but without the ability to melt. He looks angelic with the colors spilling about him the way they are.

"Go on now, Miss," Jefferson shoos. "There's plenty of men to do the countin'. They won't be too much longer. And Miss Izzy? Pay no mind to my brother. The Captain ain't no coward. I was there, Miss. I remember what he did for you."

He was right. He was there, in the back of the room when I first came, puzzling with his hat.

"Thank you, Jefferson," I say.

Part of me wants to kiss him on the cheek for sticking up for me. As for his comment about Jonathan, I don't know what to make of it. How Jefferson sees Jonathan is how I used to, before today. How do I know Jared isn't the correct one? Hiding things is deceitful, and Jonathan is unquestionably guilty of that. Perhaps Jared is closer in his opinions of Jonathan than his brother and I have been. As with Jefferson taking up my side, I know too well how hard that must have been for him. He's even more private than I am. He keeps to himself in the kitchen most days and he doesn't come into the dining room to eat with us and the other staff for our weekly dinners together. The kitchen must be for him what the library is for me—a refuge and a place of comfort. Jefferson has just shown bravery in my eyes, and I feel he deserves a reward.

"Kneading." I give him the hint as my feet pat up the stairs. "The secret to Miss Margaret's biscuits is all in the kneading."

A loud whoop comes out of Jefferson. He's finally released from his biscuit mystery. The celebration continues in the dank cellar as I am graciously released by the gloom. The outside seems livelier and more vibrant than before we went in, and I take a deep breath of the delicious fresh air.

"I was kneadin' that!" I hear him echo from the stone stairway. I can't help but groan along with Jared. "Twas all in the kneadin'. It was that simple! Oh, I can't wait till the mornin'! The house will have the best melt-in-your-mouth biscuits they've ever had!"

"You'll have a mouth full of gun barrel if you don't move over!" A gruff voice booms over Jefferson's.

"Ah! Lemme give you a hand," one of them offers. The groans and grumbles from the cellar stairs, I gather, are from men trying to squeeze weapons and body past the Fenway brothers.

I run with Tubs with my dress gathered past my ankles and continue to do so into the woods where the sun's candy-colored rays can't penetrate. The outdoors isn't the place for a lady. Maneuvering around with such weight, length, and layers, it's nearly impossible to not get tripped up. The world outside the cottage walls belongs to men and their two-legged garments. The next time I come out, I'll be sure to smuggle out a pair of Jonathan's breeches.

The next time.

When I tell Tubs, he can't stop looking back at me to grin.

It's one thing to stagger through a dimly lit room on smooth wood floors and obstacles of soft couches and chairs. I've memorized each of the rooms at the cottage so well that a bruised shin or a stubbed toe are injuries of the past. But it's another thing entirely to stagger through these unfamiliar woods. I'm not accustomed to exposed tree roots, decaying branches, and tangled vines under my feet in the day, let alone the dusky shadow before dark. Tubs isn't bothered by the woodland debris and scurries through the woods with the graceful ease of a squirrel. It's apparent he has done this many times before. I, on the other hand, tear through the woods like a lumbering bear, and I seem to find something to trip over with every step.

By the time we reach the raspberries, the sun has given the moon its turn to rule the sky. We're fortunate it's a full moon tonight. Tubs can find the path we had beaten down earlier, and we're able to push through the piercing vines with minimal damage to our skin and clothes. I do get a prickly slap from a vine right across my cheek. It burns, and when I touch it, my fingers feel wet.

Under the moon's watchful gaze, we find the lake in sparkle, and Rosemary's nose is still nuzzling through the grass.

"Do you think we'll beat father and the others home?" Tubs asks. His long fingers struggle with the knot on the rope as if it is an unsolvable puzzle. Rose snorts a greeting and nudges me under the arm.

"We should. They were just loading up when we left," I say.

He's getting frustrated with the knot. He holds out a trembling hand for me to see. I bump him aside and get the knot pulled apart with a few tugs.

Soon the house and stables are a sleepy mound on the horizon. The crickets' song and the sound of Rosemary's hooves against the pressing grass lull me to thoughts of Jonathan and his secret room. The evening's discoveries bounce around my head and block out the night sounds that I usually find so pleasant, so much so that I barely hear Tubs. He repeats the shout directly in my ear.

"Run!"

I've never run Rosemary. I don't even know how to—I don't even know if I want to, but Tubs thinks we should. Tubs kicks his heels into Rose's side, and she answers the command with a snort and a vigorous shake of her head. She digs her hooves in and works up to a speed that I didn't think possible from such a barrel-shaped horse.

My fists are full of braids. I try to get a better hold by wrapping her hair around my wrists, but it's not enough. I've never run her, and the pounding is too much for me to handle. I can feel myself tipping, even with my legs pinched against her sides. Tubs has desperately attached himself to my back and his weight is adding to the downward pull. With each gallop, I slide further down Rose's side until I have nowhere else to go but down. In an instant, the world is a swirl of grass, horse, dirt, and sky. The sound of drumming hooves is replaced with the sickening thud of bodies slamming to the earth. Tubs is writhing and moaning with his hands cupped over his face, and my sweet Rosemary lies motionless in the moonlight.

TWELVE

Once she saw I was fit enough to be left alone, Miss Margaret took it upon herself to go for Dr. Batchford. She felt responsible. I could see it in the way she was fiddling with the chain around her neck. I didn't try to remove her guilt by telling her I didn't feel the night was her fault. It gave me a strange satisfaction to keep that from her. Paybacks from everything she's keeping from me. I almost told her, when I saw her hands tremor while removing my boots before helping me lie down. The words were there, right at my lips, but I couldn't give up the power I felt over her at that moment. It was a relief when she left. I felt as if I were being torn in two from the inside. Part of me had wanted to hug into her to soothe her but the other part took a strange delight in her discomfort. I'm a foul creature. Is this how it feels to keep a secret? If so, I don't want any more of them. Let Jonathan and Miss Margaret keep them all.

The riders behind us in the darkened meadow were the Fenway brothers and Alexander. We weren't being chased. The three were just coming home at a leisurely pace, but we didn't know that. We didn't know if the brothers kept their word or not about finding me in the cellar, so what else were we to think when we saw riders behind us?

Rosemary had caught her foot in a woodchuck's hole. Alexander said her front leg and neck were broken.

"It was quick and painless, I promise you, Izzy," he reassured me.

Alexander squeezed into my shoulders, and that made the tears I cried for Rosemary come from a deeper place. It wasn't from the realization that my Rosemary was never going to get up again. It was the way he had tried to comfort me. It was the same way he comforted the young Jonathan in my room those years ago. The tears I cried were for the boy. I missed him. He was the one I trusted. I don't know the man from the castle cellar.

Alexander said it was a miracle that what happened to Rosemary didn't happen to Tubs and I. Once we were examined for broken bones and he saw that all we had were a few sprains and bruises, he grabbed his son, threw him over his knee, and gave him a sound whoppin'. In the moonlight, the wet on Tubs' face spoke his discomfort, for he didn't make the slightest sound. I could somehow sense the whipping was more a gesture of love and relief than anger. Tubs, through his silence, I felt, thought the same.

"Never, boy, ever do you run a horse full speed in the dead of night when neither you nor the beast can see a hair in front of you," he scolded as he spanked.

I cried harder. I cried for Tubs, I cried for Rosemary, and I cried for Jonathan. It was as if the walls of the world around me were beginning to crumble. Secrets have been weakening the mortar unknowingly for years. Tubs showed me more than the destroyed Gudwyne castle. He had led me to a mirror.

Alexander held onto Tubs and squeezed him tightly after the spanking. He hugged him for a long time. The father and son embraced under the moonlight. It was as breathtaking to me as the portrait of Evolyn, but lies can hide behind beautiful things as well the hideous.

Alexander wasn't exempt from the mystery behind the cellar. He was there just as Jonathan was.

The Fenway brothers slipped out of the shadows where they were quietly standing by. Jefferson came to me and helped me up onto one of their horses. He said he'd take me home.

"Don't worry, Miss. We'll come back and take care of Rosemary for you."

Jefferson mounted the horse too, to make sure I'd stay put. My sobs were with such intensity I couldn't catch my breath. My gasps alarmed the brothers, but everyone kept their heads about them, and no one ran the horses.

"We're takin' her slow and steady, Jared. Miss Izzy doesn't need any more excitement. And don't worry, Miss, your secret is still safe. Cap'n Jonathan and Hackett don't know nothin'," Jefferson whispered.

Miss Margaret's face was aghast when the brothers burst through the front door and lay me on my "fainting couch". It was the same look she wore those years ago when I first came here. I tried to get up and I told everyone I was fine, but no one believed me. Many hands pushed me back down.

Miss Margaret took up one of my hands and patted it numb while fishing for details. She couldn't keep the emotion out of her voice. Physically, her hands proved strong; her grip was solid and sure, but her strength didn't match what my ears heard.

"We must've frightened them, Miss Margaret," Jefferson explained. "The two were comin' home from an evening of fishin' when we came up behind 'em in the dark."

He whispered the part about Rosemary. He was afraid if I heard the retelling of the story it would send me into a fit of tears again. He was right to whisper, but he wasn't quiet about it. I caught every word and released another wave of sobs.

"Shh, sweet dear," Miss Margaret cooed with more pats to my hand.

I can only imagine what my hair looked like—half in its bun and half out. Miss Margaret smoothed it and tucked thick strands behind my ear while she shushed. "Oh, boys, she did love that horse. Please go see that she is taken care of." Miss Margaret's eyes narrowed when she saw Jared. She had caught sight of his pipe. Luckily, he had the good graces to tuck it from view behind his back.

"We'll take care of that right now, Ma'am." Jefferson bowed and reassured her. "We'll take care of things proper, just how they should be for Miss Isabelle."

Miss Margaret gathered her things and rushed out of the house to fetch Dr. Batchford.

It hasn't been that long since my last visit to this couch. It was when I fainted after I saw the faces in the fire. It now makes sense why Miss Margaret has the doctor come every time I'm here. It was the words she spoke to Jonathan before things went black. She doesn't want to lose me like she had lost Evolyn.

"Go on, Jefferson. I'll catch up," Jared says to his brother. With Miss Margaret gone, this is all the permission he needs to pop the pipe back in his mouth.

"Catch up nothin'. You need to come with me, straight away. We have work to do." Jefferson doesn't want to leave, and he watches Jared take a long drag from his pipe instead.

"Get!" Jared barks. To further persuade his brother to leave, he shoves into him.

Jefferson glares at him and shoulders off his brother's touch, but it is enough to get him going. He bows to me before leaving, and he pulls his hat snug to his head.

"You'll be fine, Miss. You just rest, all right?" he says. "She will be all right, won't she, Jared?" Jefferson repeats with a glare. "Jonathan won't be the only one you'll have to worry about if she's not. Miss Izzy, I'll go fetch Miss Mary to come and sit with you." He doesn't have to go far. Mary has been dusting the same table in the foyer since we've been here.

"I'm right here, Miss Izzy. Seeing to the foyer. If need be, I can fetch Mr. Tufney who's right out the window there in the garden," Mary nods. Her eyes are wide pools of blue. Jared has her nervous; the rag in her hand is twisted into a rope.

Mr. Tufney is an old man of seventy. I don't know what help he'll be if I should need him, but the name holds power and it makes Jared groan deep in his throat.

Jared falls hard on Jonathan's chair when he hears the door click shut after Jefferson. He intertwines his fingers and pushes out his palms. His gloves muffle the sound of popping knuckles.

"Mr. Tufney won't be necessary, Miss. Now scuttle along to finish your dust-shooing." Jared waves Mary off with a gloved hand. "I can keep an eye on Miss Izzy until the doc gets here."

Mary pulls the rag tight. "If you don't mind, Miss, I'll stay put where I can see you."

"Suit yourself." Jared grins and gives Mary a wink. Mary looks like a reluctant ghost. She resists the urge to float off and lowers herself into the chair by the doorway.

"Nice chair, Miss Izzy. Sit in it much? Or is it too close to the fire?" He chuckles. He rubs into the arms of the chair while looking about the room. "Is this all the Captain has left? It's hard to believe if it is. He did have the biggest share out of all of us after all."

He emphasizes the word "Captain" and in doing so, his lips sink further into his mouth. Jared leers at me in such a way it makes me uncomfortable. I wish Miss Margaret would hurry. Mary must feel the same way. She's making repeated glances towards the door.

"What do you mean, he got the biggest share? Biggest share of what?" I feel a surge of energy and I return the glare. A look of recognition gives his a spark, and he energetically points his pipe's stem at me.

"There she is! That's the girl I remember. See this?" He turns his head to show me his cheek. A smooth, white scar runs from his earlobe to the middle of his cheek. His large pores camouflaged what I didn't notice before.

"Thanks to you and that toy of yours." He puffs on his pipe and squints. "I heard about all this weeping—fainting—whatever it is you are always doing. I don't buy it. You were always a feisty little thing." He takes another drag from his pipe and chuckles to himself in memory. He puckers his lips and blows the smoke in my direction like a tea kettle in a rolling boil.

"To answer your question—we all got quite a bundle. But, your Jonathan, he came out with the most, bein' the new Captain and all. Why, we left with a ship full of copper. Plum full, Miss. Worth a pretty lot." He cocks his head and gums the pipe's tip. He looks like a starved cat trapped behind glass. "Now, there's nothing wrong with a ship full of copper; that is until you steal it. Being a seaman myself, I can tell you, there's a mighty strong fine to pay for what your Jonathan did. Crazy kid. That fifteen-year old caused a mutiny. What kid does that? He turned the whole crew on the best Captain that ever sailed the seas," he says. "If I had even a portion of his cut, I would've had my new teeth long ago. I have a whole mouth full of ivory teeth comin'—tomorrow. Maybe then I won't seem so disgusting to you." His smile is wet, and he has to use the back of his hand as a mop to dry his lips before putting his pipe back in.

The second hand on the clock next to Evolyn's picture, which had been consistently *tick, tick, ticking*, is now silent. The hand still moves but there isn't a sound to be heard. Mary isn't stirring either. The twisted rag is pulled tight in her hands and she's as still as a doll.

The room is in shock. This can't be Jonathan.

Jared puffs at his pipe, and with a smug look, he adds, "Didn't know this about your Jonathan, did you?"

No, the Jonathan I know is unselfish and giving, not the thief that Jared is describing. My heart pleads his case to my head by reminding it what he did for me two winters ago.

Winter can be a long season and a long time to be separated from the flowers that I love. One winter's night, while our garden slept under a thin blanket of snow, and I under a mountain of bed coverings, Jonathan decorated one of the walls in my room with book pages. Black and white sketches of flowers in my favorite varieties greeted me a spring's good morning. Beneath them, seven brushes ready to be dipped in the waiting pots of rainbow-colored paints. Together that morning we painted all of them, getting almost as much paint on ourselves as on the pictures. It took a week for the blue to fade off my skin.

No, this doesn't sound like Jonathan, but we all have secrets. He and Miss Margaret are both good at keeping secrets.

The room is beginning to fill with a smoky haze. Miss Margaret will be furious when she finds Jared has disobeyed her wishes and smoked in her house.

"If Jonathan stole a ship full of copper, where is it?" I ask. There isn't one item of copper visible in the room or elsewhere, except the kitchen.

We have a copper tub that gets tucked out of sight when not in use, and Miss Margaret has a few copper pots—but those are stored in a closet. A gypsy with a cart painted in the colors of summer fruits sold her those. He carries nothing but copper wares and only comes when Jonathan isn't home. It seems to me, Jonathan despises copper and wants nothing to do with it. Quite possibly, he could have gone and sold the whole lot.

"If he sold it, where's the money?"

He has to notice our modest living conditions. If this were true, shouldn't we be living in the castle in the forest instead?

Jared just shrugs and puffs more smoke.

"And if he is guilty of such a crime, why has no one come forward to accuse him? Why haven't you?" The courage I find to speak to this near-stranger in such a way shocks me. I never knew I had any. It's shocking but empowering. I just wish I had more of it to rip the pipe out of the folds of his mouth.

"Oh, he paid each of us well after he sold off the copper and after I and the rest of the crew promised to keep our mouths shut. It was enough to keep mine shut," he laughs and tugs at the sleeves of his coat. "I was able to go use my share and move to London where the respectables live, rubbing elbows with the prim and proper and the high and mighties. Look at me! I look just like one of them, don't I? Money is all it takes to turn a filthy, despicable man like me into a gentleman. Why, I bet money could even turn a savage around, don't you think, Miss?" He smiles again. I'm glad he doesn't have teeth. If he did, they would be dripping with anticipation.

I try to envision Jonathan as a greedy thief responsible for the mutiny. It is like trying to fit myself in Evolyn's petite blue dress. I begin to calculate the charges Jared said were stacked against him. Mutiny is punishable by death in England. Commandeering a ship means death by hanging. Stealing the cargo—death by hanging. He would be charged with a triple hanging if that's possible. According to Jared, Jonathan has himself in quite a bit of trouble, though oddly no one in all these years has come to look for him. Wouldn't there be a sizable bounty over his head? And a sizable number of men to collect that debt?

"Having a hard time believing me, Miss?" Jared stiffly straightens to his feet and itches a belly that's almost too big for his shirt. He wanders around the room to examine the décor. "I can only imagine how hard this must be for you. Jonathan has done an outstanding job taking care of you. Look at you and how you've grown. My, you're nearly as lovely as a summer's bloom!" He plucks a flower from a vase in his hands and squints. "Nearly." His eyes narrow and his face puckers as if he had just tasted something bitter. He lifts the vase overhead to get a look at the bottom and sneers.

He's acting as if we know each other, but I haven't seen him before today, and I certainly don't remember giving him that scar. He seems to be the only one that's bitter towards Jonathan. Jefferson works here and seems to respect him.

"I know your brother. Jonathan works alongside him and the others. From what I've seen, there isn't anything between them but shared respect and loyalty," I say.

"Captain Jonathan works alongside them to keep a watchful eye on 'em. On his investments. He wouldn't want one of them running off turning him into the royal navy. Whatever he's doing is working. He's keeping the crew happy. And happiness buys silence. Would you say you're happy here, Miss?" Jared tugs his shirt out of his breeches to take the pressure off of his stomach before sitting back down in Jonathan's chair.

"Why would my happiness be of any concern to you?" I say. I refuse to humor him with an answer.

"Oh, just curious is all. Take this vase here. I wonder what it feels like, knowin' its owner is a thief. Then again, maybe it doesn't know. We should tell it, Miss. 'Vase, your owner is a thief!'" He gasps at the news with a gloved hand over his mouth. He pulls his lips in a frowning pout as he listens to the vase's reply. "What? What's that? He has stolen things much worse—much worse than a ship, its cargo, and its crew?" He opens his eyes and mouth wide while waiting for the vase's answer. "No?! It can't be! Why, Vase, I don't think she knows. Shall we tell her? Oh, you've convinced me, we certainly shall for her sake." He sticks his bottom lip out to pout. "Miss, the vase insists that I share with you the common bond you both have, though it pains me so to do it. You must know what my new friend the vase already knows, who your owner is. Poor, poor Miss!"

"Owner?! No one owns me!" I leap to my feet to protest his lie. Mary's body reanimates from her frozen position by the doorway and she does the same.

He flips the vase upside down so I can see what he saw on the bottom. Blossoms and water spill onto the floor. He stains the floor with color when he crushes the blooms with his heel. On the bottom is a stamp, a snake-like dragon matching the one from the library rug. It's the Gudwyne family seal.

He walks up behind me and with his nubby pointer finger, he outlines the same shape out of the burn scars on the back of my neck. I don't like him touching me, yet I can't move away. I had always assumed the raised mark I had brushed my fingers against many times was just more of the healed burns. I had no reason to question that, until today. I can feel Jared's breath on my neck as he reaches for my wrist. He twists it roughly in his hands before bringing it up to the back of my neck. His gloves are swampy, and with a shackled grip, he manipulates my finger and brushes it over the raised mark. My legs threaten to collapse when the information from my finger reaches my brain. It reads the same mark that is on the bottom of the vase.

"So, tell me, Miss. How does it feel knowin' your owner is a thief?" Jared hisses and accentuates the last syllable. He sounds every bit like the dragon on my neck.

His spit dampens my ears. His words drown my heart.

THIRTEEN

Doctor Batchford gives Tubs and I a thorough check over. Tubs has a broken nose and a black eye—not from the fall but by my kicking him in the face when we went down. I came away with less visible damage—grass stains on my clothes and the palms of my hands are the only evidence of my being a part of the accident at all.

Since tomorrow was the day he was supposed to recheck me from my fainting spell, he said we could do it tonight to save him a trip. I think I have become some sort of experimental pet for the doctor. He has never seen a case like mine, so naturally, he's curious. He sets up his workspace at my desk and takes out his paper and quill pen. He runs a pen knife over the tip a few times before dabbing it on his tongue. He does this before every appointment and in the same order. His paper is neatly stacked in front at a left-handed tilt, an ink bottle (and spare) is on the right, then a sharpening and a lick and the usual series of questions.

"Any lasting dizziness? Shortness of breath? Short-term memory loss? Any new memories?" He's looking at me over his glasses. His spectacles are perched so far down his nose there is barely any nose for them to cling to. I wonder if it's even possible to breathe like that.

"No, no, no, and no," I answer in my usual way, except today it's sprinkled with extra spice. I have just found out I'm not just bound here by my fears, but I'm part of the estate.

"Do you want to talk a little more about the last memory you had?" He's already scribbling. I haven't even given him any information yet. What could he possibly be writing?

I nod yes because I remember Miss Margaret is outside and I don't want to see her. I've watched the way she cares for the things in Jonathan's home. Dusting, plumping, fluffing. I wonder if I am no different than a pillow on a couch to her. My heart screams that it isn't true, but I feel sulky and I choose to wallow in the thought of Miss Margaret being paid handsomely by Jonathan to take care of me, his favorite showpiece.

He asks me to describe in as much detail as I can of my last memory; the one of faceless people bathed in flame. I feel uncomfortable and shift in the bed. He senses my discomfort but watches curiously and pushes his spectacles back to the bridge of his nose.

Next to him on the table, the candle flickers. Liquid wax slips down the side, and its simple action frightens me. It's no longer wax, but skin dripping in globs off an arm. He can read my look and instinctively snuffs out the candle's flame between his dampened fingers. Instead of moistened cloths or pats of concern, he encourages me to describe what I saw, pen poised in the air for the newest details.

I try to describe it, but I can't. Fear has stolen my breath and gasps are where words should be. My hands claw at my dress collar in hopes the solution is as easy as loosening the material. The desk chair topples to the floor when Dr. Batchford lunges for me to get me to the window.

He instructs me on how to breathe, for it's as if I have forgotten. Breathing is something one shouldn't have to think about, and I've never given it a second thought; that is until I discover I can no longer do it. Nothing is working. In a panic, I look to him for instructions. He asks me to examine the willow and describe it to him.

"The willow?" He prods when I take too long.

Through gasps, I describe what I see to him; a head bent under the unmanageable weight of overloaded branches. I don't want to describe her any further. Not the willow. So, I don't. I watch as a puff of wind parts her leafy locks from her trunk. I want to run and hide underneath her. I wish I was there. I wish I was her. No, I don't have to wish. I am her. I'll never be anything else.

Dr. Batchford releases his grip from around the back of my neck when the gulps soften.

"Better?" I nod and apologize.

"Nothing to apologize for," he says. He sits back down, but this time he doesn't pick up his pen. His glasses have slipped again, but he doesn't fix them. He crosses his legs and narrows his eyes at me. This is what he does when he is trying to figure me out. Well, he might as well stop. He's never going to.

"Let's try again," he says. His expression remains neutral, and it feels as if he's looking straight through me and sifting through my thoughts.

"I can't," I say.

He hasn't blinked yet, so I blink for him.

"You're my only patient tonight. I have all night." He smiles and licks the tip of his pen before he dips it back into the ink. His glasses get pushed up with a knuckle.

I wonder what use a dab of saliva is to ink. Does it thin it out? Does it make the featherless pen glide easier across the paper? I decide I'll try later to find out for myself. That is if he ever leaves.

"Whenever you're ready, I'm ready." He's back to his scribbling. He isn't going to budge and give in like the others. My episodes usually produce sympathy, and he certainly isn't going to give any.

Dr. Batchford is a patient man. He could sit all night like this. I know because on a visit when I was seven, I wouldn't talk, and we sat in the sitting room all day. Miss Margaret served us lunch, tea, and then dinner while I swung my legs under the couch and the doctor scribbled on his paper. My backside was numb and my head hurt from counting the grainy lines on the wood floor, but I took it as a challenge, and I would not be the first to give in. We went on like that for three days straight, mid-morning until evening, until I finally gave in. I never did get a proper count on all the squiggly lines. My eyes would cross and feel heavy so I would close them, for just a moment to rest them, and each time my place would be lost when I opened them again. Doctor Batchford went through six bottles of ink in those three days. The two bottles of ink at our appointments now make sense.

"Willows are wonderful trees," he says. The pen scratches across the paper. He pauses to examine his work. "They're my favorite tree. We had one when I was a boy. I loved that tree." He looks up from the page to gaze out the window. His mustache stretches across his top lip when he smiles at the willow. "My brothers and I would play for hours underneath her. We could be anywhere under her: on a ship sailing the seas, in a prison full of ornery pirates, in a bakery eating warm crusty bread..." His voice trails off, and he sticks the wrong side of the quill in his mouth. When he pulls it out, a smudge of black is left behind on the corner of his lip.

"Not everyone loved that tree." He resumes his penning. Ink is growing in one spot. "My father hated that tree. Excuse me, 'disliked greatly.'" He looks over the spectacles that had slipped to the tip of his nose again and nods his head towards the door. He clears his throat and mouths Miss Margaret's name and gives me a wink. It makes me laugh, and the gesture expands my lungs. Doctor Batchford smiles.

"My father wanted to cut it down. He said it was a worthless, messy tree with no value. It wasn't like one of our valuable walnut trees that produced nuts for Mother's Sunday pie and it wasn't the maple tree that gave our family sweet syrup for our oatmeal. No. The willow to him had no value." Doctor Batchford takes a moment to admire his work, and he tilts his head to examine it from a different angle.

"A 'weak-rooted monstrosity,' my father called her. She did have shallow roots. All willows do." He shrugs in a way that shows he didn't care. "It made her more vulnerable in storms, yes, I give him that, but this tree proved him wrong. No storm was strong enough to knock her down. The old girl is still standing tall. All trees have a purpose. All trees are special."

He's done scribbling. He holds up his paper for me to see. It isn't a page scribbled full of words describing a crazy girl with scars covering half of her body. It is a masterful, inky sketch of the weeping willow outside with a girl wrapped in a leafy embrace.

Dr. Batchford's artistic skill matches those of one of my favorite painter's work. In the bottom-right corner of the drawing, initials that I recognize from years of portrait admiring are worked into the piece with precision where they would be invisible if not searched for. It is the same in every way as the initials in the portrait of Evolyn.

He corks the ink bottles, wipes the tip of his quill pen with a clean handkerchief, and places the pieces in their proper spots in his wooden case. What he doesn't pack is the stack of papers. Those he brings over to me.

"Today is the last day I'll be seeing you." Dr. Batchford hands the papers off with a grin. "It's been a pleasure, Miss Izzy. It's been a true honor to get to know you. I'm going to miss our chats," he chuckles. "And I'm quite sure you feel the same. Here. These, my dear girl, are from our time together. Please, remember me?" he asks.

"I won't be seeing you anymore?" The unexpected feeling of disappointment mingles with relief. I shuffle through the stack under his watch and notice they're all drawings. Not a word is written on any of them.

"No, you won't," Dr. Batchford narrows his eyes. "You don't know this? Jonathan didn't tell you?" His brows soften after a moment. "He does know you best. I trust his judgment." Dr. Batchford adjusts his glasses with his knuckle and points to the drawings. "I hope your willow will someday match what I have always seen."

He kisses the top of my hand, the same way he has always done at the end of every visit, to say goodbye. He nods down to the papers in my hand.

"One of my favorite portraits of you. I had plenty of time on that piece. I had three days to perfect that one," he laughs.

The picture he is speaking of is the one on the top of the pile, the one with the little girl with rosy cheeks and a bright smile. I recognize my fainting couch before I do the child. For a moment, she is a stranger to me. She sits on her hands and energetically swings her legs. The girl's skin is dark, and her mouth is open as if in laughter. It is the eyes that I recognize. It is the only part of the drawing that has any color besides black ink. They look like glistening gems reflecting firelight.

"What I see...," I ask. "It's me, isn't it?"

I wasn't asking about the little girl in the sketch. I was asking about the one I saw melting in flame.

I squeeze my eyes shut to push out the frightening image to replace it with this new one. It's like trying to re-stick a leaf back to the tree on the library door without a fresh coat of egg white glue.

I give up and let the old picture stay.

Dr. Batchford answers my question with a reassuring smile. He kisses my hand for the last time and before letting go, he gives it a final squeeze.

FOURTEEN

"Izzy, I have a hot bath waiting for you downstairs. It'll help relax those muscles of yours. Tomorrow, I guarantee you're going to be quite sore." Miss Margaret bustles about the room in her usual hurried pace and gathers fresh night clothes for me to change into.

Doctor Batchford is gone and his departure has left me quite rattled. My last session with him came without warning. I had no time to prepare for it. I wish I would have known, perhaps I would have treated our last time together differently. I might have cooperated this time. Who knows how it would have worked out if I had known ahead of time. When I have a chance to stew things over, they *never* go how I imagine them. I end up getting myself all worked up over scenarios that never happen.

"I'm afraid our little agreement with you spending time outdoors until Jonathan gets here is not going to work. There have been new developments," she says.

She's keeping her eyes from me. She knows Tubs and I weren't fishing. She's afraid I may know something. I feel awkward around her, and I can tell she feels the same.

She's unaware of it, but she's taught me something today. One can only stifle the truth for so long. Truth is a powerful thing, and it finds a way out of the captivity of secrecy, even during the ordinary everyday bustle that she distracts herself with. This is her way of running—dusting, and primping. I watch her skirt swish around the room and her active hands make quick work of things and find we aren't that much different from each other. Haven't I spent a good deal of my childhood getting lost in the library? Her industrious hands change the bed linens at a break-neck speed with skill from years of practice. She crumples the dirty ones in a ball and hugs them to her chest.

"I'm sorry, Isabelle," she says. The words rush from her lips, and she doesn't add anything else.

Sorry for what? I want to ask. Rosemary? Or did she mean to go deeper than that? Sorry for keeping secrets from me? Sorry for the burns? Sorry I have to bear these scars forever? I wonder what she sees when she looks at me. Does she see me as Dr. Batchford sees me in his sketches?

"Make haste, child. The bath is getting cold," she tries to scold in play as she exits my room.

Waiting for me in the middle of the kitchen is the copper bathing tub. When not in use, its usual place is tucked in the far corner under the kitchen shelves. Jonathan fitted it with a wooden top so Miss Margaret could store her wire baskets of potatoes on top. I suggested once when helping her put it away that she should not bother with the top and just put the baskets inside. She told me this used to be Evolyn's tub, her favorite gift from the Captain, and it just didn't seem proper to stuff her most prized possession plumb full of dirty vegetables.

To make it move easily about the room, Jonathan fastened it to a low platform with wheels. We would lock the wheels into place when the tub was in use, if we didn't we would be rolling all over the kitchen floor each time we went under the water to rinse.

When I was little, I would forget to lock the wheels on purpose. I would pretend I was a kidnapped mermaid, forced to spend her days in a copper tub. I couldn't just jump out to escape my captor. I would dry out and die. I would have to escape in my watery prison. I would grab onto both sides of the tub and rock forward, splashing waves of water as I inched towards the kitchen door. Miss Margaret would catch me sloshing bathwater on her floor and with hands on her hips and lips pursed tight, she would show her displeasure. Scolding me was futile. Jonathan had convinced her that it was good for me to play and pretend and that

I was a big help to her. What better time to get the kitchen sparkling clean than on bath day? Bath day from then on became Miss Margaret's floor scrubbing day.

It's time-consuming work heating all the water that's needed to fill the tub. Buckets and buckets of water are needed and are heated over the flame in the kitchen's fireplace. Baths are usually only once a week because of that, and it's usually at the week's end. It's only midweek, which makes this a special treat.

The water at first is too hot. It feels like needles on my feet and ankles. It takes a while to get my whole body past the prickles, but once I get myself fully submerged, it doesn't take long to adjust, and the water feels soft and soothing. Miss Margaret has put in drops of lavender oil and the floral scent lulls me to sleep. I wake to a gentle knock.

"Are you ready to get out, dear? The men are ready for you outside," she informs before opening the door.

Thankfully, she is there to help get me out. The long soak in the steaming water has left me weak and groggy. Miss Margaret helps me rub my red skin dry. The rough, line-dried towel massages my skin and feels heavenly. She helps me into my crisp nightclothes, towel dries my hair and brushes it smooth. All the day's grime is washed clean. I am put back into place. The old Izzy is back—on the outside. I just wish I could wash away today just like the day's dirt.

"We have a busy day tomorrow, Izzy. Jonathan has sent word he's coming home early and we're to have company." I can see through her overly cheerful attempt with the announcement. She's trying to bring us back to where we were this morning. "The Fredricks are coming for dinner and, oh dear, there is much to do, much to do!"

I can feel my brows pinching. I don't even try to hide my displeasure. We never have company. Jonathan prefers only the company of a few—Miss Margaret and me for starters. When he isn't working or away and if he isn't with us, he will spend it mostly with Alexander hunting and trapping. I would say Jonathan and Tubs' father are as close as Jonathan and I are. So, having Miss Margaret say company is coming is odd and scary. I have never had to keep anyone else's attention other than the people in our little family. Now my stomach is hurting again. Miss Margaret can sense my fear, and she wraps me in the waiting blanket.

"Don't worry, my dear, you'll do just fine." She hugs me tight through my wool shroud. This gesture brings back every gentle touch to memory. Maybe I'm not a branded piece of livestock to her. Quite possibly, I'm more of a pet, like Rosemary; or maybe, just maybe, she truly does loves me.

"We must not keep the men waiting, Izzy. They worked so hard for you and Rosemary," she says quietly. I don't bother putting my boots on. My bare feet cross over the threshold. She sees but doesn't say a word.

Where Rose and Tubs and I went down is where the men have dug the grave. Rose is already in and covered when Miss Margaret and I get there. Tubs tosses on the last few shovels of dirt while Alexander and Jefferson are ready to leave with their shovels and lanterns in hand. Both nod and offer their condolences.

Dirty, sweaty, and tired, these men took care of Rosemary in the most uncustomary way for my sake. Farm animals don't get burials like people do. They are just animals. I know what happens to farm animals when they die. If they were sick, they would be burned. If they had a broken leg or another injury, they would be eaten. These men knew the importance of Rose to me and took care of her in the most respectful manner they could think of, and for that I'm grateful. How could men who so blatantly broke England's laws be so kind?

Jared is leaning on a shovel. There's a smeared trail of blood from the bottom of his nose to the side of his face. His crisp white shirt is no longer pristine but is dotted with blood. I don't know what happened to him, but whatever it was, though I feel guilty about it, I'm glad.

Tubs lingers behind with me to finish up. He's patting the dirt with the back of his shovel. The mound is a smooth, perfect hill. I catch a glimpse of his grubby face in the lantern light. It looks awfully painful, and it makes me wince. His eye is swollen shut and the bridge of his nose puffy.

"You shouldn't be out here. You should be resting! Your nose—it's bleeding!" I rush to him and gently dab at his little stub of a nose with the handkerchief Miss Margaret gave me before we left the kitchen for Rose's funeral.

"Aww, I'm fine." He tries to shove my hand away. He turns his head to the side to conceal the damp trail of tears that leave a clean path of skin and freckles. Rose was just as much of a friend to him as she was to me—if not more so. He brushed her when I didn't, he fed her when I couldn't and cleaned up after her when I wouldn't. He lost someone dear today, too.

"No, Benedict Hackett, you are not!" I know progressing to the "B's" will lighten the mood and it does. I get at least a little snicker out of him.

"Nope. Still not it. I told you, you're never going to guess," he tries to tease back.

I can see behind the efforts and see the boy; dirty, bruised, and in pain. I know his pain. It's a type of pain that penetrates much deeper than skin and bone. We're in the same place and I understand him.

"Miss Margaret? Is there any stew left?" I ask.

She nods. "Plenty. No one has had the chance to eat yet. Venison stew is still simmering away over the fire," she says.

"Perfect!" I use too much cheer and volume. Both Miss Margaret and Tubs jump. "Miss Margaret, could you please go to the Hacketts and get a change of clothes for Tubs? He's getting a hot dinner and a bath," I announce.

Tubs' eyes are as big as teacups. He, for once, is speechless. Boys in general, I suppose, don't like baths as much as girls do. I know Jonathan would rather wash up in the nearby stream rather than soak in stagnant water, but I want to repay Tubs in some way, to show him how thankful I am. Words just don't seem to be enough, but a warm bath and a full tummy would be something his mother would prescribe if she were here.

"Izzy, I don't need a bath. I'll just wash up in the bowl at home like I always do." He rounds his shoulders and kicks at a loose clump of dirt.

It's pointless for him to argue with me. I'm not going to take no for an answer. I pick up our lanterns and lead him by the arm to the house. Surprisingly, he doesn't put up a fight but follows obediently. I always thought Tub older than he was, with all his outdoor knowledge and know-how. Today, he's true to his age.

He's still speechless when I usher him into the kitchen and is in complete awe over the tawny-colored tub. I direct him to the small table near the fireplace and take a bowl from a stack on the shelf where the dishes are nested in rows.

Hanging on a hook above the fire, the venison stew bubbles in conversation with itself in a chubby black pot. Jonathan and Alexander harvested a young buck and a large doe before their "trip", so venison will be on the lunch and dinner menu for a while, which doesn't bother me a bit. Venison is one of my favorites, and I ladle our bowls full.

I help Tubs get started on his dinner while I prepare the bathing water. There are multiple buckets of water waiting on the floor for tonight's dishes and the morning's kitchen work. I decide to use these for Tubs and make a mental plan to get up early in the morning before Miss Margaret and refill them. I hang them low over the fire on the available hooks to get them heating, and I scoop from the tub most of the used water with an empty bucket. I love the slapping sound the water makes when it hits the ground. I'm eager to toss the next bucket to hear it again.

The water is dirty, but not as dirty as after the three of us are done with it. Jonathan always insists that I go first, Miss Margaret is next and when he does take a tub bath, Jonathan goes last. When the tub is near empty, I sit down at the table across from Tub to enjoy my stew. With great anticipation, I lift the spoon with the steaming pieces to my open mouth. Tubs grabs my arm and freezes it mid-air.

"Wait. Did you say your thanks? I said mine already to myself," he reports with pride.

Jonathan is the one who usually prays before our meals. And when he's not home, Miss Margaret or one of the other men joining us will pray. I've never done it on my own.

I fold my hands under my chin and close one eye. The other I use to peek at Tubs. I pray, but it feels awkward and unnatural.

"Dearest Father, thank you for this stew. Please bless the hands that prepared it. Thank you, Father, for the Gudwyne copper tub that our Tubs will soon partake in, for we know, Heavenly Father, this is long overdue!" I feel a kick from under the table as I finish with an amen.

"There. Happy?" I say and shove in the heaping spoonful of stew.

"I am," he answers straight-faced. "I pray and talk to God before every meal, before I fall asleep at night, and when I wake up. When I was little, Papa would make me and have to remind me; now, I do it because I want to." He studies me from behind the bowl that conceals half his face as he drinks up the last bit of broth. "You don't like talking to Him, do you?" I snicker when he dries his mouth with his sleeve.

No, to be honest, I don't. I don't tell him that. I'll sound like a heathen. It just felt like I was talking to myself on the few occasions that I did try. When Jonathan was sick with fever and was in bed for almost a month, I was scared he was going to die. So, I prayed. God must have heard me, and I must have said something right because Jonathan got better and he's still here with us.

Now would be a good time to check on the water. I dump the readied pails in the tub along with a few drops of lavender oil. A towel across one chair, my blanket on another, I position things just as Margaret had done earlier for me near the fire.

"Your majesty, your bath awaits." I hold out the skirt to my nightdress and cross one ankle behind the other and curtsy. "I'll be right outside in the next room if you need anything."

When the door clicks shut, he shouts for me. His voice sounds small. I open the door and he rushes to me.

"I'm sorry, Izzy!"

I try my best to comfort him by telling him it was just an accident and neither of us had meant for it happen. The sobs continue, and I look around the room for help. I'm out of words.

"Do you know what I'm going to miss the most?" he sniffs. "You coming out to read to her."

He is right to be concerned. Rosemary was always the bait to get me outside. I kiss him to the forehead and make a promise to come out to read to him instead.

Miss Margaret knocks on the kitchen door before coming in with Tubs' clothes. She places them to warm on one of the chairs. She pauses to give me a warm smile before scuttling out of the room to advance to the next task.

"What?" I ask. My hands go immediately to my hair.

"I just like what I see. It's what the house felt like every day when she was here." She shines a grin to both of us before shutting the door behind her. Her words float in the air like a happy Irish song.

Tubs is struggling with his shirt. His arms are already stiffening, and he can't lift them over his head.

"Here, let me help you."

Surely, this isn't the proper protocol for a lady. Helping a boy take his shirt off would have Miss Margaret grabbing at her chest, but this is Tubs and I don't care. It's getting too hard to keep track of the things I shouldn't do versus the things I should.

"I know where everyone's going," he says underneath his shirt. "Jared was talking up a storm while we were shoveling. I think he forgot I was there. He said he couldn't wait to get back to America and be the one to strike it rich this time. He said maybe he'd even pick out his own savage to tame—that you turned out mighty fine and Jonathan shouldn't be the only one with one. That's when my father punched him hard—right in the face!"

When I pull Tubs free, he's grinning like a one-eyed jack-o-lantern.

"What's this?" I ask.

"What?" He pulls his shoulder forward to his chin and tries to peek over.

Black sores, crusty and scabbed, are stamped randomly across his back.

"Oh, that." He attempts to grab his shirt out of my hands, but I pull it back. "I didn't want you to know. Doctor Batchford says it's the same as what Mama had. He's been trying to get me to stay out of the sun. He says I've had too many sunburns."

I've only rummaged through a few medical books, but I have seen enough pictures of diseases to know that these sores aren't a good sign. My knees feel weak, so I sit down in the middle of the floor. I bury my face in my hands and through sticky palms, I see Rosemary's mound in the dark.

FIFTEEN

I never fell asleep. I tossed all night. I never got to ask Tubs about Jared's "savage" comment. The sores on Tubs' back stole that the question from me. My little friend is sick and there is no cure in Doctor Batchford's bag for what he has. Jonathan's appearance in the cellar is adding to my whirling thoughts of when Tubs will be leaving me. I am glad to finally toss off the covers to be released from the night's torture when I see the sun seeping through the cracks in the curtains.

I must replace the pails of water that I used yesterday. Margaret had prepared them for today's work. To get them, I need to go to the creek a quarter mile down the road. I wish it were easier to get. Jonathan has talked about finding a way to bring the water from the creek directly to the house. I can't see how that could even be possible, but if it is, Jonathan will be the one to figure it out.

I slip out of bed and brush my hair in a few quick strokes. I don't bother molding it into a bun. Surely, no one will be up yet. When I round the first corner of the staircase, I can hear the kitchen is already bustling with activity.

"Dear, why are you up so early?" Miss Margaret rushes over when she notices me, then her eyes widen in memory. "The pails have been filled and are already being put to use. Go, off with you, and get yourself a few more winks of sleep." She follows me and shoos me back up the stairs with her apron. "I'll have you working hard soon enough. And oh!" she gasps and claps her hands over her mouth and adds a hop on the stair. I rush down to her when she teeters. "Mercy sakes! The dresses! The dresses are coming in a few hours." She maintains her balance on her own and she giggles with a hand to her chest.

"Dresses?" I ask. I already have a wardrobe full of them. Jonathan brings a new one home after every trip.

"This is an important dinner with important guests. Occasions like these call for a special dress. Now, off with you, child!" She pushes me back up the stairs. "Back to sleep!"

I obey her in body only. My will fights her. I'll humor her and crawl back in, but I won't sleep. It can't come. Not with all that I know. I snuggle back into bed and prepare for the bombarding thoughts of the night before, but fatigue wins the battle over them, and this time, sleep comes. I even manage to sleep right up to the time the seamstress brings the dresses up to my room.

Ms. Abernathy, the town seamstress, told me Jonathan came by and picked out the dresses months ago and instructed her to have them altered to my size and ready for today.

Alexander had been with him that day, too, she says, but he chose to stay outside with the horses. He wouldn't budge from his spot even when the sky opened and released the heaviest rainfall of the season. Ms. Abernathy's eyes fall to her shoes when she mentions Tubs' father. She's been a widow for at least five years now and has been patiently waiting for Alexander to notice her. He has. That's why he stays out of her shop. It's easier to go on the way you know than to step out and tempt change. Jonathan has tried to encourage him but finally called a truce and gave up. He figures the man will move on when he's ready. Though, he warned, wait too long and the opportunity may no longer be there.

There are three dresses, though my eyes only see one. Evolyn's blue dress with the white, billowy sleeves.

"Splendid choice, Miss Isabelle," she says. If fairies were real, their voices would sound like Ms. Abernathy's; pleasingly cheerful and childlike. "But, please, try them all on. I want to make sure they fit. They're all yours."

I obey but I'm embarrassed. Ms. Abernathy is wearing the same dress I saw her in the last time she came. And the time before that—and the time before that even. I don't think I've seen her in any other dress.

"I will. Only if you promise to try one on yourself," I say. The blue dress fills both arms, and the material makes a merry swooshing sound as it drags across the floor to the dressing screen.

"Oh, miss, I couldn't!" she coos in alarm. "They're yours!"

I peek through the crack and see her looking over the dresses while chewing on a fingernail.

"Ms. Abernathy, you know how many dresses I have. You've altered every one. One person cannot possibly use all these dresses."

I can't button up the back on my own, but I at least have it on. I gather the silky material in my hands to keep from tripping under its length. It's long, but once my heeled shoes are on, it should be the perfect length.

She gasps when she sees me. My face feels warm, and I know I must have a crazy grin on my face; my cheeks are already feeling sore. Having Evolyn's dress on, I can't help but feel excited.

I wonder if I look anything at all like Evolyn. I catch my reflection in the mirror and immediately see that I don't. But it isn't all disappointing. Though I'm not tiny and petite like Evolyn, my shape is what Miss Margaret calls solid and durable. I never know how to take that. Ladies in English society desire a small stature and as a result, cinch things in and plump others out. I look healthy and natural, unlike the ladies of the day with odd, misshaped figures.

When Ms. Abernathy tugs on the strings in the back, my waist is pulled into the hourglass shape that it doesn't hold naturally. My shoulders aren't delicate and round like Evolyn's but broad and strong. I don't feel my smile fade until my eyes stop here. It's here at the shoulders that I'm brought to alarm. The dress accentuates them handsomely, but it's also where the dress reveals its cruel catch. The grotesque and uneven texture and tone of my damaged skin are also highlighted. If I wore this dress, I would be a walking testament to the dangers of bathing in fire.

"Beautiful," Ms. Abernathy compliments. "A complete vision."

A vision of horror, I say to myself. My image blurs along with the flaws. I wish they were as easy to erase as the tears I blink away.

Ms. Abernathy pulls something from underneath the remaining dresses on my bed. It is a sizable piece of the same flouncy fabric that is on the wrists of Evolyn's dress. "I took the liberty to bring this extra material just in case."

Her voice is soothing, and I feel a pulse of hope. She cinches the material together like a fan before draping it behind me. She gathers it in front of my neck, and where the ends meet, she tucks them in the bosom of the dress. A few fluffs and the wispy fabric has my scars erased from vision.

"There. This suits you better if I may be so bold," she says as she begins pinning. "I think a lady should portray a mystery about her and not give everything away." I understand her meaning. Modesty *and* camouflage. "Is this all right?" she asks before threading her needle to make the adjustment permanent.

I nod, giving her permission, and her fingers go to work. She tugs and pulls the thread through numerous places while pulling out pins and sticking them in between her teeth. When the pins are replaced with thread, she snips it free with a pair of scissors.

"Done," she says with a pleased exhale. She steps back to admire her work, and her slender fingers brush over her lips.

I didn't think Evolyn's dress could ever be improved upon. Ms. Abernathy proved me wrong.

"It's been a pleasure as always, Miss Isabelle." She offers me a courtesy and a polite grin and begins to gather her things.

"Oh, no," I say. "Your turn."

"Oh, I couldn't. Could I?" she says. It is a question that is not just directed to me.

"You can and you shall," I order with a grin. I gather up the dress's train behind me and throw it over my arm. "This one." I grab the green dress with yellow flowers. I have a feeling it will be stunning with her amber hair.

Her nails go straight to her mouth, and she chews one down to the pink on her forced journey to the dressing screen.

"What would Jonathan say? I don't want to get into trouble." She peeks from behind the screen like a scared bird.

I hand her the dress and hang her faded one over the divider when it falls to the floor. "I'll take care of Jonathan, don't you worry."

Saying his name out loud flushes my face with heat. I clench my fists to contain the anger I can feel bubbling just beneath my skin. I wonder if Ms. Abernathy is aware that Jonathan Gudwyne isn't who he says he is. Does she know that the man who summons her to alter my dresses does so not for the girl that he took in to help care for but for the girl that he stole to be part of his collection?

I don't say what my heart desires to say. I don't want to spoil this moment for her. The green dress that I picked for her was the correct choice; she looks every bit the part of a woodland fairy queen.

A gasped "Isabelle" is all she can manage when she sees her reflection.

"You look like a princess straight out of a fairytale," I say. I force a smile, but I mean it when I tell her that the dress is a gift for her and that I want her to enjoy it.

Ms. Abernathy throws her arms around me. I didn't do anything spectacular but give her something I didn't need or couldn't use. I watch as she examines herself from every angle. It may not have been a big sacrifice on my part, but the gesture gives Ms. Abernathy joy, and that is a good feeling.

"Now to have you go somewhere to show that dress off. Are you free tonight?" I ask. Alexander is going to be at the gathering. It wouldn't hurt to help him out a bit. "Tea is at five, dinner at six. I would love for you to come." I have two motives in mind. With Ms. Abernathy, that at least would make two people I would know at the ladies tea before dinner.

"I—I…" Ms. Abernathy blows out an exhale, and a smile carves out a dimple in her right cheek. "I am."

"Five o'clock then," I say and take my turn behind the screen. I attempt to get the dress off myself, but I have to slip back out when my arms fail to contort in the angle I need them to. She looks flushed and happy through the mirror as she pulls the satin ribbon loose. With each tug, my lungs release trapped air, and I'm able to breathe deeply again. I slip off Evolyn's dress and put my day dress on. With care, I guide the altered dress over the top of the screen and fluff the skirt by lifting it in the air.

Ms. Abernathy's grin grows as the air billows out of the skirt.

Now with the dresses out of the way, I can put myself to some use. Miss Margaret hands me an empty pail when I ask her what needs to be done.

"I need fresh flowers in every room," she says.

That's a lot of flowers. I'm going to be busy for the rest of the afternoon. I take a knife from the nearest cutting board and make sure Miss Margaret isn't watching when I step past my shoes to go out the door.

The flowers are in full bloom and the garden is bursting with color. It's hard to decide which to choose first, but I know for certain where not to go: Evolyn's roses. Those are sacred. If I were seeking a way to get back at Jonathan, this would be the place to do it. I walk past them and let the soft heads bob in peace. Even the dark feeling I can sense growing against him can't persuade me to cut them. Daisies with lemon-drop centers are the first flowers once out of the kitchen, so I decide this is as good a place as any to begin.

Foxgloves are second after the daisies are harvested. Their blossoms are downward-shaped bells in the pink of the sky's dawn. Lavender orchids, white water-violets with sunny button eyes, and poppies the color of cherries are all nodding for attention to be put in the bucket next.

When the bucket is full of colorful heads, I deliver them to the kitchen where they are trimmed and set in vases of water to be arranged. One bucket is nowhere near enough, so I go back outside to cut more. Maybe there will be some left so I can give Tubs a bundle. I know boys don't like flowers as much as girls, but it'll give me an excuse to visit him. I haven't had the chance to see him yet today and I have a promise to keep.

The sun is high in the sky. For midafternoon, it's still surprisingly cool. A pleasant breeze playfully rushes through the top-heavy flowers and rumples my skirt. Bed sheets are flapping dry on the line, but only for a few hours more. Our guests are due to arrive around then. Everything is to be put back in perfect order by that time to give the illusion that work doesn't happen, and that perfect order is something that occurs naturally.

The poppies are the easiest to cut. They have long, spindling stems, and it takes little effort to cut through with my knife. A cream-colored butterfly lands on a blossom. Its wings keep time like the clock in the library rhythmically opening and closing to an inaudible tick.

The beauty of the butterfly is hypnotic.

"Does Miss Margaret know that you're playing in the poppies?"

The knife I held poised to cut the poppy slips and slices into my hand. Blood immediately seeps out of the open slash, and I inhale a hiss from the pain it brings.

"I'm sorry! I didn't mean to scare you. Let me see." Jonathan helps me up to my feet and pulls out a handkerchief from his coat.

He presses it over my cut first before looking at it. I can't look up at him. The last time I saw him was from my hiding place in the wardrobe. This man who nurses me like he's done so many times before feels like a stranger. I've always trusted him, and I thought he shared everything with me. I was wrong. I don't think I'm wrong for his caring for me. For this, I have no doubt. But the man also cares for our horses, our goats—our sheep.

I muster up the courage to look at him and I'm startled. The biting words I have been rehearsing to use on him while harvesting the flowers are lost. He looks handsome, freshly scrubbed, and dressed in tonight's clothes. His pine-green frockcoat and matching breeches are striking. Jonathan rarely dresses up and this is the opposite of what I'm used to seeing him in. A cream vest like the color of the clouds that coast behind his shoulders softens his dark silhouette. The gold embroidery needled in it gives his wardrobe a princely air. Unlike most days, today his hair is neatly pulled back into a curly tail and tied with a coordinating ribbon. His bangs, however, cannot be so easily tamed, and they escape to the usual spot over his eyes.

"I'm fine," I say with a tug.

It's a lie. I'm not fine. I'm angry and now my hand hurts. I try to pull my hand free from his, but he's as stubborn as I am. He's keeping his grip.

"Just let me take a peek." He lifts the handkerchief and the smiling gap remains fleshy, for a moment, but blood soon pushes through the crevice and pools in the wrinkles of my hand.

"I think we need to sit for a bit." He adds a gentle squeeze before guiding me to a bench. He presses the handkerchief into my hand. "Are we doing all right?"

I nod, though I do feel sweaty. I know these aren't the feelings of a faint; I'm more than familiar with how that feels. This is different. Perhaps it's because my hand is pressed too tightly between his or it's the growing color of the handkerchief. The thought of blood escaping by the gallons out of my cut does make my stomach lurch when I think of it.

"I heard about Rosemary," he says. He presses his lips together and studies me from under a curl. "I'm sorry." One of his fingers feathers my wrist. He's making it difficult for me to stay angry with him.

"She was a good horse. I didn't treat her well, Jonathan. I neglected her." I scrunch my toes in the dirt to keep from crying. I make an ugly face when I cry. There'll be no hiding it if it comes; he has one of my hands.

"Part of that's my fault. I'm not good at this." He folds the cloth to press a fresh side to my cut. He's clenching his teeth. I can see his jaw pulsing. He rubs the bottom of his nose and pushes out a smile. "That had to be the most pampered horse in England. Name me any other horse that had access to a library!" He stretches his smile wider to get me to answer him and nudges into me with his knee.

I can't help but smile back at him. He always knows how to make things better.

"There. That's my girl." He takes another peek under the cloth. "You did quite the job on your hand. You may need some stitches." He chuckles at my wide eyes. "Or not."

"My girl." Jonathan has always addressed me this way, though the sound of it has morphed over the years. It wasn't just limited to the deepening tone of an aging boy. It's also how he expressed it. The warmth that usually crawls through my body is absent today when I hear it. "My girl" simply means I belong to him. The anger that he had managed to snuff out just moments ago has been rekindled.

"Do you know why we are having company today?" he asks.

I shrug. Does it matter? I didn't have a say in it and Jared has helped me understand why.

"The Fredricks are coming. I'm hoping they'll fund the rest of our trip." He tugs on my hand and cocks his head to get a better look at my face. I don't hear anything beyond "the Fredricks."

Company. I dislike entertaining. I can feel heat in my cheeks. He clears his throat and peeks again at my hand. I have never been good at hiding things from him. He knows something's wrong.

He explains that Henry and his wife, Althea, own many businesses. They own several factories. Each produces either lumber, grain, or textiles. Jonathan said Henry is an old friend of Edward's and he thinks he and Althea will be the perfect fit for what he has to offer. Jonathan has something that he feels they'll want and their purchasing it should provide him with the rest of the money that's needed for the trip. He is hoping what he has is enough. If it isn't, he said, he'll be given more of it when in America.

"I was going to wait until after dinner but—"

He stuffs his fingers inside the tiny pocket inside his coat. Pinched in between his fingers is his mother's ring. He takes his time adjusting the ring on my finger, and he doesn't speak until the turtle shell gem is centered.

"I'm leaving for America and I want you to go with me—as my wife."

Every evening at tea, I had searched the delicate hand of his mother for the ring—and now it's here, on my finger. The painting doesn't do it justice. The copper has a brighter glow in person, and the polished gem has a shine buffed so powerfully, I can see my reflection in it. Never have I had anything so beautiful on my hand.

"He had this made for her."

The "he" Jonathan speaks of is Edward, the man he never addresses as his father. The simple word is forced, and I can see speaking it is just as difficult for him as calling him by his name.

"I remember she'd read to me and I'd sit on her lap. I would twirl this ring around her finger. I didn't know much about Edward, but I knew he loved my mother. He disliked being away from her, and he told me once he felt the best half of him was gone when they were apart. That's exactly how I feel." The color in his face is growing as he adjusts the ring again. "I can't go across the ocean again without you. I need you with me. I love you, Izzy."

Trying to process the avalanche of information from the past few days is what I assume is causing the tremors that are rippling through my body. A proposal alone is life-changing enough without throwing a journey across the ocean into the mix. I grip the bench with my good hand; the garden is beginning to tilt. When did my best friend begin to love me? No, when did my *owner* come to love me? His tanned hand on top of my darker one gives me the boldness I need to confront him.

"I'm already yours," I hear myself blurt. "I'm your marked property. I found the brand, the same you use on our cattle, Jonathan." As the words tumble, I can see the brown flecks in his eyes consume the dominant green.

"I found the brand," I repeat slowly, in case he didn't catch it the first time.

SIXTEEN

I can't bear to look at him. The pained look he has is making my stomach turn. He releases his hold and lets my hand slip from his. The bleeding has stopped, so I busy myself with folding the wet handkerchief into squares. I hate this whole conversation, but I can't stop it.

"How long have you known?" His hands have his full attention. He's rubbing them together to try to rid them of the blood that's left behind on them.

"Yesterday. I was made aware of it by a friend of yours. I must commend you. You've done great work turning a savage around," I say, paraphrasing the gumming rodent.

"Jared," he huffs. "I don't like that he was near you. Mary told me you had words, but she didn't say what."

The man he named is as revolting to him as the "Snow" I made for him two weeks ago. Not the fluffy cold kind from outside, but the dessert dish of cream that resembles snow. Cream, rose water, and sugar are beaten together until it becomes a sweet, soft cloud. We serve it over fresh fruit, but since Jonathan isn't a big fruit eater, he eats plain bowls of Snow instead. Unknowingly, I used salt instead of sugar. When he ate my mistake, it was a big heaping spoonful of it. I thought he might throw up, but for my sake, he swallowed it and even managed a gracious smile.

Others at the table either spat it into their napkins or gulped down large quantities of water. I had no idea what the fuss was all about until I took a big heaping spoonful myself. I was not as successful as Jonathan at controlling my stomach. The table and the poor soul in front of me were covered with rabbit stew and biscuits.

Jonathan asks that I tell him everything and leave no detail from him. Though gentle, it is more of an order than a request.

"He told me that I'm your property, marked so by the Gudwyne family seal, or brand in my case. The same that our animals wear. You've been to America at least once before and you're guilty of thieving copper, a ship, and its entire crew—and me." My mouth is bone dry. I try to swallow, but there isn't one drop of moisture left. The trembling I had felt crawling beneath my skin is now visible, and this disturbs him.

He takes hold of my hands. The hesitancy he's had against taking them up for all these months is gone. He's also forgotten the wound on my hand, and he's squeezing it too hard.

"I want to tell you everything, but I can't. I beg you to trust me," he pleads. "This is me; please, remember who I was to you before Jared spoke to you."

He rubs his thumbs onto my wrists to get my attention. When that doesn't work, he gently taps my hands together to get me to look at him. I can't. I watch instead an ant try to carry a crumb three times its size over a blade of grass.

"The things I keep from you are meant to protect you. You must know by now that I would do anything for you. To keep you safe. To keep you from ever being hurt again."

He's desperate for me to believe him, but I don't know if I can give him that. The ant staggers on to carry his load alone down an invisible road. I watch until the forest of grass blades swallow him up.

"Is what he said true? Am I yours?" My hand has fallen asleep. I manage to wrestle it partially out of his grip, and the new position wakens it. Now it feels like a pin cushion jabbed by a million needles. The half-grip causes it to start bleeding again.

"Yes, but it's not like that." He speaks too loudly. He's trying to hide the emotion in his voice by raising it. This is what he does to try to gain control over the tears that come too easily for him. I know his crying frustrates him. That's why he used the library for it when he was a boy. He doesn't cry in front of me anymore. At some point, he stopped. I read that boys aren't supposed to cry. Perhaps that's why.

"What's it like then, Jonathan? Tell me. What am I? Am I some collectible trinket to remind you of your travels?"

"No!" He stands. My hands yank up with him. He won't let go. "I told you, it's not like that."

"Well, tell me then!" I stand to confront him. "Tell me. Do I belong to you?"

He sighs, and the place between his brows wrinkle. The transformation is happening again, and I know he will not speak of the brand or of anything else that deals with my past.

"Yes," he says evenly. He offers nothing more.

"Give back what you stole from me," I demand.

I want my hands back, too, but he won't let go. He's blurring. The tears are coming, and there'll be no stopping them. Fine. Let them come. He won't be able to resist them and I'll get what I want.

"I have stolen nothing from you, girl. Nothing. I've given everything I have to you. There's nothing here that isn't yours." I can only see one of his eyes. The brow over his unshielded one is passionately pinched tight.

"You have my memories. You said you'd give them back. I want them back. I want them back now, Jonathan." I sob my words, but they aren't working. His shoulders are still strong. "You'll tell me why I wear this mark and who gave it to me. Right now—here—today."

"I won't," he says firmly. He lets go of my hands to cradle my face, and he shakes it in beat to his clenched words. "I can't."

"Why?!" I cry and take hold of his wrists to wrestle them off. He's got ahold of my face. He's never done that before. The new touch would frighten me if I weren't so angry with him. "I'm the one who's wearing the brand! Your brand. And the memories—they're *mine*. They belong to me!"

"The memories you want aren't just yours. They're mine, too," he says. His voice is failing, and his eye is filling. "Until I'm led otherwise, I will not give them to you. It will take more than tears, girl, to get them out of me. You know better." The vein in his neck is pulsing. "This isn't me giving in to that extra slice of cake at dinner when you were six."

"You, Jonathan Gudwyne, are a thief and a liar!" I shout.

I should stop here, but I can't. The fire within is too hot, and my tongue promises to help release the pressure I can feel building.

"I hate you!" I spit. Miss Margaret's forbidden words hurt, and I gasp at its violent echo. The words thrust through him like a sword and their remnants fill my mouth with a taste more rancid than the curdled milk I once guzzled. Miss Margaret was right. It is a harsh word, and it inflicted more damage to him than my hand could have ever done to his face. Jonathan sighs from the sting of the verbal blow.

"But I love you," he croaks. He puts his forehead to mine. He grimaces. I can see I'm close to getting what I want from him. I know Miss Margaret has said my past is a burden to him. Surely he must want to be free from it as much as I want it back. He surprises me when the breath he takes helps him square his shoulders.

"I will *not* give you your memories. You're not ready. My mother couldn't handle it. How on earth should I expect you to? I killed my mother, Izzy. I told her everything Edward was up to over there. She begged me to and I gave in. I will not make the same mistake with you."

"I'm not your mother," I point out with less venom. His confession dowses some of my fire. He has mentioned her twice in one day. This is the most he has talked about her to me. My heart is begging for me to back down, to listen to him, to attempt to mend things, but it's too late. I can't take back that awful word that I said to him.

"No, you're not my mother. You're worse." He shakes his head to try to take back the words he said in haste. "I didn't mean it, I'm sorry," he says. The words roll quickly from his tongue, and he finds my hands to accentuate the apology.

"Oh, you meant it," I say with renewed energy. I step back and yank my hands from his, but I didn't need to use that much force on both. One of them is blood drenched, and it comes back with such force, I hit myself in the stomach with it. "The fainting isn't my fault. It's the returning memories," I argue. "I don't need you. Let them come on their own. I'll deal with them by myself."

"You're right. The fainting isn't your fault. I'm sorry. It was wrong of me to say that," he apologizes again. He steadies his breath and takes me by the shoulders to pull me back to him. He scowls to keep his tears hidden, but I can hear them in his voice. "I don't want you dealing with them alone—without me—but that's exactly what's going to happen. Odedeyan wants you home, Izzy. That's what this trip is all about. To bring you home. If you refuse me now, we will be forever separated. Do you understand? Odedeyan wants you back."

I don't know who Odedeyan is. He wants me back? He can't mean Papa. Papa's dead. The immediacy in Jonathan's voice is pumping me with panic. Jonathan can read it so he explains for me. "Odedeyan is Ojibwe for father. Your father is ready for you, but I'm not ready. I promised him I'd give you back to him when the time came—but I can't. How am I supposed to do this? Tell me, Izzy. How?" The tears he had been trying to fight are on his cheeks. Part of me longs to reach for him—but I don't.

"If we were married…"

"You told me Papa was dead," I interrupt.

"Never. I never told you that. I said he wasn't coming for you."

"What about Mama? Tell me if she waits for me, too."

"Don't," Jonathan drops his head into his chest, and he falls onto the bench.

I can't control my tongue. I'm hurting him, but the need to continue slashing at him is stronger than the small voice that asks me to stop.

"The months you're gone—you go there—to Papa? You said you've never stolen from me, but you have. You've been going to America to see *my* Papa. You've been keeping him from me. He's my father, not yours."

"I haven't been keeping him from you. It hasn't been safe for you there." When he looks up to me, I see that the boy is back and I feel horrible. "Odedeyan is yours, Izzy," he sighs. "When I bring you back, he will be yours alone. If we aren't married, I won't be able to stay. He will have another for you. You will marry his second choice."

"Don't I have a say?" I stomp and growl.

"No, you don't," he exhales. "I understand why he chose who he did, but I don't agree with it. He said I could ask you first. It's to be me—not that—that boy."

"I won't have either of you. I'm not marrying a stranger, and I'm not marrying a liar. My Papa," I say in a jagged gasp, "he's yours, too, isn't he? I can tell by the way you talk about him. You know him. He's taken you in? But not me—his daughter? You both led me to believe this entire time he was dead."

"Izzy…" Jonathan jumps up to try to comfort me, but I won't have him. My shoulders can square as much as his.

"Fine. Take me home to Papa. I'll marry that stupid boy and I'll be completely miserable, but at least I'll never have to see you again."

"You don't mean that. You're angry. We'll talk again tonight when everyone's gone."

"How do you know what I mean?" I sob. "How?"

"Because I know you." Jonathan takes my face in his hands and tilts it up, so I have nowhere else to look but at him. "I know you and I love you. Every fearful, spirited, passionate piece. I know that you take four lumps of sugar in your tea and yet it's still not sweet enough to make you like it. You're always barefoot because English shoes smother your feet. Every time you come down the stairs—every time— you count them, and you always hop over the last one. Look at me," he says when I dart my eyes away from him. The things he's observed of me anyone could notice with any length of time around me. Still, it touches me, and I want to hide. I don't want him to see my blotched face or even worse, anything deeper than that. "Niinimooshe, you like rainy days not because you're the troll you see yourself to be but because it allows you to stay in the library to be near the boy. The boy that's in front of you that I hide most days from you because he's weak. You need strength, Izzy—and I need it—for what I must endure every day for you. You hate him—me? You don't mean that do you?"

I don't mean it. I don't hate him. I think I might love him, even though my books say differently, but I can't tell him. I don't know how. I whimper a cry of confusion instead. The strange word he used for me is a dagger to my heart. I heard it before. I can hear the word in Papa's voice, but I can't remember what it means.

"I'll do as you wish and take you to your Papa. You'll never have to see me again, but know when I do leave you there, a part of me will die. You're a part of me. You're meant to be mine. Not because of the mark you are forced to wear but because our souls have been woven. Can't you see that? How can you not feel the same?" He says the last part with a squint as if he is trying to look inside me to check for himself. When I don't answer, he continues. "Please—keep the ring. I don't want it back. I don't ever want to see it again."

"When am I to be taken again? When will I be forced to leave?" I ask. The explosive heat from earlier is absent in my tone, but each question still wounds him. He takes a step back from me to recover.

"In the morning," he sighs. He looks exhausted, and I know it's my fault. My tongue has done it to him. "Forgive me for not telling you sooner. I thought it best this way—waiting until the last possible minute. Was I wrong?" he asks. "Forgive me if I was wrong."

"You knew I was to go when you came home last summer," I say.

Without a doubt, that was the time when things changed between us. That's when he must have discovered he loved me; when Papa said it was time to bring me back to him. He was right to wait. It would have been ten months of sleepless nights and worry for me.

"I did." I let Jonathan take up my injured hand again to mend it. The blood had loosened the ring and taken it down to my knuckle. He takes his time fixing it while putting new pressure on the cut. "Jefferson is to bring you to the ship tomorrow before dawn. He'll have instructions for you then. You need stitches, Izzy. It's your pick who does it—me or Alexander, it doesn't matter which. I won't set sail until it's done."

I pull my hand back from him, and when I do, it feels like I thrust the first stages of our separation into motion. "Neither of you. I'm fine," I say. I feel empty. My refusal of him, as a husband and as a doctor, slices the cord in two that had once bound us together.

The sound of carriage wheels crunching on crushed stone shatters the silence that the new relationship I have chosen for us has forged. There is no going back to where we were. He's destroyed any hopes of that by keeping my past selfishly to himself.

I leave him to make my journey to the house alone. I shouldn't leave him like this. I can't, can I? I should and I will. He lied to me. The world is hazy and blurred from all the tears. I disobey the voice inside that screams, "Don't look back," and I steal a glance before entering the kitchen.

Jonathan's head is in his hands and his shoulders are heaving.

I can't turn the doorknob. The blood from my hand has made it slippery. I don't want to see anymore, and I can't escape fast enough. I use my skirt to open the door, and I rush through and collide into Jefferson, whose arms are full of potatoes. Potatoes bounce onto my feet as I heave over a barrel of apples.

"Isabelle!" Miss Margaret runs to my aid. She mops my face with a damp rag, and her eyes are wild with concern. "Are you sick? Mercy sakes! You're hurt! You're covered in blood!"

This time I don't keep my tears from her. I let them come, and the wet from them collects under my face before they're absorbed by her dress.

"Papa wants me home," I weep. "Miss Margaret, Papa wants me home. Must I go?"

"My sweet, sweet girl," Miss Margaret hushes into my hair. "Sweet Merciful Lord above, the boy has finally told you," she sighs. "Yes, dear child, it's time. We must let you go and neither Jonathan nor I know how to do this. We're sorry—I'm sorry." Miss Margaret is now crying with me. "How do I give up one of my babies?"

So, it's true. My dark skin tone, which has deepened past Jonathan's these past few days, is the evidence to Jared's words and Jonathan's lack of them as to who I am. There's no denying it. I, Isabelle Gudwyne, am a savage, a Red—a gentleman's property. This is the first challenge I wish I didn't win.

SEVENTEEN

I was venomous towards Jonathan. Should I have gone back to comfort him? Part of me wishes I would have, but it would have felt unnatural and awkward. I'm always the one to be comforted. I wouldn't know how to go about it. Little boys are one thing. Soothing a brokenhearted Tubs seems to come somewhat naturally. It's ministering to the grown, the mature—the ones who seem to do the inflicting—that I struggle with. Perhaps I made the right decision. Isn't keeping facts from people the same as lying? If so, this makes Jonathan Gudwyne a double liar. It's a good thing I didn't go back. I was right to leave him there.

Mary is waiting in my room to help me get dressed. My hand has stopped bleeding, but the slightest bump can get it flowing again. She has the idea to replace the dishrag that Miss Margaret hastily wrapped around my hand with one of my monogrammed handkerchiefs. Miss Margaret had sewn a stack of them for my birthday last year.

Mary secures the material to my hand with a leftover piece of ribbon from my hair, dressing it up to make it look like a bracelet for my hand. It's rather inventive. Maybe we have just created England's next fashion trend.

"Miss Isabelle! You're engaged!" She squeals when she notices the ring resting on top of her neat bow. I must explain to her for the second time that I'm not, and that it is merely a gift from Jonathan. Mary frowns

"If you don't mind my saying, Miss, but you and Master Jonathan are an obvious match," she says while untangling the bow. She smiles and fastens it again, and this time she takes extra care fluffing the loops. There wasn't anything wrong with the bow the first time. I think she just wants a better look at the ring. "Pay no mind to the things that Jared said of the master. Jared is a sour man. He dislikes Master Jonathan—he dislikes everybody. He doesn't belong here. All of us know that and that's why none of us will let him near you. You didn't refuse Master Jonathan because of him, did you?"

I pull my hand away and cover it on my lap. The realization strikes me like lightning that this ring has no business being on my finger and I should have picked another dress.

"Mary, let's do a different dress. Ms. Abernathy brought another…"

"Miss, you know how long it took to get you into this one. There isn't time." She scrunches her face and giggles. She thinks I'm crazy for even considering changing this late.

She continues to flit around the room like a playful kitten, grabbing random pieces of jewelry for me to try. My rising annoyance with her is kept at bay with the realization she is just an excited child, a whole two years younger than myself, who would do anything to be in my place. She's a social creature and as chatty as Tubs. I unclasp the pearl necklace that she had helped me put on and ask her over to me. She gasps and giggles as I fasten the strand around her neck.

She fingers the pearls and beams. "Oh my, Miss Isabelle!" she squeals. Her smile couldn't be wider.

"They're yours," I say. They weren't mine anyway. Everything in this house—this ring and this dress—are nothing but pretty shackles.

I dip my fingertips into a small bowl of honey and twist the random strands of hair Mary left out into spiral-shaped curls. She had piled my hair on top of my head and somehow managed to create the look of curls out of my wavy hair. It looks soft and delicate compared to the harsh, neat bun I'm usually asked to wear. Mary tucks in random sprigs of Baby's Breath. I don't think I have ever looked prettier or more miserable.

Mary can barely contain her excitement as I rise from my seat and fluff the creases from the dress.

"How do I look? Presentable?" I ask. I do a quick spin for her. The train wraps around my ankles like a satin snake, and this sends her into a fit of claps and giggles.

"Stunning!" she says in an airy exhale.

I hug her and thank her as I swoosh out of the room. The guests had arrived early, and I have certainly kept them waiting long enough. The wrath of Miss Margaret is something I don't want to have to deal with. Not today.

I lift my skirt to go down the stairs, and it's heavy. I look over my shoulder and watch the dress's train slip down the steps behind me. Even with my skirt lifted, I still can't see my feet. The fear of falling is snuffed when I find my feet have memory, and they land on each step solid and sure.

Jonathan, Alexander, and Mr. Fredrick are engaged in conversation in the foyer as I round the corner to the second set of stairs. My clicking shoes attract the attention of Jonathan. He looks up from his conversation with Mr. Fredrick, who's staring at him as if waiting for an answer. He attempts to move past the short-statured man to get to me, but Alexander steps in to whisper to Jonathan. I can't see Jonathan's face; his curls have fallen again, but I can see his shoulders and they've lost their squared strength. Alexander offers him a smile and a squeeze to a shoulder before coming to meet me at the base of the stairs. He reaches for me to help me down the last few. He notices my ribbon-tied handkerchief and takes extra care tucking my hand under his arm.

"You look lovely, Miss," he smiles. "I know Jonathan should be escorting you, but he has important business with Henry, and we need his help desperately to get you home. Jonathan is the only one who'll be able to persuade him to buy off what's left of your father's copper. Is this all right with you?"

I nod while keeping a fixed eye on Jonathan. He's struggling to give Henry his full attention. Our guest notices. With a frown, Henry reaches inside his jacket. He retrieves a pipe and motions with it for the two to step outside.

"My father's copper?" I ask. "The copper on the ship was Papa's?"

"Jonathan didn't tell you? Edward stole it, but Jonathan was gifted it. To take care of you. The boy is his mother, without a doubt. He hasn't used a drop on himself. Why, both of our suits came from Ms. Abernathy's and cost us nothing.

Both were destined for the scrap heap, they were. She fixed us up mighty fine for the Fredricks, wouldn't you say?" he grins.

"Jared told me Jonathan stole the copper and the ship."

"Don't believe a thing that comes out of that snake's mouth. He's only here because Edward wants him on this trip."

"Edward?!" I shout but clap my hands over my mouth. His name isn't to be mentioned in this house. No one hears. Miss Margaret and the other women are too busy sipping and chatting to have heard my outburst. "Edward," I whisper. "I thought he was dead."

"No, he's alive. Jonathan didn't tell you otherwise, did he? Edward was part of the planning process to get you home. Mind you, the chief hid him each time Jonathan went over to visit. The boy dislikes his father something fierce." Alexander can see my confusion. "He hasn't told you any of this, has he?" His ruddy cheeks drain. "Oh, mercy sakes alive, don't tell Jonathan I leaked. I'm not one to meddle. He told me he talked to you. The boy certainly didn't tell you much." He adjusts his shoulders as if to shoo away the guilt of releasing information Jonathan had entrusted to him. He absentmindedly presses into my hand, and I pull my arm out with a gasp.

"My Papa is a chief?" I ask, and I add an unintentional moan at the end over the hot pain in my hand.

"Forgive me, Miss Izzy. Let me take a look." He reaches for my hand. "I only had the honor to meet your father once, but yes, he's a mighty fine one. I suppose that must make you a princess or—something like that." He lifts the cloth and presses his lips tight. "You need stitches all right. I'll stitch you up right now if you want. You know he won't leave until it's done, right?"

"He's made me aware of that," I say. The handkerchief is changing color again. "I'm fine. I can barely feel it." I don't bother with acknowledging his princess comment. I have no clue as to what being the daughter of a chief makes me. His guess is as good as mine.

"Well, you're to get stitches, and it's as simple as that. It doesn't matter what it feels like. A ship is a dirty place to be and that wound needs to be closed tight." The ring has twisted on my finger and he straightens it for me. "I'm sorry it didn't work out between you two. I can't picture you apart. It's an unpleasant thought, for sure. He's got a big heart, that boy does. He's given me more than I can ever repay. Not to meddle, Miss Isabelle, you know I wouldn't do that," he winks with a smile, "but Jonathan, he's the biggest man I know. He's the best of us. He would be a fine choice for a husband. The boy that waits for you isn't all that bad, but he's not Jonathan, and that makes him an ill fit in my opinion."

I didn't ask for his opinion and I don't want it. I want to tell him that he was indeed meddling and I don't care for it, not one bit, but I don't say it. It's the color that I notice swelling back into his face at the sight of Ms. Abernathy that keeps my tongue shackled. His cheeks are the color of apples press into eyes the same powdery blue as Tubs. I can see why Ms. Abernathy seeks his attention. He's a handsome man. A handsome man with loose hinges on his tongue. I got an earful for certain. It seems tongues are loose now that I'm close to going home. I wish I didn't have to go in with the ladies. I'd rather stay in the hall with Alexander and listen to his unguarded garble.

"I nearly forgot." Alexander fumbles across his jacket to find his pocket. He finds it right away once he takes his eyes from Ms. Abernathy. He pulls a paper from it and tucks it into my hand. "Tubs wanted me to deliver this to you. He says to go ahead and read it when you feel you need it most."

It feels good to have a piece of Tubs here with me. I want to cry. How fitting! I've spent most my day crying, why not into the evening, too? I find myself wishing Tubs and I were out fishing, whacking raspberry vines with sticks, or in the woods jumping over tree roots.

Ms. Abernathy is stealing glances at Alexander over her teacup. I'm happy to see her, but the feeling is canceled out immediately when I notice the two other women. If it weren't for Alexander's arm that I am offered up again and the fact the women have already seen me, I'd escape to the library and hide there the rest of the night. There is no chance of that, so I might as well make something good come out of this horrible gathering. A breeze from the open door gives me an idea. I don't want to lose Ms. Abernathy's company tonight, but there are already two miserable souls in this house. No sense in making more. A little push may be all the help Alexander and Ms. Abernathy needs. At least one couple deserves to be happy tonight.

"Oh, that's chilly," I shudder.

"That small puff of air that just came through?" Alexander raises a brow. "It feels wonderful. I'm boiling something fierce in all these layers."

"Well, I am chilled, and I don't think it wise to come down with something the evening before we are to leave. I think I may have left my wrap in the flower garden this morning. Could you find it for me?" I smile.

He narrows his brows at me. He can feel the room's air as well as I can. The small gust did nothing to change the temperature in here. With all the extra bodies, it's stuffy. I produce a shudder for him and rub the scars on my arm. This is all it takes for him to smile and agree to search.

He releases me to let me join the ladies in the sitting room where low whispers and silent sips of tea are the activities I get to look forward to. Seated in a chair next to Miss Margaret is a woman with impeccable posture and hair the color of tin. She's a tall, lean woman, who even while seated towers over Miss Margaret. Everything about her seems long. It's as if she is made of taffy candy and has been stretched from top to bottom. In the brief moments watching her, I notice her teacup must travel quite a distance from its saucer perch on her lap to her lined mouth. Every time she brings the teacup to her thin lips, she tips it ever so slightly. I wonder if she's even drinking at all.

Her dress looks expensive. Every inch of it is embellished with either lace, embroidery, or pearls, and the color of it matches the red that's rubbed onto her pale cheeks. What I see next perched on her head is what encourages me to busy myself longer than necessary at the tea service. A wide-brimmed hat dripping with all the finery of one's jewelry box is arranged around the crown and a downy ostrich feather protrudes out the back. It becomes animated at the slightest breeze or movement. I lose count of the number of sugar cubes I put in while trying to decide where to look when I'm introduced to her. Do I comment on her hat? If I were to say it was lovely, that would be a lie. To say nothing at all about something that is such an ornate spectacle could be an insult. I add another sugar cube. It's alarming how much she looks like a giant woodpecker. Miss Margaret is doing a wonderful job acting like it's the most natural thing in the world to have feathers poking out of one's head.

Sitting next to Mrs. Fredrick is a young woman that, I assume, is her daughter. She's slender like her mother, but her features aren't as stretched. Her hair isn't hidden underneath an obnoxious hat, either. Hers is up in a chignon and wound with pearls. Golden tube-curls frame her face, and I'd consider her pretty if it weren't for her stern, hard expression.

"Isabelle, how thoughtful of you to invite Ms. Abernathy for dinner." Miss Margaret opens her eyes wide, letting me know she is fully aware of the motives involved. She then winks, which is an indication that she's pleased. "Come, dear. Meet Mrs. Fredrick and her daughter." I drop two more sugar cubes in my tea before taking the empty seat next to Miss Margaret. "Althea and Agnes, this is our Isabelle."

I politely smile and nod, greeting both the way Miss Margaret had taught me and make sure to give them both proper eye contact. Althea's hat, however, is making the last step difficult.

"It's a pleasure to meet you, Mrs. Fredrick. Agnes."

Althea tilts her chin down in nod and takes a silent sip of tea. She speaks only after her teacup clicks back into place on its saucer.

"Miss Margaret, you really should keep this child indoors. Why, she could be easily mistaken for one of your servants." She's examining me through squinted eyes, and her lips are pursed in disagreement.

How can she see me? Her eyes look completely covered by their top lids.

"I find it healthy for a young woman to spend time in the out-of-doors. Fresh air, sunshine—it's the most natural of medicines. Dr. Batchford agrees. It's a habit more ladies should acquire." Miss Margaret isn't afraid of the stretched ostrich. She comes to my defense with a satisfied smile.

"I hear she has a 'delicate condition'. Does it help?" Althea whispers the emphasized words and leans in close to Miss Margaret while doing so. If she wished to keep the conversation secret, she'd be quieter about it. If she truly cared, she wouldn't have rasped it loud enough for me to hear. She has an annoying way of speech. Slowly over-pronouncing her words and emphasizing the last letter in each.

She shakes her head during her examination of me. The ostrich feather sails in the opposite direction as her head and waves for my attention. I press down on my cubes with the tip of my finger to ignore it and groan inwardly. I should have used my spoon.

Mrs. Fredrick raises her voice back to its natural volume. "If that is what the doctor would prescribe for my Agnes, I think I would find another avenue."

I believe her. Agnes' skin is as white as the sugar cubes bobbing in my cup. She looks like a pale mushroom that's never been exposed to sunlight. Visiting the outdoors, I'm quite positive, is extremely low on her list of things to do. That's the opposite of everyone here, besides Miss Margaret and myself, who crave outdoor activity and spend as much time outside as possible. Alexander, for one, can always be found outdoors, but not usually in the flowers. Alexander is shin-high in the daisies looking for a wrap that doesn't exist. Before he tires, I must send out Ms. Abernathy. I place my hand on her arm to get her attention. Today, my cold hands will work to my advantage. They're always cold, even during the heat of summer.

"Ms. Abernathy, could you please find my wrap? I think I took it off in the daisies. I'm sorry to be a bother." I add a grimace to this arm rub. I get the same obedient response from Ms. Abernathy as I had from Alexander.

"Oh, you poor dear! Your hands are like ice! Certainly, Miss Isabelle. It's not a bother at all. It'll give me a chance to admire your beautiful flowers." Her smile broadens when she sees Alexander crawling past the Foxgloves out the sitting room window.

Althea huffs at Ms. Abernathy's agreement to go outside and takes another delicate sip from her cup.

"Miss Margaret, what you've managed to do on such short notice with this dinner party is exemplary. Jonathan assured me we would be in capable hands, and he has been proven correct so far. Your staff here is impressive."

Althea went on to complain about one of her girls who burned a hole right through one of Mr. Frederick's shirts while ironing.

"But, even with Sarah and all her flaws, we're fortunate we chose her over one of those Reds that were so popular years back. I had heard they were wild and hard to tame. I didn't want to have a savage trained, so we chose our Sarah instead. She's clumsy and a bit dim, but at least she's obedient." Althea pauses to straighten her cup on her saucer and taps a long finger on the rim and tsks. "We have friends who bought a Red and they had to relinquish it last year. Nearly everyone in town had a Red. Now you're hard-pressed to find one left. Jonathan, I see, has made a wise decision and hasn't taken any of them on staff."

Althea widens her eyes with her discovery of Jonathan's wisdom, and she raises a smile in her daughter's direction. Mrs. Fredrick is a horrible woman with a forked tongue, and her heart is as homely as her overly stretched features. Miss Margaret lays a hand on my lap and our eyes catch. Her color has deepened since the conversation began. She adds a smile to her touch, and it soothes the hurt Althea caused.

"Mother, that's not what I heard. My sources have told me the savages weren't relinquished but purchased. Purchased to be freed and shipped back to America." Agnes brushes away an invisible crease in her skirt with a porcelain hand. "What complete fool would do something like that? After all, aren't we doing the good Lord's work? Taming them and giving them homes? I hear in America they run around barefoot in nothing but animal skins!" Agnes sneers and adds a shudder.

"Simply uncivilized! To walk around with unconfined feet? I cannot imagine!" Althea sputters and the ostrich feather quivers with the rest of her. "The animal skins, however, have my curiosity peaked. I have seen pieces in the shops in town and I must say, the furs are beautiful. I have yet to talk to Jonathan about it, but I think there is money for us to be found in that savage land. His father's fortune is only going to last so long. The boy needs to start investing before it's all squandered away." Althea shakes her head and clicks her tongue at the thought of a penniless Jonathan. "Tell me, Miss Margaret, how *is* Master Jonathan these days? We don't see or hear much of him. He declines all of our invitations."

"Jonathan is usually a busy man with his travels, but we've been blessed to have him home with us for nearly a year. Family has occupied his time, Mrs. Fredrick, and has kept him quite content." Miss Margaret's tone is calm, but the crimson color is growing down her neck. "As with your comments towards God's creation, Mrs. Fredrick, it offends me. We are all created in His image. The good Lord would not agree with your cutting words about the people of America and, therefore Mrs. Fredrick, I don't either. We do not speak of others like that in this house. I haven't allowed my children to speak in that manner, and I will not tolerate it from anyone else."

Miss Margaret for the first time called Jonathan and me her children—and she stood up for me and others like me. The rush of warmth I feel from her words takes my breath away. Why did it take the day before we were to leave for her to say this? How am I to leave now? How can I leave the only mother I have ever known?

"It's not like there are any here with us. They can't hear," she chuckles. "My apologies, Miss Margaret. This is indeed your home and I respect that, but my feelings towards those people will not change. They are savage and wild, and I'm glad we're close to becoming completely free of them here in England. As with Jonathan, the boy has yet to settle down, I hear," Althea adjusts the large diamond ring on her finger and glances over at her daughter. "I must have Henry speak to him about our Agnes. She's of age and is ready for a suitor."

"Mother!" Agnes adds a glare to try to further silence her mother. She looks as if she has just sucked a lemon dry, but when Jonathan and Henry walk past, her face softens. The snap and the look was merely for distraction. She agrees with her mother. The change in her makes my skin feel hot.

"Jonathan is leaving for America tomorrow. Courting for the two would be an impossibility," Miss Margaret points out. Her eyes squint when she catches sight of Evolyn's ring on my finger as if the action can help her see it better. Her spine straightens and a smile spreads. Mercy sakes, she thinks Jonathan and I are engaged!

"They can court once they're married," Althea giggles. "They could become engaged before he is to leave. Henry mentioned the boy is desperate for funds for his trip. Marriage to my Agnes could help with that endeavor. You wouldn't oppose his proposal, would you darling?" Althea purrs. "That Red infested land, my dear, is no place for a lady. You'd simply wait here for his return and put your needed touches around the house. This should keep you quite busy until he returns, and when he does, your father and I will throw you the most elaborate of weddings."

Agnes is positively beaming, and I can feel my teeth rubbing. I'm the one with his ring. I was the one who just received a proposal. How dare she think Jonathan would even consider offering her one. He isn't that desperate to get me home, is he? Alexander did say he didn't know if he'd have enough of Papa's copper.

"What's that on your hand?" Agnes asks. She leans forward in my direction to get a better look.

"I had an accident in the garden. I was cutting flowers," I say, not that my hand is any of her business. I'm sure Miss Margaret would agree that her question is a rude and nosey one.

The room is stuffy and—drat—this corset! I feel like Sunday's stuffed bird. The bow on my hand is coming loose, and attempting to tighten it on my own gives me something to do to keep my mind off all the eyes fixed upon me.

"The out-of-doors is no place for a lady, I don't care what you say, Miss Margaret. Not quite healthy after all, now is it?" Althea chides. Her pronunciation hangs in the air, and it sends prickles down my back.

"Not the bandage, the ring," Agnes says in a scowl.

I take a nervous sip from my tea and gulp down the overly sweet liquid.

Agnes looks at her mother in alarm. "That's Evolyn's ring, is it not?"

Evolyn's picture is right behind me. I feel like a complete fool. I'm wearing her ring *and* her dress.

I bury my face behind my cup and gulp down the remaining drops of brew while undissolved sugar cubes scratch down my throat. It immediately makes me cough. Miss Margaret, knowing how easily I choke, has her hands over her mouth as she waits in horror to see what level I'm going to reach.

EIGHTEEN

At least one meal a day, I swallow something wrong and end up coughing and gasping. I have discovered that there are four levels of choking. Level one is the mildest with minimal coughing and zero embarrassments. Level two is the next step up, involving the combination of coughing with the unpleasant noises that come from gasping for air. I'm headed for level three; the level Miss Margaret is hoping I don't get to. It's frantic coughing, gasping, and the burping of excess inhaled air resulting in the highest of embarrassments out of the four. Jonathan appreciates this level the most, and after a good back pounding to get my system going again, he'll laugh heartily at how unladylike a creature I am—as if I have any choice in the matter when I am moments from death, which is level four, a level I have yet to reach.

It's here at level three that I have an important decision to make. Let the excess tea dribble out of my mouth or attempt to swallow in between the swelling stomach spasms. I don't think it wise to bathe myself or our guests in spittle-infused tea, so I force it down. I cram my napkin in my mouth to muffle the unstoppable chain of coughs and attempt to make a hasty exit.

"Mother, she has Evolyn's ring!" Agnes jumps up in alarm—not to help me but to rip the ring off my finger. She grabs my hand and tears it away from my mouth. "Why do you have *my* ring?!" Her teeth are gritted tightly, and her face is red as a pepper. If I weren't choking, I'd tell her she was a fool and that it wasn't her ring nor would it ever be.

"Ladies, please! Isabelle, come." Miss Margaret swoops in between the two of us and leads me by the elbow through the room. We begin to exit the door when we nearly collide with the men who were coming to summon us for dinner.

"Oh! Pardon! Excuse us if you please, gentlemen!" All parties are startled as she half-screams our apology.

"Is everything all right?" Henry asks the question, looking up. His short stature shocks me, and it causes me to spasm even more.

When one inhales more air, and large quantities of it, there is only one way to get rid of it. There's no stopping it. I stuff the napkin into my mouth to muffle the wet burps that tumble out. The men are speechless.

I hear Althea exclaim, "Well! I never!" while Agnes clicks her tongue in disgust. Jonathan, though usually amused, watches with eyes rimmed in red from our fight earlier. He edges his way to me, but Alexander makes it to me first, for the second time. It's now obvious he's trying to protect Jonathan from further hurt from me. He looks like a giant when he steps past Mr. Fredrick's small frame and the two cups of tea, he has in his hands look like they're from the set Jonathan bought me years ago for my dolls.

"Do you need me? I know what to do! Tubs choked on a chicken bone once, and I had to whack him hard on the back at least ten times before it shot out like a musket ball. Whack her back, Miss Margaret!"

"No need for that, Alexander, she's getting air. This isn't anything we haven't dealt with before. Continue, Agnes, please, play something on the harpsichord. The gentlemen, I'm sure, would enjoy hearing some music before dinner."

Agnes' shoulders square when she takes notice of Jonathan.

"Certainly, Miss Margaret."

Miss Margaret has to guide me down the hall. My eyes won't stay open. Music pushes down the hall after us as we make our way to the kitchen. She does have talent, I think, for a rabid mushroom. The music makes me regret not trying harder with the teacher and the lessons Jonathan had set up for me. I didn't like the teacher he found. Mr. Brock was a moldy old man with bad breath and a hot temper. He'd slap my hand whenever I'd mess up. When I had enough and slapped his hand back, the man went straight to Jonathan and quit. He said I was an unteachable girl with savage manners. His comments, I see, aren't much different than Althea's. The harpsichord hasn't sung since. Funny that the only one who can make it sound the way it should is the English beauty with impeccable manners.

Miss Margaret shoulders me through the kitchen door and swishes off to get me a glass of water. Outside, Jared and Jefferson are sitting on a couple of empty barrels.

"Are you all right, Miss?" Jefferson stands to offer help, but I wave him off. When Miss Margaret hands me the water, I gulp down the entire glass.

"She's fine, boys. She just needs to get some air into her lungs." I let out another burp, and this time I don't bother with my napkin. "And out of her lungs." Miss Margaret's tone is a disapproving one.

"Jefferson, can you pour her more water? I need to check on our company. You'll be fine, dear. Just sit out here for a spell and catch your breath." She squeezes into my hand—the damp one with the ring—and raises her silver brows. "You'll fill me in on this later, I trust?"

I nod at the blurred figure in front of me. Even smeared, I can tell she is barely containing her excitement. The extra flounces of her skirt as she goes back inside make me wonder if she isn't jigging her way back to our guests.

Jefferson offers me a dripping ladle from the water barrel behind him. I take a long sip, drinking the ladle dry. I gulp the second down just as fast, but this time water dribbles out the corners of my mouth and under my chin. I dab at the water with the back of my bandaged hand. One look at Jonathan and she would be able to figure out enough of the story.

"Made quite an impression with the investors, did ya?" Jared chuckles. A cloud richly infused with the scent of spice lingers over his head. "You might want to take care of that properly. Have the doc come out and look at it. My, what a fragile thing you are. It's no wonder Jonathan keeps you locked up," Jared jeers. He steams smoke out of his nose before curling his lips to smile.

He's right. I am fragile. Blood is seeping between my fingers from Miss Margaret's grip and Evolyn's ring is slipping again. A soft and pampered prisoner is what I am. Is this who I want to continue to be? I'm no different than Miss Margaret's hidden china pieces.

Miss Margaret has a teacup and saucer, the only remaining pieces of her mother's set. She keeps them tucked away, carefully placed in her 'treasure chest'; a place where she keeps all her valuables at the foot of her bed. She'll dig them out occasionally. This makes her nostalgic, and she'll then reminisce and share stories of her mother.

Her mother was a tomboy who loved to play marbles. She had gained quite the collection of clays, winning them from her brothers and the other boys in town. On the day she lost all but four of her marbles, she also lost track of time, and it wasn't until the grass became dewy and the sun began to turn orange that she realized she was late for home and had missed her chores. Her punishment was ten wallops to the backside from her father's wide hands, and her prized marbles thrown in the latrine.

She snuck out of the house by flickering candlelight that night and picked out every marble from the foul sludge. She washed off each of them in her washbasin and the next day she won back nearly all the marbles she had lost. Miss Margaret said the sludge brought her mother's clays good luck, though never again did she tempt fate and miss her chores. I imagine Miss Margaret's mother as a little girl with messy braids and skinned knees. So opposite of myself who rarely gets the chance to skin anything.

"Here, Miss Izzy. Use this. I haven't used it yet." Jefferson offers me a fresh handkerchief of his own to replace my drenched one. I almost take it but decide against it. One must begin somewhere and my somewhere is now. I pull hard at one of my sleeves and pull until I hear it rip.

"*Tsk, tsk, tsk,*" Jared shakes his head. "Master wouldn't approve of that."

"I don't care what Master thinks," I snap. I pull until the flouncy material is free. I hate how he makes me feel like some inanimate object one can own. I sop up the blood from my palm and rub the syrupy liquid between my fingers before wrapping it up again.

"Trouble with the master?" His grin is the biggest I've seen since I've known him. He glimpses into the garden and takes a puff from his pipe and chuckles. "Too bad. Doesn't seem to be a problem with those two," he gestures with his head.

Alexander and Ms. Abernathy are sitting close together on the bench in Evolyn's rose garden sipping tea, but the tea drinking doesn't last. He must have asked for her teacup because he takes it and puts it with his own behind him. When he's facing her again, he gathers her hands in his. After a few unheard words, Ms. Abernathy is crying and laughing at the same time. My plan was successful. They've finally found each other. They look sweet together—and happy—so why does the sight of them leave me pained?

Jared snickers and looks up into the sky. "My, my! Will you look at the time! It's getting late. It's going to be a short night and a busy day tomorrow, Miss Izzy. Got to get you home to dear ol' Papa, but before I help with that, I have a new set of chompers to pick up. Until tomorrow—sleep tight and sleep sound, Miss. You'll have no problems with that, surely." He adds a gargled chuckle and leaves a trail of smoke as he walks away. He waves a hand in the air without bothering to look back.

Jefferson, however, practices better manners and bids me good night with a nod and a grinned reminder that he is the one who will bring me to Jonathan's ship.

"It'll be early, Miss Izzy. Before the sun is even awake," he warns before leaving. "And don't worry none about the ocean trip, Miss. I hear your friend Tubs is comin' along."

His comment does indeed help with the growing worry. Tubs will make the journey feel more like an adventure instead of a punishment. I don't want to go back home to Papa. I don't know him. Jonathan doesn't have to take me. What would my chief father do if I didn't show up? Come across the ocean to get me? He wouldn't. I know this because he hasn't done it yet.

Miss Margaret will come looking for me to be sure, and when she does, I want to be found fast asleep in bed. I've lost my appetite for dinner and have no desire to sit at the same table as the pompous Althea and her apprentice-in-training daughter. The only regret I have about sneaking off to my room is that I haven't had a chance to say good-bye to Miss Margaret yet. She's always up before the sun. Perhaps there'll be time tomorrow.

I have to pass the sitting room to get to the stairs, and it's in my favor that Agnes is still playing. I desire to sneak past unnoticed. It would be an impossible feat with this heavy dress bulked with crisp layers, but the music drowns out the rustling. It's nauseating me the way she's stealing glances at Jonathan. She looks like an albino spider who's just caught dinner.

Jonathan is leaning against a wall and has a boot resting on the wallpapered surface. Miss Margaret is preoccupied with Agnes' hypnotic playing; otherwise, that behavior wouldn't be allowed to continue. His arms are crossed, and his brows are furrowed as he listens to her. Henry can't persuade Jonathan to pursue Agnes, could he? He's always been mine. But I refused him. I have no right to think he'll stay single forever just for me. He wants a wife.

Though sickly pale, Agnes is indeed pretty. She looks like one of my fabric dolls—the one with the bleached-cotton skin. Her looks, however, as fine as they are, don't come near Jonathan's. In all my book studies, I have never come across another man as beautiful as he is. Together they certainly would make a sharp pair, and this thought tears my heart to shreds.

It's a long, difficult process getting out of my dress alone. It took the help of another to put me in it and now I know why. It's a struggle unfastening all the hidden buttons, bustles, and ties and I'm a sweaty mess by the time I finish. I put on my sleeping gown and the comfort of it makes me sigh out loud. It's a relief to be released from the dress's restricting confinement. I fill the washbasin and splash the chilly water on my face. The water is pink by the time I finish. I unwind and squeeze the blood-soaked dress sleeve bandage until it is free of all its rose-colored liquid and toss it with a gluey plop on my dresser.

Before it decides to start bleeding again, I reach into the top drawer for one of my handkerchiefs. I run my finger over the embroidered letter on the front. The fiber "G" feels the same to my finger as the one branded on my bumpy skin. I change my mind against covering my cut when I think of Miss Margaret and her mother, the clay marbles, the concealed china, and the stark difference the two had in taking care of their possessions.

No. I throw the handkerchief back in the drawer. I think the best thing for this wound is for it to air out.

NINETEEN

The faint sound of knuckles against wood coaxes me out of my nightmare. I sit up and squint through the sooty black and try to pick out the sound again through the drumbeat in my ears. My heart is racing, and even though my gown and hair are damp with sweat, I'm freezing. I gather handfuls of my bedding to anchor myself from the swaying motion that continues even while I'm awake. I pull the blankets up under my chin and bunch them to my chest and am disappointed when they don't bring the warmth for which my body begs in shivers.

Perhaps I'm not awake after all. I rub my cheek against one of my wrists to check for the chilly shackles that were there just moments ago. They feel free, yet why do I still hear the moans and cries? I press my hands against my ears to block out the memory of both and the adjoining chorus of clinking sounds. My hair tickles my hands, and it sends me flying out of bed. In my dream, I was chained in the haul of a ship and there were things in the water that sloshed around my wrists and ankles. Malleable and odoriferous things that were crushed under my confined limbs. I wipe my hands down my gown to cleanse them. My heart goes out to the bat that I was so afraid of days ago who was hiding in his wings behind my door. Cocooned in my blankets, I ball up in the nearest corner.

"Miss Izzy, wake up. It's time," a voice murmurs in between knocks.

I reach up and turn the door's handle and open it just wide enough to see legs.

"Why are you on the floor?" Jefferson asks. "Are you all right, Miss?" He kneels, and his body folds into a pack. He clears his throat when he doesn't get an answer from me. "Jonathan says he wants you to wear these and the only possessions you can bring with you are what fit into this bag." He stuffs the pack through the door's opening and coughs. Either the man's coming down with a cold or he's completely uncomfortable with the task Jonathan has given him. "Please, make haste, Miss. The ship's preparin' to sail as we speak. Are you goin' to be all right?" he asks again.

The weighty object in the pack's bottom sends burning pain through my fingers when it presses against yesterday's cut. I try to stand but fall against the door when the pounding in my head intensifies.

"Miss?" Jefferson rasps from the other side.

"I'll be with you in a minute," I manage to say in between the head throbs.

I light my lantern and empty the contents of the pack on my bed. I fumble with the clothes I was given and struggle with the unfamiliar sleeves and legs. My thoughts feel jumbled, and it's hard to concentrate on the simple task of deciding what to pack in the small bag. Surely, I need my brush. My thick head of hair will quickly become a bird's nest if I don't tend to it. My feather pillow and mattress are what I would like to cram in the bag, but those, of course, aren't options. The only possessions small enough to fit will be frivolous and unhelpful in the untamed wild.

These past few weeks I have heard quite a bit of hushed chatter about America from the men around the house. A few nights ago, I overheard Jefferson and another man talking about how they couldn't wait to get back to uncivilized society, though the winters in the North Country they could do without. I wonder if it'll be winter when we get there. I hope not. These clothes, as comfortable as they are, won't be warm enough.

Tubs has worn the same pair of breeches for as long as I remember. I now see why his adventuring rope is so important to him. The pants Jonathan gave me are too big, and they hang like loose elephant skin. Perhaps they are his and are what I was planning on snatching for the next adventure Tubs and I were supposed to go on. I'm not going to trollop all over America holding up my pants the same as I did in the woods with Tubs and my skirt. This is my chance to move unrestricted and free like a boy. Though I enjoy everything there is about being a girl, including my dresses, ribbons, and perfumes, I love these breeches and now see why Tubs can dart around so. My body feels free, but it's strange to be able to see my legs. I tie a lengthy ribbon around my waist, pull it tight, and let the thigh-length shirt remain untucked to keep it hidden.

A rapid knock is Jefferson's reminder to hurry things along. In the empty pack, I stuff in my hairbrush, mirror, a handful of hairpins, a stack of handkerchiefs (they seem to make nice bandages), the key from the wardrobe in the cellar (as a reminder of Jonathan's true character if I should start to think favorably of him again), and the skirt full of Miss Margaret's biscuits that I brought up last night to snack on. Before packing my mother's Bible, I tuck Tubs' forgotten note in the center and promise myself I'll read it once I get settled on the ship.

Before opening the door, I slip my feet into shoes that are a size too big. They're perfect. They're much roomier than my boots and my toes have room to wiggle.

Jefferson looks me over and growls when I cram the cap over my tangled hair.

"You need to tie that up or cut it off or somethin'. We're tryin' to keep the fact that you're a girl hidden from half the crew, and that horse's tail thrown over your shoulder is going to ruin everything."

I'm not cutting my hair. I dig around in my pack for the pins and pin it up in a high bun.

"Better," Jefferson nods when he sees that the cap conceals all of my hair.

As he pulls me from the room, I wipe away the moisture beading on my upper lip as well as the thought that this will be the last time I'll cross my room's threshold. My lantern's flickering light bounces off into the hallway to follow me. It can go no farther, and the fading light bids me a somber farewell as we slip down the stairs. I resist Jefferson's pull on the way down and take one step at a time. I let my hand slide down the glossy rail the entire length down.

We steal past the parlor where I will no longer have to wince down tea. Gone are the nightly chats with Jonathan and the evening readings as a family. In his haste through the dimly lit room, Jefferson bumps into the foyer table. The action causes the vase to wobble. In alarm, he backs into me, and his lanky body wakes up my injured hand. It roars in protest, but it doesn't bleed. The searing pain pierces as much as the realization that Miss Margaret, Jonathan, and I were never meant to be a forever family. It was all a lie.

"Wait!" I yank my arm free from Jefferson's grip. We're in the kitchen. It's the last room in the cottage. Once we pass into the gardens, I'll never set foot in this house again. "I haven't gotten a chance to say goodbye to Miss Margaret."

"You can now, child. I'm here."

Miss Margaret startles both Jefferson and me when she rises from the chair near the fireplace, hugging the only book I have ever seen her read.

"Miss Margaret?" I cry.

She drops the book on the chair to catch me when I run to her. My nose buries in the crease of her neck, and the scent of her intensifies my tears.

"I know, sweet dear. I know," she hushes.

"Come with me," I beg.

"I can't, sweet child. A ship and an untamed world? Those aren't places for an old woman. But you, my sweet girl, you are going to flourish out there. I'm going to miss you so. Both of you," she sighs. "I have so enjoyed my children."

Miss Margaret pulls back from me to hold my face. She smiles and drenched cheeks ball under her eyes as she scans over my features. It is as if she is trying to remember every detail of me for later.

"Jonathan will be back with you," I say. I smear away my wet with my fingers. The tears can't stay. My blotchy face will feel like the rash it resembles. Miss Margaret grins. She helps me with her sleeve.

I must try to remember Miss Margaret. I mustn't forget her like I did Mama and Papa. I let my fingers roll down her hair. It's tossed over her shoulder and is almost as long as my own. It feels like Evolyn's silk dress; brushed thirty times through, I'm certain, just like she used to do with mine.

Her smile wavers. She parts her lips to speak but presses them tightly instead and stretches a thin smile.

"Be kind to him—please?" She tucks a loose strand of my hair back into its place under my ill-fitting cap. "I know you're angry and you feel he's lied to you, but the boy hasn't. He's kept things from you, yes, but it was for your benefit; to spare you pain. 'He that refraineth his lips is wise,' the proverb says. There's no sin in what he did. Now, false stories about missing wraps—that, my dear, is something entirely different. It was a lie that ended up with positive results; nonetheless, child, it was still a lie. 'Death and life are in the power of the tongue', dear girl. If there were any last advice to give you, it'd be that."

Her statement was pointing to the verses in James that she had made me write whenever I talked back to her. James 3:5 and 6 are etched forever in my memory:

"'Even so the tongue is a little member, and boasteth great things. Behold, how great a matter a little fire kindleth! And the tongue is a fire, a world of iniquity: so is the tongue among our members, that it defileth the whole body, and setteth on fire the course of nature; and it is set on fire by hell.'"

Even my hand remembers the words, for I wrote them hundreds of times. You'd think both would be enough to cure my tongue's ails, but it remains a hot whip.

"The time you have together is short. Part ways in a positive light. He loves you so. Please be gentle with his heart. He's protected yours all these years. The least you can do is treat him favorably in the last days you have with one another. Promise me you'll try?"

What Miss Margaret asks of me shouldn't be that difficult. I understand her point of view. Jonathan has treated me fairly and given me above what I deserved. I have lacked for nothing here. The only things I have been denied are the details of my past. This is where the confusion and anger come in. My past is *mine*. I'm entitled to it regardless of how painful it is. There isn't time to argue or plead my case. Jefferson has a hold of my elbow.

"I'm sorry, ladies. We need to make haste. The captain is waiting, and he won't be pleased if we're late."

The captain is Jonathan and this knowledge gives me the strong urge to stall.

Jefferson relinquishes his grip when I reach to hug Miss Margaret. He exhibits grace when he doesn't take up my arm again and inwardly, I thank him for it.

"I'll try," I say.

I don't promise her. I learned that from Jonathan. I'm not sure how successful I'll be. Jonathan is wounded. When he's like this, the boy will be locked away and the man with the scrunched brow will make reaching him difficult.

Miss Margaret lets out a squeal. Not from my answer but because my shoes have crushed her toes. She pulls from me, and with a giggle, she covers her injured foot with the other.

"I'll let you in on a little secret." She takes hold of my face again and whispers, "I don't like shoes either. I kick them off every chance I get."

"Well, for mercy sakes, why'd you make me wear them?" I can feel the tears bubbling again. Miss Margaret is so much like me. It's a pity I'm just discovering it now.

"I wanted you to be better than me. I wanted you to be a real lady," she says. She covers her mouth when her voice catches. "I grew up barefoot in the potato fields. Mama and I worked hard to put what little food we had on our family's china. I promised myself that someday real food would be on those plates. My teacup and saucer are reminders to me as to where I came from and where I dreamt I would someday be. I wanted you to have more—and to be more, but you don't need shoes and teacups to be somebody. I'm sorry, child. I never should have forced this way of life on you. There has never been anything wrong with my baby girl. You were and are perfect just as you are."

"Oh, Miss Margaret!" I fall back onto her to sob.

"I love you, sweet girl. Always and forever." Miss Margaret kisses the top of my head and holds me away from her to get a final look. "Have the adventure of a lifetime. I'll be praying for you, child. Every day."

"Miss Izzy, please," Jefferson pleads.

"Mama—" There's nothing more I can think to say. This single word will have to be enough. I force myself to step away from her and towards Jefferson who's waiting at the open door.

The night's melodies are too cheerful for how I feel. The frogs and crickets are celebrating the final moments of the night, but they're wrong. The night isn't coming to an end; it's just beginning. I'll never be happy again.

Miss Margaret gasps and sputters a sob at the name I have finally been brave enough to call her. I have decided to finally give in to the desire that's been simmering within for as long as I can remember. I've never dared to call her that before today. She's been my mother and the selfless woman deserves to hear it, at least once. Miss Margaret clutches her hands to her chest to catch her breath, and when she does, the face that had been pinched with sorrow opens.

"Wait!" she reaches into the air to stop me. "The necklace!"

Jefferson allows me to return to her without complaint. He knows how difficult this is for Miss Margaret. Jonathan and I have been her whole life for as long as even he can remember.

"I have complete faith your Mama's Bible will be your two hundred and fifty-first book. Will you think of me—and Jonathan— every time you look at it?"

She asks the question with an unsteady smile. I wipe away her tears with my sleeve, and when I do, she releases a jagged exhale along with a new stream of them.

"Yes, Mama," I promise.

I let her clasp the necklace behind my neck and adjust the owl just so. The time spent making its position perfect causes Jefferson to clear his throat. This wakes Miss Margaret and she gives me a final kiss.

"Now off with you. Don't keep my boy waiting," she orders. She turns me around and nudges me towards the waiting Jefferson.

I let him pull me out of the kitchen door with no further resistance and lift me onto the waiting horse.

"Take care of her." Miss Margaret adds a nod to Jefferson's instructions. She wraps her arms around her waist to hug herself. I desperately want to go back to comfort her and have her comfort me in return, but there can be no more of that. My time with her is done.

"Oh, I will, Miss Margaret. She's in good hands. She's got more than half the ship keeping an eye out for her. Now hold on good, Miss. We have time to make up."

I wrap my arms tightly around him. My heart is so heavy that I don't even have to play Tubs' game to make it through the stone gate. I didn't give the woman the same words back. The woman I claimed as my mother. Guilt and regret burn like wildfire within my chest, along with the words that I chose to selfishly keep to myself: "I love you." Why, oh why, can't I say those simple three words?

TWENTY

The outside night is the same shadowy black that my room had been when I first woke up. Clouds cloak the skylights, and no other light is visible beside the lantern near the road that Jonathan insists be lit every night. He told me that it was a beacon—a signal—to let any wanderer in need know that our home was a safe place. I never understood its significance until now. The one man who answered its light when I was eight was a clue to its importance.

He was a dark-skinned man, heavily soiled and scratched. His knock woke us up in the dead of night. Miss Margaret and Jonathan didn't see that I watched from the top of the stairs. They let the man in and immediately escorted him to the kitchen where I heard buckets dump into Evolyn's Tub. He emerged hours later, freshly scrubbed and in clean clothes. His skin was still dark, even after all the outdoor grime was rinsed away. It was the same color as mine. The man stayed in one of the guest rooms until Jonathan left on one of his trips. The man went with him but didn't come back. Althea's comments are what polished up the memory. The man was a Red—an escaped slave from one of the English homes. The lantern was meant for my kind, my people.

I don't look back, though I desperately want to. Behind closed lids, I picture the place I had called home shrinking back further into the gloomy night as horse hooves take me farther away. The fragrance of the sweet peas that crawl up our cottage's rock exterior is quickly overcome by the intermingling stench of sweaty man and beast.

Multiple times, my hat is almost blown off my head. I'm forced to hold onto Jefferson with one hand, and it takes all the arm strength I can muster to do so. The last time I was on a horse going this fast didn't end up well. I count the number of times my head crashes into his back to keep from screaming for him to stop and to take me back. My body aches for my mattress, and every time my head drives into Jefferson's back, it feels as if my brain is coming loose.

"We're just about there, Miss Izzy. You all right back there?" he huffs over the thumping clomp of our horses' hooves.

I wonder if *he* is all right. I have counted over five hundred hits of my head to his back. He's slowing the horse and taking us off the road to a cluster of ghostly trees. The light of a single lantern glows at the base of one of them.

"There she is," he says. He points towards the biggest ship in port shrouded in black with reaching sails and a deck dotted with lantern light. He tugs up on the reins and stops us near a pair of horses with swatting tails. "She's to be our home sweet home for a couple of months, Miss Izzy."

Home. The word now has a strange weight. Home had once meant family. A place where I thought I had found unconditional love with people I trusted. I thought I would be with them forever. How can they let me go back to a man I don't know without argument or fight? A ship, America, Papa—those are the places I'm expected to find "home" again, but I won't let myself find it. Home now simply means shelter—a placc to lay my head.

With a groan, Jefferson throws his leg over and slides down the horse's side. He arches his back and twists in such a way his spine makes a sickening pop.

"Ah! That's better!" He sighs. "I shoulda prepared myself better for this trip. Years of making pies and stuffing myself with 'em have rusted me up."

It wasn't all that long of a ride, but I suppose it could have felt long for a man who's spent most of his time in the kitchen. If Jefferson feels unprepared and rusty, what does this journey mean for me? He knots our reins alongside the other horscs on the log beam and swipes his arm across his forehead. He readjusts his tipped hat back down over his head and holds up his arms to me.

"Slide down, Miss Izzy. I'll catch ya if you aren't bothered by it," he says.

"I'm not bothered if you can catch me," I smile. "We're pretty high up, and I'm not your typical dainty English girl."

"No, you're not the typical English girl. You're special, Miss Izzy," he grins. "You can't see that yet?"

If by special he means different, I certainly am. I'm not like anyone I've known before. I'm one of a kind: fearful, scarred, and hideous. It's fortunate for the world that there's only one of me. Jefferson coughs into his fist after he catches me. He doesn't know how to handle my sour face. He changes the subject instead and introduces me to the ship with a sweeping arm.

"Miss Izzy, meet the *Vrede*!"

On the ship's deck, a colony of dark shapes bustles about with ant-like industriousness. Some lean over the rails to shout to the men scurrying below with shoulders burdened with cargo. Onshore, wagons, and men unloading them vibrate the gray colors of morning.

"I hear she's become quite the ship since I've been on her last. Everyone wants to work on her. Never has Captain Jonathan been short of volunteers for his crew. Lines of men wait at port just hopin' they can be added," he says. He clears his throat and takes his hat off. He twists it in his hands a few times before speaking. "It's a fine ship now, Miss. Nothin' at all like what she was. You should have no trouble boarding her this time. We have someone here for you, too. Someone that should make it plenty easy on you. That is, if you can remember who he is."

He slaps his hat against his hand and secures it back on his head. When he feels it's good and tight, he whistles. The light that had greeted us from the road moves. Its owner meets Jefferson first with a strange handshake and then comes over to me.

"Biis Nigig?" the young man asks with a large smile.

Through the filtered light of dawn, I can see that the man is near Jonathan's age and has elbow-length hair the same color the sky had been only minutes ago. He raises the lantern to my face even though he doesn't need to, and its light blinds me. Now when I blink, all I can see is a ball of light where the man's face should be.

"Biis Nigig?" he repeats. I can't see him, but I can hear he's lost his smile.

I back up into Jefferson and shrink into him. I don't know who this man is and I don't know what he's asking me. Jefferson pushes me behind him and takes his hat off.

"She's scared, Cook." Jefferson exhales and folds his hat. "It's her. She may look different and not remember you or know what you're sayin', but it's her. Where does the captain want her?"

"In the captain's quarters."

The man with the lantern doesn't get a chance to answer. The one who offers up the information is Jonathan.

The harsh balls of light are softening, possibly helped by my rapid blinks and stretched-open mouth. It would have been better if the light had stayed. Jonathan is making his way to me, and he isn't dressed like himself. He's dressed like a ship's captain and is wearing a long-buttoned jacket and a triangular hat that's pinched in the front.

The sight of him forces a memory. I don't feel frozen with this one.

This one makes my legs ache with the desire to run.

"Get goin' you filthy pigs!"

The shout coming from behind changes Jonathan's course from me to the growing ruckus of one. A large man shoves his fist into the back of the man who was last out of a wagon bed. I can't control the shivers that come as the shuffling caravan nears. My teeth chatter along with chains that clank from ankles, necks, and wrists. Shirtless men with helmets of iron are led past us to the ship. The confining metal that the men wear is the same cold and restricting pieces that I wore in my dream.

The men can't shuffle fast enough for the grumbling giant, and he shoves his hands into the back of the last man again. This unexpected motion sends the prisoner to his knees in a tangle of chains. The guard raises a leg to add a kick, but Jonathan catches it midair and flips him to his back.

"One more strike against any of these men and I'll chain you and leave you to the mercy of the ship's haul. If the past trespasses of these men don't sound desirable to you, I suggest you start practicing immediate restraint. Release them—*now*," he spits. The sound of his threat adds to my shivers. I've never heard this tone from him before.

"Sorry, Captain. I didn't mean nothin'. These here are just Reds. They ain't nobody. They're just animals," the large man says. He has his hands up, and they're both shaking. His shirt is askew, and a bulging tummy quivers as he struggles to his feet. "Please, I'll do as you say. I'll unchain 'em."

"And you'll take off the masks as well," Jonathan adds.

"But they're savage!" The man screeches. "They'll chew on us all."

"You, maybe. You're the one who chained them. I'd be extra nice to them right now if I were you," Jonathan proposes in a bitter tease. "Jefferson, when the men are free, show them to their sleeping quarters in the haul. Feed and clothe them. Mikonan will check them over later," he orders on his way back to me.

"Yes, sir." Jefferson nods and adds a bow. "Miss Izzy, sir. Shall I escort her as well?" The hat he had been fiddling with has become a tube in his hands.

"No, I got her. Thank you, Jefferson." Jonathan reaches for my hand. "You—you are going to start the trip by getting stitches." He is successful in finding me in the haze of early morning, but I immediately yank myself free.

"No," I snap. It hasn't been but an hour and I have already failed Miss Margaret's mission for me. "You can't put those men down there. It's filthy and horrible and—and it's torture!"

"How would you know this?" Jonathan asks. "Do you remember?" He reaches for me again, but I shuffle back to keep out of his grip.

"Don't touch me—please," I choke. I add the nicety at the end for Miss Margaret's sake.

I don't mean to take it out on Jonathan. He isn't the man that I remember dragging me away from Mama. The figure was too big to be him. Jonathan was just a boy then. The uniform has me afraid, along with the restraints the abused Red men wore. I had worn the very same shackles in my dream.

Fish.

Rotting, putrid fish.

We were lined in the haul just like fish.

The smell of dying fish onshore regrettably just slaps this memory awake. My dream was more than a nightmare. It's real. I remember the big man that wore Jonathan's uniform coaxing me to lay down with an angry poke from his gun barrel. Coughs, sniffs, sobs, and moans stuffed my ears from bodies I couldn't see and the smells made by them tore at my nose. The man stomped his boot to my ribs so he could fasten my chains to the eye-hook on the floor. He laughed and called me a brown cockroach. He said I was so small he could squish me like the little bug I was. He said he'd rid the world of me if it weren't for the fact that I was worth so much. He left me to beat on a group singing near the back of the haul. They ignored his barked order to stop and to be still. I don't remember the words they sang, but I do remember it was a hymn—one that I can hear in Mama's voice. It brought me peace to hear her song, just as much as the man did who owned the foot that was pressed to my face.

The heel of the man in front of me pushed against my nose. It made me cry. The man asked me to play hide and seek with him. I asked him how since we couldn't move. He asked me to close my eyes, imagine my favorite spot, and hide there. I did as he said and as my mind drew up the spot, the ship disappeared. I was in the tight space of the rock cave that I loved to play in on our lake's edge. The man's sweaty foot became my cave's damp ceiling. I fell asleep, happy in my cave, waiting for him to find me.

Nose to toe—gill to tail—we were packed like the fish delivered to our kitchen door at home. It's funny. Part of my journey to the cottage was in the same manner as our dinner.

"You remember being down there?" Jonathan asks. When I nod, he apologizes. "I'm sorry. That's one of the memories I was hoping to keep for you. I don't like that you have to remember that. It's not going to be like that for these men, I promise. They aren't the first that I've taken back. We've known about them and prepared for them. All of them. These men will be taken care of and comfortable, I assure you."

Jonathan holds his hand out for me, but instead of taking it, I step back and collide into the man with the lantern.

"Are you afraid of me?"

Jonathan has asked the question with too much volume. I ball my fists to prepare because I know what's to come if he can't control it.

"I'm helping them. I'm helping you," he tries to reason.

I can't make out his features. His hat is pulled down tightly over his forehead, and the waking dawn is unable to cut through the dark shadow which veils his face. I assume the scrunched brow is there. I can hear it.

"No," I say, but I change it to a hurried yes when he steps forward.

"Is it the uniform?" he asks. He's trying to stunt the growing emotion. I can now see the bottom portion of his face and his jaw is clenched.

I nod my answer and the hand he let fall to his side stretches open and then balls into a tight fist.

"I don't like it either. Bear with me for a few moments longer and I promise in the captain's quarters, I'll take the coat off. We need to go now, Izzy. The sun's coming up and the men will get a good look at you. We don't need to advertise there's a woman aboard. I won't hurt you, Niinimooshe. Take my hand—let me help you." He offers his hand again and adds a "please" under his breath with the further stretch.

"I won't do it. I won't step on that ship," I say in weep. I won't be going any further than the tuft of dandelions at my feet. Tears are my weapon of choice for a reason: they're effective. "I'm not going home to Papa. I'm going to stay with Miss Margaret."

"You can't," Jonathan groans. "You know this. I thought I explained this to you."

"I don't need to go home. Let's just stay here. Stay here with me," I plead. "We can go back to how things used to be. I'll practice my shooting and not complain, and I'll hunt with you whenever you want me to."

Surely, adding us together will make my tears an irresistible brew. It does. He's drinking it in. His shoulders now have drooped and he's having trouble breathing. He glances back at the ship, and with an exaggerated puff, he clenches and stretches his fingers as he struggles to keep the tears away. They're all futile. The tears always win. He grits his teeth and snarls in frustration when they come.

"Gaawesa!" he shouts. He presses his palms to his eyes to keep the wet back, and to show further disdain for his tears, he lets out a teeth-clenched hiss.

Jonathan's emotions tend to crash on him like a sweeping wave. When the tidal wave comes, it's the rubble of him that remains after that causes him to wage continual war against it. He desires an impenetrable heart of stone, but Jonathan has his mother's heart. His battle to become something other than himself is a fight he'll never win. Shame from another battle lost is what forces him to step back away from me and the others.

He slips off his hat, and his eyes plead for help to the men in our company, but none offer any. On his steps towards the ship, he slams his hat to the ground, and his hands instinctively go to his hair where they clench into tight fists. He heaves a few breaths and the growl he makes swells into a holler. The sound bounces off the ship and it captures the attention of a sailor who takes it as a warning and puts haste in his step on his way up the ship's ramp. Jonathan takes a few moments, and on the journey back he picks up his hat.

"Mikonan…" He starts to address the man with the lantern but is interrupted.

"Quit tip-toeing around her, Waabishkaa Ma'iingan. Mashkawizziiwin-wii," the man barks. His brow narrows with the command, and his dark eyes transform into slits.

"Gaawesa, Mikonan," Jonathan groans again. "Brother…"

"You can and you will. Mashkawizziiwin-wii! Force her," the man says with added volume. He swings his lantern in my direction. "She cannot stay—you know this. If she is as full of fear as you say, she has avoided war with it too long. She must begin the battle against it. Let today be the first victory that she tastes. Help her to win, Waabishkaa Ma'iingan—stop teaching her to run. Remember who you are and your promise to Odedeyan. Gather strength from those, brother. Mashkawizziiwin-wii!"

The man with the lantern and Jonathan are addressing each other as brothers. Odedeyan is also mentioned. I strengthen my stance. If this man is my brother, this is another family member Jonathan has kept from me. He will not get me to go with him. He'll have to drag me aboard, and if he tries, I'll make it difficult for him. I'll make him wish he were taking aboard a hornet's nest instead.

Jonathan takes his time with his hat and he forces a deep inhale through his nose. As the released air steams past his lips, he extends his hand out to me. This gesture is completely odd and has me confused.

"Good morning, Isabelle. Welcome to the *Vrede*."

"I'll bid you a good morning, but I'm not going," I say with a tilt to my chin. "You will *not* get me to board that ship. I'm staying." To honor Miss Margaret and to not leave him without a hand to shake, I offer mine up.

"The other hand." He nods down to my injured one.

"It's the wrong one," I inform him with a hot bite.

"If it's the one I want—it's not the wrong one," he says through his teeth. "Who's in charge here?"

"It is too the wrong one, 'Captain'," I squint. "You're dead wrong. I'll give it to you but you had better be careful…"

The man pays no mind to my warning. He squeezes into my hand—tight. Molten pain fills my hand, and the immediate moisture from it makes his grip slip, but he doesn't let go. In between the cries of pain, I scold him in howl to let go.

"You need to quiet her," Alexander heaves as he jogs up. "Her noise is attracting attention." Tubs clomps to a stop next to Alexander and he flops in exhaustion against his father while congratulating him between gulps of air.

"One of these races, I'm going to beat you," he gasps. "What's up with her?" Tubs asks when my wails continue even after Jonathan lets go.

"You're going, girl, and that's that. Forcing you to go can't make you hate me any more than you already do. I'm sorry."

Jonathan is apologizing for the angry state of my hand and my matching demeanor. I also know the man is apologizing for a third thing. He's mostly sorry that I hate him. I know this because of how he spits out Miss Margaret's forbidden word.

"Scream as loud as you want. I'm not backing down. The men will just think you're a wild boy in need of a sound swat to the backside." He massages his hands over mine to sop up as much blood as he can. "Why Odedeyan entrusted me with you is beyond me. I ruined you. You are who you are because of me."

"Stop!" I order.

It wasn't just the smearing of his hands onto my face that I wanted to stop. It was the cutting things he said of himself. I'm who I am because of the past I can't remember, not him. If he only gave in to me years ago, things might have turned out differently. We wouldn't be isolated from each other the way we are now. Secrets build walls, and the years have built a sturdy one between us.

"How can you do this to me?" I hiss. "If you love me as much as you say you do, you'd let me stay here with you and Miss Margaret. Why are you giving me away?"

This stops his blood painting, and he pinches my face between his wet hands.

"I'm not giving you away. I'm letting you go."

Each word takes effort for him to speak. They rip up out of his throat and slice into me. I now have a wound that is a thousand times worse than the cut on my hand. Everything inside me feels shredded. He's letting me go, and I don't want him to.

"Tubs," Jonathan calls. When Tubs is in front of him, he smears what's left of my blood onto Tubs' face.

"Oh yuck!" Tubs sputters. "What are you doing?"

"You'll understand in a minute," Jonathan says while rubbing his hands down his jacket. He is freeing himself from every last remnant of me. I stomp my foot in protest and step forward to argue more with him.

"Your hat's loose," he interrupts with a point. When I grab it with my good hand, he picks me up and throws me over his shoulder and this churns out on a whole new series of shouts from me.

"Jonathan Gudwyne, put me down this instant!" I scream. I kick with my legs to get him to drop me but he curls an arm around them and clamps it tight. I have my arms left, so I use them to try to push off his shoulders.

"Boys and their rough-housing," he puffs to Alexander. It's a struggle for him to keep me on his shoulders and that's just how I want it. I'm Izzy, the human hornet.

"Put—me—down!" I growl. "Alexander, don't, please. Tell him to let me down. I can't go on that ship. I won't go on that ship," I screech.

"Sorry, Miss Isabelle," he says while grabbing Tubs by the collar. "It's the captain's way or no way. He wants you aboard, so you're going aboard."

"It's all right, Izzy. Papa and Jonathan are helping you. You want to meet your Papa, don't you? You have to get on board first and this is a doggone genius way to do it," Tubs says. "Keep up your thrashing. The crew will believe you and I were fighting and got caught."

The man with the lantern has already begun his walk to the ship. Before Jonathan follows, he adjusts my weight. I command Jonathan in between sobs to put me down, but it's futile. We're already going up the ramp. My tears always work. The man with the lantern has done something to Jonathan and now they're useless. He's completely ignoring me.

Laughter from the sight of Tubs and I mingle with the chorus sung by others as we pass. Tubs thinks my thrashing is part of the act. I'm not acting—I'm furious. Tubs' acting skills, however, are impressive. Alexander is guiding him by his shirt collar behind us and Tubs is swatting up into the air to try to get to me. His grin should be the give-away that he's acting, but the blood smeared on his face makes him look mad. In between swings, when he thinks no one is looking, he gives me a wink—a two-lidded one. He has yet to figure out how to wink.

We weave through men that are scrambling about carrying through their various duties. Men are working to pull in the thick lines of braided rope that tie the ship to shore. They sing in a chant as they heave and pull in unison to the tune.

Loosen the knot,
Pull the line,
Free the ship her tether bind!
Set her free,
Let her sail,
Set her course by twirl of nail.
The sea, she needin' To roam 'n sway Which direction go, Come what may.
Loosen the knot,
Pull the line,
Let her fate,
Be yourn and mine.

"Gotta couple of scrappers there, eh?" a voice bellows. I can't see who is speaking. It's taking too much effort to keep my head and neck upright.

"You have no idea," Jonathan answers with a groan.

"Introduce them to the cat," a gruff voice suggests. "They'll be thinkin' twice before throwin' punches again."

"Mind your work, sailor," Jonathan answers. "Once these boys are patched up, we'll be off. Be sure we're ready at my order."

"Aye, Captain." The legs belonging to the voice shuffle off in a hurry.

Several other pairs of legs scurry past to have the door to Jonathan's quarters open for us. Once inside, Jonathan leans forward and drops me. I let out a squeal but stop once I feel a soft mattress beneath me.

"None of that girl stuff while you're here," he scolds with a point, but his face softens when he gets a good look at me. "What's wrong? You don't look right."

"I'm kidnapped, bloody, and look like a boy, that's what's wrong," I say, too hot to produce the tears I usually have at this point in my outbursts. I regret my sting instantly when I see how truly concerned Jonathan is.

I don't want to be here. I want my bed. My body aches and my eyes feel swollen. I swat his hand from my forehead, but it's without the energy I had just moments earlier.

"Mercy sakes, girl!" he barks as he slides off his jacket. "You're burning up!"

TWENTY-ONE

She doesn't get sick, Mikonan." Jonathan flips off my hat to put his full hand on my head. This time, I don't swat at him. Part of his palm is on my eye and the pressure feels heavenly against it.

"She's never been sick. I've seen to it. It's that blasted cut. Girl, I told you it should have been stitched up yesterday," Jonathan scolds with a scowl.

His comment makes me bristle and I push his hand off.

"You said nothing of the sort. You said before we were to set sail. We haven't even set sail yet," I sneer. "And don't blame me. You were the one who caused all this by sneaking up behind me like Miss Margaret."

"I did not! I made enough noise to wake the dead. I called out to you. I can't help it if your head is always in those blasted stories in your books." He throws his hat again and it bullets to the floor with a muffled thump.

"Are they always like this?" the strange man asks.

"No, not usually. Well, if Miss Izzy gets her way, that is, things are mostly fine," Alexander answers. "If either of them gets challenged by the other, they can turn into battling badgers. Jonathan, for the most part, can keep his inner badger controlled and that keeps the girl in check. Today, however, isn't that day and when Jonathan unravels— they both unravel." Alexander then scowls with pressed lips. "It's cruel, Cook, what your father's doing. I don't agree with it. Not one bit."

"Odedeyan has his reasons. We must honor and accept his wishes." The stranger crosses his arms and adds his grunt of disapproval. "I wish it didn't have to be this way. I've never seen my brother like this."

Jonathan storms to the wall of shelves loaded with glass jars. He fumbles through them in search of a particular one. Most are stuffed with plants or leaves, but some have bugs crawling along the insides. A few others have frogs clinging to their clear enclosures with sticky toes.

"What do we use for fevers?" Jonathan asks with a snap. A jar teeters on its edge when it's nudged by another, and before he can catch it, it shatters to the floor. Hopping things are freed and they escape past the rubble to hide under a desk void of any ornamentation or clutter. This excites Tubs, and he scampers over to Jonathan to help catch them. "Blast it! Frogs, Mikonan? Mercy sakes, what on earth for?"

"You said to pack enough remedies for every probable and possible situation," the man shrugs. He unfolds his arms on his way over to him. "They are said to promote healing by just being present in the room. I believe it only to be true just because they are fun." The man chuckles at Tubs' joy in frog-wrangling, but his smile quickly fades when he sees it's challenged by all the frowns in the room. "Yarrow, brother. You are looking for yarrow."

"Nothing's labeled. How on earth am I supposed to find yarrow in all *that*?" Jonathan wildly points. He bends over to reach for a tiny lime-colored frog but misses it. It creeps under the lined space between the desk and the floor.

"You don't need to find it. The healer on the ship does," the man informs. He shoves his shirt sleeves past his elbows and squats down to pick up the large pieces of the shattered jar.

"Tubs, mind the glass, please," Alexander sighs on his hunched journey to his son and the other two men on the floor. "Tubs and I will handle this. Both of you, do what you have to do to make her better; but I do have a suggestion first. One of you needs to introduce Cook to her. You are in enough hot water already, Jonathan. No more surprises and secrets with this girl. She won't tolerate it."

Jonathan pushes up off the floor with a noisy exhale. He slaps his hands against his legs to free them from dust and glass shards, and with a sweeping hand, he points over to the dark-eyed man with a sigh.

"This, dear Izzy, is your brother, Mik—," but before he can finish with the name he had been using, the man interrupts him.

"Cook. You may call me Cook," my brother says with a nod.

"Why?" Jonathan throws his hands up. "That's stupid," he spits.

"Waabishkaa Ma'iingan, she's my sister. If I want her to call me by the white man's name, I'll have her do so." My brother stands to face Jonathan. Toe to toe, I notice they're both the same height.

"It's stupid, *Cook*. This whole blasted thing is stupid." Jonathan over-enunciates my brother's name and growls the rest. He shoulders past him to get to the washbasin. "She's your sister, for mercy sake."

"You said 'dear Izzy'." I pop up to face Jonathan with clenched fists to stifle the coming tears. It doesn't work. "You call me that only when you're mad at me. You hate me, Jonathan Gudwyne. I'm a vile, horrible creature and you thoroughly hate me."

"Izzy," Jonathan moans. In his stomp, he spills half the washbasin on his way over to me.

"What do I do with the frogs, Jonathan? I got' em all in my hand but I can't keep 'em like this forever. They'll have to relieve themselves at some point, and I don't want them to in my hand!"

"Mercy sakes, son. Shove them in a jar. Any jar at this point. No one cares," Alexander huffs.

"But Papa, I can't. I'm not an octopus. I don't have any hands left to open one," Tubs reasons.

Alexander picks the closest one to him, which just so happens to have a lily pad in it, and he holds it under Tubs' hands.

"Perfect!" Tubs beams. "They'll love their new home. But I need a knife to poke holes in the top. They won't be able to breathe in there if I don't. Do you have your knife? I forgot mine."

"You didn't!" Alexander barks. "That's an important thing to forget, boy. I told you to pack it. I bet you didn't forget your fishing line."

Tubs' grin tells his father he is correct.

My cries stop and most of the activity in the room ceases. Jonathan is the only one who carries on with his task. He's back to me a second time—this time with a full bowl of water. He can recognize this isn't a returning memory so his demeanor remains ruffled.

"Blast it all, girl! Now what?" He thuds the basin down on the table next to me and water sloshes over the edge. He slams in the cloth the same way he had tossed his hat and it floats there like a flat boat.

"Jonathan, if you say 'blast' in any form one more time—" Alexander starts.

"Captain," Jonathan corrects with a thunderous crack.

"Captain," Alexander says through gritted teeth. "I got it. I told you I'd call you that when we're out around the crew. What's wrong with her? Is she breathing? Do I need to whack her back? Tubs choked on a chicken bone once…"

I don't know when I took a breath last. It's a nosy inhale when I finally do. Alexander can't finish the story he's told a million times. Once my lungs are full of air, the cry I make startles all but Jonathan.

"Stop the ship! We can't leave," I shriek.

"That won't be hard to do. We haven't left yet," Tubs informs me.

"Izzy, lay back down. You're sick and you're going to make things worse."

Jonathan is frustrated. He sighs the order. My change in position is sped up when he forces me down. I don't know if the sour attitude and the grinding of his teeth are normal behavior for him when one is sick because I've never been sick before. When my head is nestled back in the pillow, he presses the damp cloth to my forehead.

"Mikonan, can you get things around for your sister's hand?"

My brother was already busy with the task, and he holds up a needle as proof.

"I have to get off the ship. I think I lost it onshore," I sob, and I try to wiggle free from Jonathan's hold. I can't see a thing; the cloth has shifted over my eyes in my struggle to get up. I can hear his feet shuffle and feel the mattress sink in next to me.

"What did you lose, girl—tell me," Jonathan asks.

He removes the cloth from my head to rub at the dried blood on my face. His tone has lost most of its heat; the rest he exhales away.

"Sit up for a minute." He tugs me up by my elbow. "Close 'em up," he says when he gets to my eyes.

Jonathan and a cloth are in front of me so I can't tell if the others are still here. When I try to look he directs my chin back to its place in front of him. If the others are here, I can't hear them; no one's making a sound.

"Tell me," Jonathan prods. "What'd you lose?"

"The ring," I sputter. "It slipped off. I lost it. I can't go home to Papa without it. I won't make it without it. I can't."

He hums and squeezes another round of water free from the cloth. He mops my face a final time and asks me to lie back down.

"So you miss it." The storm has left his eyes.

I sniff my reply and let him smear the tears away. When the flow steadies, he holds up his pinky finger. He has my ring.

"It slipped off in my hand," he says. He tries to add a smile but only one corner cooperates. "Well—do you want it back?" he asks. "Tell me yes if you do." His changing brow shifts the stubborn curls of home back to their rebellious place over his eye.

"Not if you want it for Agnes," I squeak.

"Who's Agnes?" Alexander asks. "Sorry," he shrugs when all the eyes in the room set on him.

"The pasty-looking girl from the party," Jefferson says. At some point, he had come through the door. He takes a healthy bite from his apple. "Agnes. Henry and Althea's daughter? I work in the kitchen. We hear all kinds of news back there. Sorry, Captain. I knocked but no one heard. The ship is ready, sir when you are."

"We're not ready," Jonathan mutters while squeezing the cloth free after a fresh dunking. "We have yet to stitch this girl up. How's breakfast coming? Is it ready?"

The men, who had become like stoic pieces of furniture, shudder back to their human forms. My brother groans from his perch on Jonathan's desk and Tubs and his father gasp at the announcement of food.

"Brother, you're needed here and Jared is needed down there," Jonathan explains. "I don't trust the man, and I want him busy to where he's too worn out to cause trouble. Jefferson here is just the man that'll see that it's done."

"That I am, sir," Jefferson says with a smile and a full mouth of apple. He swallows and points the half-eaten piece of fruit at my brother. "Cook, the men saw you come aboard, and they're mighty disappointed you're not in charge of our kitchen. I've heard you've made mouth waterin' meals from the fireboxes of other ships. Just think what you could do in an actual kitchen! If at any point you can be spared, I'd be honored to have you down there," Jefferson grins. "And yes sir, the morning meal is ready and waitin' for the first round of men."

"Good. Tubs and Alexander, I need you to help pass out some biscuits to keep the men's mouths busy until I can get out there. There's been enough commotion in here to wag a mute's tongue." Jonathan applies pressure to my hand and adds another request. "Jefferson, I need—"

"Boiling water, yes sir," Jefferson solemnly finishes. "It's like we've come full circle, sir. It doesn't seem right, does it, sir, to send Miss Izzy back?"

"No, it doesn't." Jonathan sighs and steals a peek under the cloth. "Sugar cubes," he adds. He offers me a glance that says he wants to examine my wound. My nod is the "okay" for him to press my fingers back to encourage my hand to open. At my gasped intake of air, the cloth gets pressed back with raised brows as an apology. "Bring a bowl of sugar cubes will you? Izzy will need that to get the yarrow tea down."

"Would you rather me give the order when you're ready, Captain? So you can stay with Miss Izzy?" Alexander asks.

"No, the men need to see their Captain. I'll be out."

Jonathan offers a smile of gratitude for the offer, but it's a poor one. It's void of any sun. Alexander returns a healthier one that shines his eyes bright before he follows the others out the door. I know them both well enough to know the gestures double as an apology from the biting remarks they exchanged earlier.

"The wound looks good. Your bleeding has kept infection from settling in. Unfortunately, this means your fever is from something else." Jonathan gives me a questioning squint, and he presses his knuckles to my cheek to gauge my temperature again. "And what's this about Agnes? Why on earth would I give that girl your ring?"

"Althea said you were desperate for money and that Papa's copper may not be enough. She was going to suggest an engagement to Agnes," I grind out. I focus on the intense dislike I have for the pale mushroom to keep the tears back.

"I had just enough to satisfy both Henry and this trip. Agnes is in no need of your ring—this time," he teases without a grin. He forces a chuckle at my disgusted "tsk" and presses a smile. "I'm teasing, girl. I told you, the ring is yours. I meant that. I'll give it back if you keep pressure on that cut."

I want it back so I handle the care of my wound. He wrestles the ring from its tight spot in the middle of his smallest finger and looks back to my brother before returning it to its place on my hand. When his fingers brush across mine, the feeling from the garden returns. It's the same strange merging of warmth and chill.

"I don't hate you," I manage to say. It's difficult to speak, and I can't seem to catch my breath. The band's weight mimics the touch that was just there. "It was wicked of me to say that. I didn't mean it."

"I know, Niinimooshe." He frowns and takes up my hands. He taps them together in time to the words he has just spoken. The dizzying, opposing feelings intensify, and I fight the sudden heaviness to my lids that demand to close with it. Jonathan doesn't notice and my brother gets another glimpse. This confession from me about how I feel about him should have brought relief to him, but his green eyes remain their soupy brown. The color is standing its ground.

"Mikonan?" Jonathan exhales. He gives my good hand a parting squeeze before getting up and letting them both go. "What help do you need to get her patched up?"

My brother lifts the crimson cloth to examine my cut and agrees with Jonathan. "The blood kept it clean. Yarrow leaves first, then stitching. I can manage both."

I know it's not polite to stare, and Miss Margaret would have something to say about it, but I can't help it. My brother's skin is the same color as my own. Jonathan notices and excuses my ill manners with a weak smile.

"Mikonan is a healer. Like Doctor Batchford. He'll do a fine job on your hand. Much better than what I could ever do. You may not even have a scar."

"What?" I struggle up to my elbows. "He's going to do it? You said you'd do it—or Alexander," I argue. "I want you to do it."

"I can't," he mutters.

Anger had blinded me to him earlier. Jonathan's face doesn't have the same rich glow it had just days ago, and there are new lines under his eyes. He offers nothing more so my brother does.

"We are no longer on English soil. Odedeyan has instructed that once you are on the ocean, Waabishkaa Ma'iingan is no longer your guardian. He is not even supposed to touch you. I am to take care of you now." My brother pinches feathered leaves from a jar and folds them in his hand. "This will stop the bleeding. Now, back down with you." My brother nods the direction I'm to go when I don't move. I obey with a hard pound back to the pillow, and this makes him snicker. "You have changed much, Biis Nigig, but there are pieces of you I recognize." He takes the spot next to me on the bed and tosses the blood-soaked cloth up to Jonathan with a smirk. He layers the frilly leaves on my wound and gently presses them flat in the pooling blood.

"But—the ring. Didn't you want to marry me? Don't you still want to?"

"I do," Jonathan says. His eyes narrow when my smile spreads. "But you don't love me—don't." Jonathan points with the cloth to encourage my open mouth shut, and it flops in the air like a war-soaked battle flag. "Don't you dare say that you do." The words rush out when he sees, that even sick and feverish, I have the strength to argue. "You'd only be agreeing to marry me out of fear. You only want to escape this discomfort. And you might be eased, for a time, but more will come. From me. I'm wrong for you. It was a selfish mistake for me to ask for you."

I clench my teeth and fight the growl that my throat wants to release. He's won the argument. There's no point in going any further with him. He won't hear me. He's locked himself away in a place I can't follow. Jonathan thinks he's wrong for me. I want to shout that it's not him who's wrong for me, it's the boy. He can't become my husband. The boy that Papa picked doesn't know me the way this Jonathan does.

"I have her, Waabishkaa Ma'iingan. Take faith she will be well taken care of. Go, tend to your crew." My brother's face is contorted with a one-eyed squint. He's trying to stick the end of an odd-looking thread into the eye of a needle.

"Sinew." My brother pulls it through and dangles it in front of me. "I cannot use English thread on you. I am not hemming a skirt." He grins up to Jonathan, but it fades when he doesn't receive one back.

"You're leaving me?" I sit up and squeak. "He's leaving me?" I ask my brother.

"Down, sister. Perhaps if you do well, we will get the frogs back out. You liked playing with them when you were little."

My panicked demeanor doesn't budge with his frog offer, and this disappoints him. He should have known that his silly frogs would do nothing for me. He's a stranger to me now and I to him. He doesn't know that Jonathan is the only one who can calm the terror that I feel—the terror of having a needle pulled through my skin—a needle with animal tendon thread. He licks his lips and exhales.

"There are other things that will work better, yes?"

"There are." Jonathan is on his way to the door and he doesn't give me a second glance. Without stopping, he gathers up his hat and coat. "I'll have it brought up for her—after the stitches and after the yarrow tea." He rakes his hair back and replaces his hat and hesitates at the open door. "She dislikes tea, brother, so expect a fight over it." He slips on his coat and speaks with his back to us. "And shoes. She detests them. Free her of them."

"Jonathan?" I ask. I could have added a bargain, a plea, or a cry along with his name, but I've tried all of those things today. They have all lost their power.

He shuts the door against my asking of him, but I know he heard me. Jonathan lets Jefferson in moments later with the bowl of sugar cubes and a steaming bucket. He hasn't left yet. He's struggling with his decision to leave.

My brother instructs Jefferson on how to prepare the tea while he adds another layer of yarrow leaves to my hand. Jefferson looks nervous. There are only three steps to the tea preparation: sprinkle the dried yarrow leaves and blooms into a cup, add hot water, and steep fifteen minutes. He's stuck on the first step. He can't decide how much of the flower to leave in the cup. I don't blame his indecisiveness. I remember the last time he was in the room with me when there was pain involved. I wasn't quiet about it. There was only one who could soothe me into silence and that was Jonathan. This time, I don't have his hand to hold for comfort. I'm all alone. Jefferson knows this could go badly.

The bleeding has stopped, so my brother picks off the soggy leaves and disposes them in the waiting wood bowl next to him on the table. He picks up the needle and smooths out the long tail of thread.

"First poke, sister. Prepare," my brother warns.

When the needle is inserted through my skin, it feels twice its size, and it zaps my hand with a lightning bolt pain. Sweat comes with the sensation, and to keep from screaming, I wad bedding into my mouth.

"Jonathan is wrong." My brother tugs the sinew thread until the loop is gone. "*You* are the one who is wrong for *him*. I have seen enough to know that Odedeyan's way is the correct way. Another poke."

This time there is burning heat in place of the lightning. Pain is a powerful gag. I don't have the strength to disagree.

"You offer nothing but weight to him. You love him, yes?" He pauses his work so I can answer.

I have to respond with a nod and an added shrug. My mouth is full of damp bedcovering. I think I do. I know I don't want to be parted from him. The princesses in my stories always cry when their princes leave for dragon slaying, so maybe I do love him.

"There is time before you are to be given to Gikto. His people will have to be appeased if you and Jonathan find each other but that will be my worry. Odedeyan desires that I learn to make decisions on my own. For my sister, today is that day. I will help you, but we have much work to do. You are spoiled and weak. Waabishkaa Ma'iingan will need a strong wiiwan—any other will crumble under what he keeps hidden. To become strong you must learn to walk on your own. You have depended too greatly on my brother. He has held you by the hand long enough."

My brother sews the remaining stitches in silence. When he's finished, he ties the noticeably shorter line of sinew in a knot and snips the needle free. I sigh from relief. The pain is over, but he doesn't celebrate with me. He scowls instead.

"You are not finished, sister. There is more pain yet to endure when your memories come—much worse than what this little needle offers. My job will be to grow you so you can battle them. Shoes. You hate them, sister. You take them off. I will not do it for you as he asked."

It isn't that difficult of a task so I don't feel it necessary to protest. It doesn't take much effort to get them off. They're too big. A few shakes to each foot and they fall with a thud to the floor.

Jefferson interrupts our family discussion with a cough. He has my tea ready. He even put in four sugar cubes. I take a sip and the partially dissolved cubes collide into my lip. It smells like flowers, but it certainly doesn't taste floral. It's bitter and it makes my tongue feel feathery. After each sip, I drop in a new sugar cube in hopes that by the time I tip the cup again for my next drink, the taste will improve. It doesn't. Much of the tea remains and the bowl of sugar is almost empty.

"Niinimooshe—the name Jonathan uses for me…" I stretch out my tongue and shake my head after a large gulp. "…is it Mama's name in Ojibwe? I can hear Papa say it. Why would Jonathan call me by her name?"

I go for another sip, but my stomach isn't ready for one and I gag instead. This makes my brother chuckle. When things settle, I force down another swallow of tea. I'm close to being finished. One mouthful more and I'll be done with this torturous drink.

"It was a name Odedeyan called Nimaamaa." My brother smiles at the memory. His eyes look happy. They have a shine like glossed chocolate. "It was not her given name. You remember her name was Elizabeth, yes?" When I tell him yes he continues. "Niinimooshe is a term of endearment. It means 'sweetheart'."

My brother nods his permission for Jefferson to inform Jonathan that the stitches have been sewn and the teacup emptied. He soon returns with what Jonathan asked to have ready for me. The plate of biscuits he had placed on my lap would have been enough. It's the scent from what Jefferson hands to me next that gets me upright in bed. I don't know what lifts my spirits more: the coffee, or the anticipation of my journey back to the person who thought to gift it.

PART TWO

TWENTY-TWO

None of us had a clue that the gifted coffee and biscuits would be the last that I would enjoy while fully awake. There were to be more of them later, but fatigue robbed me of the joy in them. The intense desire for sleep smothered me like a wool blanket as the glands on the sides of my throat ballooned. My brother told me not to be afraid of the lumps in my neck, that they were just a part of the Sleeping Sickness. He told me to give in to sleep's heavy pull. Rest and time, he reassured, were the only cure. So sleep I did.

The ocean trip is a hazed memory, of different hands and faces that came to help nurse me—Tubs, Jefferson, my brother. Jonathan, however, wasn't one of them. The times I remember seeing him, he would be hunched heavy-shouldered in a chair by the door with his jacket draped over his lap. Once, I managed to push past the current of sleep to dangle my wrist over the edge of the bed. I had hoped this would be the adult equivalent to the screams and stretches of the little girl. It may have been. His feet did manage to shuffle, but it didn't work. He didn't come to me. He couldn't. Years ago, a young Jonathan had given my Papa a promise. True to his nature, he wouldn't fold. And so my hand remained empty, matching how my insides felt, and he remained at the far side of the room. I drifted back to sleep on my own and did my part to help him keep his promise to Papa. I didn't tempt him again.

The two months aboard the *Verde* sped past, and I got off the ship the same way I got on—tossed over a shoulder like a sack of potatoes. But the shoulder was different this time. It was my brother's. The crew was different, too. They didn't scoff at the boy like they had done when I was forced on. This time, they looked on with solemn reverence. They took my lethargic limp state to be that of one coaxed into submission.

I'm now in a one-room cabin in America. I haven't seen much of it yet. Struggling to keep awake is as hard as wash day with Miss Margaret. I can only take in bits of things. Tubs' orange hair, my brother's brown skin, the stacked logs of the cabin's walls— and leaves—in the colors of fire.

Leaves? Inside? Why do I remember leaves? I force my eyes open and quickly discover why. Overhead, pointed maple leaves twist from their twine-tethers to the ceiling. A leathery, shuffling sound pads in my direction. Light and airy, like the sound my baby angels would make if their wings flapped free from their library ceiling.

"You're awake!"

It's Tubs and he's grinning down on me.

"Can you see the leaves? Do you like them? Jonathan and I did them for you. We thought we'd bring the pretty outside colors inside where you can see them. We've been waiting a long time for you to wake up."

I try to thank him for my dangling bouquet, but my throat is too dry to produce any sound. I push up to look for water but find blinding light instead. I grimace at the unhindered windows that flank the door.

"I'll get that. Are you thirsty?" he asks. "Cook told me to make you drink once I saw that you're awake."

Tubs scuffs off to handle the windows first. He's wearing a type of slipper shoe on his feet instead of his usual hard-soled pair. It's making the angel wing sound I had heard earlier. He tugs down two shirts from the line of clothes drying in front of the fireplace and hangs their shoulders over the corners of each window. He then slides over to a copper pitcher and a matching cup.

"Did you notice my moccasins?"

He holds his foot out for me to see after he hands me the water. Not bothering to pause between topics, he rambles on.

"What do you think of my hair? It's grown quite a bit since home. I'm going to grow it as long as Cook's."

I take a sip of water and swish it around to get moisture in every corner. I swallow and snicker. It's grown, all right, but not in the way Tubs is desiring it. It's got more height than length. Cook's hair is as long as mine and is as smooth and shiny as an oiled kettle. I hope he's kidding. Even if Tubs could grow it as long as my brother's, his crimped locks would look frightening that long. It would look like a boneless fox had crawled his way on top of his head and died there.

"Most of the trappers I've seen around here have hair twice as long as mine and beards as thick and bushy as Mumbert's. If Papa and I stay here, I'll never have to cut my hair again!" he beams.

I laugh, though the memory of home stings.

Mumbert was the old gypsy man from whom Jonathan bought Rosemary and the same who sold the copper wares. He had the longest beard I had ever seen on a man. He rarely spoke, but when he did, the only evidence that he had lips at all was from the quivering of his whiskers from his breath.

Mumbert drove an elegant team of gypsy horses that pulled his mobile house on wheels all over the English countryside. The strawberry-red house with the sunny-lemon door had its distinctive song to let the world know that "Mumbert the Seller of Copper Wares" was coming.

Underneath the roof of green, pots and pans of copper and the utensils that would dip inside them would clink and clatter like church bells on the Lord's Day. Miss Margaret would rarely buy anything, for Jonathan loathed anything made in copper, but she would always invite Mumbert in for tea and a bite to eat.

Tubs slides over to one of the windows and peeks under the tail of a shirt to see the cause of the growing commotion outside. The barks and snarls of dogs and shouts of men swell until there's a pound against the door. Tubs lifts the metal piece from its bracket to open it and barely has enough time to sidestep when Jonathan tumbles in. With a groan, Jonathan rolls to his side and palms himself up on all fours. My brother steps in behind him with clenched fists and a glowing eye.

"You will not take her. It is not the will of Odedeyan."

Jonathan huffs to his feet. He moans and presses the back of his hand to his lip.

"I don't care what Odedeyan's will is." Jonathan looks at the blood left behind, and with a searching tongue, he surveys the rest of the damage. "I'm taking her. We're going," he says when he notices I'm awake.

"To see Papa?" I ask. My throat feels shriveled, and my question isn't much more than a hoarse whisper.

I toss aside the covers, but my brother hollers for me to stay put. It's too late. My feet are already on the ground—well, they are briefly. I don't know if it is my weak leg muscles or the pile of blankets on the floor that causes me to fall. It doesn't hurt. I land on my backside and the blankets cushion my fall. It would have been funny if there wasn't so much anger in the room. Jonathan reaches for me, but my brother catches him by the arm and yanks him back.

Something has Jonathan shaken. He's willing to disobey Papa to touch me.

"Take her—touch her—brother or not, I will—"

"You will what? Hit me again? You didn't tell me he was going to be here." Jonathan rips his arm free, but my brother finds it again. "Let go, or this time I'll hit you on purpose. You're going to leave your sister on the floor like that?"

My brother's half-shrug infuriates Jonathan, and he runs with him towards a wall with his fists full of his shirt until they both collide into it. My brother shoves him off. Alexander takes the opportunity while they're apart to slip in between them. I'm glad Alexander has stepped in. I've tried shouting twice for them to stop, but nothing came out but a dry hiss. Tubs heard my snake-like call, and with a cautious eye on the battling pair, he skates away to get more water.

"She is not hurt. She can get up on her own. The girl is weak, Waabishkaa Ma'iingan. Weak and mushy. In no way did you prepare her for this journey. So, yes, my sister will get up on her own. She needs practice for what you failed to prepare her for."

Jonathan stretches past Alexander's chest and clutches into my brother's shirt again. With gritted teeth, he pulls him forward, and with a fist bundled in linen, he thrusts him back into the wall.

"Cook, your mouth isn't helping, and, boy, you need to control those hands. Both of you need to simmer down so we can figure this out. Whose insane idea was it to have that man here, Cook? You? The chief?" Alexander asks the question through a much bushier mustache from when I saw him last.

His palms separate the men's heaving chests.

"Both," the two men chime.

This riles Jonathan up again, and he pushes against Alexander. Alexander is a head above Jonathan and twice as broad. His struggle against him is pointless. Alexander takes hold of both of Jonathan's arms and twists them behind his back. He steers him to a chair and presses into his shoulders to force him to sit. It was authoritative but done in the same fatherly way he took care of Jonathan back at our beginning in my room at the cottage.

"You, sit and simmer down. Lay a hand on Izzy, remove her from this cabin, and I'll come after you myself. You've worked hard to keep your promise to the chief. Don't you dare screw it up now when you're so close." Alexander adds a point. "And keep your mouth buttoned. I'm talking to Cook, not you." Jonathan obeys and slumps in the chair with his head in his hands.

"Papa?" Jonathan's demeanor has Tubs shaken. He's crying. I've never seen the boy cry.

He's looking at Alexander instead of me. He, like myself, is just today being introduced to Jonathan's rage. He hands down the overly full cup, and it's shoved into the top of my hand instead of in it. Water rivers underneath my baggy sleeves and travels down my arm. I'm hot, sweaty, and feel like I've been frosted in lard—it feels nice so I don't rasp a complaint.

"Stay with Izzy. Jonathan will be fine. We just have some bumps to work out."

"Bumps?" Jonathan throws his hands into his knees and laughs. "The bump is that I'm not allowed to take Izzy home, but my monster father is."

Alexander lines his lips and forms a bird beak with his hand. He snaps it shut to remind Jonathan to keep his mouth clamped tight. "What's wrong with you, Cook? Surely you haven't forgotten who Edward is."

"Odedeyan and I have not forgotten. We remember full well who he was. White Boar took my sister. He took my people. And Nimaamaa…" My brother glances at me.

Silence. He's now staring at me and is afraid to finish. Who is White Boar? Is it Edward? He had better keep talking. I'm tired of people treating me like glass. He must've somehow heard my screamed thoughts. He continues for me.

"No," he finally says. "We have not forgotten—but we have forgiven. Edward is dead and this is a test to see if he truly is. The man you saw outside is no longer White Boar. He is no longer Edward. He is a new man with a new name. His name is Avery."

"They…Izzy, your mother, your people…were more than taken by him, Cook." Alexander squeezes into Jonathan's shoulders. "And this boy here—if the girl wasn't present, I'd remind you of the horrors he's done to his flesh and blood. You and the chief have made a grave mistake. People don't change. Edward certainly could not change, and a new name isn't enough proof for me."

"But he has," my brother argues. "The Great Spirit, your God— our God—He changed him. Come with us, Alexander. Come see for yourself."

"If Jonathan can't go, I won't go. My place is with him. The girl is coming with us, Cook. We'll bring her home."

"No."

My hoarse and emotionally detached answer startles everyone. Jonathan especially. It is a different sound for him. It isn't a defiant stomp of a word that I usually make it out to be when I snap it at him. It simply is what it is. A two-lettered word with a singular sound. I still mean it as a disagreement, but it is done without the spirited emotion that usually accompanies it.

It isn't that I don't want Jonathan to take me with him. I want him to. I don't want to be apart from him. I can't imagine being apart from him. The thought of a journey to Papa without him terrifies me, but my brother said if I want to be with him, this is the only way to do it. I must learn to stand on my own. Tubs is gawking at me. He doesn't understand my "no" either. He must think I woke up with brain damage. Tubs' face is pale—unusually pale—and this reminds me of Agnes. She will not get the chance to dig her fungus nails into Jonathan.

"I'm going with Cook," I say from my spot on the blankets.

I have yet to muster the energy to stand. I made myself comfortable on the floor because I didn't want to struggle up in front of Jonathan. He'll come to me again. He'll touch me. He'll disappoint Papa. I won't allow that to happen.

Jonathan is looking at me like I just grew an extra head. I have been in and out of sleep for a couple of months. My hair—it must be a disaster. When my fingers go to it, I expect to feel a mass of knots, like the balls of thread in my sewing basket. Miss Margaret would "tsk" every time she saw them. Hers, of course, were organized according to R.O.Y.G.B.I.V, the order of the colors in a rainbow neatly wound onto their wooden spools. But my hair isn't a tangle of knots; instead, it's weaved and orderly and as soft as my fingers remember Miss Margaret's to be. Someone has spent time brushing it. They even braided it. I question the men in the room with a look. The littlest of them grins his confession and wiggles his fingers in the air.

"Thanks to you and Rosemary," he says. "But don't let it get out that this boy can braid."

"You're willing to travel home with my father. The man who hurt you," Jonathan says in the same tone that I had voiced my "no."

"I'm willing to travel home with my brother," I say. "I trust him— and Papa. I can't imagine that my family would be willing to put me in harm's way. You've brought me up to trust and believe in a God I can't see. Papa is no different. I choose to trust him."

Jonathan releases a jagged breath and blinks away a scowl. "I don't like this, Mikonan. I don't like it all. What am I supposed to do? Go back home—or sit here—and hope Izzy makes it all right?"

"No. I have a plan for you," my brother says. He picks up the copper pitcher and presses it to his eye.

Jonathan snickers at him without a smile.

"What? It's cold."

"It's also copper. I dislike it as much as I dislike you." An edge of Jonathan's lip quivers. He's teasing. It's a sign the rage is leaving.

Jefferson steps in the forgotten open door with a steaming cup and bulging cheeks. With a full mouth, he announces breakfast is ready. I can smell his coffee, and it zaps my mouth awake with moisture. I swallow with him when he takes a noisy gulp to wash down what he stuffed in.

"Who's the bow-legged old-timer out there with the dogs?" Jefferson asks with a smack.

"Avery."

"Edward."

My brother and Jonathan both give their different answers at the same time.

"He lives. I'm surprised. When we left him, he wasn't doing so good," he snorts.

"I'm surprised, too," I cough. My dry throat feels like it's crawling with tickling bug legs. I sip what water is left in my cup and grimace. It isn't coffee. "Miss Margaret and I were both led to believe he was dead."

Jonathan scowls and crosses his arms.

"You two came up with that conclusion all on your own. I thought it best not to correct either of you. To me, the beast *was* dead. The man has always been dead to me and he'll continue to be that way. I don't care how many names for himself he comes up with."

"Well, Edward—Avery—whoever—ain't our only problem. My brother is planning to ambush ya, Cook. He wants Izzy. He's planning on taking her so he can trade her back to the chief for his copper."

"Perfect," my brother says. "Just as you and Avery said he would do."

"Yeah, well, he's my brother. I know him well," he says with a rapid pat to his chest. "He and about ten others are plannin' on taking off shortly after you do."

"And Waabishkaa Ma'iingan will not be far behind," my brother says. "The weapons we are delivering to Odedeyan are to be divided in half. My brother will take his portion when he leaves after Jared. Splitting the guns up will be safer. Less temptation for Avery and more power for you if you should need it."

"Why not take care of Jared and the others right now?" Jonathan asks.

"Your hands need no more filth, brother. God will handle them. You are to follow and act only to defend yourself or your family, yes?" he asks. "You will need at least one other. It is unwise to travel alone."

"That 'one other' will be me. Count me in," Alexander raises his hand.

"And me," Jefferson raises two—his empty one and the one with the coveted brew. "My brother is sick of seein' me. He told me to go wander off in the woods and get lost, so I will. With you two."

"Yes to you," Jonathan nods to Jefferson, "but no to you. You're heading home to Ms. Abernathy."

"Anne has the company of Miss Margaret. She's fine. She said to do what I must to see that you and Izzy are settled. A few more months isn't going to matter. This will give the ladies more time to plan the wedding," he grins.

"I can't ask that of you. Jefferson and I will be fine," Jonathan says.

"You're not asking, I'm telling. I'm coming. The house, Jonathan, I didn't ask that of you either. You didn't listen, so I'm not listening. Accept it so we can get going. Tubs, pack up. We're leaving first thing tomorrow."

"I want to go with Izzy, Papa. We're all going to the same place, right? We can all meet up with Izzy's Papa. Cook won't mind, will ya? I can help keep an eye on her and Edward the Boar-guy. I'll be her protector."

Tubs is using his big blue eyes to his advantage. He looks angelic. I hope Alexander and my brother agree. The boy has a gift. He's the only one that could get me beyond the rock wall. I need him. I'm going to need help just getting out the door.

Alexander looks hesitant, but he gives Tubs his blessing. My brother offers only a hum. Tubs reads the noise as a yes and throws his fists in the air in celebration. Jonathan has yet to voice his opinion either way. He doesn't want to leave me. The blankets I'm sitting on I'm positive are his. He did the same thing at the cottage. He slept on the floor in my room until I was well enough to be left alone. Jonathan and I aren't all that different. Sure he's older, wiser, and a hundred times more beautiful, but he's as dependent on me as I am on him. How can I encourage him to let me go?

"How do I walk out of here, Alexander? How do I leave her? Not just that, but leave her with that monster?" Jonathan asks.

I'm hoping Alexander has an answer that will fit for both of us.

"Simple: *Trust.* Trust the chief. Trust Cook. Trust God. All three of them care for you—for Izzy. Have faith that they know what they're doing. Let the girl stretch her wings, find her way. She's been cooped up in cottages and cabins long enough."

Jonathan combs his fingers back into his hair and his palms stop on his forehead. He lets his head drop over the chair's back and the pressure of his released exhale vibrates against his lips.

"Like our bat," he says.

I ball up the blankets in my fists underneath my crossed legs. I wish they were his hands instead of his blankets. I'm afraid. I'm afraid to stretch my wings, but with all the faith and trust I can muster, I'll do it. For Papa, my brother, Jonathan—for me. For us.

He leans forward and rubs his hands. He gives his hair a final tug before checking me for my response. I hope he remembers that my bat had two choices, just the same as I do. I hope this gives him—and me— the strength we need to do what we must do.

"Just like our bat," I say.

TWENTY-THREE

My brother pops in the doorway. His arms are piled high with furs. He holds them in place with his chin, and through his teeth, he announces it's time to go. Tubs runs out after him but darts back in to retrieve his pack before scurrying back out again. I am putting on the pair of moccasins my brother had kicked over to me when Tubs rushes back in, breathless and beaming.

"Look what Cook traded for me!" He pulls out a sleeve from the coat tucked under his arm. "It's fox!"

"Fitting," I say.

I wiggle my toes in the soft shoe. My feet feel massaged by the shoes' downy, fur lining and I vow never to wear hard leather shoes again.

It's time to leave. I can put off no longer what I have been stalling against all morning. I'm afraid to meet Jonathan's monster. It doesn't help that Jonathan got in another tussle over him this morning. He had wanted to say good-bye to me, but my brother refused. He said as my guardian he thought it best to start the separation. That meant no more goodbyes and delaying the inevitable. His father gets to see me— he doesn't?—Jonathan tried to argue. The unfair ruling infuriated him.

As a result, my brother now has two glowing eyes. My brother said Jonathan tightened the noose around his neck. He says Jonathan's fists are what solidified his decision to keep us apart until the wedding—or until we are back with Odedeyan—whichever should come first. Jonathan's behavior has me baffled. I'm the one who has the problem reigning in my temper, not him. The man with the quivering belly from port disagrees. His tremoring hands tell me he has seen it in Jonathan before.

My brother wouldn't answer my question about the groom. It was to be *my* wedding. Shouldn't I know which one it was to be? He told me he would help strengthen me for Jonathan. Had he changed his mind? My kick to the table leg had upset the dirty dishes from breakfast that were stacked on top. Two plates crashed to the floor and had to be tossed out in the garbage hole at the back of the cabin. The intact ones my brother made me wash and put away. He made me sweep and mop the floor, too. He said the next time I decide to abuse a table leg I should think twice about it.

When I step out the door to meet Edward-White Boar-Avery, I don't see a monster. I see an average man with a beard of silver and a bent back. He's busy tying down bundles and furs into a low carriage. It is as if a giant has ripped off the top of Mumbert's gypsy carriage and pressed down with his massive hand to compress it. The four wheels are similar to his carriage, but they aren't slender. They are thick and bulky, and instead of a team of horses, there are two lines of squirmy, impatient dogs. The strange sled stirs a memory. One that isn't welcome.

I was little but too big to be held. I remember my feet dangling and knocking into the back of Miss Margaret's legs. Jonathan had meant it as a surprise, and it was, just not the one he had hoped it to be. The old carriage in the barn was buffed and shined to its original perfection. Doors painted the same sunny-lemon as Mumbert's replaced the old ones that had dangled like a child's loose tooth. Green curtains splotched with cheerful red roses flapped in the same breeze that pulled pieces of Miss Margaret's hair from her cap and into my face. Wooden tires with strawberry-red spokes flanked all four sides of the carriage; it was the final touch needed to make this a whimsical gypsy carriage of our own.

Alexander sat in the driver's seat, unnecessarily busying himself with the reins, while a teenaged Jonathan tried to coerce me out of Miss Margaret's embrace. He tried to pull my arm free from around her neck, but the action only made me cling to her shoulders more tightly.

"Maybe we can try again tomorrow. You did a lovely job, Jonathan. I'm sure she loves it. Right, Isabelle?" Miss Margaret had asked the question into the back of my neck as she swayed. She offered additional comfort by adding a kiss.

"Please? Just one ride with me?" Jonathan pleaded.

He tried again to take me from Miss Margaret, but this time I pulled back with such force that I hit him. He had always told me my fingers had poked him in the eye. His eyes watered so. Now, I know better. I hurt him, and it wasn't from the accidental hit.

The writhing, yipping dogs bring me back, and I reach out to pet the nearest one, and instead of a wet greeting, he pulls his lips back and grumbles low in his throat.

"Whoa, now. It's best not to touch the dogs until they get to know you a bit. There'll be plenty of time for that."

The not-so-monstrous man's voice is deep and familiar, like the baritone sound Jonathan and I would make when we put our empty teacups to our chins and huffed into them. When he speaks, his voice is slow and deliberate, and his words hang in the crisp air like the puffs of white that come with them.

"Miss Gudwyne? Name is Avery."

He extends a weathered hand out to shake mine, and he shines an infectious smile so broad it nearly consumes his face. Wrinkles replace eyes that are swollen into slits.

"It's Izzy."

I hesitantly accept his hand. He's supposed to be the enemy. I take it and am surprised at the strength of his grip.

"Nice to meet you, Izzy." He gives me an unmonster-like wink and walks with an awkward gait over to the dogs. "Let me introduce you to my family. You're rearin' to get Miss Izzy home, aren't ya, Traveler?"

He grabs the face of the dog in the first row and scratches him behind his ears. Avery is greeted with a face full of kisses. The other dogs either pant, yip, or spin in their spots to vie for their master's attention. He greets each of the eight dogs with rough tickles behind ears or pats on the hindquarters as he introduces them.

"Come here, Izzy. Meet Bundle. He's the baby of the team and the most gentle. The others may not like you yet but this little dog loves everybody."

I ruffle Bundle behind the ears as I had seen him do, and with a wet nose, Bundle nuzzles under my chin. In a stiff, wide-legged gait Avery walks over to me.

"He likes you. Now, let me show you what he wants. He wants a better look at you. Like this…"

He puffs in his struggle to get down on one knee. He puts his forehead to the dog's and then gives him a generous scratch behind the ears.

"You'd never do this to a wolf or coyote, mind you, that is if you like your face the way it is. The siblings there," he points a gnarled finger at an almost identical pair of dogs, "Racer and Victory—they have some wolf in them, but they're as gentle as a black bear in a blueberry bush."

I trust Avery knows his dogs better than I do so I put my forehead to Bundle's furry one. His two eyes become a singular brown one. To see both of his, I alternate the closing of mine. His eyes change position with each wink, but from both, the same sorrowful brown looks back.

"Well, girl, you have a choice. Horse, walk, or sled?" Avery points out a spot in between bundles and furs. It doesn't take me long to decide.

"The sled. Thank you, Avery."

TWENTY-FOUR

"Haw, boys! Haw!" Avery shouts over my head to the wagging backsides of the dogs. Crimson, the lead dog, digs in and leans left. The rest of the tireless brood honors his rank and follows without question.

"Good, boys! Good!" He praises and paws at the trail a few times with his boot. Avery's empty hands are curled around the bar above my head. There are no reigns to control the powerful little beasts, just a strange language that only he and the dogs understand.

"Leave it!" Avery barks at the siblings. Racer and Victory had caught glimpse of a rabbit nibbling grass on the side of the trail, and with their heads not pointing in the right direction, their canter is off, throwing the whole team's cadence off rhythm. Obediently, they return their attention to the trotting pack in front of them.

It's a bumpy ride, but an enjoyable one. The sun is near its peak and it has melted the chill away along with the dawn's frost. I'm beginning to feel warm, so I roll the skin off my lap and let the air blow across my damp legs. Avery had said that fall temperatures can bob up and down. By evening, he promised, the temperature would be down again.

Tubs and my brother are riding behind pulling an extra packhorse. Tubs is talking in his animated way, waving his arms about something. My poor brother.

He's not one for conversation. It must be a family thing. I'm not good at making conversation, either. I never know what to say, and when I do say something, I usually regret it minutes, hours, and sometimes days later. There are only three people who are exceptions to this and one of them is here with me.

The others don't notice, but I can tell that all the jostling on horseback is uncomfortable for Tubs. The corners of his lips are turning pasty. Avery told me before we left to raise my hand if I needed to stop. He'll think I'm soft for wanting to stop already, for the settlement hasn't been out of sight long. The thought almost keeps me still.

"Whoa, lads. Whoa!" He shouts the order when he sees my arm. "Needin' a break already, Miss Izzy?" Avery steps off the back of the sled and removes his outer coat.

"If it's ok with Tubs, I'd like to switch places."

Tubs looks down in question from his horse but doesn't argue. That's all the confirmation I need to know that he isn't feeling well. Tubs' hair is clinging to his forehead. I feel him for fever as he takes my place.

"Izzy, stop!" He nudges my hand away. "I'm fine." He smiles but the corner of his lip quivers.

"Sorry, *Wilhelm*, just checking that swampy head of yours. If you'd take off that fur you'd see it's not cold enough for it."

I rumple his damp hair to shoo away his irritation with me. Like an unshorn sheep, his hair has gotten so long it stays standing. He looks like Miss Margaret's feather duster. I pat it down, and my hand gets shooed away for the second time.

"I'm not hot. I like my coat and want to wear it," he says. He wipes away beads of sweat from a scrunched brow, perhaps because I skipped to the "w's." "Looks like we're still playing. Wrong, wrong, wrong. Still not it. You're never going to guess, I tell ya," he sighs. He turns around in his seat and shines up at Avery. "Can I give the dogs the command to go?"

"Go ahead. Tell them 'hike' nice and loud when everyone's ready."

Tubs makes sure I'm situated on my horse before giving the dogs the order. The sled shoots off and Tubs gleefully raises his arms in the air with a holler. Curious birds that were watching us from their perches are scared into the air.

"Thank you," my brother exhales. I smile back my response, happy to oblige two people with one gesture.

We travel all day on trapping trails that Avery has worn down to dirt. These well-used trails, I am told, were first trampled smooth by Natives who used them for hunting or traveling from village to village.

For hours, my brother and I sway to our horses lope in silence while Tubs spends most of his time facing the wrong direction. Now and then Avery's head throws back, and he slaps a hand to his outer thigh. I bet Tubs never has to rehearse in his head what to say before he says it. I sift through my mental notes of safe topics to discuss with my brother. Weather and food. That's all I have and I already mentioned both hours ago.

I know what I would like to ask him. Why can't I call him by the same name Jonathan does? Why must it be Cook? I think I know why, but I'd like to hear it from him. I'm sure it has to do with the same reason I refused his frogs.

I wonder what it's like to be him, to be Native. I've never met one before, and if I'm going by the things I've read, he doesn't quite fit the part. His hair and eyes are dark like one but his skin isn't red like people say it should be; but then again, neither is mine. His clothes aren't right either. In place of a loincloth, he has long pants made of tanned animal skin and an English shirt. My reigns go slack with my one-sided conversation. My horse begins to crowd out my brother's, and our horses touch noses. My brother corrects me with his narrow brows.

We set camp by a wide-bodied river. The bank is high on both sides and the water is shallow and sluggish. To keep the horses' ankles safe, we lead them down the steep embankment. Tubs wades into the middle of the river. It's shallow, only to the middle of his shins. He falls backward with outspread arms and pops up to his knees with a gasp. His face is hidden by his water-soaked locks.

"We've had a dry summer," Avery explains. He limps down the edge with several buckets. "Most of the water will be like this. A blessing of sorts. It will make it easy for us to travel across 'em." He raises his voice so Tubs can hear him over his thunderous splashing. "Boy, the days of jumpin' in the water like that are comin' to an end." He puts his knuckles on his hip after handing me a bucket and continues his shout to Tubs. "If it were any colder out, you wouldn't last more than five minutes without freezing rock solid."

Just as he had predicted, the afternoon heat has gone and the temperature has shifted back to the cooler air we felt earlier in the day. I have large bumps on my arms from sticking them in the water to fill the bucket. I roll down my sleeves to dry them and briskly rub them to get the circulation back.

"Boy, change out of those clothes when you're done. Can't have you gettin' sick on us already," Avery orders. He grunts as he tugs a sloshing pail of water on the bank.

"Yes, sir!" Tubs joyfully shouts as he continues to splash. The horses pause to watch for a few minutes before dipping their noses in the running water, and the dogs above yap in jealousy begging for theirs.

"That'll do, boys! That'll do!" Avery hollers up. "Dry summers make for dangerous falls and winters," he says to me. He bends over in the shallow river to fill another bucket. "It's what I call the 'run-off effect.' Just as the rain hits a roof and trickles off, hits the ground, and finds its way back to the rivers and streams, that's how things work out here. One affects the other. No rain means no vegetation. No food means you then got hungry animals. At dinner, we're going to go over a few rules for you two."

Tubs' shoulders drop at the announcement of rules. Avery points at the dripping Tubs with the ladle he pulls out of his belt loop.

"These rules are to keep you safe out here. Skip waitin' for dinner. We're startin' now. The first one is always to be aware of your surroundin's. All animals tend to be dangerous, especially if they're mothers with young nearby. The bear is going to be dangerous because she's stockin' up for her winter's long sleep. Everyone out here is in competition for food. The one we have to be most diligent and careful about is the wolf." Avery groans at the weight of the bucket and sets it down in the river. He dips his ladle in and takes a sip. Tubs pushes through the water with wild arms and high reaching knees, scoops up the pail, and scurries up the bank.

Avery lumbers up the same bank and is mindful of his footing. At the top, he slips off his hat, and with a vigorous sweep of his hand, he reanimates his crushed locks. Spikes the color of brown sugar reveals delicate threads of the same silver his beard is generously doused in.

I was right to guess that there would be few to no visible characteristics shared between Jonathan and Avery. Besides skin color and height, they share nothing else. Avery's features are hard. His skin is like wrinkled leather; the lines on his face are deeply carved. Heavy brows match the beard that covers his broad jaws, and they shield his best feature—his eyes. His blue eyes and smile are the softest things the monster has. Are they enough to make me—and the others—believe he is a man?

Avery limps over to the sled and pulls four large bowls out of a sack and holds them out with unsteady hands to Tubs. He looks and acts old. He's only in his fifties—ten years older than Alexander. Why is he like this? A father's traits are passed down as well as a mother's. Is this a glimpse of my future Jonathan? My heart drops at the possibility that my green-eyed boy could someday morph into this bent man with angry angles and hard lines.

"Place a bowl in between each pair then get out of those clothes," Avery instructs with a shooing motion towards Tubs' clinging wardrobe.

The bowls are large enough for two dogs to put their heads in. As soon as Tubs begins pouring the water into a bowl, two greedy heads are already lapping up the cool liquid.

"Before people eat, *they* eat. These dogs will work their haunches off for you, but you got to take care of 'em. These dogs are our lifeline out here." Avery unwraps a strong-smelling bundle and the dogs bark and twirl in their spots. "Tubs, are you watchin'? This will be your job from now on."

"Yes, sir!"

Tubs leaps over. He is more than pleased to be given this responsibility. He jumps in to start his new job early and helps Avery free the fish from their paper wrappers.

My brother unfastens an axe from the back of his horse's saddle, along with a bow and quiver of arrows. Without a word, he stalks off into the woods.

"Now, let's see what we have to eat tonight."

Avery tugs at ties and pulls food items out of the packs. He tosses Tubs a loaf of bread and shoves a chunk of stiff, dark-colored meat between his teeth before sending the rest over. Tubs spreads the food out across a log. Dried fruit, beans, rice, and venison are all added to the fallen tree.

"Tubs, give me a hand. Girl, you stay put."

Avery moans in his squat to gather sticks. He wants Tubs to help him build a fire. Tubs will have no problem showing off his skills. Hunting trips with Jonathan and Alexander sometimes can last for days. I'm sure the boy has built a million fires.

"Show me what you know."

Avery adjusts his stance and watches Tubs stack up the larger pieces of wood in a triangular shape and the smaller pieces underneath.

"Do you know how to use these?"

Tubs is handed a rock and a small bundle wrapped in a leather lace. He unwinds the package and lays the pieces out: a stick, a flat piece of wood, and a small pouch packed with moss.

"You're going to start a fire with that?" I ask from the safe distance of the food-laden log. "Why not use a tinderbox?"

At home, that's how Miss Margaret taught me to restart the kitchen hearth when it would go out. Thankfully, it wasn't very often. I'm sure she thought the exposure would be helpful, as a possible cure for the intense feelings I have over a fire. Well, it wasn't helpful. My hands would shake, making it difficult to connect the flint with the steel piece, and I'd end up with nicked knuckles before ever getting a spark. By the time the fabric from the tinderbox drawer was lit, I was a sweaty, frazzled ball of energy.

With the rock in his mouth, Tubs props a stick in a small wooden tray. He winds a leather lace around its middle and saws with both sides of the leather lace. It hisses as it spins. Smoke appears first, then a tiny, red ember sparks into existence. Tubs adds a small piece of moss and blows until the brown curly wad begins to smoke. He cradles the fragile beginnings of a fire in his hands and adds the fiery newborn to the dried kindling under the little wood lean-to. A few violent puffs of air encourage the tiny fire to feed on the small debris. In moments, the fire's appetite expands to the larger branches.

"Well done, boy. Izzy, we'll let you give it a try with the next one."

Avery is trying to set up a triangular frame over the fire, but he's having trouble with his hands. He glances up and sees my gaped mouth. Nothing will come out. I don't agree with his request, but I don't refuse it. I don't have the nerve to do it either. I'm too scared. He's suddenly familiar, in a not-so-good way. The struggling increases and he growls when he can't get the pieces to fit. He traps a rod under his foot to keep it steady so he can join the other pieces to it.

"I don't like fire either. I hate it. I hate it even more so now that you're here, but we need it. We'll tolerate it together. Deal?"

The sunny grin he shines seems to instantly steady his hands and he's able to finish the frame. He hangs a pot in the middle and washes his hands together with satisfaction. He then spits in his hand and extends it out to me. Nervous adrenaline takes charge of my muscles. My arm raises without my permission. It is because I just saw a glimpse of Jonathan in the man-monster.

Dummy. It's not him, I scold. It's his opposite. It's Edward. I just shook the hand of the uniformed man from my memory. My hand feels contaminated. I don't know where to go or what to do with myself, so I get up and pace in a circle like the dogs do before they lie down. I should go sit with them, but I can't. They'll eat me. So, I go back and sit on the log with the food instead and busy myself with lining things up. I wish I could wash my hands. The food is at least organized and everything looks orderly on the log. Wonderful. I'm becoming Miss Margaret.

The horses tied a few feet away flick their tails while nuzzling their noses in the grass. Occasionally, one will lift his head, munching with ears twitching. Contented with full bellies, most of the dogs sleep peacefully. One dog snores, while another's leg swings in the dirt as if still in running mode; but for the most part, they're silent and still. Racer and Victory are the only two who pace back and forth, going only as far as their ties allow.

Avery lifts the lid to stir the beans and rice and keeps a cautious eye on the siblings. The aroma of the softening food dances around the camp, and it makes my mouth water. I can't wait for the hot food to warm me from the inside. I never fully warmed up from the river.

"Red sky at night, sailors delight; red sky at morning, sailors take warning."

A voice comes from behind describing the colors of flame in the early evening sky behind a backdrop of pine and honeysuckle. It's my brother with a large bundle of sticks on his back and in his hands, four limp squirrels dangle by their tails.

"That," Avery points with his spoon, "is a very true statement. It'll be a good travelin' day tomorrow whether by land or sea. I'm glad it's by land. No filthy, confined spaces here. The world is wide open and fresh." Avery clears his throat and shakes his head with a grumble. He spoke of filthy, confined spaces. The monster remembers me, too. His eyes divert from mine. Bet he wishes his comment stayed inside. "What about you, Mikonan? What do you prefer? Land or water?"

My cheeks flush. Avery called my brother by the name I wasn't given permission to use yet. I'm supposed to be his sister, for mercy sakes. The skin around my brother's eyes is becoming darker. Healing bruises always look worse before they get better. I wouldn't know from experience myself, but Tubs always has a multi-colored splotch somewhere. I did feel sorry for my brother. Now, not so much.

My brother unloads the stick bundle off his back and drops it next to the fire. He doesn't give Avery his answer. He says Avery is a new man and he says he has forgiven him, yet my brother holds Jonathan's father off at a distance. Tubs is back on his feet and admiring the new additions to dinner. I watch tiny red ants zig-zag in the dirt to keep my eyes off my brother's knife and focus on the sound of a crow's squawk in the distance to drown out the tearing sounds of skin being pulled from flesh. Tubs and I are startled when my brother tosses an empty fur to me. I catch it inside out and don't even flinch.

"That'll be a fine addition to dinner," Avery praises while giving the pot a final stir. "What do you say? A hat for the boy out of the skins?"

My brother nods his agreement while scrapping the excess meat off the back of the other furs.

"We have to wait for these beans to get limbered up. While there's still some light left, I need to get a line set. Tubs, how about showin' me what you know about trappin'?"

Tubs had changed into a dry set of clothes but left his wet ones in a heap on the grass.

"…After you hang up your clothes on those bushes over there to dry. Part of takin' care of ourselves out here is carin' for our gear."

"Go ahead. I'll do it," I offer.

Avery doesn't seem to be the same man that held me down with his foot, but it doesn't matter. To me, White Boar, Edward, Avery, they're all the same. I remember the man who took me and packed me for shipping with the others in the disgusting haul of his ship. I welcome the chance to have a break from him so I get up to finish for Tubs. The sooner he's gone, the better. Tubs is oblivious to the man's past offenses and he thanks me with a grin. He scampers up behind Avery, who is ahead with a basketful of traps on his back.

My brother hands me one of the squirrel-pierced sticks that he had been roasting over the fire. He nudges the pot to get better access to the flames and tells me through action what to do. When my stick gets too low, he'll reach over and lift it to where it should be. This is nice. We could sit here all night and roast a whole forest of squirrels and neither of us would have to utter a syllable.

"The boy. He is sick."

My brother's comment shatters the delicious silence.

"He is," I say. "How'd you know?"

I wonder if it is the healer part of him that can tell. Tubs does look paler than usual, but my brother wouldn't know that. Tubs is either one of two shades: creamy white or red. Red is his summer hue when the sun beats his skin this color. It's fall, so his shade is freckled porcelain.

"He told me," he says. He rotates the squirrel until its back is just above the licking flame.

"Well, he didn't tell me. I found out by accident," I say, annoyed that Tubs would divulge this secret to a stranger. I rotate my squirrel into the same position my brother's is in.

"He worries for you," he says. "He as well as the others. They have done wrong by you. All of them. They held on to you too tight which in turn has taught you to do the same."

How can you hold on to someone too tight? He's speaking in riddles. I don't understand. Instead of answering, I touch my squirrel's side, just as he does.

My brother snorts a chuckle.

"What?" I say. I didn't do anything.

"Listen," he grins.

My brother whistles. *Fee-bee-bee.* A bird behind us answers with the same three notes. *Fee-bee-bee.* They call back and forth until I cover my ears and giggle. *Fee-bee-bee, Fee-bee-bee.* They were talking and it was cute—for the first ten calls. Now my brother's notes are just piercing.

"My sister the chickadee," he snickers, "I should have chosen that name for you. Always watching. Always doing as I do."

"You chose my name?" I ask.

"Odedeyan and Nimaamaa let me choose your Native name. 'Biis Nigig'. It means 'Little Otter'." My squirrel has become too low for my brother's liking and he lifts my stick. He adjusts the squirrel on his stick and he jabs at it. "It fits you. You were playful with a bite. I recognized that part of you on my brother's ship. My name for you was a good one. It still fits," he chuckles.

We don't do any more talking until both our squirrels are done to his liking. Both look black to me, but I've never had squirrel over a fire before. When the squirrels are removed from their sticks and placed on the flat rock next to him, he takes an axe out of its leather sheath.

"Do not fear your feelings towards Avery. I had them, too. It is good to let them come," my brother says. "He was sick when he hurt you, sister. I promise you, God has made him well. Tomorrow you will see and forgive; today you will acknowledge and feel. You need *you* to begin the journey to tomorrow. We must show you who you are. Do you remember this?" My brother smooths his hand over the axe handle and questions me further with his eyes.

"It's beautiful," I say and am disappointed to have to shake my head no.

"It's a tomahawk," he says. He turns it in his hand and the corners of his mouth turn up. He doesn't have a smile as big as the sun like Avery, but it's just as warm. "This, sister, was yours."

"Mine? May I see?"

My fingers feel the story my eyes read on the tomahawk's handle. In a forest of pine, a lean wolf runs from a tusked boar. An eagle with outstretched wings watches over both as he soars over them. The tomahawk has little weight, but with the help of three copper rings, the weight it does have is expertly distributed.

"It was a gift from Odedeyan," he says. "You still remember nothing?"

I shake my head no. I want to cry. How can I not remember something so pretty?

"No fear, sister. The memories will come," my brother comforts. "I told Odedeyan this would not be a good gift for a girl. He said it was the better choice over the beaded, deerskin dress Nimaamaa wanted to have made for you. He was right. You loved this tomahawk, just like he knew you would. You practiced until you could out-throw the most skilled hunter in the village," he says with pride.

"May I try?" I ask.

Maybe throwing it again will help me to remember. Remember Biis Nigig, Papa, Mama, and my brother. He lifts one shoulder in shrug which I take to be permission. I aim for the great oak in front of us, the one with the buttery leaves. I'm not picky. Any spot will do.

Instead of sinking in, it bounces off.

"One more time?" I ask.

I'm Biis Nigig. My brother's Little Otter. Daughter of a chief and skilled tomahawk thrower. I *will* get it to stick. I get the same expressed permission from my brother to try again. I throw it—and get the same results.

"What's wrong with it?" I ask with a growl. I'm annoyed with the pretty little axe and upset that my brother even brought it out. "Why won't it stick?"

He picks up the weapon and takes great care to brush off every grain of dirt that it sunk into. He doesn't offer it back to me. Instead, he places the tomahawk back in its sheath.

"I'll teach you if you'd like to learn."

My brother looks heartbroken. My miserable throwing turned his mouth down. I brought back memories of his sister; not the one in front of him but the one who was taken. Now I feel bad for not feeling bad about his bruised eyes.

Tubs and Avery return from setting the trap line with more wood for our fire and an empty trap basket. Tubs excitedly reports the details of their trap-setting adventure. He chatters on about how he almost lost another finger setting a trap and how they could have shot the deer they saw standing in the middle of the trail if Avery hadn't broken one of his rules by leaving his gun behind. The boy is beaming. He's happy, but it's not enough to make me happy. The cottony white from his lips has spread.

We eat dinner. I eat every morsel on my plate, but find the food has no taste. It could very well have been pine needles and leaves; my taste buds wouldn't have been able to pick out the difference. My brother doesn't eat and polishes the tomahawk instead and carefully tucks it back into its leather home.

"What we need now is a little after-dinner music."

Avery pinches the last bean from his plate and pops it into his mouth. He claps his hands together as if to muster up the energy needed to stand, and he groans as he straightens.

He returns from the sled with a violin and bow. He props a leg on his sitting log and rests the instrument on his knee, plucking at the strings and twisting the knobs at the neck until the shapely structure sings in the proper key. Before he plays, he runs the bow down the middle of his tongue.

"The trick to makin' the best sound," he winks at Tubs, "is to lick the horsehair before the first song."

Tubs shudders and sticks his tongue out before digging in the pot for seconds.

The sweet sound is soothing, like a cool compress on a burning fever. The pressing weight of disappointment over my "broken" tomahawk and my brother's "lost" sister is eased to a nagging ache, and I snuggle deeper under my blankets. It's pleasant to be serenaded to sleep. In the twilight between consciousness and slumber, the violin's song is a melodic cradle, and the notes carry my concerns away.

The song persuades me to give in to the paralyzing heaviness of sleep.

The instrument's scratched whine prods me awake.

In the night's black, Tubs is as close to the fire as he can be without being consumed by it, and my brother and Avery are both on alert—Avery with his gun at his shoulder and my brother's bow drawn.

The cries continue but the violin lies mute, abandoned in the dirt.

TWENTY-FIVE

"Get out of here! Go on! Get!" Avery shouts over his rifle. He points it up in the air and shoots.

The wolves are shadowy ghosts. Their padded paws are sound-absorbing moccasins on the forest floor. The only evidence for the four-legged stalkers is the pairs of eyes that ignite in reflection from the fire's light.

"If I get a shot, I'm takin' it, Mikonan, and I don't want to hear a peep out of ya if I do! Tubs, grab a gun out of the pack—they're loaded—and get over to the dogs," Avery shouts over the commotion while trying to follow the slithering shapes with his gun. The sled dogs are inconsolable, and Avery does nothing to silence them.

"One of the dogs is gone!" Tubs hollers the same report the dogs' bark as he wrestles a gun free. His voice is tinged with terror. The screams that woke me must have been cries from one of Avery's dogs being ripped away.

"Hush, now, boys. Hush." Tubs begins to silence the noise coming from the distressed pack, but Avery corrects him.

"No, let 'em yell. It'll let these wolves think there's more of us than them. Sorry, boy. We didn't get to that lesson," Avery says when he notices Tubs struggle with the unfamiliar gun. He pulls me to my feet and hands me his. "It's all ready to fire, girl. If you get a clear shot, just point and shoot. Pull that trigger back with your finger as many times as you need to." I recognize the feel of the gun, and my hands instinctively settle into the positions Jonathan taught me. "Mikonan, you got her?"

"I do," he says. He has the bowstring pulled to his lips. He adjusts his position so his back is close to mine.

My heart is pulsing in my ears, and it must have been a while since I had last swallowed because my chin is drenched.

"You doin' all right?" Avery shouts from the shadows where I last saw Tubs. "Keep your eyes fixed on 'em. Be at the ready."

I nod, though I know he won't see my response.

A set of eyes like jeweled honey reflect into existence and keep their gaze on me. The incandescent globes float just above ground level, and while the others dart manically about much like Racer and Victory had done earlier, this one chooses to hold its position. It's now clear why Avery has kept such a watchful eye on the pair. They can smell their kin and what seems like nervous traipsing to me is a sign of warning for Avery.

"If you get a shot, take it!" Avery bellows in between his rushed instructions to Tubs.

I squint an eye shut and aim for the minuscule dark spot between the glowing eyes and exhale a prayer between dry lips for a clean kill. A shot bounds off into the woods, but it doesn't come from me. I hadn't pulled the trigger yet, and while the other eyes blink dark and flee to the safety of the blackened forest, the honey set still hovers.

"They're leaving," my brother says. He backs into me. He's not ready to lower his bow yet and his elbow jabs into my neck.

"I got him, Avery! I got him!" Tubs moves to run toward the injured wolf but Avery pulls him back.

"Whoa, there, not so fast, boy. Give him a while to lay before we walk up on him."

The shot had come from Tubs. The pack had returned for another dog but this time, Avery and Tubs were ready.

Avery pokes the wolf's eye with the tip of his gun barrel. When the animal doesn't respond, he pulls its legs over to the opposite side and rolls it over. It's female. A slender one. Even by the meager light that reaches the outer limits of the camp, I can see the outline of her ribs pushing up under her compressed mat of gray fur.

"Usually the fire keeps them back," he says. He examines her teeth and paws and runs a hand down her sunken side. "She was starvin'. That means they all are. They're desperate. The dogs are an easy meal for 'em, bein' all tied up." He grumbles under his breath and grabs a fistful of grass and throws it.

He struggles to his feet, and with an extra swing in his arms to propel him forward, he makes his way to the dogs to give them their deserved scratches of comfort. It is distressing to hear that it was Bundle who had been taken. Avery is shaken by the discovery. He bends forward with his hands on his thighs for support and exhales a groan.

The night pulses in response to our shocking loss. To the human visitors in their woods, the fall locusts hiss their eulogy of condolence while an owl hoots a sorrowful apology. We are strangers here and don't belong, but they sympathize. Their message is the salve to the one that Jonathan spoon-fed me every time game was put on the table. "For there to be life, there must be death." I didn't fully understand what he was trying to teach me, but now the saying couldn't be clearer. Bundle's death, though brutal and unfair, is just how things work—especially out here. Avery blinks away tears and dries the ones that escape with his fingers.

"I'll take care of the cleanin'." Avery pulls out a knife from the sheath strapped above his boot and points it at my brother. "You get first watch tonight. Wolf hides are profitable out here. Bundle's revenge," he says. He blows air through the corner of his lips as he saws the knife under the skin. "Most of the governors in the eastern settlements have bounties and will pay a fine price for 'em. A mighty fine price. Did you two notice all the wolf hides hangin' in town?" He doesn't need an answer to continue. "They're a nuisance, without a doubt, but this world needs 'em whether people think so or not. Even sled dog murderin' ones. Tubs, give me a hand, will you? Light the lantern and hold it so I can see."

While Tubs takes lantern duty, I take a closer inspection of the gun Avery handed off to me. I fiddle with the familiar gages, gears, and switches. I'm familiar with guns, especially this one. Jonathan was lax on many things with me, but learning to shoot wasn't one of them.

His gun collection is extensive. If the pieces were to be displayed side by side, it would be easy to distinguish the difference between the two distinct classes of weapons that he owns. England heavily produces the first class. Weighty and awkward with their drawn-out barrels, the black-powdered, single-shots are available to all and sold to the masses. Only Jonathan has access to the second class of guns— lightweight, easy to transport weapons that can be loaded with enough firepower for multiple hunts. These aren't available to all. They are the drawings and sketches from the castle cellar. These are the weapons he taught me to use but wouldn't keep at the cottage. I had always wondered where he stored them. They were hidden underneath the castle behind a false wardrobe.

I twist the star-shaped gear to load the barrel. Five clicks, five rounds. I fire three into the trees. Tubs and Avery scramble to their feet, wide-eyed and breathless. With the tomahawk in hand, my brother skids to a stop beside me. The glowing balls snuff out, and the creature makes light work of rustling leaves in its retreat as if it were just erased by the wispy breath of a fall wind.

The brand on the back of my neck is burning. I shuffle in a semicircle until I find the one responsible for the phantom pain.

The monster didn't do it. He didn't do any of the branding that day. He forced that task on a child with the cat's help. The whip with many tails turned the boy's back inside out when he wouldn't comply, and its repetitive ripping claws changed his refusals into numb obedience.

One shot should do it, but I want it done in two. A bullet for White Boar, the monster of my Native brothers and sisters—and a bullet for Edward, the same monster with a white man's name. Both beasts forced my boy with the pretty green eyes to do horrible things.

"Izzy, you can shoot that?" Tubs asks. He whimpers when Avery drops to his knees next to him. "Don't. Don't hurt him, Izzy. Cook said Edward is dead. This isn't him. I can tell. Avery's not bad. He's not Edward anymore. He's not White Boar anymore, either. Please, Izzy, don't hurt Avery."

The gun is jumping all over the place. I have two bullets but both will be wasted if I can't get the shaking to stop.

"Sister." My brother steps in front of the gun. "What did you see?"

"Jonathan said *no*, Cook. He didn't want to brand us, but Avery forced him to. He whipped Jonathan until his back..."

I can't finish because I can't breathe. I let my brother take the gun because I can't see my target.

"I didn't know," I gasp in between sobs. "I didn't know."

I crumble to the ground and dig my nails into the grass. I curl my fingers and fill them with blades. I wish I had ahold of Jonathan's hands instead.

"I'm sorry." Avery is on the ground with me, but I don't look up to see where. "I know it's not enough to be sorry, but I am. Until my last breath, I'm gonna to keep on workin'. I'm gonna work until my body stops. I'm gonna make it up to you and my boy, I promise. Forgive me, please."

"Cook?" I ask. It takes great effort just to make it upright on my knees. I know I won't be able to stand. The tremoring is too bad.

"Help me to my bed. And Avery?"

"Yes?"

"Please. Stop talking."

I can't sleep. A branch from one of the pine boughs beneath my blanket is poking into the back of my leg, and as much as I try to adjust it, it continues to be a nuisance. Avery's snores sound as if he could choke on his tongue—maybe the Lord will have mercy on us all and let him—and Tubs, not to be outdone, is breathing so hard through his mouth I'm afraid he could blow our fire out.

My brother may have had the same thoughts of Tubs. He's adding more wood to the fire. He takes a stick from the bundle by the fire and begins to whittle at it with the tomahawk. It's not the pine branch's fault for keeping me awake or the snoring and loud breathing of the men in camp. It's my aching heart. Jonathan's actions over the years—his silence, his secrets—they were all justified. I made life miserable for him. He said he loved me. How? He wanted to marry me. Why? My brother must sense that I'm still awake because he begins to tell me the story from the tomahawk handle.

"In the beginning, the Great Spirit created the animals to love one another. In the forest, all were equal. Eating not of each other, but with each other."

The fire pops and spits out a fiery branch. My brother nudges it back in with his toe.

"When man disobeyed the Great Spirit's one rule, to not eat of the fruit of a certain tree, the world and all in it was punished. In the forest, no longer were the animals equal. The wolf became dominant over all. No longer could he run with the rabbit. No longer could he chat and play with the squirrel and the raccoon. They were all afraid of the wolf that hunted them from behind the forest trees."

"There was plenty of food for the wolf for there were many old friends to eat. The wolf was fat and happy in this new world. Life was good. They did not understand the full consequence of man's mistake until the boar came."

My brother puffs out his cheeks, holds his arms from his sides, and alternately stomps his legs. It makes me giggle.

"The large, glutinous pig came as a parasite into the forest of the wolves. It dug up the forest with its strong nose and sharp tusks. It ripped up moss and sod with hoofs as sharp as stone. The boar stripped clean the wolves' paradise with its gluttonous appetite. Without food of their own, the animals that once provided sustenance for the wolf were soon gone. The wolf felt sorry for what had happened to the forest—to the plants, the insects, and the animals. The wolf finally saw what the other animals had seen all along—the consequence of man's disobedience."

"The wolves had a decision to make. They could keep running ahead of the boar or they could stand and fight. They knew, however, the only way they could defeat the boar would be through the help of the entire wolf clan—those of forests near and far. So unite they did. The white wolf, the grey, and the black fought the boar together until it ran from the forest, never to return. The wolves learned a lesson that day. They weren't the king of the forest. The Great Spirit was."

"God," I say.

A breeze whisks over the fire and fails at its attempt to snuff it out. I'm too far from the fire and chilled sitting in my bed. I wrap myself in my blanket and take the place next to him on the log. He told me the story of the tomahawk, but it was also the story of the cellar wardrobes. Life was meant to be sinless and perfect. Man ruined that with his disobedience.

"Sin. It's a horrible thing," I shudder.

"It is," my brother agrees. "It separates us from God. I tell you this story, sister, to give you a glimpse into the history of our people with the white man, but also to remind you—and me—that *all* of us are sinful people. All of us are capable of horrible things when we are apart from Him. We called Avery the White Boar because of the destruction he caused. He did evil things, but nothing so great that it could not be erased—or healed—by the work of the Great Spirit's Son, called 'Christ'. Did not Christ promise to take away *all* our sin, sister? Is Avery so bad that he cannot be forgiven? I hope not. That would mean there are limits on God's ability to save. Will there be sins of mine that cannot be forgiven? Sins of yours?"

I know Christ's blood covers all sins. I know that to become His child, all you have to do is simply confess them and He'll take care of them. He'll throw them far away. But Avery—he didn't just steal dessert before dinner or kick the gardener on the shin. He stole people. He tortured his son.

He…

"You know you are my half-sister, yes?" My brother nods. "Did you know my birth mother died while giving birth to me? The women helping my mother said there was no hope for me, that I would soon follow her. Odedeyan said when he placed his hands on my mother's belly to say goodbye to us, he felt my kick beneath his hands. An ever so subtle tremor." With his finger, he taps my blanketed shoulder. "He said he was afraid, but he knew what he had to do. Odedeyan saved me."

With a crack from the ash, a spark rises into the air, and pieces left in the dust layer momentarily shudder. I push the heels of my moccasins in the dirt and make trails while waiting for him to continue. He is unaware that in between my path making, I steal glances at him. I wonder if Papa and my brother are opposites like Jonathan and Avery. Or are they two of the same as Jonathan and Evolyn were?

"Odedeyan raised me alone. No one would help him. They said he dragged me back from The Great Beyond and I brought back evil spirits with me. No one would help him; that is until the Healer came. She came with her father, the Book

Bearer. The Book Bearer told us great stories from his book. He told us we were a sick and dying people. Not only here…" My brother motions over his body, "…but here," he taps his chest. "The Healer helped our people with the illness the white man gave to us. They brought us life two-fold."

"In medicine bottles and a Book," I finish. I pick up a stick and poke at the fire. My brother watches me for a moment before continuing with his whittling.

"The Healer, Sister, was Nimaamaa. Nimishomis, the Book Bearer..."

"Grandpapa," I finish.

I remember him. He would take me fishing at the base of a waterfall. My brother grins at the memory of him and slips the tomahawk across the stick's flesh.

"Even though the Book Bearer brought us the truth, it was still hard for the others to see me any differently than before. It takes great faith to change an ancient way of thinking. Not all accepted Nimaamaa's and Nimishomis' truth. I tried to keep proof of the 'curse' covered." He shows me a thin, faint scar under his collar bone from his father's knife. "But that did not matter. They did not have to see it to know it was there."

"Odedeyan and Nimaamaa married. Then you came and it became my job to be your watcher. I took the responsibility with honor. Keeping watch over my Biis Nigig filled the part of my heart that was empty."

Avery sits up and gasps for air. He coughs his airway open. Avery is waking, and our conversation will have to end. My brother throws what's left of the whittled stick into the fire.

"I did not watch you as Odedeyan had asked. I left you. White Boar took you. He took Nimaamaa. He took the entire village. We followed you to the fire, Biis Nigig. Never have I seen or smelled anything so horrible. Nimaamaa's screams—I can still hear her. Never will I forget."

"Tell me," I say. "Tell me about the fire. I see it. I dream of it, but I don't understand it."

"What has been done to you is my fault." My brother straightens in his grief. He takes in a jagged breath. His face is long with sorrow. "I disobeyed Odedeyan. You are this way because of me. If you cannot forgive Avery, I'm afraid you will never forgive me."

TWENTY-SIX

Avery was awake. I knew this because, even though his breathing was steady and matched Tubs, he wasn't snoring. This didn't cause my brother to shy away from sharing more. For that, I was grateful. The story of how my brother felt he wronged me didn't have the effect he thought it would. It didn't make me angry or dislike him greatly. It did just the opposite. It grew the spot in my heart that I let him settle in.

My brother didn't believe Binidee when she said she saw Stone Coat in the forest. He knew Stone Coat was just a story. He loved scaring the girls with tall tales of monsters from different tribes. He loved scaring Binidee, especially. She was the girl he had wanted to marry but would never get the chance to.

Papa was gone visiting a neighboring tribe and Mama was busy tending to sick villagers in her healing tent. That day, like every day, I was his responsibility. I was napping in the wigwam. He didn't see the harm in leaving me for just a few minutes. He and Binidee wouldn't be gone long—for the Stone Coat of the Iroquois didn't exist. He told me he thought she had stumbled upon the armored discards of the visiting white man. Not all wore them, just the warring ones. Binidee wouldn't know anything of white men or their wardrobes. She was a promised girl. She was protected and sheltered in the safety of the village. Binidee was to be a peace bride to keep the alliance strong between The Three Fires—the Potawatomi, the Ottawa, and the Ojibwe. She was to be given to an Ottawa boy.

She shouldn't have known about Stone Coat. She wasn't supposed to go beyond the village trees.

My brother was startled for a moment when Binidee pointed out Stone Coat. He could see how she mistook the struggling person for the monster. Stone Coat of the Iroquois was a giant, covered head-to-toe in rock-hard scales. This one was smaller—man-sized—with only its head covered. The monster was in a fight over his helmet. He wasn't relishing in its protection. What Stone Coat wore was a prisoner's helmet of iron.

My brother thought confronting the monster would impress Binidee. He knew this Stone Coat wasn't the beast of the Iroquois. He could see a ring of keys on his lap. His plan worked better than he had hoped, and she insisted that she go with him. Together, they met the monster with her arm wrapped around his for support.

Stone Coat didn't speak the native language of the Iroquois. He didn't speak Ojibwe. He spoke the language of Mama. My brother understood his pleas for release, and he slipped the instructed key in the awkward spot behind the monster's head. Binidee gasped when the mask came off. My brother said he should have been jealous of her reaction, but he wasn't. He wasn't even when she whispered to him in deep blush that she thought Jonathan to be a forest angel with eyes of pine. My brother told me he had no right to be jealous. Binidee wasn't his nor ever would she be.

My brother said Jonathan asked if he saw others like him. That if he did, to tell our people to run. Jonathan said the white men with him had sticks of fire unlike any other. There were no other villages in the forest but ours. My brother grabbed Binidee by the wrist and ran.

The three were too late. The white men were already there.

"Why was Jonathan in a mask?" I ask.

The sound is sharp and it feels the same way coming up from my throat. My heart is pounding, and I don't know what to do with myself again. I get up to pace, but my brother pulls me back down with him.

"Not even with me will he say. Sit." My brother tugs me down when I make a second attempt to get up.

"It's because the boy looks just like his mother. I made him wear it because I couldn't stomach looking at him." Avery rolls over to face us. "What I did out here—it killed her, and I took it out on my boy. I didn't want to see her. I couldn't if I were going to keep on doin' what I was doin'. My boy…" Emotion changes Avery's voice, and he clears his throat to hide it. He coughs and exhales to finish but he can't. He rolls over and hides in his furs.

My brother sighs at the new information, but he doesn't seem surprised. Both of us aren't surprised that it was Avery who imprisoned Jonathan in the mask. I pity the man swaddled in bear fur. He knows he has lost his son and may never get him back. I even feel hurt for him, because I understand. What if I don't get Jonathan back?

"You have learned much today, and its weight is heavy, yes? Just a taste of what Waabishkaa Ma'iingan must have to carry every day. How will you deal with these new memories? Pace a path into the earth?" My brother takes up my hands. "No. We pray. Are you listening, Avery? Pray." The bundle moves and moans its answer. "My brother—did he not teach you this?"

"He did," I say. "But you have to be still and quiet to pray. My insides never feel quiet."

"It's because Waabishkaa Ma'iingan's secrets are loud. Can you not hear that some of the noise has been taken out?"

I nod because I do notice. The new knowledge hurts, but the secrets I learned have shapes, and they aren't just noisy black blobs anymore.

"Now that you can see them, present them to Him. He wants them. Learn this, sister, and you will have something to teach Waabishkaa Ma'iingan," my brother grins. "You miss my brother?" I nod. I do. Every moment I'm out here without him. "You and Waabishkaa Ma'iingan would talk much, yes?"

"Sometimes," I tell him.

Sometimes we didn't need to. Sometimes we could just sit together in the quiet.

"That's just how it is to pray. Pray to Him the same way. From here." My brother gently presses a finger to my heart. "With your voice, tell Him everything. If you cannot find your voice, let your heart speak. We will do this with each returned memory, with each discovered secret. In doing this, perhaps someday my sister can forgive me?"

It should have been awkward. It should have felt strange. He's yet a stranger to me and I'm just learning him, but the feeling isn't close to any of those. It is exhilarating and warm. Hugging my brother feels like the most natural thing in the world.

He misses Mama, I can tell. He still hurts over her. I take out Mama's Bible to show him—to share a piece of her with him. My brother weighs it in his hands before fanning through the stiff pages. His thumb brushes across them, at moments in hesitation as if the smoke-soaked pages could burn. He tells me the strange language inside is the language of our people and that Grandpapa, the Book Bearer, taught him to read from it. Grandpapa taught me, too, my brother says, and I try reading it, but I don't remember how. Miss Margaret's necklace is still around my neck and I have yet to earn it. When I ask my brother to teach me again, the pained look on his face deepens. He doesn't like the charred places on the Bible; he tells me so, but he doesn't say no.

Tubs is asked to get up early to check on the traps. Avery has to shake Tubs to get him to wake. The boy, we're discovering, is a sound sleeper. I don't have to be encouraged to wake. I never went to sleep. I go along with Tubs because I want time away from Avery to think. I also have a body full of adrenaline to burn from last night's conversation.

"What's it like to have Cook for a brother? You're so lucky! I wish he were mine!" Tubs takes up a stick and flexes his fingers to release an invisible string. He hisses the sound of a sailing arrow.

I'm not sure how to answer him. Our relationship is too new. I could tell him it's strange to have a brother you can't call by name and that it's unfair that other people get to. A former enemy even. I could tell him I know he loves me. Well, I know he loves Biis Nigig but I'm not sure if he loves Izzy. This would just confuse Tubs. I don't want to have to try explaining things when I'm just as confused. I don't answer, and this doesn't bother him a bit. He talks enough for both of us most of the time anyway. He's used to it.

I understand my brother's struggle. I love the boy from the library, but I don't know how I feel about the man with the scrunched brow. Can my brother's love for Biis Nigig spread to include Izzy? Can the love that I have for my green-eyed boy grow to include the man with the scowl?

Toothless blades leap into the air and whip shut when Tubs pokes the same stick in the center of yet another empty trap. It's disheartening to find every trap is empty—of its bait and game.

"Looks like someone's belly was filled last night," Avery sputters.

He's trying to scrape the charcoaled layer of beans and rice from the bottom of the cast iron pot. Avery had forgotten to add the water to our breakfast. He tosses the spoon in and runs a gnarled hand through his hair, frustrated that the rock-hard mess won't budge.

"Good for nothin' but the latrine," he grumbles while throwing it in the back of the sled. "Maybe one of the dogs can lick it loose."

Avery is having difficulty with the harnesses and lines this morning and can't seem to focus. He goes from packing a few items in the sled to fiddling with buckles and knots. In between the two, he paces as if trying to remember where he left off. There's a tremor in his hands, and in an attempt to keep it hidden, he balls them in his pockets.

I choose to ride in the sled for the first part of the morning. I enjoy the rhythmic sound of leathery paws slapping against dirt. The dogs seem to have extra energy today, dipping their necks lower and pushing hind haunches harder. With mouths agape and tongues swinging, their lips are pulled back into slobbery grins. Even Racer and Victory keep their focus. I've read that animals can sense a human's emotions. Perhaps they can feel their master's misery.

We're traveling alongside the same river we camped near last night. Avery says it flows from the direction we want to go, and besides its capability to lead, the babbling beacon provides us with fresh water whenever we need it. I'm both surprised and pleased that water has been easier to access here in the wild than it has been at my civilized home in England.

When we stop for our noon meal, Avery entrusts Tubs and me to water the dogs and horses while he and Cook hunt for fresh additions to our day's meals. Tubs tosses each dog his fish while I begin the task of filling water buckets.

Looking like a wobbly windmill with a bucket attached to its blades, I hold my arms out for balance to find a place to step that doesn't include pain. The frigid water eventually numbs my tender arches, and once my feet feel twice their size, the sensation works as a cushion and the jabbing rocks feel more like smooth, hard eggs. It's when I bend over to fill my bucket that I notice the figure across the river.

The wolf looks as pitifully thin as the one Tubs shot last night. His legs look like stretched versions of the sled dogs' and his tiny waist just enhances them more. Like strings to an invisible corset, starvation has pulled his shrunken stomach up deep into his back. He paws at the rocks and darts his muzzle about. Our eyes catch while he licks his lips deep into the corners.

"The bucket! Mercy sakes, Izzy!" Tubs kicks through the water and wobbles the same wind-mill motion I had earlier. He couldn't catch up to the spinning bucket that I had allowed to get carried away by the current. "Hope Avery's not going to miss it." He watches it bob out of sight. It disappears around a bend littered with downed trees and branches.

The wolf loses interest in me and dips his head in the water. The only parts that remain air-soaked are the tips of his ears. When he emerges, he shakes dry and sneezes to snort his nose free.

"It's a good thing I didn't bring the horses down here. They wouldn't like him as much as you do," Tubs whispers when he makes it over to me. "No wonder Racer and Victory want nothing to do with their fish."

The wolf arches his back and pounces. After the drenching splash, he wiggles his head as if to empty his ears. He repeats and snaps at the water, and this time, a fish rolls into the air.

"Well, look at that!" Tubs sits on a log that has been lodged in the river's bottom to watch. "He's fishing."

The wolf lunges again. A silvery tail smacks the water's surface and when his jawing mouth goes under, it comes back out full of fat, wiggling fish. The fish thrashes in hopes of wrestling itself free from the toothy trap, but the wolf just sinks his teeth in deeper by shaking his head from side to side. When he finally decides to release it, it plops down lifeless on the rock-plated shore.

"He's alone," I say. The wolf lies down next to the fish and licks it a few times before gnawing at it. "Aren't they pack animals?"

"Maybe he's an outcast," Tubs says as he sticks his hand in the water.

The water acts as a temporary gloss, and for a short time, the dripping rock he pulls out retains its vivid and interesting hues. It's as if someone has drawn a line down the center and ordered each color to stay to its side. Tubs caresses the buttery, white side that resembles the wolf's topcoat. The other side of the rock has already begun to dry and the charcoal side that he had thought had tiny diamonds in it has lightened to a pale, moon-kissed gray similar to the backsides of the wolf's ears and the bridge of his nose. Tubs shows me his find with a squint before dropping it in his pocket.

"You know there can only be one alpha male. Maybe he challenged the leader and got kicked out of the group, or maybe the alpha saw he was weak and got rid of him. Either way, it's a death sentence. A wolf needs its pack to survive."

Racer and Victory are whimpering. They noticed the wolf, too, and are trying to pull themselves free. If Tubs hadn't unhitched the team and tied them to their trees, the two would have dragged sled and all across the river. Both dogs tug at their cords, and whines turn into hacks as harnesses ride up and push against their throats.

"They're pulling out of their harnesses!" I shriek.

I can't run. The current reduces my forward motion to a high-stepping wade. I throw the water back with my fingers in hopes of making faster work of kneeing through the water. The lines quiver and make a strange sound as the pair attempts to lunge past me with air gripping claws.

"The lines—they're pulling loose!" Tubs isn't far behind. When he reaches me, he is as dumbfounded as I am regarding what to do. "That wolf has them all riled up!" He glances back at the wolf who is no longer lounging with his fish but standing at attention with his tail tucked. Dangling the untouched pieces of fish in front of their faces, Tubs tries to distract them while I tighten knots.

Racer's eyes roll back into his head and the whites stare past the dangling treats. He staggers back towards the tree and coughs air back into his lungs. Victory collides into him and leaps over his back, showering it with spit from his flopping tongue.

"What do we do?" Tubs tosses the fish to take hold of Victory's harness but is thrashed about until he is shaken loose and thrown to the ground.

"I don't know—they're pulling free!" I shout as one of the lines burns through my fingers.

Both have managed to yank their lines free from the tree, and like a ribbon train on a party dress, they drag their ropes in the water after them. The wolf's shoulders hunch and his hair spikes but the display of aggression isn't for the splashing pair that bounds in his direction; it's for the two pudgy black balls that come stomping out of the woods.

"Bears!" I stumble backward into Tubs. "There's going to be a mauling!"

"Who? The bears, dogs, or the wolf?" Tubs yanks his sleeve free from my grip. He sprints to the sled and grabs onto the side of it to slow himself down. He slides across the ground on his backside and scrambles to his feet. "We've got to protect those dogs." He throws off supplies until he finds the weapons sack and he wrestles two guns out.

The bears lumber forward with swaying heads, planning to finish the wolf's last remaining morsels with minimal struggle. Racer and Victory make quick work of crossing the river and collide with the bears. The four become a writhing knot. From the mingled beasts come savage sounds of gnawing mouths full of fur and flesh.

The wolf jumps on top of the furry mountain and sinks his teeth into one of their backs. A bear roars in protest. It continues to back step until it rolls over and takes the wolf with him. When the skinny pest is loose, the bear swipes a razored paw across the wolf's ribby side. The blood that seeps through the wolf's fur looks like watered-down raspberry jam. He yelps but instead of nursing his wounds, he charges. He latches on to the front leg of the bear and tugs his body back before ripping his head from side to side. Bellows fill the woods as the crippled bear hobbles off in defeat.

Racer and Victory splash in their retreat to the safety of the river and bark their support for the wolf who has stepped into their position.

Tubs tosses me a gun with an attachment at the top. It looks like a magnifying scope similar to what Jonathan has at home. He says he uses it on his ship to study the stars. Without hesitation, Tubs spins the star on the gun's stock and loads the chamber full of bullets like Avery had taught him.

"Better make it a good shot! You know who he'll be coming after if you miss!" Tubs shouts over the deafening noise of the beasts.

The scope makes my target appear closer. Thanks to Jonathan, I'm a good shot. With this added feature, I surely won't miss it. I pull the trigger and instantly discover I didn't use the scope right. The end of a scope's eyepiece is nowhere for the bony edges of an eye to be. There's crushing pain and an explosion of alabaster light when the magnifying tube rams into my face. I expect to feel the warm ooze of blood between my fingers and the wet feeling of dislodged eyeball, but thankfully neither come.

"Get up! Get up!" Tubs shouts between gunshots and the hasty tugs to my body. "He won't stop!" He tries to pull me up by the elbow, but I can't see and collide into him. I end up pulling him down with me.

My eyes are robbed of their function and where the storming bear should be, fuzzy fireflies swirl in manic circles instead. The sound of roaring water and beast pound into my ears as the river relinquishes its power to let the creature pass. I fold over Tubs and wait for the impact of teeth and muscle. A loud crack rings out from behind followed by a shout of scolding.

"No! Just the bear!" my brother commands.

The whirl of an arrow replaces the sound of gunfire and the wooden projectile zips through the air over our heads. The bear roars in anger and thrashes in the water. Tubs and I both know it isn't safe to move until the river regains its courage and returns to its rhythmic garble.

"You two all right?" Avery pulls me off Tubs. His fingertips scratch as they clench my chin to angle my face for a better look. "First time using a magnifier?" I nod in an unintentional wink. "Believe me, that won't happen again. You won't let it." He chuckles and pats the side of my cheek with his rough hand. "And you two boys!" Avery waddles over to the leaping dogs. "Good boys!" His praises are rewarded with wet kisses and bouncing tails. "Fine work, boy," Avery nods at Tubs. "You kept your head about you."

Tubs hides his hands into his pockets to make them still. Now, his arms are shaking. He kicks at a tuft of grass. The way his shoulders are drooped, he doesn't agree with Avery. He untucks a hand from his pocket and tosses the two-toned rock that he had earlier regarded as a treasure onto the grass.

My brother places a cloth soaked in river water over my swollen eye and waits for Avery to take the dogs back to the tree before speaking.

"Your wolf is safe," he says. "Avery wanted to kill them both." My brother hands me the soggy cloth and pulls my eye open with his fingers. His face becomes a smeared watercolor. "Your eye is fine." He pushes air out of his nose, and a corner of his lip raises in a smile. "We have something in common, sister." He points to the faint, yellowish hue under his own eyes.

I smile at my brother's insight. We don't have a whole lot of memories to share yet, but we do have the beginnings of new ones.

"How is the wolf mine?" I ask.

He removes the leather strap of the tomahawk from around his waist and tugs at my frame as he buckles it snug around mine.

"Today is a day for gifts," he says. "White wolves are never seen. They belong only in legend. The ancients believe wolves are our spirit animals. They are said to be our guides or teachers. Is not the impossible possible with God? Can He not lead the wolf of your tomahawk to you?"

My brother can barely contain his excitement. My inability to meet his emotions should be maddening to him, but my blank look doesn't bother him. He's happy. *Truly* happy. And he's looking at me. *Really* looking at me. It's different from Jonathan's look at the cabin. My brother seems to have finally recognized me. Jonathan's wide eyes said he didn't. Both looks are uncomfortable. I check to be sure I still have one head. I feel over my hair. Nothing feels out of the ordinary.

"You are blessed, sister—you now have not one but *two* white wolves."

TWENTY-SEVEN

"What's this?" Avery supports his bent frame by placing his hands on his knees. He reaches out to the rock Tubs tossed.

"A dangerous distraction," Tubs mumbles. He keeps his eyes from Avery to watch my brother wrestle his arrow out of the bear.

Avery hums and flips the discarded rock over a few times in his hand. Like a tea kettle under pressure, he concentrates his breath out of the corner of his mouth while rubbing over the colors with his thumb. Avery massages the back of his neck, and with a tremoring hand, he offers the rock to Tubs.

"I don't want it. I was messing around watching that wolf and picking rocks when I should've been paying attention. If I had my gun with me, I could've…" Tubs steadies his breath to erase his emotion. "Avery, I wasn't ready with my gun. I could've gotten Izzy killed. I'm supposed to be watching her for Jonathan."

"Shoulda, coulda, woulda. You can't change the past, boy. What's done is done. All you can do is learn from it. The good news is, you just gained yourself some knowledge. You now know how to handle the same situation in the future."

Avery tosses the rock up and, in a surprisingly quick motion, snatches it in mid-air. He tosses it back and forth between his hands and holds his fists out for Tubs. "You did a fine job. Most of the holes there are from you."

I can't help it. The monster shouldn't have made me smile, but he did. There was no way for him to know which of the two guns did what damage to the bear.

They both shot the same bullets and the guns were the same model. It is a kind thing for Avery to say. It works. It soothes Tubs.

"Pick," Avery grins.

Tubs smiles and taps a hand. It is the wrong one. Avery puts his hands behind his back and shuffles the rock between them. He lets him pick again. He lets him pick until he wins.

The men go to work harvesting the bear. Nothing goes to waste out in the wilderness, whether it be a wicked wolf or a bear full of holes. The hide, Avery says, won't be fit for trading, but it will make a warm blanket for the dogs. Autumn in the north is a short season, and even though we're still far south of our final destination, snow can fall anytime in this country.

The smiles, the gentle instruction to Tubs, the rock game, and now his concern over the comfort of his dogs—I can see a glimpse of the man my brother sees.

With the she-wolf, my job was to scrape the flesh away from the hide. With the bear, Avery asks that I lay the skin fur side down in front of the dogs so they can lick it clean.

"You could hack up that meat quicker with this," Avery says to my brother as he tries to hand him his much larger knife.

"No. This bear is a gift. To honor it, I want to use the knife of my father and his father."

"Your gift almost killed the young ones." Avery lifts the bear's head and stretches out its tongue. With two hacks, it's free.

"That's right. Look!" Tubs holds out his hands for us to see. "I'm still shaking. How's that monster a gift?"

"There are other gifts besides the ones we hope for. We need to learn to look for them." My brother glances up to let me know he is directing the response to me. "We must give thanks for all things, in whatever form they come."

My brother could be offering an apology. Our reunion, he told me, was a gift he did not receive in the manner that he should have. Relinquishing the tomahawk back to its original owner was a powerful gesture. It shows he accepts me as his sister. He has chosen to love Izzy.

"We're not going to eat the tongue, are we?" Tubs asks. He saw Avery place it in a pot over the fire. He pinches his tongue between his fingers as if to protect it.

"Why not?" My brother looks up to Tubs as he makes the final cut to remove the bear's hindquarters. He shakes his head in amusement at Tubs' gesture. "Tongue is a treat Native children look forward to. We eat many parts of the bear. The heart, kidneys—all are good to eat." Tubs eyes dart over to the moist pile of organs.

"Disgusting! We're eating that, too?!"

I can't help but chuckle for my brother. Tubs is mortified.

My brother is enjoying Tubs' reactions to the unusual foods, and when our eyes catch, a small smile spreads when he's able to add another.

"The stomach is where we will store the bear's fat." My brother points with his knife to a furry pile of bodies. "The fat we will eat with our rabbit."

Tubs has nothing to say and this delights my brother even more.

"My snares will be filled with rabbits in the mornin'," Avery says. His shoulders are square with confidence. He picks up a silvery rabbit by his ears and examines my brother's catch. "Every snare but one— that's my guess. What do you say, Mikonan? A friendly wager?"

My brother shrugs. "I have two long ears and a bear. No beating that."

"Hey, now. The bear is both of ours," Avery says in a wide smile.

"No, it's mine, remember?" Tubs grins. His angel eyes are shining. He won't be corrected.

"That it is, boy." Avery winks at my brother and ruffles his hair. It's left standing on end. I have no braids today, so I try what works on Jonathan. I comb my fingers through my hair and gather it over my shoulder. He shoves his hands through his. The pieces are back where they should be. The monster makes me smile again.

"Six rabbits by mornin'. Loser cleans all tomorrow's game." Avery extends a hand. My brother accepts it and shakes.

"Better get busy sharpening your knife," my brother teases as he resumes his work on the bear. "Biis Nigig, come help. Rinse these in the river." He points to the bear's stomach and intestines. I run to the sled to put on my mittens. His brows narrow when he sees them, so I take them off.

My brother handles me differently than Jonathan does. Jonathan would've done the dirty job for me or let me rest in the library for the remainder of the day over the bear stress.

Not my brother. Every day, he pushes me beyond what I feel I'm capable of. Jonathan would be so proud. I'm still afraid, but I'm doing it. Somehow, I'm surviving all of my brother's challenges.

Today's challenge is the bear stomach. The slippery mass slips out of my hands and flops in the water like an enormous yolk.

"Why do we need the stomach again?" I ask. I claw my fingers into the stomach to gain a tighter grip on it and drown it until the water runs clean.

I can see my brother watching. I know he's hoping to catch a glimpse of the sister he knew. He examines my work and nods his approval.

"The stomach is the vessel our people have used to store fat for centuries. The fat makes the rabbit and other lean meats better for us."

My brother grins at Tubs. Mikonan is stretching out the intestines in the water and is trying to submerge them. When he gets one section under, the other side pops up. Tubs jumps in to offer his services without needing to be asked.

"This is our dinner tonight," my brother announces. "We will use the end sections and fill them with berries and river water."

"Delicious," Tubs teases. "No, really, Cook? We're eating this?" Tubs asks, standing on tiptoe in the water to hold the intestine as high above the water as he can.

"Yes," my brother smiles. He puts a finger to his lips to Avery. "Do you want to know what my Native brothers do with the rest?" He takes the opposite end of the dripping, rope-like organ from the river and walks out until it's stretched long. "Two play a game. We tie a lace in the middle and a man will stand at each end. The one to finish his side first to the tie is the winner."

"Finish first? You mean, they eat it? Raw?" Tubs is aghast and his freckled face is pinched in disgust.

"Oh—I have to see this." Avery pushes up to his feet, chuckling and massaging his dry hands the whole journey over.

"Come. Let's play." My brother lifts the intestine to his mouth. Tubs squirrels back so fast he trips over his heels and falls backward into the water with a slap.

Avery is howling in laughter, and my brother is grinning big enough to show that he does have teeth.

I don't join in the mischief of the others. I'm too busy force-feeding my cloth compress so I can search on the opposite side of the river. To keep suspicion at bay, after the fifth rinse I wring it free and fold it into a neat square and press it to my numb and still growing lids. I'm relieved the only lifeless mounds to be found stained in red are rocks.

"It's a good sign he is not there. That means he is well enough to find a good place to heal," my brother says when he checks my eye. He hums under his breath when he notices it's gotten larger. "The forest has medicine that will help." He tugs my hair. The simple action fills me with the warmth of familiarity.

After our lunch of assorted bear parts—the tongue was my favorite—my brother prepares medicine for my eye. What he doesn't have dried in his pouches, he gets fresh from the woods. Fall is a difficult time to find green leaves, especially the ones that he needs, but with diligent searching, he finds them.

My brother chews them until they are a warm mash, and the soggy goo is pressed to my eye. Miss Margaret would be mortified at the notion of saliva-infused leaves being used as medicine. But this isn't England. This is the wilderness and all of my brother's remedies have been as successful, if not more so, than the medicines at home. My hand is almost completely healed. All that remains is a thin, pink scar. After an hour, the mash has brought down the swelling enough for me to open my eye.

Avery thought it best that we stay put the rest of the day and start fresh in the morning. I think the day's trauma was only part of the reason. The other, I think, was to help sweeten his chances at winning the wager with a longer hang time for the rabbit snares.

When he checks them in the morning, he finds every trap empty except for one. It has a rabbit, so I guess it counts, but it is only a small piece. A padded foot. When Avery returns to find his skinning knife and sharpening rock at his place at breakfast, he pulls his hat down low over his eyes, and with a grumble, shoves the rabbit foot deep into his pocket. My brother tries his best to hide his smile.

Most of our time on the trail is spent in lessons. My brother is a living book. Each travel day, he shares a new chapter on how to live in untamed America. In Chapter One, my brother teaches us how to identify animal tracks. In Chapter Two, we learn how to find the animals who made them.

"Think of the woods as a home with many rooms. Each room is a different habitat for a different animal," my brother explains. "The tree is the room of the chipmunk and squirrel. A deer room," He points at hoof scratches in the dirt surrounding a mound of pine needles, "is this bed. There," he points ahead to a leafless, woven bush, "that is the room for the rabbit. Look here." My brother crouches down and points to a track. "Which animal?"

Tubs answers with excitement. "A fox!"

"Yes. He knew where the rabbit's house was, too."

The fox had broken into the rabbits' den and the front door is littered with dirt pilings, broken twigs, and tuffs of bloodied cottoned fur.

After weeks of traveling through woods speckled with needled pines and shedding trees, the world opens as we step into the sun. Just beyond wilting grasses that grow in sand, water as immense as the ocean tumbles. Avery won't go any further. He says he wants to stay with the dogs just inside the woods to keep watch.

"If an ambush is what's comin' our way, I'd say this is the perfect spot for one. We're cornered. Water to our front, forest to our back. There's nowhere to run. Better make this stop a quick one, Mikonan."

"The ocean? We walked in a circle?" Tubs asks. He drops the reins of his horse and runs towards the water. When he reaches the sand, his gait is reduced to a staggering jog. The boy would make a good sailor. He loves the water.

"We're back to where we started?" The crashing waves are loud, and I have to shout over them. I can't believe we're back to where we started over a month ago.

"I don't smell any salt," Tub hollers through cupped hands. He squats in the tide and lets the water fill his hand, and he takes a sip.

"It's fresh! Is it a freshwater ocean?"

"A lake," my brother corrects.

He binds the ankles of his horse and directs the answer to me to keep from shouting while he binds the ankles of his horse. There are no trees to tie them to, so my brother asks us to do the same to our horses. Tubs huffs from his jog up the beach and gets is successful with his binding on the first try. I finish mine but it isn't tight enough.

"Good, but we do not want him to be able to step out of it, see?" He tightens the knot in between his ankles. "I have no desire to track a horse today." He adds a braid tug for encouragement for my near-perfect attempt.

He reaches into one of the packs and tosses me a stiff fish.

"Here, leave this at the edge of the woods."

"What on earth for?" I ask. Bears have a keen sense of smell, and I have already seen how a hungry bear acts around fish.

"He has been following us all day."

"Who?" I ask and look over my brother's shoulder.

My heart flips with the question. It could be Jonathan. He, Jefferson, and Alexander were instructed to travel and keep watch behind us. Leaving a dead fish for Jonathan? Now that's just plain silly. Jonathan can't be the one my brother is speaking of.

"Your wolf," he says. He adjusts his bowstring to a more comfortable spot around his shoulder.

I scan the woods for silver-tipped snow, but like most of the creatures that live in the woods, he remains hidden from view. He didn't slip unnoticed from my brother, however. His eyes are sharp and his ears tuned. Before I was taken, was I like that? If I was, I'm certainly not that way anymore. My brother is always alert and aware of his surroundings. I get lost in thought. My brother says that's not the problem. He thinks while he's out in the woods too. The difference between my thoughts and his is that mine always turns to worry.

"Worry is heavy to carry. That's why you always have this look." He furrows his brow.

"I do?" I ask. I let my face relax and feel the tense muscles release. I watch the wind whip Tubs' hair around his face as he dodges the tide. I envy how light and full of joy he is.

"Come. There is something I must show you, but we must be quick. Tubs!" He shouts to the leaping boy as he pads towards him through the sand. "You have your gun?"

Tubs pats his pocket, his *yes* robbed by the wind. My brother must have told him to stay because Tubs shrugs and is back to teasing the waves.

"It is not too far," my brother says.

My brother takes the lead. His gait is graceful, even in the slippery sand. I use his footprints as a path, and between the resisting sand that gobbles up my steps and his longer gait, I begin to pant like one of Avery's dogs. My brother's lungs are strong. His breathing hasn't changed a bit.

Up ahead, he stops and waits for me to catch up. The water pushes past its beach confines and laps behind him with reduced energy. The lake has gobbled up the front portion of the beach, and the trees and sand that remain retreat further inland to keep out of reach. The water's hunger has created a cove; a haven from the wind. The numbing my ears suffered from the great lake's roar is now being soothed by the rhythmic reaching of the same waves. At the far end of the clearing, a small cabin sits and ten metal poles with rings are lined in rows in the center.

"Are we visiting someone?" I ask though it's clear no one could live in the cabin in its current state. The roof is collapsed, and the front door is crooked and holding on with the last of its grip to loose hinges.

Whoever lived here has long since been gone. The sun has erased the health from the log exterior, and it looks sick tucked amongst its living counterparts. A dark shadow seems to loom over the little clearing, and it reflects on my brother's face.

He grimaces at the pitiful building. If I were the rotting, little cabin, I'd be afraid of the stare and fall upon myself into rubble.

"Sister?" he asks. The sides of his jaws are pulsing. Jonathan does this when he's grinding his teeth. My brother is doing the same. He doesn't want to be here. "You do not remember this place, no?" He asks.

I walk up to the blackened poles. I shake my head no because I can't fully see it yet. The pieces I see aren't formed. They're just blurry blobs.

"This place does not own you. For that, I am thankful. Odedeyan is thankful. Gratitude. Such an unworthy offering to my brother who has provided such a priceless gift. I have been waiting for a worthy gift to give my brother in return. Helping you is part of that gift. More work today, sister. It is time to see more of your past. Together. Shall we try?" he asks.

I'm afraid to remember, but I know I need to. My brother's smile is grounding. It's similar to the secure feeling I have when Jonathan takes up my hands. He nods to the sand for us to sit.

"Waabishkaa Ma'iingan led us here. We came by dogs while you, Nimaamaa, Nimishomis, and the others came by ship."

"I remember," I tell him. "Avery was there."

I should have said Edward. I'm beginning to see Avery as my brother and Odedeyan see him. Edward and Avery are becoming different people to me, too.

"The branding. You remember this, yes?"

"Jonathan did it," I say, "but I don't know how he could have if he was with you."

"Waabishkaa Ma'iingan said he felt he should be the one to get you back. We should have waited for Odedeyan. He was on his way with our Potawatomi brothers, but we did not know this. We just knew we had to save you. Waabishkaa Ma'iingan was caught trying to take you from the branding line and White Boar was furious to see that he was out of his mask."

This is where I remember Avery—Edward—whipping into Jonathan's back. He was whipped for interfering with a White Boar product—me—and when Jonathan refused to brand us, the whipping didn't stop until he agreed to.

"Where did the marked people go?" I ask.

"To the copper mines or sent away to be sold as slaves. The poles behind us were for the unmarked—the old and sick—but there were a few exceptions."

I feel the overwhelming need to pace again. I get up and go to the water. The sky has never looked so blue. It would be hard to tell where the sky ended and the water began if it weren't for the strip of white that separated the two. It's a beautiful sight. Such a stark contrast to what I'm seeing behind my eyes. The pieces of memory that were blurred and out of focus are now clear.

"This is why I call Waabishkaa Ma'iingan my brother. I love him this way. You, sister, love him, too. How can we not love someone who has sacrificed so much?"

The poles are behind us, but I can still see them. I remember them. I can almost feel the fire that charred them. My brother steadies me when the new memory threatens to undo my knees.

"I was chained here. Nimaamaa jumped on top of me when the fire was lit."

I gasp when the rest of the memory comes. My legs won't move to run. I want them to, but they just wobble and buckle. I growl down at them. My brother says nothing and tightens his grip. I need Jonathan. I need to find him. It's an insane thought that I could find Jonathan out there in the wilderness on my own. I don't know which direction to go and I don't know where he is.

"I'm a blind, spoiled fool," I say.

I use the words as lashes from an invisible whip. I deserve more of it and wish I dare to spew out more of them. I clench my fists instead and let my nails punish my palms. My legs are beginning to feel less like noodles and more like how they should. My brother releases his hold enough for me to try them out. He's strong, healthy, and fast. He'll catch me if I try to go for Jonathan. I won't go into the woods. I'll settle for my circle.

"Izzy," my brother says. "What did I teach you?"

My brother didn't call me Biis Nigig. He didn't call me his Little Otter. He called me Izzy. I abandon my circle to drop to my knees. I hold up my hands for my brother to take. He takes them and lowers himself in front of me. My brother is my voice. He prays for me. All I can do is sob for Jonathan; the man with the scowl and the boy with the pretty green eyes who braved the flames to save me.

TWENTY-EIGHT

"Just until you are warm," my brother says, and he blows on the ember in its nest of golden grass. "Avery is right. This is a dangerous place to be, but my sister just received a powerful memory. We must get you warm so your legs can work how they should."

"I don't understand. Why? Why was I chained to the poles? Wasn't I old enough to be in the mines or strong enough for the journey over the ocean?" I hover my hand above the tiny fire of discarded twigs and branches from the lake and lower it until I can feel its sting.

My brother grabs my hand and scowls.

"I'm not afraid," I say, and I pull my hand free to rub at the mark. The need to feel its bite again is twofold: to honor Mama and to punish the painful memories.

"Mama. Jonathan couldn't save her?"

My brother digs in his pouch and pulls out a mussel shell tied with a strip of leather. His missing answer is his no.

"Why doesn't Jonathan look like me? He doesn't have any scars." I watch the golden blades of grass that resembled Mama's hair shrivel and turn black as he massages the salve on my palm.

"He has them, too. I have seen them. He showed me the wounds his first time back. My medicine did nothing to help. It was too late." My brother dips his finger in the salve and rubs it between his fingers. "Man has his limitations, but God does not. Do you know there were many blessings that day? The mask. If White Boar had not put it back on him, his face would match the rest. The branding. Waabishkaa Ma'iingan's hands would not have been able to release my sister from the chains without the branding gloves. The kick to you by the man at the fire closed your lungs so the smoke would not get in. Look and see, sister. Even amongst great evil, blessings can be found." My brother fits the shell halves back together. He asks for my finger to help tie the leather. He traps it. "Furry caterpillar." He nudges into me to play the same as Jonathan would do.

It was one of the games my brother and I used to play with a leather lace. We would race to see who would be the first to get the lace off their finger. The rule was that we could only use the hand of the trapped finger. My brother always won. He didn't play Jonathan's or Avery's way. The memory my brother helped me get back erases my need to ask the uncomfortable question I have about Mama. I watch the fire nibble at the blades of grass until they disappear. Turns out, I don't need to ask my question. The grass answers it for me.

At first, I thought the scent was the last remaining remnant of the burned grass that reminded me of Mama. Spicy and sweet, it revolts my nostrils and rivals the last scent of Mama that is now an unfortunate forever memory.

"Waabishkaa Ma'iingan let you out of his sight? It's a miracle! I guess blessings can come to us black-hearted people, too." Jared steps out from behind a pine snapping twigs and crunching pinecones with his boots. My brother untangles the bow from his arm and reaches back to his quiver for a feather-tipped arrow.

"Ah. Not so fast." Jared has one of Jonathan's guns and he spins the star. "Down with it, Cook. You didn't answer your sister's 'pole' question. You don't know, do ya?" My brother doesn't answer. He doesn't know. "It was that book's fault. The girl wouldn't let go of it. We couldn't let it get out that you Reds could be tamed and taught Christianity. I asked you nicely to hand it over." He flares his lips and hisses smoke through the gap between his new set of teeth. They are ivory gravestones with a pipe-stem pinched tightly between them.

"You handed me your axe instead—into my face, you remember that?" His salt-seasoned, sooty beard is gone, and the stubble that replaces it reveals a new portion of scar that was invisible before. It crawls down the entire length of his face down to the corner of his lip. His eyes narrow on my brother.

"Where's the old man and the boy?" Jared called Avery an old man. He doesn't know the old man is his former captain.

"No worry. We'll find them," he chuckles and kicks at a cluster of leaves with his mirror-shined boots. "I hate having to be out here in this wild filth." Jared sneers and brushes a dead leaf from the bottom of his coat. "But sometimes the path to riches is a dirty one."

Jared whistles and armed men step out from behind the trees. "Take her," he barks to the man nearest to him. "Get up, Red," he motions to my brother with his gun.

My brother doesn't move.

"I said get up!" Jared points his gun at me. My brother pushes to his feet and whistles the notes of the chickadee. "Keep an eye out for the old man. The Red just signaled."

An odoriferous man grabs me by my fur and drags me towards the beach where Tubs and the horses are. The wind has picked up. Tumbling clouds of fog are rolling across the water's surface like rising bread dough with an endless supply of yeast. I try to wriggle free, but it's not until I hear the gunshot explode from the direction where I left my brother that I find the strength I need for freedom. I let my legs give out underneath me and my fingers sink into the sand to catch myself. His grip tightens, and my coat becomes a constricting noose. I gargle for air and I don't get any until I throw a fistful of sand into his bulging eyes.

"Cook!" I rasp in between coughs.

"Izzy, run!" a voice shouts.

I stagger and sweep my hands into the sand in an attempt to get moving. My legs are robotic levers, and they pump my feet into obedience while my heart thrusts against the bones in my chest in an argument against them. The sound of exploding gunfire and screaming horses keep me from running to find him. Jonathan is here and right now hearing his voice has to be enough.

I reach my horse. His pupils pull back into his head. I step back when he rears and slices his imprisoned feet through the cloud that has crept onshore. My brother's horse has managed to run with his shackle. With remarkable speed and a silly, digging gait, he thunders forward until he is lost in a section of beach that has been gobbled up by the fog.

The most dreadful sounds are coming from my horse, and I cover my ears to drown them out. His high-pitched screams merge with the sounds of men reacting to flesh being torn by bullet or sword. I fight the urge to scream with them.

My pack is dangling off my horse's back, and I wonder how I'm going to get it without being stomped to death. I grab onto it when he's up in the air but I don't pull it free in time. He yanks me into him as his unified hooves reunite with the ground, and when the pack unexpectedly drops free, I stumble backward into a hole in the sand. I cover my head and roll into a ball like the poor centipedes I used to tease in the flower gardens back home. Sand sweeps over me like a tidal wave, and for good measure, my panicked horse kicks in the fence of driftwood that was placed artistically around the circled exterior.

This must have been the project that busied Tubs while my brother and I were gone. The wood piled onto my side slips off but the sand clings to my clothes and more of it packs under my nails as I claw my way out of the hole.

Jared hadn't seen him. He said so. Tubs' fiery hair would have been a signal flag to his whereabouts, and if he had stayed on the beach, he wouldn't have been missed. I search for the color, but it's impossible to see anything but horse bodies and men's legs. I toss my pack's strap over my neck and aim for the spot at the edge of the woods free from the clutter of battle.

Ridiculous thoughts go through my head as I scramble for the young saplings that I don't seem to be getting any closer to, like hoping it's all right to eat sand because I've swallowed at least a mouthful. The sand steals my steps, and it's not until the ground begins to feel firm under my feet that I seem to make progress.

When I crash through the adolescent trees, I get slapped by their flexible arms and wish I had a moment to spare to tie the moccasin lace that is dragging behind me like an emaciated snake. My feet were cold so Cook wrapped my feet with moss. I did a hasty job of tying my knee-high shoe. It's dragging across all kinds of sticky forest trash, and though the lace rejects the forest's offerings of spikey burrs and thorny twigs, it lassos around the plants that shed them. One of them succeeds in keeping its hold and pulls my shoe off.

Low lying branches pull at my hair and rip large pieces free from my braid while others seem to drop from unseen elevations to purposely whip me in the face. I trip on a root and fall onto my stomach. I lay there, shoe in hand, and crunch on the grit that's stuck in my teeth. As I listen, the muscles in my face pinch. It's the ugly face I get before I cry.

I crawl like a crab to get myself closer to the tree that tripped me to keep my eyes in the direction that I came from. The strap from the pack is digging into the scars on my neck but I leave it to keep my hands free to push up against the tree and get to my feet. Something is casting leaves aside to blaze a trail, and I wait before running like I want to.

Though it certainly made enough noise to be a person, it wasn't. After a few scampers, the squirrel sits on his feathery tail and chatters his displeasure at finding my presence in front of his tree. His nest is the one above my head, lined with leaves and tucked in the crook of the highest branch. I'm standing at his front door and his chirp-like barks insist that I be the one to move. I have no permanent plans to stay here, so this furry chatterbox will soon get his way.

The squirrel impatiently twitches his nose and scratches at the leaves with his needle-like nails. He squeaks an encouragement to himself to make the final push through the leaves to get past me and scurries to the far side of the tree. He digs up the trunk behind me and clings upside down above my head. He waves his tail in protest and hollers for me to leave. I would love to knock him from his perch with my pack, but I dare not move. The forest floor has yet to be still.

A fox-like version of my squirrel host leaps over the forest debris in a similar, effortless fashion. It's Tubs. He spies me and corrects his course through downed trees and saplings.

"There you are! We can't stay here. We have to get moving." Tubs snatches my arm and tugs me along on his journey further into the woods.

"We're going back. My brother, Jared shot him. And Jonathan— he's here." Determination can make the weak strong. I yank him back. My strength surprises us, and I collide him into me.

"And so is Jared. It's a war back there, Izzy! A downright war! We're not going back there. We're not," Tubs commands when I take a step away from him. "Cook's fine. I saw the whole thing. Jared—that slimy puffer-fish—serves him right to have his gun go right off in his face." I gasp and Tubs' face turns crimson. To hide it, he turns his head towards the beach. "Well, it's true. You don't remember him. I was awake those two months on the ship. I saw and heard all kinds of stories about who he is. Unfortunately for you, the snake is still fine."

"I don't care if Jared's still there. I'm not leaving them!" I don't care in the least that my demand is a shout.

"You would care if you knew what he did. The creep kicked you to get you chained up with the others. Who does that to a child and is never sorry for it?" He holds his hand out to signal me to stop talking, and he squats to the ground. He coughs into his shoulder. He's still trying to catch his breath. He listens for a moment and whispers. "You don't remember?" I shake my head no. I don't and that's a blessing. I've been around Jared. I wouldn't have been able to if I knew what he did. Did the others at the house know? Did Jonathan? I don't think he did. If Jonathan did, I don't think Jared would look as healthy as he does.

"Up until the time I had to I bolt after you, all of our men were doing fine. Someone must have messed with Jared's guns. None of theirs are working right." He coughs up his last word and turns into his shoulder to muffle the rest. "You've gotten fast. I could barely catch up." His cough leaves blood behind. I reach over to mother him but he pulls away.

"I'm fine. We have to get going." He gets up and adjusts his pack with a few jumps. "Jonathan told me I'm in charge. He told me he and the others have Jared to take care of. He said there's a cabin north of here and we're to stay only long enough to resupply. We're to meet up at the Great Water."

"How far is it? *Where* is it?" It's unimaginable for me to think that the two of us would make it anywhere alone.

"North. Jonathan said Thomas will give us directions."

"I'm not going anywhere until we see where your bleeding is coming from. You're hurt."

"I am? I don't feel anything." Tubs pats himself. His hand stops at the wet spot on his fur. He opens his coat, but his shirt is clean and intact. He doesn't want to be the one to break the silence, but it has to be. It's always him. "One of Jared's guns is working."

The blood, Tubs says, must be Jonathan's. He's the only one he spoke to at the beach. He reassures me that Jonathan looked and acted fine. He also reminds me of how mad Jonathan will be if I don't go with him. Think back to the cabin, he said. It's not the fear over Jonathan's anger that lets Tubs lead me away. It's remembering that I need to be a strong wiiwan. I won't be one if I don't keep going forward. Towards the beach, an occasional crack of gunfire can be still be heard, and I pray with each one it's from a broken gun. My heart leaps with each rustle and snap from the forest floor behind us but it sinks when I discover it isn't Jonathan.

After a day of brisk walking, we make camp and get a fire going in a hollow stump. The fire would be concealed enough to not attract attention. Tubs' skin is clammy and the corners of his lips are blue, so I wrap him in my blanket as well as his.

Neither of us has any water left. Our leather pouches are both empty and the place we were supposed to fill them was at the lake. Dinner tonight is uncooked rice and jerky.

The crushed pieces of grain are hard to swallow and they scratch going down. My back teeth are packed with them and the tip of my tongue is becoming raw from trying to push them clean. I dig out the rice with my finger and am grateful Miss Margaret isn't here to see it.

"Do you think wolves would like rice?" Tubs asks in a shiver. I haven't heard him crunch any dinner down. I look over and see his piece of birch bark is still full of the stiff grain.

I swallow my freed pieces. "I think you know the answer to that. They like meat. Little boys like you," I say in tease and I fall against his padded frame to nudge him.

"I'm in trouble then." Tubs' movements are slow. He reaches for his gun and pulls a pine branch from his bed. "We have company."

Tubs shivers from what he can see in the shadows. He drapes the branch over the stump. The fire reaches the needles and burps an explosion of hisses. For a moment, the night is gone. Pudding-thick smoke races into a night sky of the same hue. Matted in blood and illuminated in heavenly light is my white wolf.

TWENTY-NINE

I sniff my hands. They reek of the fish I left for him back at the lake. The scent must have lured him to us. He either hopes I have more or he thinks I'm a fish with legs. I reach for my piece of jerky but Tubs smacks my hand away.

"Don't feed him!" His angled brows ask if I'm crazy. "Stay still and don't move."

He pulls the gun from his belt but before he can prepare to fire, I grab his wrist. He sighs.

"He's hungry. Look at him," I say.

I feel sorry for him. The wolf's situation isn't much different from ours. He's all alone and left to fend for himself. Tubs doesn't have an ounce of pity towards him—he reminds me of the one who killed Bundle. Tubs' attempt to pull me to his side doesn't work. I still feel sorry for the wolf.

Shadows tuck in the ridges of his ribs. Even when the wolf lowers his head and growls his agreement with me, I still have no fear of him. Tubs didn't notice, nor did he care when I point out the wild canine doesn't bare his teeth like we've seen his domesticated versions do. A few of Avery's sled dogs still won't let us touch them, and they'll flash their teeth like battle-ready knights if we get too close.

"Hungry is right! It's us he wants, not that little bit of jerky!" He slaps my hand again.

"Stop!" I grit my teeth. The second smack layered on top of the first hurt. "Let's just watch him and see what he does." Tubs lets me have my way because he says I'm older and he has to. He isn't as convinced as my brother that the white wolf is mine.

I toss the jerky and the wolf paws at the chunk and flips it around in the dirt a few times before licking it up. His growl changes tone as he swallows the morsel without chewing. He licks the sides of his mouth to be thorough with the snack. He opens his jaws wide and yawns deep. The action morphs his growl to a high-pitched squeak.

"Now you did it. You gave him a little taste. Now he's going to want more. Izzy!" Tubs barks my name when I grab the gun away from him.

"Just wait a minute," I snap back.

Tubs presses his lips into a thin line, crosses his arms, and mimics the wolf's growl.

"All right, I'll give it back, but don't shoot him unless you have to."

The wolf doesn't come any closer, but he does forge a trail around our camp. He paces back and forth in a half-circle, sometimes even making it all the way around. I wonder how a half-starved creature can have so much energy.

Tubs tugs both blankets closed and balls his knees to his chest. He leaves the blankets open enough to expose the gun and the knees that are helping to balance it. He yawns without making a sound.

"Have you eaten yet?" I ask.

He shakes his head and snuggles more deeply into his wrap. "Not hungry."

Even though I insist he try to eat, he just yawns and shakes his head. I'm worried. He didn't eat this morning either.

"Get some sleep, Bartholomew. I'll watch him."

This time when I take the gun from him, it's without any arguing. He goes to bed right where he is. I tuck the blankets tightly around him and fold an extra set of my clothes to serve as a pillow.

"Still not it," he mumbles while pulling the blankets up over his nose.

"I know," I say with a kiss to the top of his head.

I tuck the gun away and wave my hands over the fire. I hover them over the flames until they tingle and sweat. When I take them away, the air kisses them cool.

"Why are you alone?" I ask. I dry my damp hands across my breeches and wait. For him to answer? I almost laugh and the feeling feels odd. It's been a while.

Without missing a step on his circular journey, my wolf turns his head towards the sound of my voice and flops his tongue out in a pant. The expression pulls the back the corners of his mouth and it looks like he's smiling. I extend my arm out towards him. He growls and freezes, and I draw my hand back. His growling stops when my hand is to my lap. He looks past me, smacks his tongue to the roof of his mouth, and resumes his cadence. His tongue slips out between his teeth when he regains his rhythm.

"Cooks says you're the ma'iingan from my tomahawk. Are you?"

My brother had taught me the name for him, and it sounds odd coming from me. When my brother speaks Ojibwe, it sounds like a beautiful song. When I use it, it feels as unnatural as the leather shoes I wore back home. I wonder if my native tongue will ever feel like my moccasins. I glance over to see if Tubs heard it. He's breathing the heavy way he does when he's asleep. I like saying the wolf's name. He shares Jonathan's Native name. I don't know what the "Waabishkaa" part of his name means but I like having an excuse to say the second part. It makes me feel closer to him.

"What are we supposed to do with you?" I ask.

His skeletal appearance concerns me as much as Tubs' coughs and skin sores. The meager rations Avery tucked in our packs were only meant for a few days. An unknown amount of days separated from Avery's well-stocked sled and a hungry wolf wasn't part of the plan for our provisions. The ma'iingan stops trotting to look behind me. He licks his mouth shut. The beginnings of a growl adjust into a whimper as he lowers his head to submit to someone—or some*thing*.

I swivel to look behind me, but the only thing I can see is a waving fern that has been coaxed into greeting by the wind.

"If you're truly hungry, you'll eat this," I say, and I use my foot to shove forward my birch bark with the rice I had left.

The wolf licks it clean but is startled when I yawn and rub at my burning eyes. The dry discomfort is more from fatigue than from the smoke that keeps blowing into them. My eyes water from the throaty stretch, and it is soothing, for a moment, so I shut them to help the tears penetrate the balls of my eyes. Each time I repeat the process, it gets harder to force them open.

The wolf scampers back to his trail with his tail tucked and resumes the rhythmic padding that has the same effect on me as Avery's violin. Before my eyes shut for the last time, I watch the wolf lie down. He balances his chin across his front legs and he kicks his rear legs out from underneath his belly.

When he's comfortable, I practice his name once more.

"Ma'iingan."

His ears twitch and his eyes twinkle in the firelight as they blink.

In the morning, our fire is just a finger of smoke, and Tubs is a shivering wool shroud. Autumn leaves shudder and glide to the ground from their weighty burdens of painted crystal. I watch a leaf coast into the pile the wolf had used as a bed. Avery had said winter can come anytime here, and this morning's frost is a warning that winter is near.

I revive the fire, and when Tubs' tremors are reduced to an occasional shiver, I leave him to search for water and to try my hand at hunting, for the first time, alone.

Deciding to leave him is difficult, but someone has to look for water and find more to eat. I don't want a repeat of last night's meal. I reassure myself as I check the gun's position in my waistband that Tubs isn't capable of its use and it's better off with me. To soothe my growing unrest at leaving him helpless, I tell myself I'll hunt only within sight of camp.

There are no signs of water in the circle I make around camp. With the toe of my moccasin, I move aside curled leaves that have been frosted by the night's breath. I uncover a bed of moss at the base of an oak. I take a seat and close my eyes. The dark is comforting to the hammering in my skull from my skipped breakfast.

I don't expect to see any deer. I didn't take the special precautions required to see them. Jonathan will change into scent-free clothes before going out, to not smell like Miss Margaret's fried potatoes or onion-rich fritters, and then after a light-footed forest entry, he'll sit near a deer run. Jonathan calls deer, "Ghosts of the Forest" because they have a keen sense of hearing and smell and are tricky to hunt. They have sound-funneling ears, moist, odor-seeking noses, and are dressed to disappear. Jonathan says they are outfitted for forest-dwelling but the trees themselves will give them away if you know what to look for. He told me that to see one, you must look at the forest horizontally and watch for movement.

I catch sight of two white branches floating among the naked trees. The buck they're attached to blends in near perfection with the drab forest around him. Regret prevents the "fever"—the feeling Jonathan describes when he sees "the big one." I never went hunting with him. Ever. I always said no. I'm able to ready the gun with ease. I curl my hand in hopes of hiding my fishy scent and wait for the owner of the rack to come into full view. I watch the buck with the reaching crown stride with ease through the forest entanglements and wish for Jonathan.

He noses through a pile of leaves and I ready the gun. It doesn't feel right, and when I try to spin the star to load the chamber, it doesn't move. I turn it over in my hands and notice an object is flattened in a piece of the gun that should be turning. My stomach muscles tighten when I realize it's a bullet. The realization that the damage could have been absorbed by Tubs causes me to shudder, and I toss the gun into the leaves.

The buck hears the disturbance in the leaves and he adjusts his ears to catch the direction. He licks his nose and his nostrils flex. He stomps his hooves into the ground and the hollow thud can be felt beneath my feet. He thrusts air out of his nose like an angry dragon and the warmth from it creates a violent cloud of steam. The noise is thunderous and I lean further into the tree, wishing my pressure could open it.

Even before his breath has a chance to be consumed by the cold, the buck leaps out of sight. In the disturbed leaves, a squirrel rushes to pack his cheeks with the acorns left behind. My body is trembling, but the rumbling in my stomach gives my hand the courage to try my aim with my axe again. After all, I am the owner of it and my brother did say I was a skilled thrower.

I steady my breath and place my hand on the handle where it feels most comfortable, with the axe's end at my wrist. I flick it with a quick motion, and when it lands, the leaves rustle as they swallow it from view.

I prepare myself for another meal of tooth-chipping rice with the trail I kick through the leaves to my tomahawk. When I pick it up, the squirrel with the rounded cheeks falls loose.

I hadn't noticed that I had company on my hunt. Perhaps it wasn't me that the buck had discovered but my starving, new friend. From somewhere behind the trees, I imagine with hungry eyes that he cheered me on, knowing his shrunken muscles had no chance with the beast. When the buck bolted, my wolf wasn't disappointed for long. Breakfast of squirrel may be a smaller morsel, but it's an easier meal to steal. I put the squirrel down to begin the cleaning. The white wolf snatches it and like a puppy with a new toy, it bounds off towards the woods. He zips away and his tail expresses his joy in the upright wag behind him.

A muffled chuckle and a chain of wet coughs cue me that Tubs, still bound in his wool cocoon, has seen it all.

"He just stole our breakfast!" I stomp. "Did you see that?! That sneaky fur ball! Bad, ma'iingan, bad!" My stomach gurgles along with my shout. The noise bounces through the forest and chases the wolf for me.

"He's hungry, too," Tubs says. For, for once, the boy is sympathetic. He looks like a fragile caterpillar in the beginning stages of rebirth with just his eyes peeking out from the blankets.

I have words I could say but I choose to hum instead. I remember Miss Margaret's reminder to reign in my tongue. My stomach is talking and it's a strange feeling. I've never felt it do this before. It rumbles long and hard until the evidence of the squirrel is wiped from my tomahawk.

The disconnected look in Tubs' eyes drives me to scrub the blade with newfound diligence and I won't stop until the metal is mirror clean. I torque the weapon with my wrist and hope the earlier throw was from the Native me and not just a lucky throw from the pampered English version. My stomach rumbles in agreement. We can't afford for it to have been.

I have never known hunger. In England, the kitchen was always open and fully stocked. Fruit in open barrels could be harvested with zero effort by just passing through the room. I enjoyed them in their original packages but loved them just as much when they were transformed into jams or desserts. Crates of carrots and potatoes were stacked high in the corners begging to be munched or thrown into stews. Miss Margaret's biscuits could always be found in a covered bowl, and a warm pot of coffee would hang above the kitchen fire from dawn until nightfall. All of it left out in the open and ready for the taking.

I poke into the fire to make it grow and press my stomach into silence with my free arm.

"Don't worry. You got one. You can get another." Tubs buries himself deeper into his blankets. "After we eat, we need to get going. We can't stay here. Jared's still out there and your Papa's waiting." The grey bundle quivers and rolls into a ball when seized by a series of wet, barking coughs.

"You're in no shape to travel, Tubs," I say, but I know he's right. Somehow, we need to keep moving.

I spend the rest of the morning gathering wood for our fire—and squirrel. Tubs' prediction was correct. I could get another. I get three more, all as easily as the first.

The smell of roasting squirrel revives Tubs enough to where he can sit up and rotate the sticks. I find the stash of handkerchiefs from home at the bottom of my pack and give them to Tubs to cough into. His hands are getting sticky from what isn't getting smeared onto his pant legs. His birch bark is getting low. I busy myself replenishing that next, though, without water to make it into tea, it's close to worthless.

My brother began treating Tubs' condition as soon as he was made aware of it. Every evening since we've been in America, my brother has made Tubs drink a medicinal tea made with birch bark. When I asked my brother if this would make him better, he didn't hum a reply. With this new symptom of coughing up blood, I understand why.

When the leather pouch is plump again, I get to work building a mobile bed. I've never built one before, but I know how it should function and what I need it to do. It needs to be comfortable for Tubs and easy for me to pull. I begin with the bed's rectangular shape. I find a tree tall enough to provide for all four sides and yet slender enough for me to handle chopping through. It's a young tree with a healthy supply of limbs that can be used as support branches for the mattress.

To fasten all the loose pieces together, vines that were once viciously laden with thorns are skinned and used as rope. A twin set of juvenile trees with a natural crook in the middle provides the perfect set of runners for the base of my bed, and once they are tied into place, I add a mattress of pine boughs.

"Ready to try it out?" I ask and step back to admire my work. It has taken me the entire day but I finished it and I managed it all on my own.

"Not bad for a girl," he teases. I help him onto the needled mattress. "And you put the branches in the right direction." He tries to smile, but his muscles form a wobbly grimace instead. "The other way and it would be a long, pokey ride." Tubs chuckles and snuggles into the nest I prepared for him and lets out a contented sigh. "It's just as comfy as Avery's."

His compliment warms me, though it fails to reach my toes. My feet are cold, and they feel like blocks of ice.

"Give the order, Master Musher, and we'll be off," I say with a wet sniff. My words form a cloud, and when I bend over to pull Tubs' adventuring rope around my waist, my face sends the white puff in dance before it dissolves. I make a swift nose swipe before I reach behind my back and wrap the rope once around my mittens.

My little friend musters up enough energy to play along and a small voice orders me to hike.

"Which way?" I ask. I don't like that I have to ask the boy at all. I don't want to disturb him, but I need to know which direction to go.

Tubs untangles himself and squints away the sun's unwelcome light, though it isn't harsh in the least, and points out the direction. The sun is low and its light is pleasant. It looks like a giant orange, and if the trees weren't in the way, I feel as though I could grab it. Just a drop of its juice would help loosen the grip my swollen tongue has on the roof of my mouth. I know Avery wouldn't approve of my decision to travel this late in the day, but I feel it's worth the risk. We can't go another day without water, and we must find this Thomas and his cabin. Tubs won't last another night out in the cold.

The load is heavy, even with a skinnier Tubs aboard. To get the sled to move, I have to run and push with my toes. It slides a few feet and takes most of my energy with it. The bed isn't moving as easily as I thought it would. I struggle with the bed for a few tugged steps more and drop the rope with a grumble. I step out of it and kick it. The leaves scatter but the rope barely shudders. All my frustration went into the gnarled root hidden under the leaves. My jaw-clenched growl scatters my ma'iingan who was watching from a tree infested with mushrooms.

The white wolf circles and trots up behind the sled while I rock and hold my toes intact until the pain subsides. I pick up an acorn and throw it at him as if making him disappear again would do the same to me. When the tears fall, great pressure is relieved, and I don't want to stop. My face is drenched, and not wanting to wear snot on my sleeve for the rest of the journey, I use a leaf but all it does is smear wet around.

What if I was *supposed* to burn? I should have. I should be with Mama. I pull my thumbs free and clench my fists in my mittens. Why me? Why am I here and not Mama? I growl again and I let it turn into a scream. This time it is directed at Edward for hurting Jonathan, to White Boar for hurting me, and to the bed when I see the tired little body on top of it. The sight pulls sobs out of me. He's going to leave me and I can't let him. The journey ahead is too great to do on my own. I lay on the ground and plan on never getting up again until my bundle stirs and calls my name. I've frightened him, and it makes me feel a kinship with White Boar that I didn't think possible. I am a loathsome, selfish creature and I hate myself for it.

THIRTY

"Going forward, no matter how small the step, is how you do it," Avery had said when I asked him how we were going to make the daunting journey to Papa. We had stopped multiple times that first day, and I remember Tubs' growing frustration.

"If every day's going to be like this, we'll never get there." Tubs refastened the dropped pack back onto the horse and took his anger out on the strap. He had pulled it too tight and the horse swung around and knocked Tubs to the ground with his strong backside.

Avery laughed, undaunted by the day's trials. "Overcomin' obstacles is part of the journey, boy. You travel by puttin' one foot in front of the other, and you tackle problems that come the same way; one at a time to the best of your ability." He helped Tubs up and brushed him off. "A sour attitude clouds judgment and just adds opportunity for more calamity. Don't know 'bout you, boy, but I like to keep my calamities to a minimum if I can help it."

Tubs shuffled off to the sled without another word. When we had to stop to clear a twig from a horse's hoof, he remained quiet and helped keep the horse still.

"Izzy?" Tubs' arm is raised. Our last clean cloth is hanging limply from his hand.

When I try to take it, the buoy under the blanket keeps hold and even summons enough energy for a giggle. He pulls the blanket down to reveal an eye.

"Good thing we got one left. Your face is nasty."

I snatch it and nudge the mound with a *thank you, James,* even though I feel his care for me is undeserved.

I harvest the mushroom tree before reattaching myself to the sled and then, like I did a lifetime ago in England on our first adventure together, I pick a spot. A conjoined tree with two trunks is my first goal of the day.

My wolf didn't take offense to the acorn I whirled at him when I threw my fit, and at a safe distance, he trots behind. Without stopping, I free a handful of green leaves from the only healthy tree in a forest of brown. I pop a couple in my mouth for moisture and drop one for my ma'iingan. He sniffs at it. It sticks to his nose when he looks up to see where I am. He shakes his head and scrapes it off with an oversized paw.

A blue jay screeches the late hour. Winged forms, void of color from the coming night, take heed of the warning and coast to their nests for the night. The woodland floor bustles with its activity a little while longer as squirrels abandon their hunt for food and run for their tree-top homes that will soon be lit by lamps of starlight.

A decaying oak missing all of its branches is my last goal tree of the day. It looks like one of Miss Margaret's sewing needles. The forest is hushed now that the bed is no longer plowing through its rubble.

A distant tapping pauses my nightly camp set up. I twirl like a minute hand to determine its direction. It was a different sound from the *rat-a-tat-tat* I've been hearing all day from the woodpeckers. It is a knocking sound with rhythm. I head off in the direction I think it's coming from with Tubs in tow, and as the sound grows, the delicious, comforting scent of fire strengthens. The scent holds hostage any thoughts of danger and forces me forward with hopes that it's Jonathan, my brother, or any of the men from our two traveling parties.

A large man with a fur hat as large and obnoxious as Mrs. Fredrick's is spotlighted by the light of a single window. A robust fire is lighting his work. The small cabin that it belongs to is crouched behind him in the dark. The leaves rustle behind me and the sound of running fades away. My ma'iingan must have seen the two dangling wolf carcasses hanging from one of the trees.

Tubs wakes in a fit of coughs and this stops the man mid-swing. The woodsman twists in our direction with axe still raised. The tail from his hat bounces over his shoulder like a women's braid.

"Who's there?" He hollers into the dark.

"Isabelle Gudwyne, Sir." My voice sounds small following his booming one. My face is prickling with heat. I feel foolish about giving him my name. I could have given him Agnes' name and I'm sure it wouldn't have made any difference. "My friend is sick and he needs shelter," I add. I scrunch my toes until they cramp to keep from crying. I pray that this man is a kind and merciful one and hope I haven't made a grave mistake.

"Gudwyne you say?" He lowers his axe. "Come closer," he asks.

I step into the light.

He gets a good look at me and hums. He can't possibly recognize me. I don't know him. The man hammers his axe into the balancing log. It splits in half and tumbles off the stump table, but the axe remains lodged. He makes his way towards me, much like the black bears back at the river, lumbering and heavy-footed. The Goliath-frame cloaked in shadow frightens me and having nowhere to go, I back into the bed. The back of my calves collide into it and I lose my balance. I fall on top of Tubs. He lets out a moan but doesn't kick me off.

"You said 'he.' Who's with you?" He bends over Tubs and lifts the edge of the blanket so he can get a better look.

"Well, I'll be. It's a boy." Without another word, he reaches down and cradles Tubs in his long arms. "Come. Follow me."

He kicks at the cabin's door with a fur-wrapped foot, and though much force was being used, the fluff absorbs most of it and the sound is reduced to a soft thump. The man rushes past the person who opens it and lays Tubs on a bed in the corner of the cabin.

"Boil some water for tea. These young-ins need warming up." He instructs a wide-eyed girl with strange markings on her chin.

She brushes aside a ratted section of hair and rushes to the kitchen portion of the cabin, and with swift hands, she dips a ladle into a bucket of water. She fills a copper kettle that teeters at the top of a stack of dirty dishes and hangs it on a hook in the fireplace.

The girl dips the ladle back into the bucket and with a hand underneath to catch the drips, she brings it to my lips.

She doesn't watch where the ladle lands. It hits me in the nose and most of the water spills down my neck. She's immersed in the activity at the bed and the unbundling of Tubs.

"What's wrong with him?" He asks. "He's mighty pale. My lands, look at those freckles, Maddie!" He removes Tubs' shoes and covers him with a heavy blanket.

"He's sick," I answer. I don't need to tell him how bad Tubs is. The man sees the dried blood smeared down his chin.

"The Red Cough?" He asks. My nod drains his face as pale as Tubs.

The girl takes notice that the ladle is empty and when she returns with another, I stop her.

"Please, the boy."

Her skirt swishes to a stop and it exposes child-sized boots. Her eyes finally see me. A droplet from the ladle slips into her waiting hand and like a witch's potion, it transforms her delicate features. Her lips purse and the bridge of her nose folds in a deep wrinkle. Like the hottest part of a fire, her blue eyes blaze and match the inked lines under her lips. The white near her temples and thin fan of wrinkles at the outer corners of her eyes tell me she isn't a girl at all, but a woman of at least thirty.

She changes course and rustles over to Tubs and lifts his head to guide the ladle to his lips. At first, a stream of water trickles down the side of his mouth, but with Maddie's careful guiding, the remaining water manages to get into Tubs.

The woman grabs the man's shirt sleeve and yanks him down until his ear is to her lips. She whispers and his eyes dart over to me. He scratches at his head but the itch isn't reached. His hat is still on his head. He pulls it off and fumbles it in his large hands. His black hair is a fright. Spiked and standing on end, he looks like Percy, the black cat that lives in the stables at home. I tried many times to catch that cat and give him a good brushing the same as I did for Rosemary, but I could never catch him. He'd watch me with those sharp, green eyes and the slightest movement towards him would send him racing to the rafters. He would lick his fur from the safety of his perch in an attempt to fix his disorderly hair on his own.

The man combs his fingers through his hair and parts his lips as if to speak. He shuts them and averts his eyes to the floor as if in search of the lost words.

"Please, sit. We'll…" Maddie throws the ladle into the water bucket and the violent splash interrupts the fumbling giant. "…*I'll* get you something to eat. Name is Thomas. Thomas Coley. This is my wife, Maddie."

He fills two plates from the pot over the fire. Thomas places a plate of stewed meat and cooked potatoes in front of me and hands his wife the other. He takes his place behind his wife and squeezes her shoulder as she scatters the food with her fork. A potato falls onto her lap. She picks it up and throws it back onto the plate, and the shoulder squeeze becomes a massage.

Maddie mashes the vegetables with the back of a fork and she feeds Tubs the soft mash. His eyes are closed but his mouth opens after each bite like a baby bird ready for more. In between forkfuls, Maddie smooths back Tubs' curls with her fingers.

Without taking her gaze from Tubs, she speaks in a guarded tone. "Get your fill and warm yourself up, girl. When you're done, I want you out of my house. The boy is free to stay." She gets up and moistens a cloth with the water she tips from the kettle and lays it on Tubs' forehead. "You hear me, girl?"

Her eyes look like my china doll's eyes—the doll that I never played with that sits on a chair in the corner of my room. My doll at least smiled with her empty, glazed stare.

"Maddie, please...." Thomas interrupts.

"Please, nothin' Thomas." Her controlled tone raises to a shout. "I will not have a savage in my home." Her lip trembles. Thomas pulls her to him.

"She's Jonathan's girl. We can't turn her out." He buries her small frame in his arms and whispers words that I can't hear into her hair.

She sniffs and studies me from over Thomas's bent arm. She shakes her head and buries it deep into his chest.

"No matter. She is who she is. You know I can't have her here!"

"I know, I know." He soothes her with sways and pets to her wild locks. He presses his lips in apology. "I have a shed out back that I store all my furs and traps in. When you're done here, we'll get you settled there for the night. You'll be plenty warm out there." He offers a faint smile of reassurance. I have a feeling the last part was added more for himself than for me.

I push away from the table and stand by the door. I don't want to stay where I'm not welcome. I'm making the woman miserable, and I know too well what that feels like.

"I'm ready. Just, please, take care of Tubs. He needs his tea."

"Birch bark, I know." Maddie backs out of her husband's embrace and takes down a jar from the kitchen shelf.

"I know all about your kind and their remedies." She stomps over to me with the jar of birch bark clutched in her hand. Her grip is so tight, her marbled knuckles look as if they could pierce through her skin.

"Maddie!" Thomas rushes over to grab her raised arm, and for a moment, she's motionless. Her eyes are as wild as her hair, and as they sweep over me, I can feel energy building. Like a loaded wind-up toy, she slams the jar down, and with as much momentum as she can muster, she swings. With the same intensity of the shattering glass, her hand explodes across my face.

THIRTY-ONE

Thomas opens the door to the shed, but he doesn't step inside. He reaches in with the lantern to show me inside. A frog blinks away the unwelcome light from his winter home in the moss tucked between the logs. Its skin is as green and lumpy as a walnut with its summer shell.

I had missed this year's walnut harvest. By now, the cellar floor should be full of the drying nuts and the room's air spiced with their sharp scent. I try to picture Miss Margaret in her old apron, the one with the tulip-fabric patch. She wore it every year when she shelled walnuts. She called it "walnut birthing" for it was hard work coaxing the tender folds of nut out of their protective wombs even with a hammer. I remember how in years past she would sweat with the work it would take to muscle her way through the blackened layers. I look hard at my memory, but I can't see her eyes. My heart sinks when I realize I don't remember their color.

The lamp's power to reveal the mystery of my sleeping quarters is hindered by a wall of hanging hoops. All its energy is concentrated on illuminating furs that are stretched tightly on handmade frames made of willow. Thomas moves enough of them to make an opening. Behind the hoops is another layer of obstruction. Thomas sweeps his arm into a

a curtain of hanging traps and holds them aside. Shadows lurch from the deadly chimes. They're ghosts of the creatures that were trapped in life. They flee into the dark corners of the room.

With a nod, he encourages me to pass. "Be mindful," he says.

I hunch through and collide into the back wall of the shed. On my knees, I massage my head.

"You were told to be mindful." He drops down an armload of wolf pelts and apologizes for my tight sleeping quarters. "Just until I can reason with her," he reassures. "I'll get through to her. She's a hard-headed little thing, but she's got a heart. I remember her from before. She wasn't always like this." His mouth pulls and it elongates his face even more. "The soft part of my Maddie is still there. I'm certain of it. You saw the way she looked at the boy." Though not stated as a question, it was meant as one, and he waits for my response.

"I did," I say as I feel the throbbing spot for a lump. It matches the side of my face that pulses from her slap. She has a heart, but Thomas is wrong. It's as black as the squirrels my brother and I scorched those dinners ago when the trees outside were dressed in the color of the cheeses that age alongside the Gudwyne walnuts.

"I never should have brought her here," he says. "It's my fault she's this way. I've been meaning to get her—us—back to England, but it costs. I got a good start here with these pelts but I have quite a way to go. Got me two more just the other day. Thinkin' I might need to expand out a bit. You comfortable—warm enough—get enough to eat?"

No, I'm not comfortable. But I don't tell him that. This place smells like a wet animal, like a million Rosemary's left out in the rain. The pelts have their heads still on, and their eyes, void as a starless universe, have a consuming grip. They tell me what I already know— that he's going to leave me out here in the dark. I loosen my fur to get air. Like that blister on the side of my smallest toe that has come and gone and come back again, the irritating weight in my chest is back.

Thomas reaches outside for the lantern to see if I had received his pelts with a soft hand. I had, and while I smooth one over me, I force my eyes to glean from the direct light. I don't shut them until they water and are blinded white. I let my fingertips roam in the soft fur. They remind me of the backs of Bundle's ears. This is as fine a place as any to stay in. A clink of the chain that Thomas' shoulder nudges into reminds me of where I could be instead.

"Thank you. Tubs and I both appreciate your hospitality."

"Tubs!" Thomas says with a snort. "That's some name! It isn't his real one, is it?"

I don't answer. I can't summon the will because I fear I may never know.

"Your Tubs will be taken care of, I promise."

I can't see his face because the light I had stolen from the lantern is in the way. But I can see his fingers disappear in his beard in his hesitation to leave. The way he rubs his beard is the same way Jonathan runs his hand through his hair.

"You'll be good and warm, Miss." He clears his throat as if the action could force himself into belief.

"Sir, the lantern. Will you leave it?" I ask. I shift my position to my other hip and the pelts beneath me bunch into a ball beneath my leg.

"Sorry, Miss. I can't do that. These pelts are the path to bring my Maddie back, and I can't risk a fire in here. Besides, it's a full moon tonight. That should be all the light you need." He nods towards the rectangular window near the roof and tosses my bag on top of the deflated wolf pack.

As the door clicks shut, I hug my pack and squeeze my eyes closed. I watch the ball of light I had taken from the lantern fade into the dark. When I open them, I blow out a breath. Though not as penetrating as Thomas' lantern or as comforting as a fire, the moon does provide enough light to see by. My awkward giggle stirs the silence. I, Isabelle Elizabeth Gudwyne, the girl with the flame-pierced skin and eyes of crimson, miss fire.

I didn't get a chance to eat any of the mad woman's dinner, so the mushrooms at the top of my pack are a welcome sight. Just underneath the soft caps, I can feel Mama's Bible. With a mouthful of mushroom, I give up reading after trying to sound out a handful of the nonsensical words with too many vowels. I fan through the book instead and breathe in deep the scent of Mama. The pages stop falling in the center of the book, and Tubs' note stands erect like a knight's banner.

I had forgotten to read it. To snuff out the guilt, I reason that there hasn't been enough time. Fingers don't bend well in the cold, and it takes a bit of tugging to get the stiff paper to unfold.

There aren't any words to puzzle through in the light that is almost too dim to read by. It's mostly pictures and a few letters in a child's unsteady penmanship.

He had drawn a picture of me reading to Rosemary. I can tell it's me from the bare feet and exposed ankles. An eavesdropping Tubs with a head full of corkscrew shapes for curls is raking hay in the stable. The note simply reads "I" with a lopsided heart filled with ink, followed by the letter "u". The unsteady signature that follows fills my limbs with the humming energy of a busy hive. It reveals the reason why my young friend has been so impatient with our game. He had wanted me to know his name months ago, the day I was handed the note at the gathering when my world began to unravel.

Overcome by the buzzing in my ears, I wade through the hanging debris until the joints in my fingers crack against the door. I fumble with the handle, but the door refuses to give, even after I slam my good side against it. Thomas locked me in. I pound until the flesh on my clenched fists is numb and I scream for Tubs until my throat burns. Regret fingers through pages of memory and realization point to the stables where I would read to Rosemary. Tubs was always around to listen. He loved hearing me read to her because he couldn't.

I wave my hand through the beam of light and watch the dust particles twirl in a frenzied dance. The frog has pushed his way through the moss during the night, and the morning ray that speaks warmth offers none.

I warm the insides of my mittens with a huff before putting them back on. Last night I had fallen asleep looking at Tubs' letter. When I woke in the night with iced hands, I chose to tuck them under my arms rather than fully wake and search for my mittens. I rip one of them off when I discover the frog's new living quarters.

"They aren't too far ahead. Just a day, so expect me in two."

I crawl to the peephole and see both Thomas and Maddie. He has his wife's tangled mane in his hands. He lets the knotted mass slip over his fingers before he pulls her to him. Together they sway, and they communicate this way until the horse next to them snorts its impatience. He kisses the top of her head before he pulls away from her.

"I know this is difficult for you, but please, feed the girl and keep her alive. She's no use to us dead."

Maddie tugs her coat tighter around her neck and drops her face into it. She nods once to acknowledge him and balances on tiptoe to reach for a final kiss.

It's not until the beam of light disappears that she comes to the trapper shed. She doesn't have food in her hand, but a gun instead. One of Jonathan's. His guns seem to be everywhere.

"I'm not afraid to use this." Her threat has no energy, and her eyes are swollen and red. "Get up."

Her voice is similar to Ms. Abernathy's—pixie-like and sweet. It doesn't match her hard exterior. I dress her in one of my gowns from home, the yellow one with the cap sleeves and high waist. With the aid of a brush and a soaking bath, she'd be a stunning beauty. The angry brow and the twisting clicks of the star encourage me to my feet.

Breakfast is on the table, though the sun says it's past noon. She motions for me to sit. The oatmeal is cold and stiff, but I eat it as if it were the eggs and biscuits of home.

Maddie tucks the gun in the waist of her skirt and takes the chair next to Tubs. The room is heavy with the vibrations of a mother's yearning, and she combs his curls back the same way she had done the night before.

"He's dying," she says.

"He'll be fine," I reassure *her* to reassure myself. "He just needs rest."

The oatmeal isn't settling well. His motionless body is telling me I'm wrong.

"I don't like you here." She labors on each word. "But I won't be able to live with myself if I don't let you see him—to say goodbye." This time when our eyes meet, the eyes that had once flamed with disconnected hate now burn with regret. "I know what it's like. I never got to. Come," she beckons.

Last night, I would have done anything to be near him. Now that I'm here, I feel I'm close enough. I'm afraid of Tubs' stillness. I don't know this quiet stranger.

"Please. Come." This time, the spoken word transforms her features. She offers her open hand as a peace offering.

I accept the chair near Tubs and fold my hands on my lap to keep from touching him. His face is as milky-white as the bed pillow. It's the pale universe to the galaxy of freckles that sparks my heart into recognition. This silent boy is no stranger. This porcelain child, who exceeds the beauty of the cherubs on my library ceiling, is my beloved friend.

"Go ahead, take his hand. He'd like that." Her tone is soft, but her face is etched with struggle. It's taking work for her to sound this way.

I take his hand in mine. He responds to my touch and his chilly fingers bend over my knuckles.

"You bear the mark," she says.

She can see Edward's dragon brand. I had put my hair in a bun last night. She exhales and turns to the kitchen to begin the chores that haven't been done in weeks.

"The one who took me had the same—but his was burned onto his arm." She works to free a dripping plate from its aged dinner layer and forces a misplaced giggle. "We're mirror images of each other, Isabelle Gudwyne."

She shakes her head and tsks. I straighten at the noise. Is it because she has something in common with a Red or is it meant for the fossilized conditions of her dishes?

"I was taken just like you, but the Red who took me didn't treat me as nicely as I'm sure Jonathan treated you." She itches her nose with the back of her wrist. "Thomas and I gave up years of our lives for them, and without a flinch, they do this to us." She sounds another misplaced chuckle for the memories only she can see. She doesn't move for the longest time. I think she has fallen asleep standing. She wakes when the dish slips from her hand and sloshes in the water. The plate becomes her focus and she digs at it with the tip of a spoon.

"While I was gone, my son became sick. Thomas tried everything he could. He tried every remedy out in these woods but nothing could fix him. That filthy Red kept me from my boy." She thrusts the plate underwater and the water waves over the edge. She holds it there, much like I had done with the bear stomach as if to drown it clean. She falls asleep again, with her eyes open. I cough and shuffle my feet. She wakes and seems startled that I'm here. Her nostrils flex but a soothing breath relaxes them when she sees Tubs.

"My husband has been stationed on this trap line for more years than I care to count. Jonathan planted us here to be a beacon—a lighthouse—for any survivors of White Boar. A place to resupply. It's been a noble cause but it's one that has come with a heavy price."

"Jonathan—have you seen him?" I ask. Ready to meet this woman halfway towards peace.

"He had a delivery this past spring. Saw him then." She wipes her forehead with the back of her hand before reaching for the next plate that's fuzzy with mold, "He said one more trip. This must be it. Looks like you're the last."

Tubs stirs and Maddie's brow narrows. She fills a skillet with glowing embers and places the covered pan underneath the blankets at his feet.

"Thomas wants us to return to England, to start over and forget this place. But leaving here would be leaving my boy. I don't think I can do that." She glances at the door before tucking the blankets tighter around Tubs.

"Your son," I ask. "How old was he?" I don't ask where he is. I know where he is. He's gone. Tubs will join him soon. Will I mourn as Maddie? Will I ever wake from the pain of losing him?

"About his age. He was a sweet boy—curious—energetic. He loved it here." The corners of her lips raise from the memory, but they fall back to their sorrowed position at another.

"I was feeding the dogs when the men and 'The One Who Took Me' came back from hunting. That's my name for him. Thomas changes it up when he talks of him and adds a 'you' at the end." Maddie chuckles without a smile. I give a weak one, too, because she laughed.

"The One Who Took Me came back empty-handed. He was an awful hunter, but we gained a deer after he promised to loan me out. I don't know for sure, but I saw him point me out to another…" Her sentence winds down like the exhausted lights in Jonathan's cellar. She tucks a wad of frizzy hair behind her ear while her tongue sweeps into the bend of her parted lips. "It was a dry summer. Like this one past and all the animals, predators especially were agitated and on edge. The wolves. They came into camp. In the daylight. Terrified mothers shielded their screaming children. The chaos and the cries were perfect for my escape. While the men battled, I ran." Maddie is held captive by the memory. The only part of her body that seems to have permission to move is her lips.

"I ran into the woods and didn't stop—not even at night to sleep. I followed the river, just as Thomas had always told me to do if I were to ever get lost. 'Follow the river,' he said, 'It always leads somewhere.' It wasn't until I heard Thomas' axe that I knew I had made it home. It was like I had reached the shores of heaven. That is until I heard my baby was gone."

She's asleep again. She goes to the shelf of remedies where the birch bark was once tucked. She reaches for a jar and empties some of the dried ingredients into her palm. Her cupped hand hovers near her chin, but before the medicine has a chance to make it to her lips, she wakes. She brushes it into the dishwater, and with sobbing gasps, she shakes the jar's contents into the same water.

After the episode passes, she looks around in wild realization and whispers just loud enough for me to hear.

"I can't." As the words purge from her throat, Tubs jolts upright. His lips are as pale as the moon. The unexpected action and his unearthly look startle both of us.

"Papa!" He cries. "The wolves are coming and Izzy's outside!"

Tubs whimpers as he kicks and pulls at the blankets. Maddie rushes over to help me keep him in bed.

"Tubs, here I am. I'm here." To force the direction of his gaze, I frame his face with my hands. Translucent eyes the color of a turbulent sea separate me from him.

"Papa, please! We have to get her inside!" His chest heaves against my own as I hold him close.

Why the wolves? Did he hear Maddie's story in his sleep? Or maybe it was my sleeping arrangements outside away from him. Whatever the cause, I should have the power to bring peace to him, but my attempts only make him struggle harder. He moans with the effort it takes to stretch his arms past me. His fingers fan through the air for grip as he reaches with longing towards the door. I look to Maddie for help. She nods with understanding and asks permission with a raised brow to sit next to him. I slide down enough to give her room but stay with him by resting my hands on his legs.

"Shhh, sweet boy. Your Izzy's here. She's safe." Maddie smooths Tubs' damp hair back with her hands. She cradles his face in her hands and smiles. It's the first true smile I've seen her shine.

"Mama?" His drenched eyes lock onto her in the hope that what she speaks is truth. "Izzy's safe?"

Maddie sighs at the name he called her and she holds him close. She comforts him with a kiss to the forehead and a lullaby of hushes. She's rocking him. It's a breathtaking scene. A picture of love, loss, and healing. Her touch calms him and his eyes regain their depth. This time when he looks at me, recognition shines through the fog. He exhales in relief.

"Did we make it? Did I get you home?" He allows Maddie to lay him down and he closes his eyes in contentment.

I avoid the truth and answer the only way I know that will not shatter his heart.

"Rest, Tubs. Please," I beg.

He opens his eyes and notices Maddie. "Is this your Mama?" he asks. His outburst has depleted his energy and he now reaches a new shade of pale.

"No, Tubs. She's a friend," I answer. I have his iced hands between mine, but it's more for the touch than to try to bring his circulation back into them. My hands are always cold and will be of no help to him that way. I hope there are no more questions. I can't tell him I'll be alone when he leaves and that I'm nowhere near home.

"I'm tired," he whispers.

I swallow the urge to cry. I don't want him to go. I rub his hands between mine before I wrap them snugly between my laced fingers. I secure the grip as if I had any power to keep him here.

"Did I do good? Getting you home?" He tries to summon the strength to smile, but his lips can only tremble.

"You did. No one could have done better." I kiss his bloodless cheek and lay next to him. "I love you, *Jonathan*," I say, as I put my arms around him and hold him tight. The burden of regret threatens to pull me from him to take to me to places where I failed him. I hold him tighter. "I've never told you and I'm sorry."

"You finally read it." A tear disappears into a damp curl.

"Yes, I did and it's a fine name. It fits you." I dry the moist trail on his cheek with my thumb. My dear sweet Tubs shares the same qualities as his namesake.

"You love him too, don't you?" he asks. He opens his eyes and forces a snicker. "I know you do. You're going to tell him when you see him, aren't you?"

Why is everyone so certain about the way I feel toward Jonathan except me? How can I give the man my top three most difficult words to speak when I'm not even sure yet? Tubs is the first person that I've ever uttered the words to. Let's say Tubs is right and I do love Jonathan. How on earth will I ever tell him?

"Read to me?" He asks.

I look to Maddie. With her apron balled in her fists, she shakes her head and shrugs.

"Read from your Mama's Bible. I know you remember how," he whispers into his pillow.

I ask Maddie to get it from my pack. I open to the center of the Bible where I had returned Tubs' letter. I look over the foreign words and work on sounding out the vowels and letters. Maddie frees her apron long enough to pull out one of the kitchen chairs but once seated, her hand seizes the material up again. I can't do this. She gives me a nod of encouragement to keep trying. I sound out another word. It's a struggle, but through the stammering, I think I can hear my brother.

"Izzy, you read just as pretty as Cook." Tubs' compliment is sweet. It isn't as pretty as my brother's. It is choppy and rough. I work until I read an entire Psalm. I close the book to free my hands. I want to hold him, but he shakes his head, "No, please. Don't stop."

I read until his chest rises for the last time and the last bit of warmth leaves his body.

I kiss him goodbye and the tip of my nose is moistened by the sweat of his laboring. My sweet little friend has gone home without me. I'm all alone.

THIRTY-TWO

It was Miss Margaret's song. She used to sing it to me back when healing burns made sleeping difficult. The melody was her own, but she told me she borrowed the words from King David. It was in the style of the Irish folksongs she would hum around the house. Most of them made me want to try her high-stepping dance, but this one made me feel as if I were swaying in a cradle. When she sang, I could see the emerald green fields of the childhood home she sometimes talked about. In my sleepless dream, cottoned sheep with lowered heads munched in time to the sorrowful swing of her notes, and sleepy lambs nuzzled through the grass with searching noses, the same way Miss Margaret's fingertips massaged through what was left of my hair.

Give ear to my prayer, O God
Attend unto me and hear me
My heart is sore pained
With fear and trembling

Oh, that I had wings like a dove!
I would fly away
I would fly away
I would fly away

If I had wings of a dove!
Unto Thee will I cry, O Lord;
Hear my voice when I cry unto thee.
Thy face, Lord, I seek
In my hour of need, O, Cradle me 'neath thy wings.
Comfort my soul
Comfort my soul
Comfort my soul
'Neath your wings, Lord, comfort my soul.

I stir from a sudden chill, and a blanket slips from my shoulders. I had fallen asleep at the table. While I slept, the air had grown heavy with moisture from the drying floorboards and bed linens. The hanging material rustles, shuddering from the door's unwelcome breeze as the cold mingles with the room's damp discomfort. Maddie must have made another quick exit and left the door open. She's been making frequent trips outside to relieve her stomach.

"I'm sorry. I thought I shut the door. Did the cold wake you?" Maddie thumps the toes of her boots against the threshold before coming in. She hangs the lantern back on its hook and shuts the door with her foot. Hunched in shiver with her arms wrapped around her, she shuffles to the kitchen to get some water. She sips from the ladle and grimaces.

"You need to drink it all, Maddie," I instruct. "It's snowing?" Gloppy flakes are clinging to her shoulders and hair. Their existence is brief; in moments they're transformed into smears of wet.

"Pretty hard," she says. She gulps down the rest of the water. The fluid immediately causes havoc to her stomach and she leans to her knees. "I hope it stays down this time. I don't want to go back out there." Her gaze reverts to the developing puddle underneath her boots. "I'm glad the snow held off for as long as it did." She stands upright while smoothing back wet pieces of hair from her face and checks me with a glance to see how I took her last statement.

"You need to lay down," I tell her. The floor's wet has chilled my feet, so I dry their undersides on my pant legs before pulling on my moccasins. "Do you have mint?"

When she nods, I look through her remedy shelf until I find its jar.

It was sunset when we finished burying Tubs. We laid him to rest next to her son, amongst pencil-straight pines, and beneath what Maddie says come summer will be a canopy of ferns. The clouds were swollen and inked, like the heart Tubs colored for me. They looked like harmless grumps. The clouds coasted in a sky of the same colors that gave my sleeping friend his supernatural quality back at the castle cellar.

I sniff the inside of the jar and the scent softens the jarring thought of a life without Tubs. My tongue curls against the roof of my mouth in anticipation of the treat Miss Margaret and I would make in winter. The hard-boiled sugar looked like thick shards of glass when it was cooled and broken into pieces. The first time we made them, I crunched down on one and the hard candy packed into my teeth. For a frightening moment, my teeth stuck together in a glued clench, until my jaw popped them apart. Miss Margaret told me I had missed the joy in the candy and that I was supposed to let it dissolve in my mouth. I followed her instructions the next time and was delighted to find that after the harsh candy's exterior melted, it relinquished the best part of the candy, a mint leaf.

"A lovely note to my nose just as your voice is to my ears," I sigh. The delicious memory doesn't last as long as the candy. A growing ache within turns it sour. I inhale the jar's perfume again and pretend it had just been filled with the hard candy of home.

"Pardon?" Maddie takes a seat with her brush and gathers a handful of ratted hair to work on. She brushes the ends into her palm before working her way up.

"I heard you sing." I pull down a teacup from its shelf home and drop in two leaves.

"Make two cups," she says. She hisses the 's' and scrunches her nose after a pained tug. "You were dreaming. I don't sing."

While Maddie works on her hair, I play a game with my tea. I try to hold my breath as long as the leaves are held under with my spoon. I never win. It's a tie every time. When Maddie nears the back of her head, where the knots are at their thickest, I offer my help.

"May I?" I ask.

She studies me and wrestles for an answer. She slides the brush across the table and takes interest in her mint leaves.

"You know you can't stay," she says with a stir to her cup. Captivated by the twirling leaves, she places her hands on her lap to watch.

"I know. When I'm finished, I'll sleep in the shed."

The brush is useless against the aggressive state of her hair. I pull a section apart and find the reason. Briers are working in clusters as natural hairpins to keep her hair in an eternal knot.

"No, I didn't mean that. We're beyond that, wouldn't you say?" She nods to the gun that's hanging next to the lantern. She takes up her cup and poises it for a sip. "I meant, you can go." She sips with the same face I have made many times before with the same drink. She leans over the table until the tea settles. "Not that I was ever holding you here anyway. You could have left anytime you wanted," she chuckles.

She was right. I could have. Her head has been to her knees for most of the night. She says the posture helps ease her rolling stomach.

I've never seen anyone vomit so much. It's like her body is trying to rid itself of the medicine she has been taking. Puking aside, even when she had the gun, she wasn't a threat. It was obvious to me the moment I saw her twist the loading star, she didn't have a clue as to what to do next.

"You're still here for the same reason I'm still here," she says looking towards the empty bed. "It's to be near him. But, he's gone. They're gone. The boys aren't here—not anymore." Her eyes are bagged and swollen from the cleansing trips outside, and they still have their unhealthy look from earlier, but they can see.

Maddie explains in between tiny sips of tea that Jared had come through two days before and offered a handsome price for my return. Thomas had told Maddie I was to be their shortcut to England.

"Why didn't Thomas take me with him?" I ask. It seemed to me to be a waste of provisions and time for Thomas to go for Jared without me.

She tips her cup and plays with the sip that's left inside. "He should have. That doesn't make sense." The portion escapes past the leaves and puddles onto the table. She absorbs it with her apron and her mouth parts in realization. "Unless he didn't go for him." She looks about the tidy room and down at her hands, which are still pink from their scrubbing. Her face brightens. "He's bought time—for both of us." The vigor she had during our cabin clean-up returns, and in haste, she gathers our cups and puts them in the empty washbasin.

"There's much we must do. We have to get you ready," she says in gasps, but her skirt swishes to a stop when she sees her reflection in the blackened window. "But it's night." She seems confused by the time of day and she shakes her head in frustration.

"You need your rest. Don't worry, I'll see to it you're on your way at first light. You can take the bed." I open my mouth to object, but she holds her hand up to stop me. "I'll be fine on the floor. My Thomas is a big man. I find myself more often than not sleeping on the floor and then sneaking back before he wakes."

She makes her way to the door to gather the wolf pelts from the shed but pauses when she sees me fiddling with the tassel on my moccasin. The bed is a barren, naked reminder of who's missing. Stripped void of its coverings, the bed is nothing but a skeleton and can offer no more comfort than a bed of bones.

"We can both sleep on the floor," she says, and before she leaves she presses her lips together. It's as close to a smile as she can muster.

Sleep finds Maddie, but it avoids me. The bed tucked in shadow is the elixir that keeps me awake, along with the lingering odor of the mint tea. Damp rooms hold onto their scents, so I press my nose into the fur to keep the smell from penetrating. I pretend the slumbered breath coming from the lump of fur next to me is Tubs, but I stop because it hurts. If it wasn't for the sheep and the cradle's sway, I never would have found sleep.

Fear not, for I am with thee,
Do not be dismayed for I am thy God
I will help thee,
I will uphold thee,
Child, on my strong wings I shall mount you up!
I will strengthen thee,
I will strengthen thee,
I will strengthen thee,

Child, fearless and mighty with me you shall be.

The subtle rustle of pages wakes me. Maddie has a book propped on her chest. She must not have slept long, because it's still dark.

"I thought you didn't have a Bible," I say with a yawn.

"Never said that I didn't. I didn't give you mine because I made a promise to Tubs—that I would let you try to read from yours." She closes the cover and wipes it with her hand. "I've been away too long. I've been lost, but I've been shown the way back." Maddie props herself up on an elbow and pulls a fur closer. She smiles and leans in towards me. "Much like the Ash Princess. Have you heard of her?" Maddie rubs at the markings on her chin. I would say by the way the firelight is dancing on her fair skin that she's the princess she's so eager to speak about. The inked lines that can sustain a lifetime of rubs no longer look savage but ornamental, like pieces of jewelry.

"Thomas can understand them and he says they all ask the same question. And it doesn't matter which, the ones living here or the ones just passing through on their way to your father. They all ask it. 'Have you seen the Ash Princess?'"

"I haven't heard my brother speak of her," I say. Curious, I lean on my own elbow and mirror her. "Truth or legend?" I ask.

"Listen to the story and you tell me." She tucks a smooth strand of hair behind her ears and snuggles deeper into the furs. "I've heard it enough times to know it word for word. I hope I do the legend justice." She clears her throat and her eyes widen. Mine feel wide, too. My brother says our people write nothing down. Stories are passed down from generation to generation by mouth. Maddie is helping pass down the tradition. Word for word or not, she's bringing great honor to my people. My grin is an encouragement to her. With a great inhale, Maddie repeats the old tale.

"In the midst of the Great War between the Wolf and the Boar, the claws of the black wolf and the grey fought against the ivory tusks of the gluttonous pig. The once fertile soil that the boars had ravaged turned red with blood from the pawed creatures as well as the hooved. A chief prayed to the Eagle for help. His once-peaceful paradise was now shriveled brown; the music of the forest was choked silent and replaced with the howls and grunts of warring.

"Peace between the two beasts, and his forest's return, is what he longed for. While his heart was lifted to the Eagle, and his ears plugged with sounds of battle, a boar crept past and found a prize among him. The chief's eyes were blinded by the tears of great sorrow he had shed over his fallen allies. He didn't see that White Boar, the grandest of the boars, had entered his wigwam and had stolen his only daughter.

"The princess was the guardian of the light of the black wolf and the grey. White Boar greatly desired her light, though the boars had possession of their own. They were selfish, greedy, and ravenous. They wanted both. When the princess refused to give up the light, both were given to the fire to do with them as it wished.

"Fire was different back in the days of the Great War. It gave great heat, but it had no light of its own. The flames consumed the girl and in moments, she was reduced to ash. The light it swallowed changed the fire's form forever.

"Though he lost much, the chief kept faith in the Eagle and continued to send up his prayers. The Eagle heard and had mercy on the great leader. He sent a white wolf to bring the girl back from the Great Beyond. With the touch of the wolf's great paw, the girl rose out of the ashes a woman—a mighty warrior armed with a copper axe.

"Gifted with claws of copper and teeth of iron, the black wolf and the grey call him 'White Wolf'; for he is the greatest of them all with the power over flame and ash."

She reaches into a basket and holds out her hand to show me a cluster of tiny pine cones. She tosses them in the fire and the flames around them turn blue. I gasp with delight. She grins. She's pleased by my reaction.

"Your people say the Eagle in the story created White Wolf to be the princess's forever guardian and companion for as long as her earthly journey lasts. A romantic notion, wouldn't you say?" She snickers. I give her one back. I find it funny that the legends of my people aren't much different from the stories I heard back home.

"Thomas says the Natives are eager for the day when White Wolf and the Ash Princess will return to them and present their two gifts. The first is the gift of freedom from the white man's chains through the power of fire and the might of axe. The second is a book the Great Spirit forged from the light meant for your people." Madeline clicks out a tune with her tongue. "So, what do you think? Truth or legend?"

"Surely legend," I say with a chuckle. A princess who rises from the dead and a wolf who can control fire? It's an outlandish tale from an imaginative mind just like the ones back in the library. "It's a great story, though."

"It is a great story. It's yours." Maddie throws aside the furs and twists her hair up into a bun. She cups it in her hand to hold its shape while she fishes through a bowl on the bedside table. When it's pinned in place, she makes her way to the kitchen.

"Mine?" I can't get free from the pelts. I'm having to beat through them like a hatchling.

"Yes. You're the one they're waiting for. You have the axe..."

"Tomahawk," I correct with an aggressive tug to Thomas' prized pelts.

"The book...your Mama's Bible; and the White Wolf...you must see that!" She grins at my inability to see the comparisons and adds a laugh for my fur entrapment. I do indeed have all of them but my ma'iingan—how could she know about him? "Come, we have much to do. There are many miles left for you to travel."

"I'm not her. I'm no princess and I'm certainly not a warrior. I'm just—me." Hearing the words out loud is a reminder of what I'm not. I do know what I'm *going* to be. I'm going to be a huge disappointment to my people and my father.

Maddie puffs noise through her lips. "You're much stronger than you give yourself credit for, Isabelle Gudwyne."

Thomas and Maddie have hiding places all over the little cabin. She's pulling food from places other than cabinets. Bags are under the floorboards, the bed, and on nails hanging in dark places in the ceiling. By the time my pack is bulging with shape, our reflections are gone from the windows and the world is beginning to wake in shades of grey.

"You must stay away from the eastern trail where Thomas and Jared are. Follow the pointing trees on the western trail instead." Maddie's steamed breath points the way towards a cluster of birch trees. "They were made to bend by the ancients and they will direct you. They will take you to where the land ends. When you see the Great Water, cross it. It should be frozen enough for you to cross on foot. Once you cross, have faith; your people will find you. And, Isabelle, one last thing…" She lifts my fur to check for my tomahawk's presence. "I must warn you. The western route is a dangerous trail. It belongs to them. If they don't recognize you as the Princess, they'll recognize the mark of White Boar. Keep it exposed. It's the common ground you have with them. It should keep you safe, but be ready for any action that you may need to take."

"Them?" I ask.

"The tribe of The One Who Took Me. Potawatomi," she says. She tugs my coat closed and helps secure the enclosures.

Potawatomi. Gikto's people. No wonder Papa wants me to marry him. Mikonan told me I have white blood as well as the blood of my people. I can see now why my brother said my union with Gikto will be valuable. It will strengthen ties with the Ojibwe but it's also to help mend relations with the white man. Maddie's mistreatment by The One Who Took Me reveals how strained the relations are between the white man and the Potawatomi. The new realization feels like the shackles I wore on the ship. How can I refuse Gikto now?

Once I pass her inspection, she follows me out to the sled where she fastens Tubs' pack with my own. His, too, is swollen with provisions, and both packs promise to provide enough food to fund my solo journey for months. It would be easy to pretend Tubs isn't gone. His pack is here. I can even see him bounding through the forest, leaping over limbs and scuttling over logs on his way back from some adventure. Maddie doesn't say anything as I watch for him. She understands. How many times has she done the same? I miss Tubs. It's a yearning that makes my body feel sick. The journeying I have left is making the sickness worse. How am I to do this alone?

Folded in neat bundles next to our packs are the wolf pelts from the shed. Maddie asks me to wait as she ducks back inside the house. She returns with the handmade bedcovering that covered Tubs. It's dry from its washing last night, and I can feel its warmth from the fire through my mittens.

"I made this when I found out that Thomas and I were going to have a child. I made it for our boy, Seth."

The name shrouded in cobwebs grinds out of her throat like rusted metal. She pulls at the corner of a loose nail and exhales. When she looks up, I notice the doll-like stare is gone. Eyes that once kept me at a distance with the help of an herb-pierced spear now pull me close.

"I'd like you to have it. Consider it a gift for the Ash Princess." The corners of her mouth tremble before they stretch into a smile.

I hug her goodbye and kiss her on the cheek. She returns the kiss. My, how people can change. Just yesterday she couldn't tolerate my presence. Thomas will be pleased when he returns home. His Maddie has returned, and it didn't take a trip across the ocean to find her.

THIRTY- THREE

The snow is clinging to the trees in clumps. The world is heavy with cotton. The trees are unhappy with last night's snowfall, and with encouragement from the wind, they shake off their unwanted coats. My moccasins and sled leave behind a wet trail in their discards, and as the length of my trail grows, so does my fear. If Thomas doesn't keep Jared from back-tracking, this will be as obvious a trail marker as the crooked trees I follow.

It's foggy and difficult to see. The fog is eerie. My hood is down and the icy fingers of morning are adding to the anxious prickles on the back of my neck. The snap of a twig proves that the eyes I feel *do* exist behind the ghostly trees outlined in mist. My wolf friend is back. He follows behind just within sight in the gray haze. Besides the phantom eyes, he is my only company and it brings me at least a crumb of comfort.

I walk until the arches of my feet throb. The entire day has passed and I only stopped once to dig out a piece of Maddie's hardtack to nibble on.

At camp, I ignore my wolf's hesitant steps towards the fire and keep my attention at my feet and the growing mound of slushed, dirty snow. I scare him when I come back with an arm-load of pine boughs. The waving branches send him scurrying past the fire's reach, and a frightened hop is added when I drop them on the spot I had cleared. When my activity settles,
he crawls back to me on his belly; close enough that I can reach out and touch him.

In a swift movement, he snatches one of my mittens and shakes it the same way he shook the fish at the river. He tosses it in the air and when it lands at his feet, he crouches behind it and waits for my reaction. Avery's warning keeps me still. The wolf could snap off my hand as fast as he had picked up my mitten.

The white wolf tires of waiting for me and he pulls in his panting tongue. He snatches the mitten again and pulls at it with his great teeth. When he's satisfied with the size of the hole, he proudly lets it dangle from a tooth before tossing it back into the air. This time it lands farther from him, and I feel confident enough to take it.

"Do you want it?" I ask. I shake the matted mitten before I toss it over his head. He twists and his lanky legs throw chunks of mud and slush.

He returns in a muffled pant. His tongue ejects the mitten and with his monster claws, he digs it into the ground. Satisfied with the mess he has made with it, he steps back and sits.

"You destroyed my mitten!" I laugh. It was like popping a yeast bubble in a rising loaf of bread. The laughter relieves some of the tension that's been growing in my chest. "Can I have it?"

My fingers brush against the wet mass before he snatches it. I scream in surprise and then am lost in laughter when the tossed mitten flops into my face.

"Disgusting!" I shriek while rubbing my face free of slobber. "But thanks for giving it back." I put it on the end of a stick to let it dry over the fire in hopes of salvaging it. I'll have to mend it somehow; these mittens are my only pair.

"Are you hungry?" I ask. "I think I have something better in here than that mitten."

I fish around in my pack for the dried meat Maddie had packed. I throw him a piece, and instead of running off to eat it alone, he lays and tucks it between his paws.

The day is fading, and for the first time in months, I'm homesick. At home, it would be time for tea. Jonathan would be coming in from the snowy outside and hopefully would have wiped his feet well before traipsing on Miss Margaret's clean floors. I'd be waiting in the seat farthest from the fireplace to win another of our games, and maybe Evolyn's ring would be on my finger. After dinner, we'd have our Bible reading. I stare with longing past the fire and see him. As he bends to read, he swipes the hair from his eyes. I strain to hear his voice, but all is quiet besides the licking coming from my ma'iingan who is still relishing his treat.

I remember my own Bible and tug it from the confines of my pack. I read aloud to my wolf until the forest is settled in silken black; all the while, missing the man who daily fed me from it and the boy who gave me the courage to glean from it on my own.

It's snowing again, and flakes are landing on my exposed nose and cheeks. They melt and run down my face like cold tears and I wipe them away along with the warm ones. I'm near sleep when I feel a nudge against my back. I hear a squeaked yawn before a contented exhale.

The eyes I had felt in yesterday's fog are real. I catch fleeting glimpses of child-sized figures with dark features darting between the trees. Only one child is brave enough to be seen; a whistling girl with swinging braids that collide into her waist with every hop. Following behind with long, confident strides is a man with a bow threaded over a shoulder thickened by fur.

My wolf doesn't seem to be bothered by the dark strangers. He follows behind the sled in a horse-like trot. My feelings are his opposite and my pulse quickens when I think of what they did to Maddie. If they try to take me, what can I do? I have my tomahawk. Would I be able to use it against them? It's silly to act like they're not here. There's no point in prolonging the inevitable. Knowing someone has to be first, I pull out my tomahawk and face the pair.

"Do you speak English?" I ask.

They don't. The man eyes me with a look that's as sharp as an arrow's tip. The little girl, however, smiles with her eyes, and with hands covering her mouth to hold back a fit of giggles, she steps out of the woods. Bobbing against the top of her thighs are a pair of caramel-colored mittens. She lifts them over her head and takes them off their strapped tether. Unafraid, she holds them out to me as an offering.

Arming myself was the wrong decision and the man responds by positioning an arrow in his bow. I am no match for this man who looks like a cold version of my brother. I kneel and lay my weapon between us. This encourages the little girl to approach and she looks from me to my tomahawk with wide-eyed wonder. She drops the mittens at my feet and scurries to hide behind the thin-lipped man with the stern face. Without a sound, he motions with his weapon towards the sled.

"Book," he grunts.

"So you do speak English," I say.

"Book," he insists louder. He tucks back the bow but he keeps the arrow in his fist.

The only book I have is Mama's Bible. He allows me to go to my pack, but it's under a watchful eye. When the book is exposed, he's in front of me in two giant leaps.

"Book," he barks holding out his free hand. The little girl shifts her large spooled eyes from me to the raised hand with the clutched arrow.

He lets the pages fall past his thumb and with the arrow still in hand he crumples the pages into a mound as he leafs through them. He pauses on a page and struggles in a whisper to pronounce a word. His brow narrows deeper with every fumble. He growls in frustration and slams the Bible into the slush and the book pages feather into the snow.

The little girl scrambles after it and picks it up by the spine. She brushes off the clinging snow and turns a limp page. She searches the words with her finger. She picks one and her expression turns to sorrow when after several attempts, she can't make it out.

The little girl forces a smile and returns the book to me. She nods to the mittens to encourage me to take them up. I do. She takes hold of the man's hand and tickles it with the tip of her braid. His eyes narrow at her, but her added giggle causes the corner of his almost invisible lip to twitch. They converse in front of me in a language different from the one Cook had begun to teach me. Her influence encourages him to tuck away his weapon but he continues to hold his ground.

It's been an awkward day of travel with my bare hand tucked under my arm for warmth. I huff into the mittens before pulling them on and the inside layer of rabbit fur comforts the hand that had become red with cold. This gift has fulfilled a great need and somehow this little girl was aware of it. Perhaps she was one of the pairs of eyes that I had felt watching through the mist.

"Thank you," I say. I speak nothing more for our languages are too far apart.

With a nod and a raise of a hand, I let him know that I have understood him and I replace my tomahawk in its belt. Without looking back, I resume my trek. The little songbird resumes her notes. Distance softens them into a soft lullaby. My ma'iingan is choosing to travel closer to me now. I let my mitten brush across his back.

The cold is too bitter to be traveling with a bare head. A gnarled tree was one of my goal spots. A bird whisks to safety with manic pumps to its wings when I pass. My heart is thrust into my throat. I'm startled more by what I discover when I tug at my hood. The fur rests high on my neck and even with my hair in its English bun, my neck's brand hasn't been exposed at all. The Potawatomi pair recognized me as the Ash Princess and let me pass.

THIRTY - FOUR

The cave that ma'iingan and I discover brings back the memory.

The lost page of my childhood is returned to me on an unseen current as swift as the one that had brought in the torrent of storm clouds overhead. The sky has become an ocean of turbulent gray, and the clouds in them race past like battle-ready ships.

I remember reaching for the dandelion's yellow top with my toes. My brother called me his "little otter" and laughed when I plucked the flower free. The English dress my mother had me wear was itchy, and I distracted myself by letting the grass tickle the bottoms of my feet. I was little and I shouldn't have taken much room but with help from the full-bodied skirt, I consumed my brother's lap.

"Mikonan!" My laughter and his name came out in staggered breaths as he bounced me on his knee. I bobbled and the earth moved with me. His moccasins were muddy from the morning's hunt and as I watched them dance, I remember thinking how silly his boy's feet looked trouncing around underneath my fancy fabric.

It was my birthday and Papa said we could celebrate the day in Mama's customs. My first cake was baking in a pot over the fire and the smell was making me impatient. To help me pass the time, my brother shared an ancient story from the time before Mama and Grandpapa. A time when my brother andPapa believed in spirits and monsters. It was a story that Papa, Mama, or Grandpapa would not have approved of.

My ma'iingan sniffs the air before taking sure strides inside. The cave is empty. I make camp outside even though the cave promises to offer as much comfort as any cabin. It's been weeks since I was with Maddie, and my body craves any covering other than furs. My brother hadn't meant it to, but the tale he shared for entertainment scared me, and now the fresh memory of my childhood keeps me out in the cold. My brother's story may be a tale for the fireside, for big brothers to tease their little sisters, but I've learned many things on this journey. I choose to sleep outside because I believe even the tallest of legends can contain a grain of truth.

I brush the snow from the cave's doorway before piling down every fur from the sled for my sleeping cocoon. I tuck my fingers in my palms and squeeze them tightly to try to force warmth into them. Working with my hands is uncomfortable. Even handling soft things like pelts and blankets brings about a strange, prickling pain. Yesterday my fingers were itchy; today they're numb and patched with white. Avery had warned me against frostbite. Frustrated I didn't think of it sooner, I double up on my mittens and wear my damaged pair underneath my gifted pair.

My snow-water isn't ready, and I haven't had anything to drink since breakfast. I shove a handful of snow into my mouth. It makes me shiver, and I remind myself not to do that again, no matter how thirsty I get. While I wait for the pot of snow to melt over the fire, I chew on my frozen strands of hair and hate on winter.

Winter is no longer my favorite season. Gone are the feelings of an enchanted world covered in sugar and whipped egg whites. It's a time of runny noses, numb limbs, and a consuming cold that fire cannot reach.

The Wendigo of my brother's tale thrived in winter. Perhaps because it no longer lived. The dead are already cold. At the fire that day, my brother had told me the Wendigo was a skeletal creature whose hunger could never be quenched. It was once a man, he said, cursed to a monster's form for committing the unthinkable—feasting on the flesh of his kind. I tighten my hood against the invasive thoughts of the forbidden story. My rhythmic breathing replaces the ear-stuffing silence of the forest, but the tale is not so easily thwarted.

Nature sleeps, the legend says because it fears the Wendigo. I have noticed the trees seem to be nothing more than barren sticks. Their feathered companions that once flitted about their leafy arms in musical conversation have left for nests hidden in secret places. The nails of the scampering pests have also gone silent. All seem to play into my brother's story. Even the air itself portrays a character, as an ally of the Wendigo who threatens to snuff life out of those who dare wander in it. It's sharp with ice. With every inhale, my nostrils stick together.

Like the storm that swells above, so does the fear of my wandering this frozen wasteland alone. I try to gather courage from my ma'iingan, who appears content in the isolating cold. He seems unfazed by the world's desolate appearance. He doesn't even seem to mind his new harness.

Not willing to succumb to the wooing's of the cave, my wolf only allows his tail inside. He blinks at me and licks his nose. His ears twitch, and the short-howled bark he sounds is a reminder for me to take my tomahawk out. He gives the all-clear when he rests his chin on his legs. I reach out and scratch the bridge of his nose and he nuzzles my hand. His chin is still sticky from yesterday's honey.

"I'm sorry about the harness, but I need you. I can't pull anymore," I say. "May I, dear sir, remark how handsome you look in your leather vest?"

His ears telescope in my direction at the compliment.

Yesterday, we had come across a trapper's cache, a box made of logs that looked like a miniature cabin for a forest troll. I knew what it was because Avery had them in strategic places on his trail laden with extra traps and supplies. This one was his, too. I know this because a dragon was burned to the outside, which matched the dragon Edward had burned into my skin.

There is an unwritten law amongst trappers. They are willing to share, but no one takes anything for free. If you take an item from a fellow trapper's box, out of courtesy you must leave something behind. The box was Avery's musher cache. I took the harness and line that was inside and left my hairpins and a pelt for trade. Rules are rules and they must be obeyed. New friends, even if they were once enemies, are included in the un`written law.

It took me an entire jar of honey and most of the hardtack Maddie packed to entice my ma'iingan into his harness. I waited until his tongue went into a smacking frenzy before I tried putting it on. At my first attempt, he nipped me. It didn't hurt, and he hadn't meant for it to. He was just as nervous and afraid as I was. When he saw the harness was harmless, he let me tighten the straps. I wonder whether he would have cooperated if he hadn't been given a belly full of nectar. The way he hovers like a furred Miss Margaret makes me believe he understands my body is weakening and my ailments are growing.

I coax my ma'iingan over to me with a soft tone and he responds by crawling over and cuddling into my back. My neck makes the odd popping sound I have become accustomed to when I look back at him. I'm not Dr. Batchford, so I can only assume that it's from the long days of looking down at my feet and not up at the trail ahead.

My scars have also become a problem. The skin on my damaged arm fits more tightly than the rest. The muscles beneath don't have the range of movement that I have in my other arm. I was told by Dr. Batchford to never baby my arm and to exercise it daily, even if doing so is painful. If I failed to follow these instructions, he warned, I could risk it freezing. Miss Margaret had made sure I stretched it every morning and it had always been part of my morning routine right before the washbasin. But that was before when I was a slug. Now I'm nothing but active. My arm's pain and further decline can't be from underuse but the long days of travel and daily work for survival.

A layer of snow has formed over my pelts and I feel ridiculous not utilizing the cave. I've come across the first decent shelter in weeks and here I lay, huddled outside underneath the clouds' spigot acting like the little girl on my brother's knee.

"There are no bones, are there, Ma'iingan?" I wrestle off my blankets with wild kicks and my wolf stands to his feet in curiosity. He eyes me with a jeweled stare when I grab the pine-knot torch I keep within reach near all my fires and stomp into the cave with it once it's lit. "You know the story, don't you? You wouldn't have come in here if there were any."

My ma'iingan whimpers his reply.

"Just you wait, dear brother." I thrust the torch into all its corners and find it's the same clear as it was earlier. "Papa isn't going to be the one to deal with you; I am." I grumble a few more threats to my absent brother as I shake my things free from snow and move them inside.

According to my brother's fearful tale, Wendigos sleep in caves on beds of discarded bones. "There is no bed, brother, because Wendigos don't exist."

I hear his response, for I had said the same thing to him that day. "Something like it, Little Otter, must exist for the story to have been born—yes?" he had said with a tug to my braid. "Perhaps, little sister, *I* am one."

My brother curled his lips to bare his teeth and roared. He had looked frightening, but I knew I could do better. I copied but I felt my growl was fiercer.

"No, *I* am!" I giggled. I remember chasing my brother around the fire snapping my jaws until Mama scolded us both.

The fire and the snow outside are horizontal. To keep the fire strong against the angry forces of wind and snow, I toss four logs in. The wind is wicked, and it threatens to steal what I haven't been able to wrestle inside. The sled is the last to be brought in and my ma'iingan takes it upon himself to try to pull the line with his teeth. He digs at the dropped line with a paw.

"You want to try to pull?" I shout. He doesn't hear me. *I* can't even hear me. Without a struggle, he lets me put the rope around his neck, and through the blinding snow, he pulls the sled into the cave while I push from behind.

"Good, ma'iingan!" I praise. He is rewarded with a kiss to the forehead and a vigorous scratch behind the ears.

"Good, indeed," I hear.

I trip over one of the sled's runners in my haste to face the voice. Both my ma'iingan and I are on all fours in front of a dark shadow. Its girth blocks out the fire behind it but one simple step forward brings a corner of light to the beast. It's wearing clothes, tattered ones, and loose articles rumple about the figure like the dancing arms of an octopus until it's safe inside from the wind.

My ma'iingan lowers his head and sneers at our surprise guest. The bridge of his nose creases in a wrinkle as he pulls back his lips to expose a gummed armory of ivory. With a wet growl, he charges towards the creature.

A gunshot echoes through the cave and my white wolf is thrown back. The creature's arms reach out for me, and I swing my tomahawk to discourage it from coming any closer. The sharp blow I receive to my head spirals me into a jumbled, dream-like state. I'm asleep but somehow I know I shouldn't be.

The creature's face is grey but over its nose and cheeks, it wears the mask of a raw wound. Frostbite has painted the portion purple and crimson but the dying tissue on the tip of its nose forces the colors into black. Grotesque eyes tinted in yellow peer over cheekbones that no longer have the flesh to plump them. This creature would fit the description of my brother's Wendigo if it weren't for the porcelain teeth.

"I got one more shot," Jared spits as he clicks back the hammer of his black-powdered pistol. His speech is garbled and wet, and spray from it lands on top of the frozen dribble on his beard. "I can either finish him off or use it on you. Matters none to me."

He twists his face to adjust the bobbing dentures while waving the gun back and forth between me and my ma'iingan. Jared had shot ma'iingan—where, I can't tell—but it's bad enough to keep him panting in the corner. I see my swing had been true. My tomahawk had done damage to Jared's stomach. The pressure he's using with his arm isn't working. The red stain is growing.

"Tie the beast outside," he commands.

"He stays where he is," I tell him. I scan the cave for my tomahawk. It's between us. I creep up to standing and plan to reach for it, but the cave begins to tilt. I fall against the leaning wall and reach up to touch the throbbing spot on my head. My fingers are wet with blood.

"Try that again," he says with a point of his gun, "and I *will* shoot. But *who* I choose is my seee-cret," he grins and shushes me with a dirty finger. Blood thinned by saliva veils over his dentures from gums puffed with scarlet blisters. The sight makes my knees weak. He kicks the tomahawk further away.

"Got food?" He digs around in my pack until he finds the leftover rabbit from lunch. He spits his dentures to the ground and stuffs the pieces in. He grimaces when he tries to gum them. He swallows the pieces whole instead.

"You know that rabbit won't help. You're a dead man. You have scurvy," I say. I don't have any of the oranges that my brother said were given to the men aboard ship to keep scurvy away, but I do have some uncooked rabbit livers. My brother says those have the same healing effects as the citrus.

Jared laughs when I make the suggestion. "I'm done with raw meat. Ah, this rabbit tastes a whole mite better than a man does." He licks his fingers and chuckles. His lizard eyes water in the delight he takes from his humor. He notices my horror and huffs with a smile. "Ate more than one." He reports the news as if he had consumed something as common as chicken. "The one with the gun has all the power."

He dreamily examines another piece of the rabbit before popping it into his mouth. He mumbles past the meat. "I had ten men. Ten men, mind you, back at the beach. Plenty to do a little mining and enough to bring a nice little harvest back to England. But thanks to Gudwyne, most of 'em were killed. Crafty boy—he rigged the guns. I should've known—they were his. Four of my men survived and got away with me. They were mighty helpful, I must say." He chuckles again and scratches at his face. The blood from his nails leaves a smeared trail behind. "Didn't want to waste my last two shots on huntin', so..." He licks his lips and pats the midsection of his bloodsoaked shirt, looking much like a molting lizard who's been stomped on. "…need I say more? My men have served me well."

"How were you able to get on the trail?" I ask, shocked the stern-faced Native let him pass.

"Out of fearful respect. They remember what happened to them— what the white man can do." Jared stands and rubs his hands before smacking them together. "Pack this stuff up. We're going to see your Papa. I'm gettin' my copper."

"Now?! In this storm?"

"I have to get you to the chief first. Jonathan and that savage brother of yours are still lurking out there."

I push myself off the wall to show him I have the strength to fight him. "You're going to have to use that last shot. I'm not going with you."

Jared cocks his head and squints. "My, my, looks like you *are* back. At home I got a glimpse; now I see she's here to stay." He lifts his arm to check his wound and his sleeve hangs heavy with blood. "Fainting days behind ya now, are they?" He spits onto the ground and dries his lips with the back of his hand. He snarls when he sees the red left behind. "Fine. I'll be honored to forever snuff those flames out of your eyes. I'll shoot you, pack you up on the sled and eat you next. Papa will get ya back as a bag of bones."

He smiles and bends a finger towards the trigger of his raised gun. I straighten at the moment of clarity washing over me just before the gun powder ignites. Jared was one of Avery's men. That's why my father wanted him here. He knew greed would overrule his common sense. God would take care of him, my brother said. God would invoke justice, and he used his creation to do it. Jared has been reduced to a Wendigo and his slow death is an ugly and gruesome one. For me, it'll be different. It'll be at rest with Mama, Grandpapa, and the God that I've grown to love. It's not at all scary and awful like I had once thought.

I brace for impact, but nothing comes. The smell of sulfur is in the air, but it's without the damaging sphere. Jared's eyes are wide with surprise—not from my lack of injury but the wound in his neck. He tries to form words but the only sound released is a series of wet gargles. In the front of his neck, the triangular stone of an arrow juts out. Jared falls to his knees, and he gropes for the shaft that's jutting out from the back of his neck. In his struggle, his cracked lips contort. Moments after the muscles have formed them, a word bubbles out from his swollen lips.

"Red."

His shoulders heave in an attempt to laugh, but before the sound has a chance to escape, he falls forward like a downed tree.

A young man with a turban of fur enters the cave while a bear with a man's legs drags Jared's body out to a large fire that lies beyond my own. Jared's fate is to be that of every Wendigo. My ma'iingan sways on his feet and takes a few unsteady steps before bolting out the cave opening past the two men.

"Princess." The young man lowers himself to bow. It's done in an awkward motion, and he teeters before his hands steady him. "We found you. Did the Wendigo hurt you?"

"No, I'm fine." I check my head again. Still wet. "Please. Don't call me that. I'm not the princess."

"Heck if you aren't." The bear ducks in the cave and pushes back his head. My heart does a strange leap. Avery winks with a grin as large as his face.

"We heard the Ash Princess was on the trail. Heard Jared was sniffin' around, too. Looks like we found you just in time."

"Jonathan. How is he?" I ask.

I wince when Avery presses too hard on the top of my head. He holds his hands up in apology and lets me take over applying pressure. The man warming his hands at the fire is Gikto, the man who is to be my husband. Why, oh why, didn't Jonathan come to me instead?

"He was shot. But don't worry, Mikonan was patchin' him up when I left. He looked to be all right to me. He talked to me, Izzy," Avery grins. "I'm a blubberin' old fool. I'm excited because my boy said words to me. Civil ones, at that. He wanted my help. *Mine.* Imagine that."

The cold has shrunken my fingers. When I arrange pelts for the men to sit on, my ring slips off. It lands near Avery. He picks it up and twists it around his bent fingers. He sighs at the reunion and falls heavy on the pelts.

"My boy gave you her ring?" He hands it back and mutters under his breath. "Looks like I didn't help much at all now, did I? Might have even made things worse." Avery shuts his eyes to hide from the man at the fire.

I put the ring back on with the same care that Jonathan had used when he put it on me.

"Things are pretty messed up, Avery, and I don't have a clue as to what to do."

"All I know is what my boy said. Get Gikto—tell Izzy," Avery says. He looks confused. He leans forward and rakes his hands through his hair. He leaves them there and tugs. "He said you need to try. You got my boy's ring. I don't think you want to try." He pulls his hands down his face when he looks up to me. His hair isn't in his eyes like Jonathan's. It's standing on end. The men have so many differences, yet there are traces of similarity in each.

"I don't," I say.

I remember Gikto and I quickly add an apology. I don't want to offend him or make him angry. I may not have a choice to marry him. According to my brother, peace brides aren't given a choice. My brother isn't here to help with another option like he said he would be. My time to work my way to Jonathan may have worn down.

"It does not matter what you or I want. It is what our fathers want." The boy shrugs. "Matters none to me. I have no one, but I know the princess does. I know the legend. Waabishkaa Ma'iingan is said to be your guardian until death. Why is this no longer so?"

"Waabishkaa. The first part of Jonathan's name," I ask. "What does it mean?"

"Waabishkaa is Ojibwe for white. Jonathan is White Wolf. The princess does not know who he is?"

"No, she doesn't," I say. My brother did say I had two white wolves. My ma'iingan isn't the one from the legend Maddie told me. It's Jonathan. According to everyone here—the white man, the Potawatomi, the Ojibwe, and the Ottawa—Jonathan is my White Wolf. I am his Ash Princess.

I want my brother. I need to pace again, but there isn't any room in the cave with a giant Avery-bear, my promised husband, myself, and my sled. Avery takes charge and digs in my pack. He takes out Mama's Bible.

"What did Mikonan say to do?"

"Pray," I say, "and read." I add the last because that's the part Jonathan had tried to teach me.

"Then that's what we're going to do. Pray for wisdom and read for comfort. Good plan?"

It is a good plan. Gikto seems to be on board.

"Our people greatly desire the words from your book. The two that met you on the trail say the book is in Ojibwe only. My village is angry with my Ojibwe brothers and sisters. The book was to be for all of us. Perhaps, princess, the time for you and Waabishkaa Ma'iingan has passed? Maybe it is God's will that you and I are to be together to share the Ojibwe words with the Potawatomi?"

"What about the Ottawa?" I say. "They're left out."

"Well, if that wasn't a princess-like thing to say. If there were any doubt, girl, who you are, it should be gone," Avery says. His grin is warm and should be comforting, but it isn't. Jonathan sent him to make sure Gikto and I found each other. Does this mean he's found something, too? A life without me?

I don't want to waste any more time. I can't. The need to run is growing. I notice two others by the Wendigo fire with my ma'iingan. "Would they like to hear, too?" I ask.

"They?" Gikto casts a questioning look to Avery who looks back at him blankly. "There are no more of us here."

The figures with my ma'iingan were visible only to me. Gikto and Avery saw only a wolf guarding a Wendigo's flame.

I settle to read and take glances at the men outside. I read until the storm's rage is quenched and the sun has victory over the exhausted clouds. Out from underneath a pile of leaves in the cave's corner, a mouse noses about for a morsel. With full cheeks, he scurries past the discarded dentures and out into the cold.

THIRTY-FIVE

The cave's mouth looks more like a painting than an opening to the world. Yesterday, the forest was void of life and the grey that coated it was smothering. Last night, the storm had cleansed the forest of its drab and its morning's gift of snow in flawless white is luminous. Now that the clouds are gone, the sun is free to stretch its beams and its reaching light gives life to the cave's mural. It's as if the world has been summoned awake by the wave of the Great Hand that formed it thousands of years ago. Death has been conquered and today life celebrates its deliverance.

The morning is just as brutally cold as yesterday, but the sun looks warm. I can't resist a visit. I shield my eyes on the way out and startle a pair of cardinals sunning themselves. They flutter in play into a sky of robin's egg blue. The tiny prints they leave behind in the snow are sweet, and they resemble the initials of love carved into the bark of a tree. I trace over their scratching and scribble my hopes next to them. Even though I know it may never be, the letters I nestled together in the same space makes my heart flutter. Meeting Gikto has shown me who I want to marry. It's not the Potawatomi boy in the cave with the fur hat; it's the man who I'm paired with in an Ojibwe legend.

Gikto explained to me the marriage custom of the Ojibwe. Courtship is similar to the English way. Both sides must approve and the couple's contact is under strict supervision. Beyond this, the similarities end. A marriage ceremony isn't required. In most cases to seal the covenant vow, all that is needed is a mutual agreement between the families, and the union is accepted. The new husband simply moves in with his wife's family where they stay for a year. After the year, the couple then moves into their wigwam. Our union has been approved. By Jonathan even. He sent Avery to get Gikto for me. There is nothing more to do. Gikto and I, according to custom, could be considered married; but my promised husband is kind and merciful. He assures me we won't be traveling to Papa as husband and wife. He says out of respect to Waabishkaa Ma'iingan and our legend, we won't be married until he has gotten Jonathan's blessing. He knows our fathers will not be pleased, but he says he not only honors Waabishkaa Ma'iingan but he feels the same way towards the Ash Princess. He wants to please me just as much.

"Is that wolf out there with you?" Avery asks. "He's got a harness on. Mercy sakes, how on earth, girl?"

Miss Margaret has great power over the vocabulary of many. She wouldn't find it funny that the man she detests uses her words, but I do.

"Honey and lots of it," I say.

"Can he pull?"

"He pulled the sled in the cave," I shrug. He did that on his own with very little coaxing from me. I have no doubts about my ma'iingan pulling further. To Papa, even.

"The sled that you *made*." Avery shakes his head with the final word. "I wouldn't believe any of it if I didn't see it for myself."

Avery turns his back to me and coughs. I know he's fighting tears. He had stopped at Maddie's. He had missed us by a few days when he stayed behind with Jonathan. In the short time he had known Tubs, he had grown to love him. I told him I didn't know how I was going to tell Alexander. He told me not to worry myself over it. He already instructed Gikto that either he or my brother will take care of it.

My ma'iingan seems fine. The Wendigo fire and the strangers that tended it are gone, but ma'iingan remains near the abandoned debris that continues to smolder. He's rolling over his breakfast and he doesn't seem injured in the least. He jogs his legs through the air to help himself change positions. Once upright, he washes his face and neck with the scent of his prey.

"Ma'iingan, come," I call. With two new traveling partners, he may not come. This will be the first test of whether he will be a successful sled wolf.

My wolf nudges the furred body through the snow with his nose before he picks it up with his mouth. He trots over and the limp catch animates beneath his chin. He pays no mind to Gikto and Avery and drops an intact rabbit at my knees. He's proud of his morning's harvest, and he shows this by rubbing his face onto mine to share the game's scent.

"That's a fine breakfast, Ma'iingan, thank you." My hummed tune keeps him calm. I bob past his head to search through his soaked fur to find the origin of the blood. With one swift glance, I can see what kind of catch the rabbit is. "I see you have given up stealing from traps. My boy is growing up." I nuzzle into him before expanding my search area across his skin.

My ma'iingan has brought home breakfast every morning for us since we've been on the trail. At first, they were frozen bodies missing a head or a limb; signs they were taken from the jaws of a trap. As of late, however, they have been limp and whole. My ma'iingan has matured past scavenging and is learning to hunt on his own without help from a pack.

"Where is your wound?" I scratch into his neck and my fingertips get lost in his thick coat. He scoots into my lap and covers my face in wet kisses. The growls that accompany them make Gikto uncomfortable. He shifts to the farthest portion of his pelt and has his hand on his knife sheath. "There's nothing. How's that possible?" I ask Gikto. Avery's nervous, too. He has a hand on his gun.

"The men you saw last night," he said, "were heavenly messengers sent by the Great Spirit to heal him. The book—it mentions that He uses them."

Gikto has proven he has great retention, even while being read to. When Jonathan would read, I found it hard to pay attention to him. Even though his reading was done in a tone that I remember as musical and full of volume, it wasn't enough to keep me from drifting. He knew this and would add silly sentences to see if I was listening. Miss Margaret would frown upon this but it did help—a little. When I needed to keep awake, I had the most success observing Jonathan. I found he licks his lips often, will scrunch his nose before he sniffs, and a part of him has to be in motion at all times. It was a mystery each night which part of him would be free from the bondage of stillness.

"There can be no other explanation," I say. "Jared shot him. I saw it."

Ma'iingan is at my feet. I rub a cloth into his fur, and the vigorous massaging required to remove the color puts my friend to sleep.

"So it was you who found my musher's cache," Avery says. He recognizes the harness as his. "The hairpins should have been the give-away. Not used by any trappers that I know of—not that they'd admit it if they did. What's mine is yours. I want no payment from you, girl."

Avery's words are like Jonathan's—the ones he used when we fought in the garden. I regret not heeding Miss Margaret's advice to be gentle with him. Since the garden, I've been impossible. Avery recognizes the look of regret. He presses a smile.

"Let's see if he can pull. If a sheltered girl can build a sled, mercy sakes, an untrained wolf should be able to pull. He's not going to understand the commands my dogs get. Let's see how he is with Racer and Victory. If he tolerates 'em, we can pair him up with one." Avery rubs his hands together. He's happy with his new project and his blue eyes have sparkle.

We don't need any honey—not that we have any left to use. My ma'iingan lets us hook his harness up to the lines with no disagreement. I must admit, my little sled looks impressive with an elegant white wolf at attention, ready to work. My sled looks cute next to Avery's larger one. His sled has changed from fall. The wheels are gone and there are runners like what I have on my sled. Avery notices my admiration of the two sleds, and he winks. He brings over the twins. Ma'iingan chooses Victory by starting a playful wrestling match with him. Victory is placed in the lead position. All my ma'iingan has to do to be successful is to mimic his new friend.

Ma'iingan wants to play, but Victory is a professional. He growls and nips at his new partner. Avery had warned not to wait too long once the two are situated and harnessed. I shout 'hike' and Victory digs his paws in. Ma'iingan follows. He's a natural puller.

Avery grins when we come to a stop next to him. "Never would've dreamed I'd see a modern-day Noah. You can build and can even manage wild animals."

He makes a few minor adjustments to the lines and lays out our traveling plans. Gikto will go with him. I give Avery a mental hug. This whole peace-bride thing is just plain awkward. I feel for my brother and the girl he loved who was forced to be one, too.

"It won't be long and we'll be at the Great Water," he says. "Gikto will escort you across. I won't go any further. My boy will be there. He talked to me and all, but I still don't think he's warmed up to me quite yet." Avery messes with his hair and runs a gnarled hand over his beard. "I guess goodbyes will be comin' soon, so I'm gonna do this now. I don't dare ask for your forgiveness. That's too much to ask, but I do hope I've been able to ease just a smidge of the hurt I caused you."

There's no thought whether it is earned. The hug I give him is an action learned by what I've discovered reading Mama's book. Forgiveness isn't easy. It's hard. It's not a feeling. It's a choice. I choose to forgive Edward. I choose to forgive White Boar. I choose to forgive Avery. I do this because of what was done for me by Christ. Is the pain gone from what he's done? Certainly not. But forgiving is letting go. It's giving it over to the One who wants to carry it, to mend it, and to seek justice for it. Jonathan has yet to learn this. He has yet to see who his father has become. I want to teach him—I want to show him what I learned—but my promised husband is here. If Jonathan gives Gikto his permission, I won't get the chance. My Waabishkaa Ma'iingan will be forever lost—to me and to the peace that comes with letting go.

Gikto has kind eyes, and when he smiles, his high cheeks smoosh up into them. He's a mish-mash of my two favorite people. He's chatty and energetic like Tubs, but he doesn't move as gracefully as Tubs out in the woods. He has a handicap. One leg seems to be shorter than the other. This doesn't seem to slow him down, and it doesn't slow our progress. We've been taking walking breaks from the sled with the snowshoes he brought. I had a hard time getting used to them, but once I did, I felt like a snow pixie. I could walk right on top of the snow! Gikto moves quickly on them, even with his odd gait. Gikto is smart like Jonathan. He isn't as well-read as Jonathan, because there aren't any books in his village, but he has taught himself five—*five*—languages. He knows his own Potawatomi tongue along with Ojibwe, Ottawa, French, and English. He said he collected them from the many different men that have stumbled upon the trail of his people. He wants to learn Dutch next. He'll get his chance. Avery says some Dutch trappers are staying with the band of Ojibwe over the Great Water. He doesn't yet have another Native name. I found the perfect one for him. Owl Tongue. When I told him, I could tell he liked it: his cheeks hid his eyes.

Avery has gone for a different route over the Great Water. Gikto and I are alone with only Ma'iingan as a chaperone. Miss Margaret would be livid. My people would be as well if they knew we were traveling unmarried. Gikto tells me not to worry. We won't be alone for long. My people are waiting just over the water in an abandoned village.

"A decision will soon be made, Princess."

I hum and smile. I pat at a solid structure with my mitten and admire the artistically stacked blocks of ice. Several of these stand across the snow-covered beach, and to me, they look like majestic Lake Guardians. I've been preparing myself to be Mrs. Gikto. Jonathan will be giving his blessing. He wants me with Gikto. He wouldn't have made Avery get him for me if he didn't.

"The ice harvesters have been here. We must watch our footing," Gikto warns. He adjusts his hat. He squats down to tighten the laces around his moccasins—again. He's not eager to cross.

My promised husband doesn't know me as well as Jonathan, but he knows who has my heart. He knows marriage to him will be a difficult transition for me. I don't like secrets, so I made sure it was me who told him this. I also told him I thought him to be a friend. Jonathan was once my friend and I grew to love him. I asked for Gikto's patience. I pray the Lord will have mercy and allow the same to happen to us.

"My brothers were lost in the Great War. My father's first son was a mighty warrior. My father's second son was a skilled hunter. His third son is nothing but a cripple and an 'Owl Tongue'." The name I gave him draws a smile from his pained look. "Father says it is my time to provide for our people—to assure our position in the Counsel. I just wish there was another way to help my people. I am sorry, Princess."

The ice, as far as the eye can see, resembles jagged pieces of broken glass. We step onto the ice and Gikto becomes uncharacteristically quiet. My people are on the opposite shore. It feels like we're on our way to a wake instead of a marriage.

The lake is in a battle to rid itself of its icy armor. The uneven surface groans and crackles with each step. Even when I stop, the frozen lake grumbles and bemoans the trespassing.

The ice is making ma'iingan's job difficult. The runners on the sled are consistently getting stuck, so I detach him from it. It takes both Gikto and me to maneuver the sled over the sharp mountains of ice. Only patches are smooth, and on my way towards one of them, a breathless Gikto pulls at my arm.

"Mind your steps. Harvesters have been on this side of the water, too." He points out the shapes on the other side that guard the shore like the ones we left behind. "Smooth sections are the areas they cut. We do not know how long it has been since they have been here."

I heed his advice and stick to the path ma'iingan pads out for me in the fresh snowfall. He seems to have experience crossing frozen lakes and is confident in his journey to get to the other side.

Ma'iingan has made it to the opposite shore and is avoiding the advances of the humans camped there. They are but specks, but I can see them clustering together against him. I leave the sled and run as well as one can on jagged mountains of ice.

Gikto scolds me as I run across a smooth section. Ma'iingan's footprints have marked it safe so I don't give its stability a second thought. I slip and fall face-first on a square of snow-covered slush. When I push up to my knees, I see ma'iingan stretched in full sprint coming back to me. From behind, Gikto shouts for me to stay still. In my crawl to Gikto, the thin sheet gives way.

THIRTY-SIX

The shock from the severe cold pushes what air I have left in my lungs out into large bubbles. The transparent orbs race like a flock of confused birds to the surface and pop against blue mountain peaks that have grown upside down under the ice. The water is a level of cold that burns, and I have foolishly wasted the tiny amount of air I had on a useless scream. Its sound is as alien to my ears as this world is. My garbled plea is a dismal waste. There isn't anyone here to hear it. The sun curiously steps forward as if it has heard me and peeks down to tell me so through a square of swaying slush. It can't offer a hand but it does offer something. The water may make attempts to distort the sun's features from me, but it can't disguise its light.

For months, the ball of light has been my clock and my traveling companion. It has become a consistent friend. I dig upwards and wage war against the water's lies. I battle against its dual grip—against the wet and the toxic temperatures holding my clothes and muscles hostage. I feel above my head for an edge and grab on. The piece crumbles with my touch and bobbles overhead like ice in a glass of water.

I try for another edge, and when this one proves stronger, I'm able to pull until my head is above the water. I gasp for air too soon. The cold water scalds my throat as it rushes down to dump into my lungs. My retching drowns out Gikto's orders. My eyes feel like they're bulging. It's only after I get the air I need that I press into them with my waterlogged mittens.

Through a watery haze, I make out a blurry Gikto on his stomach. He's reaching for me, and our hands seem miles apart. He slides his snowshoes over.

"Use the shoes!" he shouts.

"Izzy?" Jonathan appears behind Gikto with my brother close beside. Jefferson and Alexander stagger up breathless next to him and heave over bent knees. "Get that sled clear and the furs ready!"

"Aye, Captain." Alexander and Jefferson answer in unison and disappear from view. Jonathan's fingers fumble with the buttons on his coat and he grumbles in frustration through gritted teeth when he can't pull them free.

I use the ends of the snowshoes as picks. They give me the much-needed grip to pull out, but when my chest is on the surface, the ice, yet again, gives way. The swirling water crashes into my ears and drowns out the shouts from the men that abandon their duties and cluster behind Gikto.

"Keep trying! Pull! Pull!" Gikto screams when I emerge with a violent gasp. Jonathan is at the sled sawing free Tubs' adventuring rope while keeping a fixed eye on me. When it's free, it takes him several attempts to get it around his waist.

I try again, but it ends with the same result. I let go of the snowshoes and they float back into my face. I splash them away with monstrous hands that are so numb, they can produce no other function. Jonathan's hands must feel the same. He can't seem to form a simple knot.

"I can't," I sputter. The words I had meant to follow gargle when my mouth and nose go under again.

My whimpers mingle with ma'iingan's, whose movements are like an insane dance. His direction is indecisive, and his nose searches the air above the ice for an answer. The pull to my ankles has intensified now that my legs no longer have the strength to kick. I inhale more of the frozen brew when I tip my chin in the settling slush to tell Gikto. I know it's hopeless, but I reach for him anyway. This time, he creeps past the point he had felt was unsafe and catches hold of my sleeve. A chorus of shouts loud enough to be heard underwater ring out when my head goes under. This time, I don't fight, and I let the water have its way. It doesn't feel as cold anymore, and the quiet is comforting. The water shifts around me when a body joins me in the cold abyss. The push I feel from underneath works in time with the men's pulling. With laborious groans, I'm pulled to the ice like a caught fish.

"So this is what ice fishing is like," I try to tell the men, but my lips refuse to move.

"She's so blue," I hear someone say.

"It's because she's not breathing," Jonathan answers. He has my chin pinched between his fingers. His beard scratches against my cheek when he puts his ear to my mouth to make sure. "Someone help him with that animal!"

I try to turn my head to look but my muscles won't let me. Something's wrong with ma'iingan. He's wailing like a heartbroken ghost. Jonathan positions me upright. Gikto is struggling to pull ma'iingan out of the hole by his harness. Alexander rushes to his side and together they pull the wolf free. They collapse together in a heap on the ice and ma'iingan continues his sobbing without any attempts to get up.

"Quiet him!" Jonathan snaps his order. "Rub him down and run him. Use this if you must." He tugs a gun from the holster strapped to his thigh and tosses it to anyone with the reflexes quick enough to catch it.

It's alarming how floppy my limbs are. My body is at the will of the direction that Jonathan pulls it in. He pounds on my back to encourage my lungs to release their water. My head falls limp on my shoulder. My fur is providing a hindering cushion against his efforts. He manically works at releasing me from the puzzle of material. Once free, I topple backward, but his arm catches me before my head hits the ice. Nature trades places and a head of orange dusts the sky where the ice should be. A face of ivory artistically spattered with freckles peeks out from behind elbows and shoulders.

"Breathe, girl, breathe," Jonathan moans.

He carries me to the waiting fur and once on my back, he straddles my legs and pushes into my stomach. I am at the mercy of the unpredictable head positions caused by the pumping, and I lose sight of my friend.

"On her side, brother." My brother drops to his knees at my side to instruct Jonathan.

I see bare feet. My little friend squats down and cocks his head to see me. Tubs shines a smile with such light that his copper freckles glow. "You can't come home yet, Izzy. Let Jonathan help you. Take a breath. I won't leave you. I'll stay with you until you do."

My brother shifts into Tubs. The boy's body shimmers into transparency as my brother walks through him. Tubs' gaze keeps its promise. He doesn't leave me even when his father steps in front of him. This causes me to wonder who this child is. My little friend is either the creation of my brain's final sparks or he's an angel like the two at the Wendigo fire. An angel dressed as a human to soothe His children and to do exactly as He asks.

"Help them. Breathe," he says.

Jonathan growls in frustration, and the sky is back to where it should be. Lumps from the ice jab into my back and are pierced further when my brother and Jonathan take turns pushing on my stomach. I feel the repetitive rubs from the uneven surface, but it doesn't hurt. I feel light and my body is no longer a concern to me. My angel friend leans over and his face takes precedence over the view. I want to go with him. I'm ready. I want to be with the God of my Mama's Bible. The One I have grown to love.

"Take a breath," Tubs smiles. "He's told me you must stay. Breathe—now."

My lungs obey, even when I don't want them to. The water, warm from its resting place in my lungs, rushes out of my nose and mouth.

"There. That's my…" Jonathan's smile lasts longer than his thought. His teeth look like elegant soldiers in their military best contrasted against the dark of his beard, but they disappear. He doesn't finish. I'm not his girl. I'm Gikto's. "Get everything off her," he commands to any hands that will fit in the tight space.

My body is back to its anchored weight against the ice and it feels as though it's on fire. The cool air on my bare skin feels nice, and I moan in disagreement when I'm bundled in pelts and placed on the sled.

The men take up their positions and together they lift me. Jonathan glares at Gikto when he doesn't get up to help. He thinks we're married. He thinks Gikto's place is to be by my side and not by a half-drowned wolf. My brother. He needs to help Gikto. My ma'iingan will die if he doesn't stay.

I thrash on the lifted sled and the unexpected motion startles the men. The sled tips at an angle that threatens to throw me off but it's corrected before it has a chance.

"The squirrels are burning," I slur. I can't get my tongue to cooperate. It feels heavy and lifeless.

"What?" Jonathan asks. He looks to my brother for an answer.

"The squirrels are burning," I repeat with added force, though it comes out the same as the first.

The blank looks are irritating. Is everyone hard of hearing?

"The squirrels, Mikonan." For my brother's name, my tongue's muscles effortlessly slip into their positions. My brother notices and his grin could battle Avery's.

"I think she is concerned for her ma'iingan," my brother guesses. "Yes?" He nods to me with arched brows. I nod and sigh in relief.

"I will care for him," he beams and plants a kiss on my forehead. "Go, brother, I trust you will care for her." He squeezes Jonathan's shoulder to encourage him to go without him. Jonathan grunts his answer and orders the men forward.

My brother has our mama's healing touch. I can see him watching her—learning from her. This should comfort me, but it doesn't. Ma'iingan had lifted his head in response to my voice but has made no attempts to get up. I close my eyes and pray to be deaf to the gunshot.

The longhouse is dark and murky. The windows in the roof above the fires aren't doing their job venting the smoke and the air is thick with cloud-like streaks. My stomach is rolling from the sooty air and from the hot, sweetened drink my brother is forcing me to swallow. Each sip makes me gag. I almost wonder if it wouldn't be better with tea leaves in it.

The dress and leggings the woman put me in are warm but not warm enough to keep the "tremors" from happening. Mikonan warned me they would come. He says he'll have to watch me. If the shivers get too severe, I'll have to have my mouth packed with moss. He has helped many who have fallen into icy waters, and he told me that several have chipped teeth from their violent chattering. I think I'll try my best to disguise my shivering. I don't want dirty, wormy strings in my mouth.

My shoulders are becoming sore from the heavy load of pelts my brother piles on each time he comes over. He's avoiding the woman who helped me get dressed. She lingers in the shadows, sometimes pacing, watching for ways to be helpful. He's about to add another pelt.

"Binidee?" I ask.

"Hush," he shushes, and the heavy pelt goes over my shoulders.

"She's here?" A shiver speeds through my body and steals my breath. I get it back just before he leaves for another pelt. "She seems curious about you. Does her husband know she's nosing around?"

"There is no husband. She is widowed."

"That's wonderful!" I shudder and sink deeper into my ever-thickening shroud. It's still not enough to warm me. I'm beginning to think I'll never get warm. "I mean, that's awful—but wonderful for you. She sure seems to be interested, so that's wonderful—but awful her husband is dead. Is she still in mourning? Are you going to talk to her?" I'm rambling. I feel like Tubs.

Ojibwe custom says one must mourn for a year after losing a spouse. My brother says she's past the mourning period. It's been eight years.

"You have been shivering too long," my brother says. He layers on another pelt. "You need your husband. The pelts and fire are not going to be enough."

"I don't have one yet. Gikto is supposed to talk to Jonathan." The thought of snuggling with Gikto by the fire terrifies me. I toss off a pelt and grin up at my brother. He isn't fooled. He piles it back on with a scowl.

People are gathering at the far side of the stretched dwelling, sitting on the floor or benches. They mingle together, the young with the old, murmuring amongst themselves. Young girls with whispers and giggles behind cupped hands and boys busy kicking each other on their backsides are mixed in with layers of dark, stoic faces.

"What are they waiting for?" I ask. It is a struggle to form the words and it sounds chopped and strange. My teeth have clanked together and I pray he didn't notice.

He hushes me and asks me to rest and not to speak. My brother had noticed my teeth. He answers my question while peeking into his moss pouch.

"To see if you will accept him," he says. "The boys, however, have no interest in that. They are just curious as to how the Ash Princess escaped the Water Lynx. Remember that story, sister?" he grins.

"The underwater monster that drowns men. Another story big brothers pass on to their younger siblings to terrorize them," I squint at him and shiver. He hushes me again, and in play, he does his best scowl back.

"You remember much now—yes?" he asks. "On the ice—you called me by my name."

I nod into my chest. Memories of my limited time here come back like a spring mist for the most part. Steady and almost unnoticed. I was a small child of six or seven when I was taken, so most of the memories, like the mist, which seemed insignificant at the time, really aren't, it turns out. The pleasant memories of Papa's hand-carved pipe, stained fingers from gathering blueberries with Mama, and the call of the cranes in summer are needed to offset the traumatic ones: the murders by fire and my travels in the bowels of filthy ships. It's disappointing. The lost memories didn't bring back the feelings I had hoped they would. My heart is still heavy, and I feel a gaping hole within my chest. My brother hasn't been able to fill it. Perhaps Papa can.

"You said they are waiting to see if I'll accept him. Accept Gikto?" I ask with a deep shiver. My teeth collide into each other in rapid succession, and I can no longer hold the tremors back. Mikonan holds up a pinch of moss. "Brother, no!" I shrink back and try my best to invoke sympathy, but it doesn't work.

"Open," he orders and opens his mouth as an example as if I am the six-year-old version of me. "Your Waabishkaa Ma'iingan needs you. Will you help him?" He stuffs a wad in my mouth and he keeps on stuffing until my mouth is packed full.

I nod. Ma'iingan must be the one Mikonan has been leaving me for as he paces over Binidee. I hold my hand out for him, a signal that usually brings him bounding to me for a treat, but he doesn't come.

"It is not your ma'iingan who needs you. You must know by now who the true White Wolf is—yes?" He raises a brow, and when I don't answer soon enough for him, he nudges me. I do know who White Wolf is.

"Will you help him now?" He asks.

"I can't. Gikto," I say through my mouthful. It is a muffled mess, but somehow my brother understands me.

"Jonathan got him for you because he did not want you and Tubs to be alone. He was wounded—badly—but my brother sometimes forgets my abilities." My brother straightens his back with a smirk. He pushes up to his feet and gathers me and my fur wardrobe in his arms. He takes me towards the darkened portion of the longhouse that stole his attention when he wasn't with me. Jonathan is sitting on a wide bench with his back to the corner. He has his head buried in his arms.

"Gikto received permission from Waabishkaa Ma'iingan but— hold out your arms, Jonathan, if you still wish to have her—Gikto has now refused you."

"What?" It's another muffled response from me but one that both Jonathan and my brother understand. This makes my brother laugh. Jonathan moans. My brother lowers me down to him and takes my pelts from me to cover us both.

"See how she fills your lap? She must also be the one who fills your heart. Brother, you cannot have both the love of my sister and the vengeance you seek against your father. Which do you choose?"

"Take her." Jonathan's protest is merely verbal. His arm is around my waist. "Where is that coward of a boy? Tell him he's a fool. He must come and take her."

"The boy is no fool. He is brave going against tradition for you. You owe him gratitude for his generosity," my brother scolds.

"She knows where I came from. I can't have her." My brother must have told him what I remember. Jonathan is speaking as if I'm not here, but he knows I am. He pressed me to him when he said he couldn't have me.

"Sister, you know who Edward has become. Jonathan does not. Help him find his father just as he has helped you get to Odedeyan. Can you do that?" Mikonan tugs at my hair and smiles at my nod. He removes the blanket from around his shoulder and drapes it over his arm.

"This is much like the blanket that wrapped Odedeyan and Nimaamaa when they made their promise to each other. Odedeyan had always said with your

English blood and upbringing that you may marry in their custom, but our way is just as binding. Are you both in agreement? Do not be a fool, Waabishkaa Ma'iingan, if my sister accepts you."

My fingers are hesitant to reach for him. I'm afraid. Could he possibly still love me? I know where to find his hand; I can feel it resting on the top of my leg. My fingers slide over his until they slip between the spaces. They're so cold; the touch adds fuel to my shivers. His fingers squeeze into mine to perfect the fit of our laced hands, and his arm tightens to help warm me against the added chill. Our fingers fit just as they did when we were children. Mikonan can see our answer and lowers the blanket over our shoulders.

He closes it tight and informs us that nothing else needs to be done—that we no longer are two, but one.

"Ninaabem?"

Mama's Bible has helped bring back much of my old language. The Ojibwe word asks if he is my husband. I don't know if he understands it. The word is a pitiful, spitty-sounding mess.

"Niwiiw."

He knows the Ojibwe word. Jonathan curls up into me and buries his face in my neck. He called me his wife.

I didn't notice that my brother led the procession out the door. I didn't feel the many eyes sweep over us in approval as they passed. Jonathan takes in a great inhale, and the controlled release of his breath warms my neck. I feel the same. It's as if we had both been pulled from the ice today and we're taking our first breaths together.

THIRTY-SEVEN

It didn't take long for me to see what my brother had meant when he said that Jonathan needed me. Both of us, exhausted by the physical and emotional strain of our journey, had fallen asleep in our embrace. At first, I thought he was just re-adjusting to get comfortable. It was a subtle movement and it would have gone unnoticed by me if it weren't for the person choking in snore at our feet. The shrouded figure on the floor sounded like an angry raccoon, and even though I felt tempted to swing my fist down to silence him, I didn't. After all, I reasoned, we had taken his bench.

My new husband's stirrings turn into moans but can be calmed back into the depths of sleep when I find his hand. I wish Mama were here. This is all I know to do, and it seems childish. The moss that's still in my mouth silences my crying, but it does nothing to the rapid rise and fall of my chest. I'm further frustrated when, even in his sleep, Jonathan knows what to do. He pulls me tighter to him and massages my neck where healed burns press into his father's brand. Already, I can see my shortcomings, and I wonder if I'll be a help to him at all.

In the morning, the bags under his eyes show his sleep wasn't a sound one. Jonathan holds his hands out under my chin and asks me to spit. The tremors had left during the night, but my body still feels chilled to the bone. He catches the sloppy mess and tosses it into the fire.

"Better?"

He swipes my tears back with his thumbs. He thinks I'm bawling over a mouthful of moss, and that just makes more fall across the ones he had smeared away. I nod and bury my head in his chest. I get a comforting squeeze and kiss to the top of my head.

Gikto had gathered all my things from the ice and has them packed on my sled. Jefferson and Alexander are putting dogs into their positions at a second larger sled. Jonathan is impressed with my little sled. He kisses my hair again. He knows why I had to build it.

I haven't seen Alexander since the cabin. I'm not sure what to say to him. His footsteps crunch in the snow. He stops in front of me and hangs his head. He's unsure, too. I'm not good at words—never have been and never will be—but perhaps they're not needed. Out here, I've learned to act. Actions can be my words. I hug into his waist. His large frame melts over mine.

"Gikto told me what you did for my boy. What a remarkable girl." He pulls back enough to try to offer down a smile, but it comes out like Maddie's did at first, pressed and pained.

I don't feel remarkable. I couldn't save him.

"Tubs had the adventure of a lifetime. No one could have given him that but you. Our separation will be but for a moment. Eternity is forever. I'll be with my boy again."

His eyes are red and glossy. He squeezes my shoulders like he has done for Jonathan many times. I can hear him through his grip. He's telling me he loves me. He sniffs and rubs a finger under his nose. He tries his smile again, and this time I can see my young friend in it. The blue eyes that he had once shared with his son shift to a noisy Jefferson who's working one-handed. He won't let go of his unfinished apple. Alexander's shoulders droop and he rolls his eyes. Jefferson is unaware of his talent for brightening difficult situations. Alexander shakes his head and adds an amused snort on his way to help.

Gikto is coming along and is ready to go in one of the sleds. He's been lost in a book all morning. He traded his snowshoes for it from a Dutch trapper and is learning his sixth language. Mikonan says Gikto holds the key to please his people—not through marriage to me but through Bible translation. Gikto has agreed to help translate Mama's Bible into the language of his people and in the languages of all the nations of the north. After all, God's Word, my brother said, is for all nations, not just the Ojibwe. It will be a monumental task, but it's one that Mikonan sees a great need for. Gikto was relieved to be asked to come home with us. He wasn't looking forward to facing his father empty-handed. He seems excited about the work and not bothered in the least that he lost his promised wife. When my brother came up with the marriage alternative, Gikto looked at my brother the way Tubs had, and the way most that encounter him do. I must admit, my brother's posture and presence are commanding, like a chief-in-training. If he weren't my brother I'd be enamored as well, but I remember frogs in my moccasins and snowballs down my back.

Jonathan says we should be with Papa within the week. He's insisting that I ride on my sled for the rest of the journey.

I don't argue. The cold had stolen my strength yesterday, and I still don't have it back. I feel like a rag doll with most of its stuffing pulled out.

My sled now has four dogs panting waiting to pull. Ma'iingan could do it on his own if he were here. I ask about him. Mikonan reassures me that he's fine. He and Gikto rubbed him dry. A shot to the air got him up and he went the opposite direction of where I was taken. He disappeared into the woods and hasn't been seen since. When I tell Mikonan that I have faith my ma'iingan will find me, he just answers in his usual hum.

Jonathan is wanting to get me in the sled, but I'm "using" the bush again. I filled my water pouch three times. I guzzled it dry twice waiting for the dogs to be attached. I did it on purpose as an excuse to go into the woods. Four times so far—just to be sure I'm good and "empty." Jonathan doesn't comment on my small bladder but grins instead. He can see through my antics. He knows I don't want to travel apart from him. We've just found each other. He must feel the same. He has a solution.

"Your faithful steed, Princess." Jonathan leans over and holds back his arms. He wants to carry me on his back like he did when I was little.

"I'll break you," I giggle.

"He will break himself," my brother corrects. "The bleeding has finally stopped. Carrying my sister will surely open you again."

"Then you'll patch me up. That's why I brought you along," Jonathan says. "Just for a little while, sour-face."

He makes me laugh. I haven't heard that sound in a while. Jonathan hasn't either. I won't be going into the sled yet. He squeezes my legs to his side to let me know we both got our way. Mikonan isn't amused, and he grumbles on his way to the second sled.

The village is out to see us off—everyone from the smallest swaddled in cradleboards to the oldest who sit bundled by the fire. An elderly woman with a bronze face pinched with wrinkles starts a chant. The others in her fire circle join her. Drums from the other side of the village pound out a rhythmic tune to showcase the women's words. The song sung by a few is felt by the whole. Needles cease their weaving and are left to dangle over baskets of waiting beads and quills. Skins are left to their stretchers without the stones to scrape them. Dangling pots over popping fires are left without spoons to stir them. I bury my face in Jonathan's neck to hide from the serious faces and dark eyes. It's too much. I don't feel like their princess. I'm just me.

"Don't hide from them," Jonathan instructs softly. "Their princess has come home. They've waited so long for you. Let them see you."

I face them, but I keep my cheek on Jonathan's shoulder for safety. One by one, they drop to their knees in the snow. I smile at them to show my appreciation, but I know the postures aren't all for me. Jonathan won't admit it. The knees are for Waabishkaa Ma'iingan, too. He's the one who deserves their gesture of gratitude. He's the hero of our legend. He released them all from the captivity of White Boar.

Jonathan couldn't carry me long. The pain in his side became too great. The rest of the day, we travel apart, I on my sled, and he with Mikonan and Jefferson at the end of the caravan with the three horses. By evening, we're together again. I miss the longhouse. Camp set-ups and tear-downs are tedious. Just one more week and we'll be with Papa in his dwelling.

The men make up their beds just as I had done on the trail. They scrape snow away with their boots then pile the pelts on top of pine boughs. Jonathan isn't interested in the way of the masses. He's making his, his way. He uses a downed tree as the back to his pine mattress. Pelts are layered on and it looks just like a furry couch. Our library couch. My brother is the first to test it.

"Not bad," he grins. "My brother chooses an upright bed because he does not sleep. Room for three?"

Jonathan grumbles and buries Mikonan under a beaver quilt. My brother rips it off. His grin has grown. The man looks giddy like Miss Margaret had been at our last tea. He looks completely silly, too. His smooth hair is standing on end and pieces float about his head like the down in a baby bird's feathers.

"Wound check." My brother tosses his pack in front of me. "I need you to take a look at him and tell me what he needs."

"Me?"—"Her?" Jonathan and I voice our shock in harmony.

"Yes. Unless you are planning on letting me move in with you. Both of you, sit." My brother rolls up and motions with his hands for Jonathan to lift his shirt. "Ishpinan."

"The girl is going to faint straight-away. I'll do it. Hand over…"

"Bizaan ayaan!" My brother gestures for Jonathan to shush.

Jonathan is reluctant. He drops to the pelts and opens his fur. He lifts his damp shirt just enough to expose the sticky wound. It had done exactly as my brother said it would do.

"Mercy sakes! You're bleeding like a gut fish, and you weren't going to say a thing were you?" I scold.

"A gut fish?" he laughs.

"I'm not happy with you."

My face feels hot, and my body feels prickly. He's right. I might faint. The hole is oozy with fresh blood and crusted with old. No. I will not faint. I'm the Ash Princess, daughter of an Ojibwe chief. I'm Little Otter, sister of Mikonan. I'm Izzy, wife of Waabishkaa Ma'iingan. The feelings of a faint pass, but the heat in my face remains. That's when Miss Margaret says my eyes blaze, but they can't be. Jonathan's smirking. I huff at him and he tries his best to stop.

"Yarrow leaves," I tell my brother.

"Good, but that was easy. We used those on the ship. I did not stitch him with sinew. Tell me why."

"Gunshots are dirty. Sewing it up would be trapping things in. It will heal best by keeping it clean and covered," I say. My brother hands me the leaves. Jonathan tries to intercept them, but he's too slow. "Your wound isn't covered. How's it supposed to get better?"

"I couldn't breathe with it. Mikonan wrapped me too tight." The incorrigible man is using the eyes I used to use on him. They work just as mine did. He's gotten the leaves out of my hand.

"Boonitoon!" I take them back with a poor attempt at a scowl. It doesn't stay. He's smiling at me. I can see why Binidee gasped. I could do so myself. He is a forest angel with eyes of pine. A tired one.

His shirt needs to be lifted higher, but I don't press him. He doesn't want me to see beyond the gunshot wound. I understand scars and the embarrassment that can come with them. I press the leaves on top of the hole that sinks into healed burns, and the green tips curl over his shirt. I'm only allowed to see a small portion but it's enough for me to know that his torso is undoubtedly covered in the same scars that plague my arm and neck. Raised scratches as thick as my finger curl around his waist and add to his odd skin patterns. These must be the scars from the whip. He doesn't like me looking. He's pressing his shirt tighter to the rest of him.

"Giizhiikan, Ogimaakewens," he says in tease.

He wants me to finish. He added the princess at the end to detract—to lighten the situation. My husband is uncomfortable and ashamed, and I don't want him to be. His scars are a part of him, and I want to love them, too.

"I'm trying, but you need to sit up. You're heavy." My attempt to bark my order fails and I laugh it instead. I need to wrap him, and he isn't offering any help. He's nothing but dead weight.

When I'm done, I'm dripping wet and flustered. I shouldn't be. It's freezing out here. Jefferson and Alexander are already asleep, wrapped like mummies in their pelts. Gikto is reading in his. Jonathan has a soft smile. My brother walks off to tend to the fire he just fed moments ago. My husband pulls me down to him on the couch.

"Miigwech, Niwiiw."

He kisses me and it misses. It lands on my cheek. His beard is rough. It scratched into my lips and tickled my nose. I know I look as silly as my crazy brother. My eyes are closed. I know Jonathan's looking at me, but I don't care. I don't want to open them. His flawed kiss was beautifully perfect. He's gathering my hair, and it does nothing to encourage my eyes open. The cold air feels heavenly against the wet on my neck. The finger against my collar bone and the gentle tugging to my neck is what works them open.

"What's this?" Jonathan has found Miss Margaret's necklace.

"My reward from Miss Margaret's dare. Well, a dare I have yet to complete." Jonathan presses the owl's beak and it wakes. "Mama's Bible is to be my two-hundred fifty-first book."

"And how's that going?" He's adjusting the chain, and I can feel his fingers on my scarred skin. This is where he and I are different. I don't mind him seeing mine; but then again, he's always seen them. He's the one who nursed every burn.

"It'd go faster if I had your help," I say.

He snickers. "You never pay attention when I read."

"I'm a mature, married woman now," I grin. "Try me."

He lifts his arm as a signal for where he'd like me to be, and he tucks me in the crook of his arm. "See you in the morning," he teases.

His Ojibwe is beautiful and read in his tone, it's warm and lulling. It makes my chest ache—not from the anxiety that sometimes settles there, but from the discovery that the love I have for him isn't so new. I have always loved him, as my best friend—it's just evolved into something deeper and richer. He's playing with the ring around my finger. The soft, feathery feeling is too much to fight. He's right. I still can't pay attention to him when he reads. I feel his beard brush against my cheek before I give in to sleep.

"Gi zah gin."

I don't know if it is Jonathan or Miss Margaret who says the "I love you". I give in to sleep to dream of Miss Margaret and the thirty strokes of her hairbrush.

THIRTY - EIGHT

It's our last night on the trail. The travel week has been a joy. It's been pleasant traveling in a group. The chores are thin now that the men are here and life on the trail isn't the struggle that it once was. Sleeping is the best that it's ever been for me. I feel the warmest and safest that I've felt in months. I'm still failing to keep awake during Jonathan's Bible readings. I'm hoping that will change after we've been married for a while, and he isn't such a distraction anymore. Jonathan hasn't slept much. He stirs every night. The cure to his moans is still my hand, but it's not enough to give him the amount of sleep he needs. The dark smudges are growing under his eyes. Once we get home, I'll take care of him. I'll talk to Papa and my brother. There must be something we can do to get him to sleep.

Jonathan's daily kisses continue to miss, but Althea helped me discover they're not mistakes. They're strategically planted. Althea had made a funny comment at tea about Jonathan and Agnes courting during marriage. Jonathan wouldn't know this. He wasn't there. He thought of it on his own. She had meant it as a joke. My husband is doing it to be thoughtful. He's giving me time to adjust to my new feelings towards him. He's courting me.

I keep Miss Margaret's necklace hidden under my shirt. I don't take it out in front of him anymore. I found it upsets him and seeing it has made the few nights I've been with him worse. It took some coaxing on my part, but he finally told me why the necklace troubles him so. It reminds him of the young

Jonathan in the cellar. The necklace was the last happy thing he made before Edward forced him to make the weapons. I asked if he missed it. The creating. He said yes. I asked if he'd make me something. He didn't say yes, but he didn't say no either.

Last night, we talked about Miss Margaret. I told him I was worried about her missing us. He told me by early summer, she would have two more in the house to keep her company. Alexander and Jefferson will be going back in the spring. To ease my missing her, he told me the good news: the cottage and the grounds now belong to Alexander and Ms. Abernathy with the agreement that Miss Margaret can stay. Jonathan said he gave Alexander the house as a wedding gift—to encourage him to propose to Ms. Abernathy. I thought my wrap brought them together. Turns out, it took both of us to do it.

Jonathan told me that everything he had is spent. This isn't a disappointment to him—it tickles him. He said Althea will be relieved that her match-up didn't work. The Gudwyne estate now belongs to a housekeeper, a stable hand, and a seamstress. He said Papa's copper is gone. He spent it mostly reversing Avery's sins. He used it to buy back my people and he used it to care for me. He sold the *Verde*. He sold it for our supplies here and to fund Alexander and Jefferson's trip home. I told him I didn't care about the cottage or the copper. I don't miss any of it. England and all its fineries were like my old leather shoes. They were an uncomfortable fit. Jonathan squeezed me to him and he told me the surprise he has waiting for me at Papa's should be as fine a fit to me as my moccasins.

I'm about to drift off, but Jonathan's reading stops.

"Ma'iingan's here." He tightens me into him to further wake me and is humored when I shoot upright.

"There," he points and keeps his voice low. "Underneath the oak."

I squint through the dark and see ma'iingan crouched low near the tree's base. I slip free from Jonathan's arm and wiggle my fingers to coax him to come. He's acting strangely and is bobbing his head as if deciding whether or not he will obey. When he decides that he will, it's not with an energetic bound; it's a belly crawl over.

"What's wrong with him?" I ask. I'm alarmed by the drastic change in his character.

"It's a submission posture," Jonathan says. He takes hold of my shoulder to keep me back. "Be careful."

"Come, boy." I stretch my arm to him. He's fingertips away. His attention shifts back and forth between me and Jonathan. I can see he's in a battle with himself and the sight is heartbreaking.

"He's afraid." I move away from Jonathan to help close the distance, but he pulls me back by the arm.

"No. Make him come to us." Jonathan takes out his gun as a precaution. "I promise. I won't shoot unless I have to."

My ma'iingan creeps forward the inches needed for me to reach him, but he looks miserable. His ears are plastered back and his eyes are bulging. My touch brings a growl from his throat, but he softens the threat with a whimper. He still has his harness on. He allows me close enough to undo the buckles and straps. It falls to the ground and his body ripples through a series of shakes. Freedom from the strapped vest takes him back to the edge of the forest. With a whimper, he lowers himself to the ground and he crawls back to me. He stretches his neck to reach my hand and he gives it a swift lick before flailing to his feet. He scampers off to a safe distance before looking back. I call his name and it gets caught in the lump in my throat. He pulls in his tongue and yips a goodbye before trotting off into the dark.

I fall back into Jonathan and cry over the loss of my friend. I sob a pathetic apology and tell him I understand if he feels like marrying me was a mistake. I feel it is. My brother says Jonathan needs a strong wiiwan. Crying isn't strong.

How will I ever be a help to my Waabishkaa Ma'iingan?

Papa is everything I remembered him to be. He is Mikonan but with eyes wrinkled from the extra years. When I see him, I run to him. I wonder if he saw the six-year-old he saw last. He catches me in an embrace, and his deep laughter vibrates into my chest.

Jonathan greets Papa next. When Papa takes sight of Jonathan, he says the days of celebration he has planned will have to wait. We've been apart again for most of the day, and my heart drops when I see that the inked smudges under his eyes have grown.

"There will be a time for us, daughter. Take care of him." Papa cradles my face in his hands and smiles my brother's smile. He kisses my forehead. "Mikonan, help your sister." My Papa's face may be smiling, but his eyes aren't. They're dark with concern. They remain so, even after Jonathan insists he's fine.

We walk past rows of wigwams to the edge of the woods where a trail leads inside. Nestled in a clearing is a cabin. The ground is thick with snow, but come spring, I imagine the forest floor will be breathtaking when bunched with ferns. Clusters of my beloved birch trees are here. My brother raises a hand and shakes it in the air without turning around. It makes me laugh. Birch leaves in the summer shimmer in the sun when the wind whispers through them.

"Close to your trees and far enough so your brother can't bother you," Jonathan teases loud enough for my brother to hear. He grins down to me and tugs at our hooked fingers. "What do you think? Leather shoes or moccasins?"

"Definitely moccasins." I wrap my arms around one of his and my excitement nearly topples him. He has lost much of his strength this past week.

Mikonan is already at the door. He heard Jonathan's remark and he hurls a potato at him from the basket balancing on his shoulder. He misses.

"I am out of practice," my brother laughs. "But now that you are back to stay, I will get plenty."

Jonathan takes the chair in front of the fireplace and sighs as he stretches his legs out.

"Let me catch my breath," he says. He adds a wink to ease the worry he can see I'm cultivating. "I'll show you around in just a minute."

"He finished the cabin this past spring," Mikonan says.

"We," Jonathan interrupts with closed eyes.

"We." Mikonan smiles and pokes into the fire that someone had waiting for us. If I were to guess, I would say it was Avery. There's a pile of pelts in the corner with my hairpins on top, but it's thicker than the one I left in the musher's cache. My brother prods the fire until its light licks bright. He glances at Jonathan to be sure he isn't looking and mouths the same name that I had thought. He points to our library clock on the mantle. Avery had delivered that, too.

"This man is as stubborn as you, Little Otter. He would rather stay with grandmother in her wigwam than stay here without you." My brother gravels out a snore and laughs at his sound.

"I never did get any sleep." Jonathan peeks with one eye and yawns. He adds a weak laugh to soothe my look.

When Jonathan closes his eyes again, Mikonan nudges into me with the armload of pelts before he goes out the door.

"We will not let him see these yet. He is not strong enough to deal with Avery. Worry not, Biis Nigig. Your Waabishkaa Ma'iingan will be whole again. The load he carries is a heavy one. We are not built to carry such things for so long. Rest is what is best for him now."

I let out the breath I had been holding and let his diagnosis nurse my anxiety. He leaves, and what little confidence I had in being the wife of Waabishkaa Ma'iingan goes out with him. Jonathan's care is now mine. I don't know if I learned enough, if I'm strong enough, or if I'm even worthy enough to nurse him back.

I take the few moments I have alone to explore the room. Jonathan is asleep, and I'm thankful for my moccasins' light touch on the floor. The room is calming and comfortable. It feels this way because most of the things here are from home—pieces that he must have smuggled out over a long time for me to not notice they were missing. The clock, however, is the masterpiece of the room. He'll notice it and will ask who brought it. He'll know it wasn't any of us. It wasn't on our sleds. It was on Avery's. This is where I need to practice my brother's teaching. I'll pray for wisdom. I won't lie to him. I won't ignore it, and I won't keep it hushed and quiet. Keeping a secret is like raising a dragon. They start innocent enough, but they grow. Wicked teeth grow through naked gums, claws grow from tiny fingers, and whipping wings grow from infant sails.

On both sides of the mantle where Avery tucked the clock, shelves are tight with books. I scan the titles and look to see if any of the dragon books made it. It doesn't surprise me there aren't any. Jonathan hated those books, and he made sure to keep them on the in highest shelves to keep them from me. It didn't work. They became the forbidden fruit of the library, and I secretly read every one of them. I found reading them exciting and not much different from my other fantastical tales. Why he kept the books is something I never understood. Why not destroy them if you despise them so?

The seventh wardrobe from the castle cellar is here—the one that Tubs and I had noticed was missing. The carving on this one is clean and simple and matches our world here better than the other six would have. It's a simple pine tree that represents Jonathan's symbol for rest. He has always told me pines were his favorite, and being among them always brought him peace.

It doesn't open when I pull on it. It's locked and there isn't a key. I remember my key, which I had brought from home. Thankfully, I had brought my pack with me, and I dig to the bottom until I feel the rib piece. It knocks into my wrist as I adjust the key to fit into its matching hole. The lock makes a click when I turn it, but before I can peek inside, Jonathan begins the usual stirrings that happen when he's asleep.

I go to him but decide it best to let him squeeze every ounce of slumber that he can. I work on making him comfortable rather than taking hold of his hand. I work on loosening the laces of his boots and by the time they are both slipped off, he wakes.

"Go back to sleep, Jonathan. Things are fine," I say.

"I hate sleep," he yawns.

"I know you do."

He rubs his fingers into his eyes, and he tries to blink away the fatigue. His eyes look painful. They're shiny and red. He smiles at me as he stretches his arms behind his head. He messes his hair and unruly locks fall into his eyes.

"Sleep. Who needs it?"

"You," I say. I've only been alone with the man for a few minutes, and frustration is already tempting me.

He holds his arms out for me to come to him and I do, even though I don't think I should. I slip onto his lap and my weight pulls down the neck of his shirt. I start to correct it, but my fingers freeze when they touch skin in the same bizarre patchwork as my own. The damage done to him engulfs the entire front of him. It's consumed more of him than I thought.

How badly burned was he?

"I'm sorry," I choke.

You weak, fragile girl! My brain screams. I bite into the inside of my lip for punishment. Jonathan needs me to be strong. Comforting me isn't what my tired husband needs.

My throat is tight, and I know no other words are going to be able to fit to explain myself. I wind his shirt's lace over my finger until my finger fills it. He can't possibly know what I'm sorry for. I watch the tip of my finger turn red and I rehearse what I'd say if I could. *I'm sorry your father was horrific and sorry you haven't been able to see the man he is now. I'm sorry the same flames that tore into me, tore into you, too. I'm sorry that as a boy you had to care for me. I'm sorry about your mama. I'm sorry for not thanking you. I'm sorry I'm me—and nothing more for you.*

"*I'm* sorry," he says as his fingers glide over the top of my scars.

His eyes close when I slip my fingers across his forehead to put his locks back where they should be. If I can't say what I should, I need to at least say what my heart is screaming.

"Gi zah gin, Waabishkaa Ma'iingan."

He can't answer. I don't give him a chance to. Our kiss is becoming salty, and when I peek, I can see that his lashes are wet. The tears are his and not mine. This makes me hug into him tighter with a vow to forever share his burdens and help him direct them to the One who wants to carry them. Jonathan has always been my home, but it took a journey to Papa to see it. The gaping hole has always been the Lord's to fill; I just had to let Him.

For the moment, my insecurities are snuffed. My husband is telling me through his tears what he needs. He needs me. Imperfect, scarred, fearful me. I'll give him me for as long as our earthly journey lasts. I'll pray for him. I've found that prayer works. I'll read to know how to serve him better. The Word instructs. I have all I need to be successful. Right now, there is nothing but satisfying contentment and an overwhelming confidence that I am the perfect help-mate for him.

After all, for the past eleven years, I've had the best teacher.

AUTHOR'S NOTE

My eyes are still blurry this morning from the tears. I can't count how many times this book has made me cry! Out of frustration, exhaustion—joy. The tears I cried last night were over the pages that go here—under the Author's Note.

My poor husband. He blinked as I choked, "What do I say?" And, "When I figure it out, will I sound stupid?" This one really got the liquid flowing. "I don't want to bother him (my editor) with something so teeny. Something so "easy." Great. It's going to be just— me."

My note to you will look rough—my editor is getting his much-deserved rest. This note is straight from my laptop to your book page. I'm not a grammar queen or a punctuation princess—you'll discover this quickly. My editor is the one who made my book sing with the proper marks. I'm going to be brave. I'm going to be bold. I'm going to use this as another opportunity to reveal myself—this time without any make-up and without the perfect selfie-angle.

It was never my intention to publish a book. I mean, really, come on—Me? *White Wolf* started as a self-appointed dare, like Izzy's two hundred and fifty books. My son's tenth grade English course, One Year Adventure Novel, promised a novella by the end of the school year. I thought, sure, why not? Austin finished his sophomore year, but both of our books didn't

make the finish line. It took the following year, and the one that came next, to finally finish. Some days, I had only fifteen minutes to write. Most days, I put in an hour. I wrote every day (minus the weekends) and did it just how Mama taught me. One scene at a time; one chapter at a time. Each chapter is to be mini-story, she said, with an end to make the reader turn the page or to "bring them back." Finishing a chapter in *White Wolf* was reliving my childhood in Children's Church in that metal chair. It's what she used to do every Sunday.

The book—its plot and its characters—became more vivid and clear as the years passed. *White Wolf* became an extension of me. It became an outlet for my fears, a sounding board for my beliefs, and a place to exercise my creative muscles. I didn't realize how much of me was in *White Wolf* until I had to think about my Author's Note.

Izzy—is me. I "dislike" tea, though I love the thought of it. I don't like wearing shoes; I'd much rather clog around in my husband's too-big pair. I have a temper. My eyes don't flare like Izzy's; my nose itches instead. My husband has to fight his amusement, just like Jonathan has to when my finger brushes manically under the bottom of my nose. I enjoy reading like Izzy, though I did more of it when I was younger. There are times, even at forty-something, I still stomp in frustration and let out a spirited growl.

Izzy and I are most alike because we both have scars. Hers, however, are visible. Mine—aren't. I always felt like people could see them. Their eyes would look, but they couldn't see. No one knew of my soul's scars but Jesus and the one who put them there.

Izzy is quick to discover beauty in others (Maddie, Miss Abernathy, and Agnes)—I find myself doing the same. Both of us, sadly, fail to see any of it in ourselves. I let Jonathan give the clues that suggest Izzy is indeed pleasingly pretty. Her honey-rich eyes and tanned skin rival the princesses of her books with their fair skin and golden hair. The glance Jonathan steals at Izzy in the library when they examine the bat and the look he gives her at tea are the hints that point us in this direction. At some point, Izzy must have referred to herself as a troll. Jonathan mentions this at tea. I'm sure her negative view of herself bothers him as much as it does my husband. I often describe myself with the same cutting descriptions. I must be pleasingly pretty to Kris, too. He'll shake his head and groan his disagreement with me.

Jonathan is based on my husband, but he also has pieces of me. Both men share amazing traits: they're patient, they're nurturing, and both exhibit a silent strength. Like Izzy, I will never tire of holding my husband's hand. I understand Jonathan because, like me, he has secrets. Me—well, I had secrets. Jonathan keeps his for the same reason I had kept mine—to shield and protect his loved one from pain. It sounds honorable enough. Turns out, it's not. Jonathan's silence of both his past and Izzy's births a dragon. In *Letters from the Dragon's Son*, we'll get the chance to meet it. Izzy says that harboring a secret is like raising a baby dragon. I agree. Secrets are always damaging—even if they are kept to protect. Secrets are heavy.

Secrets are debilitating. Secrets are consuming. I know, I kept one. I raised a dragon of my own.

Tubs isn't anything like me. Well, besides the chatty part. My husband says I can hold a conversation with a stick. His exact words, not mine. Tubs' character was my opportunity to envision what it would be like to say good-bye to my brother. Henry committed suicide in the fall of his senior year in high school. Izzy was fortunate. She got to see Tubs' sores. She had warning his time on earth would be short. I wish I saw warning signs in my brother. I had no clue that behind his sunny smile, he struggled. He kept his pain and depression a secret. We had something in common and I didn't even know it. He had a dragon, too.

Miss Margaret is a delightfully, beautiful "Frankenstein." She's a "mother" with two hearts—the one I have by birth and the one I gained by marriage—and she's draped in the soft, cushiony flesh of my Dutch grandma. Grandma Bolhuis is the one responsible for my love of baking sugary delights, and she's the inspiration behind Miss Margaret's irresistible biscuits. Grandma and I ate a whole peanut butter pie together once. My tummy wasn't happy. That's my only memory of throwing up—though, my Mama, I'm sure, has memory of others. Grandma stayed up late one night and underlined her favorite verses in my Bible for me. I saw hers. It was pretty with all its colored markings. I wanted mine to match hers. I learned that God's Word is nothing to be afraid of with its big words and lists of "begats." It's God's love letter to us. Remember Miss Margret's marble story? That was my Grandma. That's a teensy peek at how colorful she was.

Like Izzy, my tongue doesn't work. I rehearse often what I'm going to say. I have a list of "safe topics." Moses and I would have been good friends. I can't remember when I discovered that my fingers could replace my tiny, timid voice. Perhaps it was in middle school when my English teacher forced us to journal in her class. I'm not sorry that the connection between my brain and mouth isn't wired like most. I found out what works for me and what I was created for— for action—for servanthood. My hands and feet work just fine. Once I started serving my "Papa" (Jesus), I was able to push past my fear ("push past", dear friend. I may always struggle with fear, BUT I'm not afraid of it!). I found a way to fight once He pulled me out of the ashes. Galatians 5:13 is the tomahawk my "Papa" gave me—"You, my brothers and sisters, were called to be free. But do not use your freedom to indulge the flesh; rather, serve one another humbly in love."

Three years ago, I started a novella about a half-Native American girl's journey to her father in America.

More specifically, back to her home in Munising, Michigan. The story was to end at our favorite place to vacation. I never knew it'd grow into a full-length novel with me infused so deeply in the story's fibers. I'd love to pluck out each one and show you, but it'd take another book to point out all the hidden "Easter eggs." Words were chosen with care. Every aspect of this book has a purpose and meaning to me. Perhaps this is what coffee dates are for—to "sip" on the book's messages. You know where to find me if you'd like to chat!

White Wolf isn't as original as I thought. My story is deeply etched in its pages. I see from both, *White Wolf* and the story of me, how much the Lord loves his children. He held me in his lap every time I cried out to him (Zeph 3:17). I see that the Lord is merciful. He gave me the strength I needed while I waited for my own White Wolf (Heb. 4:6; Ps. 29:11). I see that the Lord is giving. He gave me the best mate imaginable (James 1:7). My husband loved me before I knew what love truly meant, and he patiently waited for me to learn to give it back. I see that the Lord gives power. He gave me what I needed to forgive my own Edward (Eph. 1:19). I see that the Lord gives peace. In all circumstances, the good, the bad, and the ugly, our Abba Father offers it generously (Phil 4:7).

What about you? Do you have wounds of your own that need healing? Or are they now scars that have long since crusted over and are in need cleaning?

Please, go to Jesus today. Ask for His help. He wants to mend you and make you whole. Let Him edit your past, polish it, and make it clean. Let Him write the rest of your story. With His touch, I promise…

…YOUR STORY WILL SING!
Tammy

ABOUT THE AUTHOR

Tammy lives in Michigan's Upper Peninsula near the shores of Lake Superior with her husband and three teen/adult children. Currently, they are working on their "new" home just outside the Hiawatha National Forest that she writes about in her stories.

Tammy enjoys hiking, kayaking, beach wandering, "hunting" for birch bark, and spotting migizis.

She is the author of *White Wolf and the Ash Princess, Letters from the Dragon's Son,* and the short story *Eagle Eyes* from the Descendants of White Wolf series.

OJIBWE AND POTAWATOMI

NAMES WORDS AND PHRASES

Biis Nigig (Ojibwe) - Little Otter.
Bizaan ayaan (Ojibwe) - Be still! (Enter 'bizaan', click search.)
*Boonitoon (Ojibwe) - Leave it alone; quit it.
Gaawesa (Ojibwe) - Impossible! No way! It can't be done!
Giizhiikan (Ojibwe) - Finish. Finish with it.
Gi zah gin (Ojibwe) - I love you.
Gikto (Potawatomi) - Talk.
Ishpinan (Ojibwe) - Lift it high.
*Ma'iingan (Ojibwe) - Wolf.
Mashkawizziiwin wii (Ojibwe) - Force her.
Miigwech (Ojibwe)- Thanks!
*Mikonan (Ojibwe) - I find it among many other things
Niinimooshe (Ojibwe) - Sweetheart.
*Nimaamaa (Ojibwe) - Mother.
Nimishomis (Ojibwe) - Grandfather.
*Ninaabem (Ojibwe) - My husband.
*Niwiiw (Ojibwe) - My wife.
*Odedeyan (Ojibwe) - Father.
Ogimaakwens (Ojibwe) - Princess.
Vrede (Dutch) - Peace.
Waabishkaa ma'iingan (Ojibwe) - White wolf.
*Wiiwan (Ojibwe) - (his) wife.

*You can hear these words spoken in Ojibwe @ ojibwe.lib.umn.edu

Dictionary Sources

The Ojibwe People's Dictionary @ www.ojibwe.lib.umn.edu, A Cheap and Concise Dictionary of the Ojibway and English Languages: English-Ojibway 1907 by George Buskin; International Colportage Mission, A Dictionary Of The Ojibway Language by Frederic Baraga, Potawatomi Dictionary @ www.kansasheritage.org, Freelang EnglishOj

You Can Connect With Author Tammy Lash Via

http://facebook.com/tammylashauthor

http://pinterest/tamlash5

http://tammylash.wordpress.com

http://instagram.com/tamlash5

If you enjoyed White Wolf and the Ash Princess, would you please consider leaving a review on Amazon or Goodreads?

Made in the USA
Columbia, SC
23 September 2022